Review of *Delilah Cross* by Adelle Bradford

Delilah Cross is an important and engagingly written novel. The characters are sketched carefully and the plot unfolds with a combination of eventfulness and subtle rhythm. There is no marked peripeteia but that which constitutes the prologue, perhaps the most provocative passage in the entire book. The reader makes sense of the secret long before the other major characters, yet it is still worth watching them work together to get their answers.

On the whole, I believe this is a highly publishable manuscript that would appeal to a wider range of readers. It is precisely the kind of book that could conceivably make Oprah's book club list and should therefore catch the eye of a publisher who can take the risk. I think there is also tremendous potential for a screenplay. I regret that I am not of much help on the first count but I would very much like to attempt to assist you with the latter.

Please contact me at your convenience to discuss the matter further, if you would like. I would like to close by acknowledging the depth of what you've offered here and encouraging you to seek publication with a reputable press.

Dr. Emily Plec, Associate Professor
Communication Studies
Western Oregon University

About the Author

Adelle Bradford lives in Virginia. She has blue eyes and is owned by a possessive cat. She finds both animal behavior and the human condition fascinating. Writing is a way of life for Ms. Bradford and she writes because she cannot help it, as she attempts to paint her "mind pictures" in words for others to see.

DELILAH CROSS

A Novel by

Adelle Bradford

Other Published Works by Adelle Bradford

"About Small Things", Article published in The Mississippi Crow Magazine Summer 2007 Issue
http://mississippicrow.com/index.html

"The Traveler", a Science Fiction Short Story, published April 2007 as an Amazon Short by Amazon.com

"*Jacob's Ladder*", published in The Writer's Net Anthology of Prose, Volume one, Fiction, edited by Gary Kessler for the Writer's Club Press (December 2002), available at Amazon.com, ISBN 0-595-65040-6

"Legends of Nevermore County", an anthology of eight short stories published January 2006 by PublishAmerica **ISBN-10:** 1424103703 / **ISBN-13:** 978-1424103706.

"All About Eve and Other Things", a volume of poetry and essays published December 2005 by PublishAmerica **ISBN-10:** 1424103398 / **ISBN-13:** 978-1424103393

"Rejection Slips", Article published in The Mississippi Crow Magazine Winter 2006-2007 issue
http://mississippicrow.com/index.html

First printing 2009
Paperback

ISBN:

Printed in the United States of America

PROLOGUE

The man was deeply asleep, far down in that dark place where life reaches its lowest ebb, the place sometimes called "the little death", the place most of us visit almost every night- -or wish we could- -without truly knowing the nature of the place we seek or what we seek there. His return to awareness was slow; he resisted, first incorporating the sounds disturbing him into dream scenarios that seemed to last for minutes . . . or perhaps only seconds in that place where time sets its own rules and flows in its own directions. He tried to ignore them, explain them away as something other than what they were, but by then he was awake, his mind fully engaged in identifying the sounds.

When the long, quavering wail came again, he grunted in disgust. It's her, he thought, his irritation at being roused slowly escalating into anger. He sat up on the edge of the bed, clumsily fighting the dangling folds of the mosquito net. Grunting, he finally managed to find the opening and shoved it to one side. He felt it rip as he did so, and irritatedly pawed at his gummy eyelids before reaching to snap on the bedside light. His body felt old, heavy, slow to respond as he shoved his feet into slippers, picked

11

up the heavy-duty rectangular flashlight sitting on the nightstand, and left the bedroom.

He cursed loudly when he stumbled over the kitchen stool as he reached for the pull chain on the dangling kitchen light. He didn't need this shit, he thought. It was probably nothing more than a bad dream, but he didn't dare take a chance that it wasn't. Opening the door at the back of the kitchen, he turned on the dim overhead light in the long, narrow hall that ran the rear width of the building, and ended in a small bathroom.

"Just shut up," he yelled, as the anguished wail came again, louder now that he was closer. "God damn it! I'm coming!"

His slippers made hollow slapping sounds on the bare wood floor as he walked, shuffling and scuffling noisily as he approached and opened the door to the second of four rooms that lined the right side of the hall on the outside wall of the building. The bottom of the door was solid wood; the upper half consisted of one-inch square chain link mesh nailed to the frame. The same kind of mesh covered the single glassless window in each of the four side-by-side rooms. The door swung inward. There was no knob on the inside, and he left it standing open as he snapped on the flashlight. Mentally he damned the German architect who sat at a drawing board in Berlin years before and decided that three thousand miles away in these four rooms in Africa that he would never see, no light fixtures were needed.

She was curled up in a whimpering ball on the cot in the corner. There were no covers on the cot, and no mosquito netting to deter insects. There was just a bare, much used, mattress covered with dirty blue and white striped ticking, and she was naked except for the thin, cotton shift she wore. For just a moment, no more, he felt a flash of pity. She looked so small and defenseless in the harsh, white glare of the flashlight. Then she wailed again and the anger returned.

He balanced the flashlight on its square end on the floor so it reflected light back from the white ceiling, and seated himself on the cot beside her. "What's wrong?" he asked, as he roughly grasped her ankles, turned her on her back, and pulled her legs out straight. Then he spread them so he could examine her pelvic area.

"Oh," she moaned. "It hurts." Her arms were up, her hands concealing her face.

"What hurts? Where do you hurt?" He quickly ran his hands over her distended belly, checking for contractions, then slid an exploratory hand between her legs, checking for wetness, assuring himself that nothing was overtly amiss with her pregnancy. He needed to be sure. It was much too early for labor and delivery, and almost anything could complicate matters. He still felt clumsy, not fully awake, anxious to get this over with and get back to sleep.

13

"My ear hurts," she whimpered. "Here." She cupped her ear with her hand. Her voice was high and delicate, childlike.

He slid up on the cot beside her and leaned over close to her face, his neck almost touching her cheek as he tried to get a good look at the ear in the dim light. I hope it isn't an infection that will require heavy doses of antibiotics, he thought disgustedly. That's all I need this late in her pregnancy.

Those were his last coherent thoughts. Her arms were around his neck in an instant, holding his head in place with a strength that surprised him. So strong . . . ! Why is she hugging . . . ? Oh, she's biting . . . ! My ne . . . . Chew . . . ing . . . .

The disjointed fragments were swept away in a sensory whirlpool of sounds and pain. She was growling deep in her chest, a vibration more felt than heard as, with mouth open wide and lips peeled back from her white teeth, she chewed through his jugular vein, ripping and gnawing with mechanical ferocity. Gripping his head tightly, she ignored the wild flailing of his arms, the kicking legs that sent the flashlight flying across the room, the agonized grunting, gargling sounds he made. She didn't stop chewing until a gush of hot, coppery-smelling blood sprayed across her face, and splashed up the wall at the head of the cot. She held him then, until the rhythmical gushing ceased, the blood flow became a trickle, finally stopped, and he became still.

She pushed him from her then, and sat up on the edge of the

14

cot as his body flopped grotesquely to the floor, the blood looking black in the diffused light. After a moment, she rubbed her side. He had hurt her in his flailing attempts to escape, but she felt a sense of urgency now and ignored the pain.

Her movements were methodical, deliberate as she unhurriedly walked from the room and went down the hall to the bathroom at the end. Stretching upward on her tiptoes, she tugged the dangling cord that turned on the light; removing her blood-soaked nightgown, she stood looking at it for a moment before dropping it to lie like a wet, crimson and white flower garishly blooming on the gray cement floor. She moved to the shower, and turned on the water, then stepped in, carefully scrubbing with her hands to remove the blood from her body and hair. Then she turned her face up to the spray, and stood for long moments letting the water run in and out of her mouth to wash away the blood taste.

She was small, perhaps five feet one inch tall, but perfectly formed, the swell of her pregnant belly graceful, a natural part of her inherent femininity. Her dark brown hair was raggedly cut short, and wet wisps lay darkly plastered on her forehead. She was neither dark skinned nor fair, her complexion lying somewhere in between; dark eyebrows arched gracefully over eyes of an unusual shade of blue, and her features were small and regular. Looking at her as she stood there, it would be difficult--if not impossible--for anyone to envision her having any part in the

15

bloody, violent scene that had just taken place down the hall.

She had only one blemish . . . high on the left side of her chest, halfway between the point of bone by the hollow in her throat and the point of her shoulder, was a neat row of inch high, reddish-white scars. For a moment, touching them one at a time, her fingers traced the four distinct X's there. They were neatly drawn thin lines, deeply etched. No cutting tool had made them, and no burning brand had left them there. They had been very slowly, carefully, and painstakingly traced with the tip of a surgical probe dipped in acid...without benefit of anesthetic.

There were no towels in the bathroom, and naked, still dripping, she stepped around the bloody nightgown and walked back down the hall to the kitchen without glancing right or left. She didn't notice the bloody footprints she had left on her way to the bathroom; even if she had, it would have meant nothing to her.

Almost as though dazed, she stopped in the center of the kitchen and slowly looked around. After a moment, she went to a small board nailed to the wall by the back door. Selecting a large key from the half-dozen hanging there, she turned and walked out the screen door. The black coiled spring attached to the door jamb pulled it shut behind her with a thud, momentarily dislodging the moths and flying beetles attracted by the light. Stepping off of the back porch, she rounded the building, walked to the high iron gate in front that was the only opening in the high walls, and used the key to open the heavy padlock that held it shut. After tugging at it a moment, she managed to remove it from the heavy hasps, and, without removing the key, dropped it in the dirt beside her bare feet.

The moonlight was silvery bright, painting deeply etched shadows, illuminating and tracing the well-worn ruts of the single track dirt road leading to the right of the gate. She looked down at her feet. The heavy red dust of the yard had coated them to the ankle, sticking to their wetness, giving them the appearance of being shod in some strange kind of soft, form-fitting shoes. To the left beyond the compound, the road continued, but it was scarcely more than a faint track nearly overgrown by the jungle. A dark threatening tunnel, the thick hanging vines and pressing trees swallowed the moonlight before it could penetrate more than a few feet.

She had been born inside the walls of the compound, and never in her short life been outside of them. She hesitated just inside the gate now, whimpering, filled with fear of the unknown. Then quickly, without looking back, she pulled it open just enough to slip through. Barefoot and naked, silent tears running down her face leaving silvery tracks in the moonlight, she stepped through the gate, turned down the track to the left, and entered that unknown dark. She felt her way slowly, carefully, pausing

17

often to listen. A few hundred feet into the dark, leafy tunnel, she turned off the track and pushed her way into the undergrowth. Ignoring the unavoidable pricks, jabs and scrapes from rough and mostly unseen vegetation, she steadily made her way deeper into the jungle.

Once she paused as the baby stretched and changed position inside her. Her arms protectively cradled her bulging stomach for a moment. Then she raised one arm and touched the scars on her shoulder. "You are my babe," she whispered to the child inside her. "No one will hurt you or take you away."

After a moment, she moved on and disappeared into the darkness.

CHAPTER ONE

The day was warm with that distinctive late spring balminess that lasts only a few days. The feel of it seemed to make subtle promises that this time it would last forever, never slipping over the dividing line into summer's sweltering heat.

A few puffy clouds did a languid slow dance across the sky, coming close to each other, almost joining, then moving away, engaged in a teasing mating ritual that would, somewhere over the horizon, consummate itself in a sudden, brief, orgasmic downpour. The light breeze that urged them on touched the trees as they elbowed each other for position close to a small stream, and the faint susurrus of green leaf hands rubbing together accompanied the soft, musical gurgling of running water.

She stood quite still, looking upward at the clouds, fascinated by their seeming sensuality, wondering why such familiar surroundings had taken on such a strange aura. Even the touch of the breeze on her skin had a teasing, stroking quality. Then, without warning, the stream muttered something she was quite sure was obscene, and the stepping stone she was balanced on shifted slightly with a hoarse, grating chuckle as it nudged its underwater neighbor knowingly. In the shallows, a gentle current stirred, rippling in amusement as it curled suggestively around a gnarled, waterlogged root. One of the clouds slid over the sun, slyly running its elongated shadow fingers down one side of the stream, briefly caressing three of the moss-covered stepping stones and raising a ripple of goose-flesh on her thigh before it moved on.

After a moment frozen in an instinctive defensive crouch, she straightened slightly, long, bare toes cautiously seeking a new purchase on the rock she now knew to be treacherous. Her toes seemed to take on a life of their own. Sensitive undersides responded with a sudden awareness to the velvety softness of the damp moss as they pushed their way into it, feeling their way, searching for the rough, granular surface of the stone beneath. Finally, feeling once more safely balanced, she started to step to the next flat stone, the third in the six that crossed the stream in a casual arc. Before she could make the first tentative forward movement, a small, brightly-feathered bird settled itself on one of the overhanging branches that drooped above her head.

She gazed upward, surprised at its boldness, intrigued as its colors shifted and changed in the sunlight that now dappled this side of the stream. Looking closely, she could see that the feathers themselves were not actually brightly-colored, but the play of the sun created a kaleidoscopic shift of colors across them . . . bright to dull to rainbow iridescence with each subtle change in its position. A sudden memory of another place, another time, a different reality, threatened to overwhelm her. Almost angrily, she shoved those images aside and concentrated on this bird, here and now.

It looked back at her, turning its head from side to side, taking its time as each obsidian eye appeared to deliberately inspect every intimate detail of her naked body. Then, with a rude, dismissive, downward jerk of its tail, it cried raucously, "See your tits and wee-wee! See your tits and wee-wee!" and flew away in an explosion of color.

She stood without moving, feeling bits and shards of its ridicule cutting at her body like brightly-colored pieces of broken glass. The stream formed a small whirlpool mouth, spinning a fallen leaf in a dizzying spiral before hungrily sucking it under with a small, wet slurping sound. Gurgling mirthfully to itself, it hurried off toward the holding pond behind the barn.

Ignoring the stream now, feeling strangely detached, she looked down at her body. It seemed to have all the normal hills and valleys. Looking at herself was something she avoided as much as possible, especially her naked body. Something about it made her uncomfortable; somehow, in some indefinable way, what she saw, the body she saw, was not real, not who she was at all. For a moment, a vision of another belly, a belly covered with straight, coarse dark hair, the navel a mere suggested indentation behind its dark screen, flashed across her mind. Impatiently, she pushed it away and cautiously poked a finger in her navel. That felt real enough even though it looked funny with her finger sticking in it.

Then she thought about pieces of colored glass, and raised her hand to her waist, laying it flat against her stomach. If enough of them stuck in my flesh, I could become a stained-glass replica of myself. The little trickles and blobs of blood from the cuts would hold them in place, and I would become something quite different and unique, especially with the sun reflecting through all the colors and rainbow patterns of my naked vulnerabilities.

That last bit was jarring. Had she unconsciously made a pun? If so, now was really no time to be engaging in wordy witticisms, not in her present precarious predicament. She frowned. There it was again, that niggling-naggling juxtaposition of words, the playing of alliterative notes like bits of silent melody as she spoke the words soundlessly, saying them only in her mind. Or had she actually said them aloud? Sometimes it was hard to tell for sure, especially when she felt certain she was alone. Even that was dangerous because she could never be completely sure when, or even if she was alone.

She smiled wryly, little more than a fleeting grimace marring the smooth skin around her generous mouth. Delusional behavior? Or maybe even paranoia? She had read about them in psychology books, but when you had been overtly watched for years, was it paranoia to suspect that someone might be watching you covertly? And react accordingly, especially when you had something to hide? Perhaps . . . and perhaps not. Surely, being subjected to intense scrutiny over long periods of time could turn the most normal, well-balanced, clear thinking, intelligent person into a cringing neurotic. The books told her that, too. No, she didn't think she was suffering from delusions or paranoia. Something was not right here.

She dropped her hand from her stomach and raised her head, slowly turning it from side to side as she carefully inspected her surroundings. The first day, she had made it to the second stepping stone, the one on which she was now standing, before retreating to the safety of the bank. Yesterday she made it all the way to the third before succumbing to the gut-wrenching, yellow-green-black fog of fear that enveloped her. Snake-like, creeping up her legs, coiling around her body, penetrating her pores, invading her cells, it devoured her until nothing was left of her self but a small shrieking voice urging her to run! Get away! RUN!

Before yesterday's horror could fully manifest and repeat

itself, she forcibly dragged her attention back to the present. Everything was the same as it was yesterday and the day before, except, of course, today she was naked. She considered that. What had given her the idea that attempting to cross the stream would be easier if she came unencumbered by clothes, one on one against the stream, the water, and her fear of it? From where she stood now, naked and balanced uncertainly on the second stepping stone, it seemed like a very bad idea, a downright stupid idea, in fact.

Then it hit her. Her clothes! Even if she got all the way across, her clothes would then be on the other side. She considered the situation. Her options seemed to be two in number, if you didn't count the possibility that she might stand on this stone forever, unable to go either forward or back. She could go back now, or cross if she could, then cross back again to reclaim her clothes. Or, and she couldn't help grinning slightly at the mental picture, she could cross the stream and stroll naked up the path across the pasture. After climbing over the stile to the road, she could make her way up Palmer Road to the farm driveway, waving nonchalantly to any passing cars or tractors, of course.

Then, she could walk up the long gravel driveway, past the big gatehouse where the Clement family lived, past the currently unoccupied bunkhouse, to the main house. And all the while she could casually pretend that such naked strolls were everyday occurrences in her life. Her grin grew larger as she pictured the look on Sarah's face. Naked strolls were not the order of the day in Sarah Clement's calm, well-organized life.

She sobered. That was one walk she really wanted to take, but not naked. There was no choice but to go back. Rather than confronting her own lack of planning, she somewhat petulantly decided that it was the bird's fault. If it hadn't distracted her with its vulgar remarks, she would have easily made it all the way across this time . . . and back, too. She sent a shaft of angry disgust arrowing after it. When I get back, I'll look you up in my bird book. It will serve you right if I find you there with your beautiful colors done in lifeless pastels, all washed out and frozen on the page with precisely meticulous little pen strokes. Did you even know, you dirty bird, that that man, Audubon, only did dead birds? He had to catch 'em, kill 'em, and stuff 'em first! Only death held things still enough for him! How do you like that?

Another thought struck her. Did they stuff him when he died? Judging from some of the pictures of him she had seen, he could just as well have been dead and stuffed, perching on the edge of a chair while he waited to be immortalized like one of his famous birds. The thought both amused and saddened her. Death was a hurting thing, a lesson she had learned early and well. Death was final and irrevocable. The bird had been a lovely, innocent creature and had certainly said nothing obscene to her. Neither had the stream. The sexual innuendos she had been feeling all around her, from the clouds to the downright obscenity she had attributed to the bird, were hers and hers alone . . . and totally out of character. She frowned. Why would she be thinking like that? What was causing it? What were her instincts trying to tell her?

In her mind, she went over her last two aborted attempts to cross the stream. Now that she thought about it, even with her clothes on something hadn't felt quite right. She had come as far as the stream many times during the last two years. She was intrigued by the distinct seasonal changes that almost magically transformed the same places on the farm into four different worlds for her to explore, each with its own distinctive colors, sounds and smells. She often followed the stream up to the place it splashed out of a culvert under Palmer Road to begin its journey across the farm, and traced its path down to the murky green holding pond behind the barn. From the pond, it was a gentle, easy-flowing, willow-lined stream that meandered along the edge of the acres of cropland to disappear quietly into the culvert in the old stone fence that marked the boundary of the next farm.

Of course, she always kept a safe distance from the water, watching the banks closely. She never went closer than a hundred feet to the pond either, even though she would have liked to get closer to the mallard ducks that made it their year-round home. Indirectly, the mallards contributed to her determination to cross the stream. One day, shortly after she arrived at Bent Tree Farm, she followed the stream and became aware of the ducks that lived in the pond area. Her first reaction was a sense of horror and fear, a feeling that the ducks were in terrible danger there on the murky water. But, as she watched them, reasoning replaced her emotional reaction. She saw this was their natural habitat, this was where they lived; logic told her that these were water-fowl, the pond was an ideal place for them to be, and they were in no danger . . . but she never went closer than a hundred feet because her fear wouldn't let her.

But she did explore the corollary in her mind: water was also a part of normal human environments. Water, in and of itself, was vital and necessary for survival. Cleanliness was necessary. No, she was not afraid of water at all. She was afraid of what was _in_ the water. Even though her logical mind told her there was nothing in the water here that could possibly hurt her, deep, visceral instincts told her something very different. That was her phobia. Yes, the mallards had caused her to really think about it over a period of time, and, in her own way, try to overcome it.

So, she thought, everything had been all right then. But the last two times she tried to cross the stream, and today particularly, there was . . . what? She paused, trying to put a name to something that was scarcely more that a slight, uneasy lifting of the hairs at the nape of her neck, a something both known to her and unpleasant.

What had she thought the bird said? "See your . . . ?".
Something about that was familiar. Then she remembered.
Sammy Truesdale had said those exact words to her at Hiller
School about three months after she arrived there from Bhutu.

The scene was suddenly clear in her mind. She was following
the rules and taking a shower in the upstairs bathroom shared by
four other Hiller resident students. As she stepped out of the
shower and reached for her towel, he was standing in the doorway
watching her, a simpering smile on his vacuous, moon-round
face. In her mind, she could still see the string of drool that leaked
from the corner of his mouth, working its way toward his chin
even as she stared at him.

"See your tits and wee-wee," he said. Then he giggled and
took a step toward her.

Without thought, she jumped toward him, not away. Her fists
were clenched and both arms were locked straight out in front of
her. Although she was a full head shorter and fifty pounds lighter,
she was stronger, much stronger. The force of her stiff-armed
shoving blow sinking into the doughy flesh of his belly forced
him back out the door and across the narrow hall, where he hit the
wall with a loud thump. She stood there as he slid down the wall
into a sitting position, watched as he gagged painfully and
vomited into his lap.

She felt no sense of outraged modesty, no violation of her personal privacy, and no insult. She did not know what tits and wee-wee were. At the time, she had no concept of these things, but he had broken the rule, and she knew the importance of rules. There was no lock on the bathroom door, just as there were no locks on most of the inside doors at Hiller School, but when the bathroom door was closed, a light came on over the doorway. The rule said that when the light was on, you waited until the person came out. You did not open the door. If you could not wait, you found a grown-up person and they would take you to another bathroom.

That was the rule. She did not know why this was. It made no sense to her because the shower, toilet, and basin were three different things meant for different uses. She had learned that at Bhutu. But logic told her that someone could use the toilet while another used the shower and another used the basin. The fixtures could even be used at the same time by even more people if necessary, that much was clear to her. But there was the rule, and Miss Agnes had taught her well at Bhutu. Violation of rules, any rules, brought swift, painful punishment.

Her nose had wrinkled in distaste as the smell of his half-digested breakfast wafted across the hall. Stepping back inside, she closed the door firmly. Now she was irritated. She had to take another shower to wash off the wad of gooey saliva that had flown from his mouth and landed in her hair when she hit him. Being in water was an ordeal for her, but being clean was also a rule. She decided, as she quickly scrubbed at her hair using as little water as possible, that she did not like Sammy Truesdale. He broke the rules and he didn't smell good.

Still standing carefully balanced on the stepping stone, a small, sad smile tugged at the corners of her mouth as she remembered the innocence of the little girl she had been. Then, everything had been black and white, good and bad. Good meant not hurt. Bad meant hurt. There was no other state of being. She was still learning about all the shades of gray that exist in human behavior, exploring and trying to understand the long, complex, perplexing gradient that lies between black and white, good and bad . . . hurt and not hurt.

Apparently, in Sammy Truesdale's mind, she had become some kind of avenging demon that he had to appease. For a week he followed her everywhere around the school, trying to get her to take the stuffed teddy bear he offered her. She ignored him. Then, Nurse Romer finally noticed the urgency of Sammy's pursuit, the anxiety on his face as he cautiously edged to within arms-length of Delilah, holding out the teddy bear with a combination of fear and supplication on his face.

"Sammy would like you to have this teddy bear," Nurse Romer said, taking it in her hand. "See what a nice, new teddy bear it is.

See how soft and cuddly?" Nurse Romer stroked it and rubbed her cheek against it. "It's a lovely teddy bear, Delilah. Why don't you take it? It will make Sammy happy."

She took it because she had not yet learned that there was a difference between a suggestion and an order. And there was another reason, one even more compelling. She recognized the words teddy bear. She knew those words although until that moment she hadn't known what they meant. It had been a glorious moment of enlightenment and discovery for her although she had given no outward indication of her inner excitement.

Yes, she had never been sorry that she took Teddy Bear. Sammy Truesdale never came near her again, and Teddy Bear became her dearest friend and comforter. She still slept with him every night.

Suddenly back in the present, she knew what her unconscious was trying to tell her. Without hesitation, she turned toward the bank, toes now gripping the hitherto treacherous rock firmly as she smoothly changed positions. Balancing easily, responding now, not to thought but to finely tuned reflexes, she bent her knees slightly and leaped. Clearing the first stepping stone, she landed far up the grassy bank in a crouch from which she instantly straightened, smooth muscular legs propelling her up the tree-lined path toward the small clearing to the right of the path where she had left her clothes.

Lifting up a branch that drooped languidly ground-ward from one of the larger trees, and sliding sideways between two slender saplings, she entered the clearing. Dressing swiftly, she replaced her clothes in the reverse order that she had removed them . . . first her panties, then bra, loose khaki Bermuda shorts, and an over-sized, no-particular-color plaid shirt that hung loosely to well below her hips. Finally, she shoved her feet into worn brown sandals. Fishing in the pocket of her shorts for a moment, she came up with three large hairpins, and deftly, with the speed of long practice, twisted her long dark brown hair into a sleek bun. Holding it in place with one hand, she tightly secured it in place with the hairpins.

Almost finished now, she took a pair of large, heavy-framed dark glasses from her shirt pocket, noticing, as she always did when she put them on, how dismal and lifeless they made everything appear. They relegated her to a kind of shadowy half-world, both concealing her from the world outside and it from her. Most of the time, she considered this a more than fair exchange.

Finished. Here stands the prim and proper Delilah Cross, she thought, an interesting creature at times, even when the stained glass portions of her anatomy aren't visible. Her thoughts were sarcastically mocking, echoing the resentment she felt. Although it hadn't happened recently, she still felt a deep smoldering anger over the times she had been observed, tested, and casually discussed in her presence, referred to as 'she', relegated to the kind of un-person category reserved for furniture, or idiots . . . or animals.

Yes, she thought, and 'she' has an irrational fear of water, too. And, of course, 'she' is mute you know, simply cannot or will not speak a single word.

"Can speak, and very well, but will not," she said very softly in a high, sweetly melodious voice as she moved from the clearing and started up the path toward the farmhouse. "And, do you know what?" She continued to sarcastically emphasize the pronouns. "Someone is watching 'her' without the courtesy of telling 'her' that 'she' is under observation. And do you know what else? 'She' knows who it is, too." She almost sang the last words, not loudly, but defiantly, her customary caution overwhelmed by her anger.

* * *

Dr. Casey Lowell slowly lowered the small pair of binoculars from eyes he somewhat belatedly realized were aching from the unconscious pressure he had been exerting on them as though pressing them tighter against his eyes would bring things even closer. Although he didn't need visual verification of his state of arousal, he glanced downward at himself anyway. He rubbed his eyes none-to-gently, causing them to water. Well, so much for that professional scientific detachment I was so proud of, he thought disgustedly as he stepped away from the old fieldstone wall against which he had been leaning while watching Delilah. He straightened his back with an involuntary grunt. The whole episode at the stream had taken only ten minutes or so, but his back felt like he had been fixed in place against the stones for hours. He was sure the lumpy outlines of some of them were permanently etched in his back.

His sexual reaction annoyed him. It was a betrayal, an unconscious response, libido sneaking up on him when his mind wasn't looking, so to speak. No, he had been looking, totally focused physically and mentally, intent on her every move. His aching eyes and back muscles were proof enough of that. But who would expect her to take off her clothes? And he was, after all, a normally virile young male.

He snorted and shook his head. His excuses, while truthful as far as they went, were both feeble and trite, and to find himself making them irritated him even more. The truth of the matter was he hadn't even been aware of his arousal until now, and certainly not when it happened. He mentally reviewed the sequence of today's events.

When Delilah left the farmhouse by the back door and headed down the path toward the small woods that clustered near the stream, he left the main farmhouse behind her just as he had the two previous days. He stopped to get the binoculars from the shelf in the shed by the kitchen garden, but instead of following her down the path, he went diagonally in the other direction, around behind the big, renovated barn, and followed the cow path to this site by the old stone wall. He put the binoculars in the garden shed the first day, not wanting to be seen carrying them in and out. From here by the barn, he had an almost unobstructed view through the trees to the place where the stream slowed, spreading itself into a small, clear pond crossed by the stepping stones.

The stepping stones were a continuation of the path that started at the back of the farmhouse and wound through the woods to the stream. Beyond the stream, it continued across a pasture and ended at an old-fashioned stile over another fieldstone fence beside the road. Clearly very old, and almost obscured by encroaching grass and shrubs, the path was still defined enough for the eye to follow. Over a period of more than two hundred years, generations of farm children had used it as they walked to and from the one room school at the crossroads less than a mile from the farm. Their feet, bare in the summer and shod in rough leather in winter, had left their mark on the land, wearing and packing the path well below the level of the earth on both sides.

A carefully-preserved historical monument, the old school still stood alone on its corner, clean of line, economical of structure, its purpose clearly defined. The original bell still hung on the small porch, and two wooden privies, complete with half-moon cutouts in the doors, sat at a modest distance to the rear, partially screened by hedges. As soon as the opportunity presented itself, Casey intended to visit the school, following the path from the farm. He was sure that from some vantage point on all the surrounding farms, you would still be able to see traces of similar old, overgrown paths, all of them eventually converging on the crossroads like spokes on a wheel.

In contrast to the school, a gentle reminder of a quieter time and a slower pace, Crossroads Gas, a self-serve station, Crossroads Market, a twenty-four hour convenience store, and Crossroads Diner, a small cafe, occupied the other three corners of the intersection of Palmer Road and Brookline Avenue. The latter didn't actually become anything resembling an avenue until the city limits sign of Centerville. Firmly planted in a circle of flowers surrounded by whitewashed rocks, and backed up by Rotary Club and Chamber of Commerce signs, it announced that you were entering an incorporated municipality with strictly enforced speed laws.

In addition to a small commuter train station and an even smaller bus station, Centerville's latest (and only), claim to fame was a big, new, shopping center whose centerpiece was a sprawling general merchandise store. Part of a successful chain, it had metastasized and spread itself across the entire country in the last twenty years or so. Casey was sure that if each store's location were plotted on a map of the United States, it would form a huge, follow-the-dot picture of a dollar sign. The store was surrounded by several locally owned businesses, and while the owners probably didn't share Casey's follow-the-dot dollar sign picture theory, they had been astute enough to take advantage of the location, as had a large super-market chain. The shopping center drew customers from the whole surrounding area, and while this exodus of shoppers and their dollars created a great deal of chagrin in nearby towns, it put satisfied grins on the faces of the businessmen and elected officials of Centerville.

Casey arrived at his viewpoint before Delilah reached the place where the path disappeared into the woods; he saw her enter the leafy, sun-dappled gloom where the trees grew close, sometimes meeting overhead to form sweeping green arches. It was only a few moments before she came back into his first shocked then bemused sight, naked now, and walked slowly down the bank to the stepping stones across the stream.

Nude or not, she seemed to have no problem at first, stepping to the first stone, pausing a moment, then stepping to the second of the six that spanned the stream. She had stopped there, looking upward at the sky, apparently watching the clouds. Then the second stone appeared to shift slightly under her weight, and she stood crouched, motionless for some time until straightening up and moving slightly to look up at a bird on a branch over her head, staring at it with rapt attention. When he moved the binoculars to get a better look at the bird she found so fascinating, it flew away, its colors so bright in the sun, it left a brief prismatic flash dancing in the binocular lenses.

She moved again, looking down at her naked body, then slowly explored her navel with one finger in a surprisingly child-like gesture. After a moment, still looking down at herself, she placed the hand, open and flat, on her bare stomach, and stood that way for some time, apparently lost in thought.

Only now did Casey realize, as he mentally reviewed the scene, that it was those simple, almost child-like gestures that triggered his sexual response. Although they had no slightest suggestion of the sexual or erotic about them, there was something in her unselfconscious appraisal of herself that struck him as being both innocent and sensual . . . a combination that, on some deep, primal level, he found irresistible. He filed this bit of new information about himself away for future examination.

Then, she looked up and around. He could see her expression clearly; she looked puzzled, at least that was how he interpreted it. Unexpectedly, she turned and exploded in a jump that landed her well up the bank, giving him only the briefest glimpse of well-formed buttocks, tanned, well-proportioned, muscular legs, and long, dark brown hair that hung nearly to her waist. She disappeared with surprising speed up the path and into the shelter of the trees; in a very short time, she appeared, fully dressed, walking rapidly back up the path to the farmhouse.

Sarah Clement introduced him to Delilah when he arrived at Bent Tree Farm four days ago. Delilah and Sarah were in the kitchen preparing lunch when he walked in, and Delilah had acknowledged the introduction with a nod of her head, not looking at him as she continued to chop celery on a big, old-fashioned cutting board at the sink. He had seen her again on the previous three evenings at the communal dinners at the big table in the farm kitchen, but she had eaten quickly and left the kitchen, spending, he assumed, the evenings in her room.

Although he watched her attempts to cross the stream on the two previous days, knowing that she was in her own way trying to overcome her water phobia, nothing had prepared him for the sight of her small, finely modeled but somehow sturdy naked body. In the dappled sunlight of that perfectly natural setting, he had been a rude intruder into the unique privacy of her own personal battlefield.

Dryad, he thought, or nymph, a fey creature that belonged in the woods, and deserved her privacy away from prying eyes. The thought had come unbidden, and it made him uncomfortable. Yet, when she reappeared, fully dressed in her usual baggy, nondescript clothes with the omnipresent dark glasses firmly in place, she had transformed herself back into Case 38, File

41

Number 362, Brighton Foundation Special Attention Group, Sub. A. And he, Doctor K. C. Lowell, Junior, was here to observe her, evaluate her, and present his recommendations for her future to the Board of Directors a month from now.

It was a thoughtful young man who made his way slowly back to the farmhouse. After pausing to put the binoculars back on the shelf in the garden shed, he went in the back door, through the kitchen and up the stairs to the second floor. Entering his room, the "green" room, he closed the door, and stood there thinking. After a moment, he sighed deeply, blew the air out through pursed lips with a small whistling sound, and gave a desultory shove to the unruly forelock of brown hair that dangled just above his eyebrows. It promptly fell back, but he didn't notice. As he looked at the stack of file folders sitting in the middle of the small desk under the window, he wondered how in the hell he was going to word today's report on the outdoor activities of Delilah Cross.

Kicking off his shoes, he flopped on the bed, closed his eyes, and relaxed. Interesting name, Delilah Cross, he thought dreamily, rolling the syllables of Delilah over his tongue, tasting the fluid movement of the vowels. A sensual name that made the almost harsh abruptness of Cross seem shocking and abrasive by contrast. Like her name, she was a fascinating creature, an enigma. As he drifted off to sleep, his mind went its own way,

42

filling itself with the swirling greens of trees, the variegated blues of running water . . . and the naked body of Delilah Cross.

CHAPTER TWO

Delilah jerked awake with a loud intake of breath just as the whistling blow of the long, supple, still-green switch wielded by Miss Agnes was about to connect with her bare buttocks. Taking another deep breath, she propped herself up on her elbows. It took a deliberate effort to relax all the muscles automatically clenched in anticipation of the blow. *Oh Lord,* she thought, *haven't I been punished enough for one night?* She rolled over and sat up on the edge of the bed. The luminous hands on her bedside clock pointed to half-past three. This was the third time tonight she had abruptly awakened, each time escaping from painful scenarios that were not so much dreams as a reliving of past realities, all of them unpleasant and more than a little hurtful.

Hasn't anything nice ever happened to me, she wondered? As she thought about it, it seemed like the only really nice, truly enjoyable things happened long ago in her childhood. There time flowed easily, and she never woke with a gnawing knot of anxiety in her stomach, the ever-present sense of unease that had colored her days for the last eight years.

"Gnawing knot," she whispered to herself, smiling a little. Two good words that ran playfully together, but how aptly they described her feelings. Even her trips to the stream were tense affairs now, serious and purposeful. But she didn't want to think about that right now; it was enough to know she was being watched, and surreptitiously. That was something that hadn't happened in several years. Usually they were polite enough to announce the fact that they were watching her.

After a moment, she chuckled softly. Telling herself not to think about the stream was like telling someone not to think about pink elephants with purple polka dots. For a moment, she contemplated the parade of fanciful elephants she had conjured for herself, then banished them by returning to thoughts about her happiness, or lack of it.

Maybe everyone's childhood assumed that easy quality when looked at across the chasm eroded by passing years. Maybe childhood was the time before we learned to worry about tomorrow, she thought, then tried to remember just when it was that she learned about tomorrow. She couldn't remember exactly when she first understood the meaning of tomorrow, but she did recall clearly when her childhood ended. It vanished forever in the space of one hour, on one hot afternoon, on one day in the season of 'not rain', in the year she later discovered to be 1995.

Maybe that was when she learned about tomorrow . . . and the meaning of pain in all its guises.

She abruptly stood up, using the movement to close the door that started to open in her memory. She was wide awake now, and unwilling to risk reliving any more painful scenes. *Those dreams are actually bits and pieces of my life*, she thought sadly. *Maybe that stained glass imagery this afternoon bubbled up out of my subconscious to talk to my conscious self about my feelings like it dug up Sammy Truesdale to tell me I was being watched. So memories can be useful, too.* She sighed. Sometimes, she felt like someone had turned her whole life into a jigsaw puzzle and set her the task of recreating a picture of herself that they considered acceptable. Early on, as far back as Bhutu, she had been smart enough to glimpse the pattern they had in mind, and she had really tried to follow it, to be whatever it was they wanted to see, wanted her to be.

Her grin was a bit unpleasant, a tightening of her upper lip that exposed white upper canine teeth that dipped slightly below the line of her other teeth. The problem was that Delilah Cross knew exactly and in detail who she was, had known since that long-ago day when Auntie first explained it to her. And Auntie had repeated it to her every night over a period of years, always stressing that it was a secret that could never be told. When she was very young, it had just been a story that Auntie told, and it wasn't until her time at Bhutu Holding Facility that it became reality; it was there she realized it was not just a story Auntie told, it was the truth.

As she turned toward the foot of the bed, she caught a glimpse of herself in the dresser mirror. She paused, looking directly at her reflected image, something she usually avoided. Her eyes narrowed, and the grin became a grimace. For a moment, the wavering image of a small girl, eyes wide in terror, mouth wide in a silent scream, superimposed itself over her own. She blinked hard and turned away, not noticing that her right hand rose toward her left shoulder, gently rubbed the area to the side of her collarbone, and returned to her side.

Well, she had kept the secret for Auntie. For eight long, confusing, heartbreaking years she had kept the secret, carefully putting the scrambled puzzle pieces together for them, each time holding up a picture of Delilah Cross for their inspection and approval, always hoping they wouldn't notice the missing piece, the secret she so carefully guarded.

Over the years, she had created three separate Delilah Crosses and was working hard on the fourth. Would there never be an end to it, she wondered? And who was she? Who was she really? Right now, right at this moment, how much of her was really herself and how much was acquired from the parade of characters she played? She grinned, an honestly amused grin this time . . . parades of charades. Always playing with words, fascinated by them since her first attempts as a baby trying to understand and imitate the sounds Auntie made.

The grimace changed to a wry grin. Enough, she thought, and shrugged into her sloppy old bathrobe, belting it over the baggy gray sweat pants and shirt in which she slept most of the time. The robe was clean, but faded to an indeterminate no-color, and decidedly old and tacky, as were the sweats. It wasn't as though she couldn't have all the new, properly fitting, stylish clothes she wanted, whenever she wanted them. While she was at Hiller School she had had them, too. She just didn't want them now.

Brighton Foundation was more than generous in providing for her every physical need, and she supposed as her legal guardian they were required to do so. But they more than provided for her, she had discovered, they were lavish in catering to her every expressed wish for reasons she had never been able to understand.

Well, at the moment, new, modish clothes didn't fit her latest persona of a baggy, colorless, self-effacing, self-erasing non-person, not worth a second glance let alone the close scrutiny to which she was usually subjected. *It is excellent protective coloration,* she thought; *blending into the background is almost like fading into the wallpaper, or vanishing into the foliage as a chameleon did, and easier to do.* The thought of struggling with pantyhose crossed her mind. *And a lot more comfortable, too.* She grinned widely, honestly amused, the tension caused by her bad dreams banished for the moment.

When she was getting ready to leave Hiller School and come to Bent Tree Farm, she packed only the oldest and most worn of her clothes and a few treasured personal things into two medium-sized suitcases. The rest of her belongings, clothes, shoes, junk jewelry, some fairly good costume jewelry, several unopened bottles of perfume, and all of her make-up, went into cardboard boxes and plastic grocery bags which she carried over to the Newcombes' house and presented to Becky. It took three trips.

Becky Newcombe had helped Delilah shop for most of the things in the first place, and the things she chose for Delilah were almost always things that pleased Becky the most, and which her own clothes allowance wouldn't stretch to cover in a million years. She was a reddish-blond with very fair skin, and though she and Delilah were the same height, Becky was slender with a very small waist that exaggerated the size of her breasts. Delilah's hair was a glossy dark brown, her complexion a shade or two darker than Becky's and her build more stocky and well-proportioned because of her heavier bone structure. Delilah wasn't fat, far from it, and of the two of them, she actually had the better figure.

Somewhere down deep, Becky harbored a small, selfish resentment of the fact that a person like Delilah, who had little interest in clothes and no sense of style, possessed a seemingly endless clothing allowance. This didn't seem fair to her, and it was not surprising that many of the clothes she insisted were just perfect for Delilah were totally unbecoming to her, but just right for Becky, who borrowed them almost incessantly. If a person could actually wallow in happiness, then Becky Newcombe wallowed as she spread the contents of the boxes and bags on her twin beds and squealed her delighted thank-you's to Delilah.

So, it had been the new Delilah who was delivered to Bent Tree Farm almost two years ago. She had arrived in one of the ubiquitous small, neat, dark blue, Brighton Foundation cars, of which they seemed to have an unending supply, and left standing on the wide front porch with her two suitcases sitting on either side of her like small, brown, totally ineffectual guard dogs. And that is how she felt as she stood there on that day, a total non-person. The suitcases seemed to have more reality, more solidity, more identity.

The sour-faced young woman who met her at the small regional airport after the commuter plane from Philadelphia made its bumpy landing had picked her out of the scanty group of passengers by taking her arm none-too-gently and saying, "Here, come with me."

That was the entire extent of her conversation during their sojourn through the airport, the stop at the luggage carousel, and the fifty-mile drive to Bent Tree Farm. They arrived well after noon and the only time the woman acknowledged her presence was to throw a disgusted glance in her general direction when Delilah's stomach growled loudly, notifying her that breakfast was long in the past, and she had fed it nothing on the plane.

When they turned into the gate, drove up the long, gravel driveway, and stopped in front of the main house, the woman took the two suitcases from the back seat, marched up the steps, and deposited them on the porch with a thump. Still without a word, she returned to the car, wheeled it around in a smartly executed U-turn, and with a crunching of gravel, abruptly zipped out of Delilah's life in much the same way she had entered it.

Not knowing if she was expected, if she should knock, just walk in, or simply wander around until she encountered someone, Delilah felt completely lost and disoriented. In the back of her mind, she could hear Auntie's voice clearly. "Not know what do, not do."

So she sat on the top step between her suitcases and simply waited. It seemed reasonable because by not doing she was less likely to violate any rules or customs of proper behavior that might be in effect here. Doing, if it was the wrong thing, might get her off to a bad start in this new place. Although not doing had also gotten her into trouble in the past, Auntie's "not do" philosophy had worked for her more often than not, and she had no reason to think it wouldn't work now.

She was sitting on the step, chin in hand, when Sarah Clement discovered her an hour later. Delilah was expected and Sarah had been waiting for her arrival, thinking that the person who brought her would bring her in and introduce her, or at least announce her presence before leaving. Talking a mile a minute, her round, ordinarily pink face suffused with the red of indignation, she grabbed the suitcases and clucked Delilah into the house. She paused in the hall to indicate the bathroom across the hall from the spacious living room, and continued on, depositing the suitcases at the foot of a wide staircase on the right. "Go ahead and use the bathroom if you need to, dear," she said. "I'll be in the kitchen getting you a bite to eat. It's past lunchtime, and I'm sure you can use it." She moved on down the hall to where a wooden swinging door closed off the end of the hallway.

Delilah gratefully used the small, spotless bathroom, taking time to wash her face as well as her hands. The towel was very soft and white, and she pressed it to her nose to inhale the pleasant, fresh smell, a different odor from the ones she identified with Hiller School and the Newcombes' home . . . and Bhutu. None of them were home smells, group smells, but this one was a good one, she thought, different but definitely good.

She had been getting desperate to go to the bathroom, almost to the point of leaving the porch and looking for a bush to squat behind. The sour-faced woman hadn't bothered to inquire about the matter as they went through the airport, and Delilah was too intimidated to make the request on the little writing pad she always carried with her. As her growling stomach proclaimed, it had been a long time since breakfast at Hiller School.

She had managed to remain outwardly calm and swallow the orange juice offered by the stewardess, but Delilah could not force herself to use the bathroom on the plane and face another one of the horrors that seemed to be tucked away in nooks and crannies all around her brain. She didn't know what it was, she only knew something terrible would happen to her if she went into an airplane bathroom, although she had no conscious memory of ever being inside an airplane before.

When she left the bathroom at Bent Tree Farm that day, she walked down the carpeted hall, pushed open the swinging door to the kitchen, and stepped into the nicest, most welcoming, friendly room she had ever seen.

It was large, well equipped, and, it seemed to Delilah, swirling with sunshine and good smells. If it isn't the center of life here, it should be, she thought. She looked around the big room. On the left there was a huge, oval wooden table that comfortably seated eight without using the leaves. It was polished to a high gloss and a hanging lamp provided light directly over the table. The pale yellow curtains at the windows that spanned most of the wall over

53

the big double sinks gave the room a light, sunny cast, and the dark, beamed ceiling contrasted nicely with the line of copper-bottomed pots and pans that hung over the big electric range. It reminded Delilah of something she might have seen on television or in a magazine picture, but certainly never in person, a real farm kitchen with all its warmth and good smells.

The small, shiny glass and stainless steel kitchen of which Dee Dee Newcombe was so proud came in a poor second in Delilah's opinion, but she felt a surge of loneliness wash through her. There had been some good times, fun times in Dee Dee's kitchen. She quickly stifled the thought. Now was no time to drift; she needed all her wits about her.

In a remarkably short time, she found herself seated at the table hungrily eating a cold lunch. Tuna salad liberally laced with chopped celery, topped with slices of hard-boiled egg, a huge scoop of cottage cheese sitting on a slice of pineapple, and a thick slice of what could only be home-made bread spread with what could only be home-churned butter soon occupied her full attention.

She had read somewhere about bread and butter like this, but never tasted it. Before she caught herself, she raised the buttered slice of bread to her nose, inhaling deeply to get the full aroma of the combined smells. When she raised her eyes, suddenly aware that she had violated one of the rules of proper table manners so carefully beaten into her by Miss Agnes, and more gently prompted by Dee Dee Newcombe, Sarah, who had been watching her, laughed out loud.

"It does smell something like heaven, doesn't it?" she asked. "I think the smell of home-made bread is the biggest reason I bake my own. And, as far as I'm concerned, there's nothing that can beat the taste of home-churned butter, even if we do use an electric churn and only have enough cream to make it once a week. Just wait until you taste a really fresh egg or a tomato still warm from the sun. Why snitching fresh vegetables from the garden is such a habit around here, we keep a salt shaker on a little shelf out there by the water faucet."

As Delilah visibly relaxed under this shower of warm approving words, Sarah turned away, thinking as she busied herself at the counter, *if I didn't know better, and I don't, I would think that child is scared out of her mind.* Her usually smooth forehead wrinkled in thought. Something about the way Delilah kept her head down concealing her eyes bothered Sarah. From the few glimpses she had caught, Delilah's eyes were quite beautiful, a very unusual color. There was much more going on here than she had been led to believe, but one thing she knew for sure, this child needed a friend, and being a friend was something Sarah Clement was very good at.

Before Delilah was quite finished, Sarah placed a platter on the table. It was piled high with sugar cookies, big, round, hand-sized cookies, their lightly browned tops liberally sprinkled with sugar. She poured two big glasses of milk, and lowered herself into the chair nearest Delilah. Taking a cookie for herself and handing another to Delilah who was still chewing her last bite of bread, she sighed and brushed her gray bangs back from her slightly moist forehead. Then, quite unselfconscious, she reached under her practical, loose-hanging smock to ease the stretch band of her denim jeans.

"Judging by the way you were dumped off like so much baggage by that . . . that . . . ," Sarah fumbled for a word to suitably express her disgust without resorting to an obscenity, " . . . by that twit, you probably don't have the slightest idea about Bent Tree Farm, what goes on here, and what you'll be doing here, do you?"

When Delilah shook her head, she did so without a twinge of guilt. She did know quite a few things about the farm and what she was doing here. Part of her information had come from Harold Newcombe, Hiller School Director, and the rest came from her unauthorized, surreptitious entries into the Hiller School computer. That system had led her, after much trial and error and help from Paulie Newcombe, into the Brighton Foundation computer network through the "back door". Actually, she knew quite a bit about Bent Tree Farm, but she wanted to hear what

Sarah had to say about it, so she waited expectantly.

Munching cookies and drinking milk, Sarah explained, touching Delilah on the arm from time to time, patting gently to emphasize a point. It was this contact upon which Delilah focused because it was such an unusual experience for her. Since she and Becky and Paulie had crossed that arbitrary invisible line from childhood where rough and tumble play involving physical contact was acceptable, and entered that strange land known as adolescence, she had had little physical contact with other people.

She suddenly missed Auntie and her comforting, touching closeness with a sense of loss that was near physical pain. These kind, reassuring touches by Sarah satisfied a need she hadn't realized had been there all along. She needed touching and physical contact, her body was hungry for it. She leaned closer, taking comfort from Sarah's nearness, inhaling the smell of her - a good smell, a pleasant combination of food mixed with a light talcum powder - as Sarah explained the workings of Bent Tree Farm and what was and was not expected of her while she was here.

Delilah paused in the act of twisting her hair up into its customary bun, the graceful line of her body emphasized by her raised arms even though camouflaged by the sweats. That had been her introduction to Sarah Clement and Bent Tree Farm and these were good memories. Sarah had become her friend, a real friend, treating her with affection and respect, expressing genuine interest in her as a person, and a great deal of concern about her well-being. So did her husband, Joe, and their son, Jordan. In a strange sort of way, Bent Tree Farm had become her second home and Sarah a kind of surrogate Auntie. Sarah, Joe, and Jordan had become her family, her group.

While Delilah was aware that Brighton Foundation owned the farm, she was only peripherally aware that the entire Clement family was employed by Brighton Foundation. She knew this, but in her mind the farm belonged to the Clement family. They simply didn't fit her mental picture of the report-writing, order-taking types she had encountered continually during the previous six years. They were too easy-going, too relaxed . . . too human.

Even Harold Newcombe, who, she was now beginning to realize, had been a kind of savior in her life by almost literally making her a part of his own family, occasionally gave the impression that he could only make decisions up to a point. When that invisible line was reached, he seemed to feel it necessary to consult someone higher up, someone authorized, someone with more power than he was permitted to exercise. In a way, it reminded her of how Miss Agnes had continually consulted her God, asking His forgiveness, asking His permission, always seeking His approval . . . and they all wrote reports.

She only started to understand Harold's position as Director of

Hiller School after she had penetrated deeply enough into Brighton Foundation computers to comprehend their bureaucratic structure, to get an idea of the flow of power up and down. In her mind, Brighton Foundation was some unbelievably huge, monstrous tree whose branches cast shadows across half the world, its sap a transport system that carried information up and money and orders down. And Delilah could not find a place in this structure for the Clement family, even though she puzzled over it from time to time.

What she really thought about was the identity of that all-powerful being who sat on the very top branch of the Brighton Foundation tree. Or, she wondered, were they buried somewhere in the roots, tapped into the life juices of the tree like some burrowing parasite? Or maybe it was really the God of Miss Agnes?

The comparison had never entered her mind, but had she made it Delilah would have realized that her mental picture of the great Brighton Foundation tree was nearly identical with those tree-diagrams used by genealogists and others to delineate the roots, trunks, branches, twigs and leaves in family records. Or the chain of command charts in businesses where the most powerful sat ensconced at the top. Or the natural order chains used to illustrate the divergence of species, among other things.

Bhutu Holding Facility occupied one of the lower branches, as she saw it, while Hiller School was solidly sitting several branches above it. But she couldn't seem to find a branch for the Clement family, even though Bent Tree Farm, itself, nestled in a leafy bower somewhere near Hiller School, across from it but higher up.

Sarah, Joe, and Jordan lived in the big remodeled gatehouse near the road. Joe ran the small farming operation, mostly experimental organically grown crops, with the occasional seasonal help of a hired hand from Centerville. Jordan also helped when he wasn't busy with the various hydroponic crops in the big state-of-the-art greenhouse.

From time to time, various visitors, mostly Brighton Foundation employees and grant recipients, spent up to a month at a time at Bent Tree. Some stayed in the bunkhouse because their experiments with test plantings in the greenhouse required that they sometimes work strange hours in the small but well-equipped lab partitioned off at the rear of the greenhouse. Their comings and goings would be disruptive for the other Brighton people using some of the six bedrooms upstairs in the farmhouse proper, so they followed their own routines and schedules, and took their meals with everyone else, a very efficient system that took care of the needs of everyone.

Sarah was responsible for everything else, and, with the assistance of two women from Centerville who were called in when needed depending on how many people were in residence, she did an excellent job, planning meals, buying groceries, cooking, and, in general, keeping everything running smoothly.

Life at Bent Tree Farm had a feeling of normality and permanence, and some of the knots of tension and anxiety, those gnawing knots, had been slowly coming undone as the months went by. Delilah had the run of the farm, free to come and go at will, and she derived a great deal of satisfaction from pitching in and helping Sarah.

She went along on the twice-weekly shopping trips to the Centerville supermarket at the shopping center, happily pushing the carts around the huge building. She thoroughly enjoyed these trips and looked forward to them. For some reason she didn't understand, the lights and background music, the mixed smells of baked goods, produce, and even furniture polish, combined into a kind of carnival atmosphere that excited her. Becky and Paulie had taken her to a couple of carnivals and she had had a wonderful time there. The music and occasional announcements over the loudspeakers heightened the impression of carnival, and the shopping carts reminded her of bumper cars as they made the rounds. Sarah always started on one side, going up and down each aisle, and Delilah pushed the carts, carefully avoiding bumping or being bumped by other carts, until, having successfully negotiated the entire course, they came at last to the check out counter. She always felt a little sad then, sorry the fun had ended.

She had even learned to bake sugar cookies, carefully following Sarah's instructions. After solemn deliberation and much tasting, Sarah had declared them to be almost as good as her own. To Delilah's taste and sensitive smell, they were identical, but she gave no indication. Sarah was the dominant female here, the main cookie-baker, and it was not her place to challenge that position in any way, not even about a cookie.

Delilah also spent several hours each day working on her college correspondence courses, and she spent many late night hours in the large office at the end of the upstairs hall a few steps down from her room. There, with growing expertise, she continued to prowl through Brighton Foundation computers, reading files, compiling information in her head, and carefully erasing all traces of her back door entries when she logged off. Had anyone found her there, using the front corner office space she had chosen for herself, there was always a textbook open on the desk beside her, an innocent explanation of her presence. She was careful, very careful.

Sometimes, filled with an energy that must be expended, she grabbed her flute from the dresser, and simply ran. Across pastures, down overgrown paths, through the woods she would fly, until, out of breath and exhilarated by the simple knowledge that she had the freedom to run, she would drop to the ground wherever she found herself. After taking a few deep breaths, she would play the flute.

The pan flute was her own private joke, one she would never share, and it always made her smile. Dee Dee Newcombe had included her when she decided that the children should have training on some musical instrument as part of making them "well-rounded," as she put it. Paulie had made finger-down-the-throat barfing motions behind his Mother's back when she made the suggestion; Delilah knew that his choice of a trombone as his instrument was pure maliciousness. Whenever he was angry, he practiced long and loud, eventually driving everyone out of the house until he had vented his frustration.

Becky and Delilah had drifted around the musical instrument store without much enthusiasm, looking for something they might like to play. Becky eventually settled on a guitar after she had tried it out in one of the soundproof rooms provided by the store, paying far more attention to the young man assisting her than the instrument itself. And Delilah, though she really preferred the plaintive tones of a recorder, chose a pan flute, knowing she would the minute she heard its name.

She enjoyed the lessons, though Becky and Paulie considered them a drag and bore. Sometimes the songs she played were recognizable, sometimes they were lilting and happy melodies she made up as she went along. But, at other times, they were little more than plaintive pipings full of minor tones, expressions of sadness and longing. After a while, she would lie back, empty of thought, satisfied just to be.

As she stood there with her arms upraised, Delilah suddenly realized that Sarah, Joe, and Jordan must have been hearing her music all this time, the haunting sounds of the flute drifting and carrying in the still air of the farm, sure indicators of her current emotional state. She remembered all the times- -mostly when she was upset or frustrated and had expressed it in her playing- -that one of them intercepted her with a request for help with some chore, or to ask if she would like to ride into town for ice cream. Funny how she saw that now, but didn't at the time.

She stopped twisting her hair up, and removed the hairpin she had put in place. Why in the world was she bothering to do this? Who was here to see her in the middle of the night? She sat back down on the edge of her bed and slowly stroked her brush through her lustrous waist length hair. Yes, it had been good here, and if a feeling of contentment and belonging was happiness, then she had been happy here. But now she was being watched again.

That thought sent an almost imperceptible shiver through her body, and the hairs at the nape of her neck lifted slightly. They always did that when she was confronted with something new or strange that made her uneasy or frightened. At the same time, her ears always felt tight, somehow closer to her head. Being watched

64

meant danger in the world she came from. Only a predator focused that intently, and only after picking its intended prey. This knowledge went soul-deep, and had caused her endless anguish over the years.

She had been watched a lot over the last eight years, watched intently for every flicker of movement, every response to stimulus. Observing is what these professional watchers called it, watching her, then attacking her with words, precisely-written words on charts, graphs, and reports. Words, she discovered early on, whether true or false, held power over her, tremendous power. When once she had refused to cooperate with some testing procedure, she was told that it was 'for her own good'. Yes, all for Delilah's 'own good', with never a mention of all the professional curiosity satisfied, or all the professional esteem acquired as a result of learned papers and articles filled with words, words accurate or not, all supposedly based on these observations of her.

Just like Miss Agnes, she thought with resentment. Every blow she struck with her correctional implementer had been accompanied by a 'it's for your own good'. It was done, too, with a pious upward glance, as though she was either basking in her God's approval, or sneaking a look to see if He was paying attention as she fulfilled her mission. How many times, Delilah wondered, had Miss Agnes explained to that her holy mission was to find some infraction of her rules. However small such violations may be, she always reiterated that she needed to do something for Delilah's 'own good'.

Sadistic old bitch, Delilah thought, laying her brush back in its place on the dresser, serving a sadistic old God. Now she would personally do something for her 'own good'. The memories of her arrival at Bent Tree Farm and the warmth and good feelings evoked by her first memories of the kitchen brought her thoughts back to sugar cookies and milk. She padded barefoot down the stairs and turned right toward the kitchen. She didn't turn on any lights because she had made this late night trip downstairs many times before on restless nights when sleep came hard or nightmares rode her from her bed. She didn't notice that she rubbed her backside with one hand, responding to body memory of old pain, as she pushed the swinging door to the kitchen with her other.

She stopped in mid-movement, one hand on the door, the other on her backside, totally still, scarcely breathing through widely flared nostrils. She smelled him, and knew immediately who it was, but not why he was sitting in a dark kitchen at four o'clock in the morning drinking coffee. She could smell the coffee, rich, strong, and fragrant, and the faintly toasted vanilla of cookies.

Her first instinctual reaction told her to flee, scurry back to the safety of her room like some small, frightened animal. No, I won't run, was her second thought. I have a right to be here. And I

66

baked those cookies this afternoon. A flash of irritation accompanied that thought as though the cookies were her personal territory and he was trespassing without her permission. Sliding silently through the partly open door, she eased it back into place without a sound. Finding the light switch on the wall with one hand, she raised the other to partly shield her eyes.

She was prepared as the light from the hanging lamp over the table flooded down, spotlighting the table while leaving the rest of the kitchen in easy, softly shadowed illumination. He wasn't expecting it, hadn't heard her, and the light was painful to his dark-enlarged pupils. With a startled exclamation, he jumped up, overturning his chair with a clatter as he turned to face her.

"Don't you know how to knock?" he yelled. Then he seemed to realize where he was. No one was expected to knock on the swinging door of a dark communal kitchen at four o'clock in the morning. He hadn't when he came in an hour ago, so why should she?

He grinned at her apologetically, then bent to right his chair. "Sorry about that." Embarrassed now, he reached down, picked up his coffee mug, took a big swallow, and promptly choked as the coffee and a few residual cookie crumbs went down the wrong way. Fortunately, it wasn't serious, but he managed to spray coffee over a large area of the table in front of him, barely missing the plate of cookies. Adding to his humiliation, when he involuntarily snorted, a trickle of coffee ran out of his nose and made its way down his upper lip.

He didn't see Delilah's grin of delighted amusement as he quickly turned to the sink and grabbed for the paper towels, first taking care of his dripping nose, then wetting a handful to clean up the mess on the table. When he turned back in her direction, the grin was gone.

She stood quietly, unmoving, watching him from her place by the door, finding that she was thoroughly enjoying his discomfiture. It was very seldom that she saw anyone without their public mask firmly in place, and this was the first time she had ever seen a professional, a doctor, no less, even if he did seem awfully young, lose both his professional and personal composure at the same time. She couldn't help feeling a bit smug. Served him right for spying on her! She raised her eyes from the table and Casey's furious cleaning efforts, to his body.

She had learned the hard way from Miss Agnes to keep her lids lowered, looking upward without raising them much or tipping her head up from the slightly lowered position it assumed through years of practice. While this gave her the appearance of being either humble or shy, or both, it also had the advantage of shielding her thoughts from casual view, an indirect bonus that had served her well during her years of deception.

Eyes are the windows of the soul. How many times had Miss

Agnes said those words to her? She always managed to imply that Delilah had no soul, that nothing looked out of her eye windows, that the space behind them was somehow empty of that invisible something everyone else seemed to have. Certainly, soul or not, Miss Agnes had found Delilah's eyes to be unpleasant and distasteful. With an act of will, Delilah shoved Miss Agnes back into her dark closet. She wondered, not for the first time, why Miss Agnes always seemed to make sneaking, hurtful appearances whenever something was bothering her.

She concentrated on the man. His brown hair was sleep-tousled, forelock hanging over one eye. He, too, was barefoot, and he was wearing only a loose-fitting pair of faded gym shorts that hung low on his hips, exposing a line of dark hair that rose to his naval. It was quite fine and silky-looking in comparison with the dark curls of hair descending from his chest. She controlled an urge to smile. Certainly, his sleepwear wasn't any more presentable than hers, and at least she was completely covered now, even if she hadn't been this afternoon at the stream.

She could smell him, too. The inherent male musk, which she associated with all post-pubescent males, mingled with the light pine scent of bath soap. There was a faint sweet-sour odor of sleep sweat, the fading tang of adrenaline. There was also the distinct smell of cat, and something else, something she couldn't quite identify. She took a deep breath. It wasn't the odors, she thought, it was the hair, the dark body hair that bothered her, triggering something deep and disquieting. Suddenly, her fingers twitched involuntarily. She wanted to touch it, touch the hair.

Danger! Danger! The alarm bells in her mind went off so loudly she nearly jumped. Surely he could hear them, too? Breaking off her inspection, she inclined her head slightly up toward the light, then back toward him.

"Oh, why was I sitting here in the dark?" he asked.

Thank God she's stopped examining me, he thought. Casey was thoroughly embarrassed again, both by her intense scrutiny and by his own thoughts. During that long moment while she was studying his body, making no attempt to conceal what she was doing, he was having vivid mental pictures of her as she stood naked, immobile as a small perfectly-sculpted statue, on the stepping stone in the stream. I better get some control here, he thought. This young lady is only sixteen years old, and she's my professional responsibility. These reactions are totally out of line, he told himself sternly.

In response to her slight nod at his question, he babbled. He could hear himself babbling, and he couldn't stop. "I couldn't sleep for some reason, so I came down, made some coffee, turned the light off, and sat in the dark to drink it." He looked down at the still damp spot on the table, and the cookie crumbs sprinkled around.

"I guess it's pretty dumb to eat and drink in the dark, but I do some of my best work in the dark." Oh God, he thought, double entendre. Will she get it? He scanned her face quickly and professionally this time. No, not a flicker, at least he didn't think so. He couldn't see her eyes. She seemed to habitually keep them concealed for some reason.

Delilah was still standing where she had first stopped. Her stillness bothered him. "Oh, I'm really forgetting my manners," he said. "Would you like a cup? It's still hot." In response to her nod, he quickly busied himself, pouring a cup, getting a spoon from the silverware drawer, cream from the refrigerator, and the sugar bowl from the side counter.

She slipped into the chair directly across from his, watching him as he made two trips, placing everything in front of her with small flourishes. His body language says he is very nervous, she thought, but if something about me is upsetting him, I don't know what it is. Then, again, his sitting in the dark kitchen at four o'clock in the morning drinking coffee and eating cookies had nothing to do with her, of that she was sure.

She reviewed what she knew about him aside from the fact he had been spying on her for the last three days. He had been at the farm for four days, he showed up promptly for lunch and dinner, and carried on a lot of laughing conversations with all the members of the Clement family at the dinner table. Although

Brighton Foundation employees frequently spent varying periods of time here, they usually kept pretty much to themselves, preoccupied with the contents of their own minds with no interest in keeping up social banter at mealtimes. Casey's socializing was unusual, she thought. Then, of course, there were those others, those who came here to study Delilah Cross, but they had always announced their intentions, and there had been fewer of those, the last one over six months ago, much to her relief.

So, what else did she know about this man? Well, his name was Doctor K. C. Lowell, Junior, although he insisted that everyone call him Casey. He was observing her without the small courtesy of telling her so, and no matter what his hypothesis or theory about her, she was sure that he would take her apart and put her back together again to substantiate it. It had happened many times before, and she was sure it would happen many times again, until . . . until what? Until they decided to set her free? Until she died of old age?

Anyway, he seemed awfully young, and not wanting to be called by his title was unusual in her experience. For some reason associated with ego, all the doctors she had encountered, male and female, seemed to insist on their titles, and frequently assumed a kind of pedantic, pompous, know-it-all attitude they felt in keeping with their degrees and learned importance.

Delilah had always found this funny, and assigned each one

her own private name, ranging from plain "Worm" for Doctor Robin Early, to "Dunghill" for old Doctor Dunhill because he always, to her sensitive nose, smelled of unwashed underwear.

When she was younger, first learning about the importance of deodorants from Becky, she had wondered why normal body odors didn't offend her, while the smell of worn clothing disgusted her. Later, she had decided that body odors are a sure-fire method of communication, clear and unequivocal. Simple, direct, and they don't lie, while clothes carry signals that come from this morning, or yesterday, or, and she wrinkled her nose, from last week in Doctor "Dunghill's" case. Too bad so much of human sensitivity to smell had gotten lost somewhere along the evolutionary trail, and how fortunate for Delilah Cross that no one could smell out her deceitfulness as she could theirs.

Casey resumed his seat across the table, and Delilah nodded her thanks, as she added a spoonful of sugar and a splash of cream to her coffee. All this mulling, another good word, hadn't gotten her anywhere. She looked down into the mug as she stirred, intent on the spiral patterns made by the heavy cream. A brief, clear picture of the stream swirling around before it swallowed the leaf flashed in her mind.

Casey watched her, assessing the focused concentration she was giving the cup. It reminded him of the way she had looked at the bird at the stream. What does she see, he wondered? What is she thinking about what she sees?

Quite without warning, almost before he consciously thought them, the words were out of his mouth. "Delilah, why don't you talk?"

She froze. No other word could describe the sudden cessation of movement. He saw it happen. In a split second she became totally still, the spoon held upright in the cup, coffee swirling around it. He had never seen anything quite like it, outside of catatonia, and that wasn't the case here. She had actually stopped breathing, and he thought of a panicked animal caught in the beams of headlights, unable to move out of harm's way. One beat, two beats, three beats, he counted the time. Then, she slowly relaxed, took a deep breath, and raised her head. Her eyelids were fully open, and she gazed directly at him, allowing him to really see her eyes.

He sucked in his breath involuntarily, unaware of the sound it made in the quiet kitchen. He was staring, and she returned his look, her eyes steady and unwavering. The irises were large and a startling blue, nearly the color sometimes seen in Siamese cats or girls wearing specially tinted contact lenses. They were ringed with darker brownish-blue, and showed a slightly less than average amount of white around them. The long, full dark lashes she used to such advantage to conceal provided an almost unexpectedly startling contrast.

They're beautiful, he thought, totally, amazingly beautiful. But it wasn't just the color or their beauty he saw. There was pain there, pain so deep and pervasive it hit him with an almost physical impact. And there was an unmistakable maturity there, a cynical, intelligent knowing and strength of will that pierced him and held him impaled.

Still holding his eyes with hers, Delilah smiled, a small, mocking smile that showed the barest flash of her upper canine teeth as she raised an eyebrow. She rose then and was gone, leaving Doctor K. C. Lowell, Junior watching the kitchen door swing to and fro, sitting there with cold coffee and cookie crumbs, trying to sort it out.

CHAPTER THREE

Delilah scampered down the hall and up the stairs, reaching the haven of her room before the kitchen door had stopped swinging. She sat down on the edge of the bed, took a deep breath and told herself to take it one step at a time, consider one thing at a time. That had always worked for her before, and, after all, nothing terrible had happened, not really, just a series of unusual occurrences that's all.

First of all, in the slow, almost dreamy days here at the farm, she had relaxed the rigid, almost impenetrable armor she so carefully built for herself during what she still thought of as the time of Miss Agnes. It had grown considerably thinner during her years at Hiller School. But it was still operative enough when she got here to give her a feeling of being in control over what she would allow to be known about her and what she would keep concealed behind her shield.

Here at Bent Tree, she had not been pressured in any way, not forced to perform to anyone's expectations except her own; she had been allowed to set her own pace. When she thought about it now, she could see how easily she had succumbed to the quiet, easy-going life-style and the open, genuinely accepting friendship offered by Sarah and her family. It had been easy because she wanted it, needed to relax, needed to feel safe, if only for a while. And there was nothing wrong or dangerous about that.

So, what was the first thing? The uneasiness and irritation caused by Casey Lowell's sneaky observation. It had been nearly six months since the last official observer was sent out from Brighton Foundation. That time, it was an earnest, bespectacled young lady intent on finishing her doctoral thesis in style by using first-hand information that she personally gathered by observing and interacting with the one and only Delilah Cross. She departed, clutching her precious computer printouts like crown jewels, and there had been no one since...until now.

Delilah's mouth turned up at the corners as she remembered. Margaret had been fun. It was certain that very up-tight young lady had never been called Margie, or Maggie, or any other less than proper form of address, of that Delilah was sure. She arrived with her preconceived ideas as firmly anchored in place as the thick glasses that clung bat-like to the bridge of her large, feature-dominating nose.

At first, Delilah had taken great pains to bolster every one of those ideas, no matter how weird or outrageous. It was almost too easy because Margaret conscientiously used one of the office computers to record each day's observations, painstakingly arranging her daily notes to fit the detailed outline of the thesis she carefully entered into the computer the first evening of her two week stay. If the facts she observed about Delilah didn't fit her outline, or contradicted it in any way, she simply discarded the information as irrelevant. A very handy way of conducting observations to prove any point you wished to make. Margaret's work was an exaggerated but accurate example of everything Delilah had found to be true about most of the observations she had been subjected to across the years.

Just as carefully, after Margaret went to bed each night, Delilah went down the hall to the office, booted up the computer Margaret was using and read each of her day's entries. Across the years, Delilah had developed an almost obsessional fascination with the reports that were written about her. When she could do so undetected, she was not above altering a word here and a statement there to put herself in a better light with the faceless people to whom the reports were sent. These people were not nameless, not any more, because she had their names carefully memorized, they were just faceless because she had never seen them.

Delilah wondered what kind of grade Margaret finally got on her effort. After all, she had helped, even going so far as to correct spelling errors - of which there were many - and straighten out some rather bizarre grammar. She also changed some of the information, thinking at the time how the addition or elimination of one little word could change the meaning of a sentence, and how that altered sentence could change the whole thrust of the entire piece of work. That Margaret didn't seem to notice the alterations was the best part of all. Delilah loved playing games with words.

Her grin became almost wicked, puckish and full of mischief as she recalled a conversation she had accidentally overheard between Sarah and Margaret, one that had caused her to ease up a bit on poor Margaret . . . a bit but not much.

On that particular morning, she volunteered to collect the laundry bags from upstairs and take them down to the basement laundry room, a chore she didn't mind at all. Soon after her arrival, she invented a kind of game that consisted of placing all the laundry bags on the banister, giving them a starting push, then running down the stairs to the landing to catch them before they fell off. Certainly a simple kind of game, but one she enjoyed because it amused her, as most games did.

Apparently, Sarah and Joe were amused by it, too, because on one such occasion she had lined up four bags on the banister leading to the ground floor, having successfully caught them at the end of the first half of their sliding trip from the upstairs hall.

She had given them a particularly hard push, and was partway down the stairs, intent on catching them, when Sarah and Joe, deep in conversation about some farm matter, came down the hall from the kitchen.

They stopped short as four bags of laundry shot off of the banister and plopped at their feet. With very straight faces, Sarah and Joe turned to look at a breathless and embarrassed Delilah, who came down the last few steps and stood waiting for the expected scolding.

Turning to Sarah, Joe asked, "Sarah, I realize that it was a close race, but did you happen to notice which color bag hit the floor first?"

"Yes." Her face and voice were serious. "As a matter of fact, I did. The yellow laundry bag hit the floor first."

Joe bent over and picked up the full yellow laundry bag. Holding it by the drawstring, he held it out to Delilah, who automatically extended her hands to take it. "I hereby announce," he said in a solemn voice, "the winner of this week's race to be the yellow laundry bag, with special mention to rose, green, and blue, who also outran their jockey, Delilah Cross."

Sarah applauded vigorously, reached over and patted the yellow laundry bag, and laughing good-naturedly, they stepped over the rest of the bags and went out the front door, leaving Delilah standing there. She looked down at the yellow bag for several moments before finally understanding the joke; then, she burst into laughter, surprised and delighted at the nonsensical humor.

On the morning Delilah heard Sarah and Margaret in the kitchen, she had just successfully completed the weekly laundry bag race all the way to the basement with six bags without missing a single one. She fished her notepad and pen out of her pocket as she hurried up the basement stairs to share this silly accomplishment with Sarah. Just before she pushed on the swinging door, she heard Margaret's voice raised in complaint. She paused when she realized she was the subject of discussion.

"It's very frustrating, Sarah." Margaret's voice, as always, was a nagging nasal whine. "How can I gather any really meaningful information about her when she doesn't talk?"
Much to Delilah's surprise, Sarah's voice had a cold edge she had never heard before, the words clipped and sharp as she answered. "Her name is Delilah Cross, and she most certainly does talk. What do you think she is doing when she writes on her notepad? And I am sure you have found Delilah to be cooperative?"

"Oh, those scribbles? They're almost illegible and so short they don't give me hardly any information at all." The whine became more evident and anger sharpened the pitch. She sniffed loudly, wrinkling her nose as though the words had a distasteful smell before she continued.

"Do you know what she did? I prepared a whole list of essay questions that I spent a lot of time developing, questions designed to elicit much meaningful information that I could use." Margaret's tone had become self-pitying and she paused, apparently mourning all that wasted effort.

On the other side of the door, Delilah's grin was so big it hurt her mouth a little.

"So, what did Delilah do?" Sarah's voice was still cool, and the insistence on using her name was very deliberate, but Delilah detected an undercurrent of amusement in it now.

"Essay questions," Margaret repeated, "and she gave stupid one or two word answers to every one of them!" The last words were a squawk of outrage.

"Oh my!" Sarah said. "That sounds very unlike anything Delilah would do. I've never known her to give a stupid answer to any question she was asked. Are you sure she understood that they were essay questions? Could you, perhaps, give me an example?" Sarah was almost overtly patronizing now, but Margaret didn't seem to notice.

She was silent a moment, trying to think of an example that best substantiated her complaint. "Well, this one question, in particular, was designed to elicit her feelings about, you know, her background. Actually, it was sort of the key question, the most important one of all." The tone was disapproving, as though

Delilah's background was somehow offensive to her. "It basically asked which primate she thought the most outstanding, and why." She paused, collecting herself.

In the hall, Delilah had doubled over, holding both hands over her mouth to stifle her laughter. She remembered that question, and she knew she really should leave before they heard her, but she wanted to hear Sarah's reaction when she heard the answer she had given to that stupidly-phrased question, one of dozens on Margaret's so carefully prepared list.

"She said," Margaret's voice moved into the upper registers in her outrage, "she said 'King Kong', and for why, she answered 'Big'!"

With Sarah's unrestrained whoop of laughter following her, Delilah hurried down the hall, out the front door, and ran all the way down the slope to the barn where she collapsed on a pile of straw with tears of mirth running down her face.

It was some time before her sides stopped aching and the laughter degenerated into intermittent giggles. At last, interrupted by an occasional hiccup, her thoughts became organized enough to make a decision. She would be a bit easier on poor Margaret, even though Margaret was abrasive and irritating, and exuded an offensive odor in the bargain. The vivid mental picture of Margaret's nasally-whined words flying like angry hornets from the thick, yellowish, almost-visible moving smell-cloud of disinfectant soap that surrounded her had sent Delilah back into a giggling fit that lasted for several minutes.

Delilah was still smiling at the memory when she took a deep breath and returned her thoughts to the present. Now, she was ready to deal with tonight. She had not been mentally prepared for her encounter with Casey Lowell or any other half-naked man drinking coffee in the dark kitchen. This was unusual, as was seeing anyone without a public face firmly in place. She couldn't help grinning maliciously as she thought about the stream of coffee running out his nose. Served him right.

Get serious, she told herself. She should have been able to handle that situation, and, as far as she could tell, she had handled it, remaining calm and composed, feeling superior in the face of his obvious discomfiture. Yes, up to that point she had been in control of both herself and the situation.

What had gone wrong? She didn't want to face it, but she had to. Look at you,
Delilah, smell yourself. You wanted to stroke the hair on his chest and belly. You knew he was responding to you sexually, you knew it. He's a mature male, and he saw you naked today. Come on, she told herself, the air was thick with pheromones…and his weren't the only ones. It was the hair on his body, she thought reluctantly.

The hair.

Suddenly, an image of hairy bodies moving together in an urgent sexual rhythm filled her mind, blotting out thought. She could feel the heat, the humid, dark, almost-liquid heat, smell the dank, earthy, layered odor of sex, of decomposition and fecund growth, hear the rising-falling undertone of background noises made by myriad life-forms living and dying . . . and the sounds of mating. She was nearly overwhelmed by the familiarity of the heat, the smells, the sounds, the feeling of rightness and belonging that the image evoked.

She sucked in a harsh, involuntary breath and pushed the picture away with all her mental strength. Please, she thought, not now. Not now! Then, after a moment, she smiled, a complete smile that reached her eyes, an honest smile. Lying to herself was a luxury she couldn't afford. The last eight years of her life had been one continuous lie, and in order to maintain it, she had to be scrupulously honest with herself.

Yes, she knew the odor that permeated the air in the kitchen. And, as the momentary flashback her subconscious forced upon her made clear, she knew many other things about sex, as well. In the group it was a daily fact in everyone's life, a required social gesture of bonding among all members, from youngest to oldest. In addition to lust-driven estrus matings, sex in all its permutations was simply acted upon at will and scarcely noted.

Even though Auntie had kept them both distanced from all but the most token gestures of the socially required group sexual activity, seeing it, hearing it, smelling it daily made it familiar to the point of disinterest to her. But clearly the impressions and knowing were still a part of her, part of who she was. Early imprinting, she thought. I read about that. Her eyes went to the row of books neatly lined up on the bookshelf fastened to the wall above her small desk.

And then, of course, there were the adolescent boys and girls, both at Hiller School and around the Newcombe house. While Paulie Newcombe entered into puberty without the usual fanfare of cracking voice and pimples, her nose had duly informed her of the fact long before his parents became aware of it. She still marveled at the omnipresent group of teen-aged boys that almost magically appeared when she and Becky were thirteen or fourteen. They always announced their presence to her nose first, occasionally before she actually heard or saw them, especially if she happened to be downwind.

The few weeks she attended the local high school with Becky and Paulie had proved to be too much, the assault on both her nose and ears more than she could stand. There were just too many sexually ready young people confined together in small spaces, the air too heavy with the smells of arousal, lust, anger, and frustration. The territorial battles waged between both males and females kept Delilah in a continual state of anxiety and the struggles for dominance never stopped. The loud voices and shrill laughter that continually echoed both indoors and out were, to Delilah's ears, the unmistakable mating calls of human adolescents.

Even though she did not tell him the real reasons, Harold Newcombe had been very understanding when Delilah indicated that she could not attend the high school with his children. He made arrangements for her education to continue through correspondence and computer education courses. Actually, she progressed faster and learned more this way, concentrating on the subjects without outside distractions. Just one more thing to thank him for, she thought. He was a nice man and she missed their talks.

Delilah's eyes narrowed and small wrinkles appeared in her forehead as she once again considered the odor of sex. There had been another one, too, a doctor with facial hair that hung down over his shirt collar. Old Doctor Beard she had called him to herself after she learned what a beard was.

For the first few months after she arrived at Hiller School from Bhutu, there were frequent and detailed medical examinations. She wondered at their apparent interest in her blood, feces and urine. At first she thought that the sometimes painful probing and always painful shots and blood taking were intended to protect her from illness that might be transmitted to her by other students

87

at the school. Then she had heard them discussing her, and it became clear that they were much more concerned with protecting the students and themselves from contamination by her. Even in her innocence at that time, it emphasized the difference between her and them, her strangeness, her not belonging. Delilah's need for Auntie and home was a constant, almost physical pain then, one that she still experienced, though not so strongly. It had never stopped, only now it was a deep, aching, sadness, a longing for what had been, but could never be again. She understood that now.

Eventually, she had received a clean bill of health, everyone relaxed, and medical examinations were only routinely done at intervals. She had no clear recollection of them, but she did remember old Doctor Beard. She remembered him because of that particular smell and what he had done to her. As he had touched her in the course of what was noted on the chart as a routine "pre-puberty pre-menses exam", his fingers had wandered. They stroked and fondled, gently probing in all those places that Miss Agnes said she must never touch herself, except, of course, for washing, which must be done quickly and never lingered over because Miss Agnes's God didn't approve.

Delilah remembered her confusion, remembered raising her head and looking around the room for the nurse and the Hiller Schoolteacher who brought her here. She didn't see them, but she could hear their voices in the distance, in another room, talking about potted plants. Strange how clearly she remembered wondering what potted plants meant.

Then, she forgot about them. What Doctor Beard was doing was very pleasing. Small jolts like little electrical currents were coursing down through her abdomen, centering in that forbidden place between her legs. When she spread her legs slightly to give him freer access, he groaned softly, and, taking her hand in his free one, he moved it up and down the front of his pants. It was then that she became aware of the smell, nearly overpowering in its intensity. It mingled with her own odor as she became wet and slippery under his fingers.

Even though she was intent on her own pleasurable feelings, Delilah's mind was working on the problem. Miss Agnes had taught her many things, one of which was that she must always cooperate or be punished. Whatever was done to her, painful or not, was always for her own good, and must be endured in order to avoid even greater pain. Well, this was the first enjoyable examination she had ever had, and she was not touching herself, so it must be for her own good. She shut the door on Miss Agnes and accepted this examination as just one more strange, incomprehensible happening in a life that seemed to consist of strange, incomprehensible things.

As she remembered the incident, she smiled, not at the

incident itself, but at the total innocence of the Delilah child she had been. It was not until much later when Becky Newcombe told her mother how totally dumb Delilah was about sex, and Dee Dee, in turn, mentioned it to Harold, that she had been enrolled in a sex education class. It was only then that she discovered that old Doctor Beard had done something very wrong, had crossed a criminal behavior line, and had molested her. She hadn't even considered it important, and by the time she learned that other children might have been seriously traumatized by his activities, he had quietly died of natural causes, slipping away while quite properly tucked in bed beside his devoted wife of forty years.

That was about all she actually learned about sex from the class. Other than an understanding of the sexual customs and sexual behavior required in this new life she was living, and an understanding of the proper names of the physiology involved, she found that she knew far more about sex, itself, than was taught in the course.

Pushing these old memories aside, she forced herself to look at the rest of the problem, the most important part. Sex she could handle. It was forbidden to her, and forbidden it would remain. She would pay closer attention to her natural body rhythms and cycles, and be more aware of the subtle rise and fall of hormones within her system. Understanding how they affected her behavior made them easier to deal with and control. It was all very straightforward and logical; she could even chart it out on the computer and tack a printout on her bedroom wall if she wanted to. But about the other part of the problem, she wasn't so sure.

This half-naked, pheromone-emitting man, this Peeping Tom of a Doctor Casey Lowell, who snorted coffee out of his nose and ate her cookies, had cut straight through to the question she had been seriously grappling with for nearly a year. It was a question, a simple five-word question no one had ever bothered to ask her before.

"Delilah, why don't you talk?"

Hunching forward, she softly asked the question out loud. "Delilah, why don't you talk?" She muttered the response. "Because Auntie told me not to." Straightening up, she spoke more clearly. "Because Auntie said if I talked it would bring death to me, to her, to the group." The words seemed to hang in the air, almost visible, she thought, like little ghosts of the past.

But Auntie told me that as far back as I can remember, long before I was taken away. It was the group she was afraid of. Auntie spoke, they did not. My mother and her mother, and her mother's mother before her spoke, and they did not. I spoke, and they did not. She was afraid of what the group would do if they found out about the speaking.

Delilah dropped her head into her hands. When Auntie visited her at Bhutu, she had said it over and over again. "Not speak!"

Even then she said it, even after it was clear to Delilah that she could never go back to the group. Auntie made it clear that she would have to stay and deal with whatever happened and not speak, even if there was no longer any physical danger from the group if she did speak. In fact, not speaking had made things infinitely more difficult for her, was still making things difficult.

_So,_ she thought, arriving at the same conclusion she had reached dozens of times in the last year, _once I was taken away from the group, it wasn't the fact that I might talk that frightened Auntie so. It was fear of what I might say if I did talk. It was the fact that someone might discover the secret thing. That was what Auntie feared . . . the damnable secret thing._

Delilah made a low, keening sound between her clenched teeth. She had been over and over this in her mind for months, and it always came back to the same thing . . . the secret thing. Even though she knew that Auntie was no longer with the group, Auntie was right about the secret. It must never be told. She had been a child then, and the only way Auntie could safeguard her and the secret was by ordering her never to speak at all. That way, she could never innocently say anything that might raise questions or cause an inquiry. Yes, Auntie had been right all along. Everything Delilah had learned through her endless hours of research, starting when she was so young that she spent more time with the dictionary looking up words than she did reading the text, only served to emphasize how right Auntie had been. The secret must be kept, no matter what happened and no matter what it cost. *But, on the other hand,* Delilah thought, as she had many times before in the last few months, *I'm eight years older now, much wiser in the ways of this world, and much more wary.*

She crawled under the covers. She was sleepy again. In her mind, at this moment, the matter was settled. She would talk when and if she chose to talk. She would give it more thought, but for now, it was settled. Besides, there was the quest, the mission she had set for herself on that terrible day at the zoo. She would have to talk in order to embark on it, and the time to begin was near.

Thank you, Doctor Lowell, for asking that question, she thought, and yawned widely. She reached for her friend, Teddy Bear, curled up in a ball, and went to sleep. There were no dreams, at least not any that she remembered.

* * *

While she slept, Casey was finding out more about Delilah Cross, aka Case 38, File Number 362. He could see that it would take a while because the files, which had been delivered yesterday afternoon, covered six years. There were, strangely enough, no files covering her time here at Bent Tree Farm. He would have to ask Sarah about that later. He had requested that original files be shipped to him, remaining politely firm in his insistence when told that it was not Brighton Foundation's practice to release original documents from the archives. Perhaps not, he agreed, but it was his practice to work with original documents, and if they wanted his services they would have to make an exception in this case. Eventually they had reluctantly agreed, but only after he signed a legal document accepting full responsibility for the return of the records, complete and intact.

Casey really didn't mind the trouble because he found that original handwritten reports often gave a clearer picture of both observer and subject than clean, impersonal computer sheets filled with information entered by a disinterested data entry clerk. Sloppy, hurried writing, coffee stains, error corrections- -or the lack of them- -all added to the overall feeling of participation, of being there on the scene with the subject at that particular moment in time.

Substitute victim for subject, Casey thought, and it came closer to the truth. His work, more often than not, consisted of detective work, ferreting out facts, putting them together in coherent patterns, and arriving at conclusions based on the information he gathered. He gave himself a small, approving mental "Attaboy". So far in his career, he had made some very good decisions on behalf of the subjects, even though, from time to time, he was very uncomfortable with the idea that he was drawing conclusions and making decisions that would most likely affect people for the rest of their lives.

The last report in the files was his own, a very brief, sanitized version of Delilah's three attempts to cross the stream. He had written it in the dark hours this morning, just before he went down to the kitchen. He made no mention of her taking off her clothes, and he was still not sure why he hadn't. He simply stated that she had made three separate attempts to cross the stream on three consecutive days. There were six stepping stones across the stream, the water was clear, the current not too swift, and it was only knee-deep and could be easily waded. In the comments section, he said she appeared to be working on the water phobia on her own, and recommended that she be allowed to continue without outside interference for the time being.

After he finished rereading it, Casey leaned back in the comfortable swivel chair. He didn't like his report one bit, and he wondered how many other reports like his he would find in the files, clear, concise . . . and totally worthless. He had spent more time describing the stream than he had on Delilah. As he looked at the report, he realized that anyone reading it would know far more about the stream than they would the subject of the report.

He looked at the folders stacked on the desk. When he stopped to think about it, it wasn't a very big stack considering the fact that it supposedly covered, in detail, six years of a human being's life, and a pretty unique human being, at that.

He swiveled the chair further around, looking at the room. It had once been the master bedroom suite in what, for its day, was the fairly modest country home of a wealthy gentleman farmer, one who maintained his primary, more elegant residence in a town. It was huge, compared to the size of the six bedrooms that lined the upstairs hall, three on each side. They shared one bathroom at the end of the hall, tucked in almost like an afterthought. Casey grinned. It probably was an afterthought because this place had been built in the days of chamber pots and outdoor privies. While it had been in continual operation as a working farm for more than a hundred years, as he understood it, it was now devoted to largely experimental crops, both in the fields and inside the big greenhouse. The original owner had been Thomas Bentry, but the name Bent Tree Farm was what the locals had called it from the beginning, based on both the Bentry name and the huge, gnarled tree that still stood between the house and Palmer Road.

In Casey's opinion, the remodeling job done by Brighton Foundation architects was superb, keeping all the ambiance of age and elegance, while incorporating all the latest in equipment and conveniences. He had noticed it in the kitchen, and as he gazed around this huge corner area designated as "the office", it was apparent here, too. Windows filled the east and south walls, allowing good, natural light on even the darkest of days, and this was augmented by unobtrusive overhead lighting in each of the four separately-defined working spaces. Each area had its own desk, phone, lockable file cabinets, and computer set up, complete with printer, scanner and fax machine. It was separated from the others by shoulder-high shelves upon which were neatly arranged reference books and plants, creating comfortable spaces that allowed four people to work privately, undisturbed by others who might be there.

A small bathroom opened off of the main area, utilizing what had once been a dressing room. A comfortable sofa and chairs were grouped around a large coffee table in one corner near a compact service area complete with coffee maker and under-the-counter refrigerator. All in all, Casey thought, a really pleasant and private place to work, which is exactly what Brighton Foundation intended it to be.

In any given month, so Sarah had informed him, one to six different people might spend a week or two here, each pursuing his own line of inquiry, finishing work that required intense concentration or quiet time for thought. While Casey assumed that most of them would be Brighton employees or Brighton grant recipients, he was only indirectly an employee, more of an outside consultant, but obviously he was being accorded all the benefits of a regular employee.

Sarah also said that the people who came here tended to keep to themselves, sleeping in the small bedrooms, working in the office, and occasionally strolling around the farm. Their time here was expected to be highly productive, and certainly not social. They occasionally met at lunch, and everyone gathered around the big kitchen table at dinner where they exchanged polite pleasantries, and separated again into their private worlds.

Sarah had grinned when she told him that this was exactly what Brighton Foundation wanted. Bent Tree Farm, in addition to its experimental farming operations, was a kind of individual think tank, one of dozens of such places they maintained in various locations around the world. While her words were off-hand and relaxed, her tone and expression conveyed the clear message that while none of these brainy personages were currently in residence, should one or more appear on the Bent Tree scene, Casey should keep his attempts at socializing to a minimum.

Casey sighed. He didn't feel insulted by Sarah's warning. It was her job to keep things running smoothly. All in all, Brighton Foundation took care of it's own. And that brought him back to Delilah Cross. As things stood now, she was their ward, and they, in effect, owned her. His report would play a large part in whatever subsequent actions they took about her, and he was already in trouble, and he knew it.

His professional objectivity had wavered dangerously when he

98

saw Delilah naked at the stream, and he had lost it entirely in the kitchen when she raised her head and let him see the real person in her eyes. She was no longer the "subject", a tidy, impersonal case number. Delilah Cross was a real person to him, an intriguing, fascinating, sensually magnetic girl-woman. Oh yes, Casey thought. I'm in trouble here, real trouble.

CHAPTER FOUR

The act of observing an intelligent creature when they know they are being observed, no matter how unobtrusively it is done, defeats its own purpose. The individual first tends to observe himself, evaluating their own actions in context with what they believe the observer thinks or wants to see. Then, they tend to perform both for themselves and the observer. This is especially true when individuals are able to reason and feel threatened or vulnerable, either by the act of being observed, the observer, or both. While their performances can offer the knowledgeable valuable insights into how both the observer and the act of being observed itself is perceived, it offers little real insight into the actual normal behavior of the individual in question. In effect, they both become players in the scenario, actor and audience in turn.

From The Changelings

The official record began in 1994 with a very brief notation included in a routine report filed by a Brighton Foundation research station in Zaire, Africa. "We have received," it said, "an unauthenticated report regarding what appears to be a human child traveling with what appears to be a troop of chimpanzees. Suggest recovery team investigate when convenient."

"Well hello there, Delilah!" Casey said aloud, and flipped to the next report. It was brief and to the point.

"Small female child recovered and taken to Doctor Mellich at Timbo for preliminary examination." He puzzled over a notation that read, "No problem with recovery other than prolonged and violent struggles by the child and repeated attacks by a very large, adult female ape, obviously defending the child. This is quite unusual, as adult females usually retreat with only token resistance. Apparently the bond between these two was very strong. Had to use tranq gun on both of them. Later, we were attacked on the road by two armed men who appeared to be interested in taking the caged child. Scuffle ensued, but we managed to drive away. Only damage was to vehicle . . . two bullet holes in the boot."

The reference to the child being in a cage bothered him, and shooting at the vehicle endangered the child as well as the men.

The whole thing about the fight with the adult ape was odd, but the observation about someone trying to take the child was even more so. Casey couldn't help grinning at the typical British understatement and tone, as he turned to the next report.

It was more revealing. According to the notes made by Dr. Mellich at Timbo, the effects of the tranquilizer dart had worn off by the time they got her to him, and she had fought them ferociously, kicking, screaming, hitting, biting, and defecating. This last caused Casey to grin. Typical ape behavior, all right. She had shown unusual strength and staying power for her size, which Dr. Mellich attributed to fear-induced adrenaline, and had continued to fight until heavily tranquilized. The doctor reported heart, lungs, liver, eyes, ears, nose, bone structure and general reflexes all within normal parameters for a female Caucasian child of approximately eight years.

Casey grinned broadly as he read the next few lines. Doctor Mellich reported that her kidneys, bladder and bowels were also functioning quite well, often and unexpectedly. He had not actually discovered that she was Caucasian until after she had been bathed and most of her long, matted hair cut away. In his words, " . . . she was incredibly filthy and infested with parasites inside and out," a situation he went about remedying as quickly as possible.

As he read between, through, under, and around the lines, it was clear to Casey that Delilah had been a real handful. For some reason, he found this not only understandable, but admirable as well, especially when he read the comment scribbled across what appeared to be a small, time-browned bloodstain on the bottom of the report.

"She bit and scratched all three of us," it said, "so we all get tetanus booster shots, and will probably need rabies shots, too!"

Way to go, Delilah, he thought, closing the folder and placing it to one side. He stretched his arms high above his head, then tipped his head back a moment to relieve tense neck muscles before reaching for the next folder. It was considerably thicker, and the dates on the cover indicated that it covered a period of two years from September 1994 to October 1996. The first item was a receipt signed by Agnes Kittridge acknowledging delivery of one female feral child to her at the Brighton Foundation holding facility in Bhutu, Zaire, Africa.

Although feral children were not common, they did show up from time to time in various parts of the world. With the fierce wars and famines that had swept Africa since World War II, and the attendant displacement of entire starving populations, they had become even more common, whether due to the death of the parents or deliberate abandonment. This was the first time Casey had heard of a Caucasian feral child in recent times. This uniqueness was probably part of the reason she had stirred up such intense interest in the scientific community . . . that and the fact that she had made such a remarkable recovery, if that word could be used to describe it.

As he mentally reviewed what he knew about the Delilah Cross case, Casey decided he preferred the word adaptation to recovery. She had not had some strange disease from which she recovered. As he saw it, she had adapted, not once but twice, from civilization to jungle, then from jungle back to civilization.

The search for her parents or some relative, or even a clue as to how she got to where she was found, had been intensive and fruitless. The general consensus was that her parents were dead and the child had, by some miracle, survived the ordeal by being more or less accepted by the troop of chimpanzees with which she was found, probably adopted, nurtured and protected by the female who had fought in her defense. It was conjectured that the female was a dominant or high-ranking troop member, and had possibly lost a baby of her own.

Casey agreed with this theory. He was young, but not so young that he had not already made a name for himself in the dual fields of human and animal behavior. Crossing over between the two fields made him especially qualified to work with feral children, but until now his work had dealt with impaired or dysfunctional adolescents who, due to severe abuse or some form of retardation, had to be expertly evaluated so decisions could be made about their future. His father, Doctor K. C. Lowell, Senior, was considered to be the outstanding expert in this rather narrowly defined field. Casey considered himself lucky to be working in a profession he had loved since he was a child while following in his father's footsteps at the same time.

He didn't feel like he was working in the shadow of his famous father, either. He never hesitated to consult him with questions, and they often discussed his cases in great detail. His father was called K.C., the letters carefully pronounced to distinguish him from his son, and using his dad as a sounding board and mentor garnered the benefits of his experience as well as giving him needed feedback that was extremely helpful.

No, Casey wasn't working in his father's shadow. At thirty-two, he brought his own style to his work. Like becoming just plain "Casey" instead of Doctor Lowell. He had observed very early on in his career that the subjects, and he didn't like that word either, frequently became guarded, not responding easily or naturally because of prior painful or unpleasant experiences connected with doctors. Casey became just a friendly guy who came on the scene, stayed a while, interacted with them overtly, observed them carefully covertly, then went away, leaving only pleasant memories behind . . . at least that was what he hoped.

He was young enough, laughing and relaxed by nature, and, sooner or later, he evoked the same responses. He was himself, and they soon became themselves because he was totally non-threatening. When this happened, he got down to his real work, doing the job to which he was assigned. In most instances, it was to evaluate the subject, determine how well they were adapting, how well they interacted socially, and how close they were to being able to function in society on their own, under supervision or, as happened in some cases, not at all. Then he submitted a detailed report, made his recommendations, and moved on to the next assignment.

This particular assignment was, in effect, a hand-me-down from his dad. Brighton Foundation, for reasons not explained, had gone outside their own large employee pool, specifically requesting the services of Doctor K. C. Lowell, Senior. However, at the time the request was made, he was deeply involved in research for his latest book, and when he suggested that perhaps his son, who possessed the same qualifications though not the long experience, could properly handle the job, the powers-that-be at Brighton Foundation had accepted the substitution.

Casey sat for a long time looking at the Bhutu delivery receipt. It reminded him of a receipt for a package, an inanimate object, and not a living human being. Then he realized that the child had probably been transported from Doctor Mellich at Timbo and delivered to Bhutu Holding Facility in the same cage he had found so disturbing. After a while, he began his journey through two years of a child's life as seen through the eyes of Agnes Kittridge.

He took his time, occasionally going back to re-read something, and when he was through, he leaned back in the chair. He was frowning, the usually unnoticeable vertical lines between his eyebrows deeply etched, his eyes narrowed, and his ordinarily slightly up-turned lips were pulled tightly against his teeth.

According to her reports, Agnes Kittridge had given Delilah both her first and last names shortly after her arrival. While it was usual that a first name was somewhat arbitrarily assigned in these cases, it was highly unusual that a family name was also given, especially long before the official search for relatives was completed as it had been in this case. And the reasons she had given for doing so were completely unacceptable as far as Casey was concerned.

Pulling a yellow notepad close, he began to write. First of all, Kittridge said that Delilah not only made the sign of the cross, she made it clearly and insistently. Those were the words she used. But how did she make the cross? Inwardly, as a Catholic would? Outwardly, as a benediction? Exactly what had she done that Kittridge so clearly perceived as making the sign of the cross? Then it struck him. Of course. Although she didn't say so, that was where the name Cross came from, directly connected to the sign the child made.

107

He paused a moment, then wrote some more. Why would Kittridge assume that this sign she made had anything whatsoever to do with a devout family? And why should anyone in any way be grateful for it? This was a false note, an apparently biased personal assumption that no respectable observer would be caught dead making. And, why the name "Delilah", for that matter? It was a biblical name that seemed to go right along with the other religious connotations he was finding here.

He printed in bold block letters, "Who is Agnes Kittridge? Ask Dad," and continued reading down that page in the report. Then he slowly and carefully read through the others again. According to these reports, Delilah had arrived at Bhutu with her water phobia already firmly in place, and she had never spoken or attempted to speak a single word during her two-year stay there, no matter how much encouragement she received.

Apparently, the water phobia and the not talking were the only things that had remained constant during the last eight years. As he read further, Casey puckered his lips in a low whistle of amazement. According to these monthly reports, most of them scarcely more than a tightly handwritten paragraph, Delilah had been properly toilet trained, learned to eat properly, stand properly, sit properly, walk properly, dress properly, and, in general, behave like a properly civilized little person . . . and all within the space of two years! In addition, while she didn't seem to be able to write, she had learned the basics of reading, showing remarkable skill at following simple instructions, whether written or delivered verbally . . . and done it all without ever saying, or attempting to say, a single word!

It seemed transparently clear to Casey that no one had ever read all these reports in one sitting. No one could have read them together as one piece as he was doing now without seeing the anomalies that leaped from the pages. And the use of the word "properly" struck him as being the worst. Properly? What criteria had been used to determine the meaning of that word? What did walking or standing or sitting "properly" mean in connection with an eight or nine year old feral child?

Suddenly, quite unbidden, he saw Delilah's eyes, the pain and knowing he had seen in them. Without a doubt, she knew and remembered clearly what "properly" meant to Agnes Kittridge. She knew what it meant, and the experience of acquiring that knowledge was still there in her eyes.

He made more notes. According to the various articles he had read about her in preparation for coming here, Delilah had made a wide range of sounds from the very beginning and she still did. Both early and later examinations found her to have completely normal vocal apparatus. Her hearing was superior, and it was noted that she appeared to have an almost supernormal sense of smell. He remembered thinking at the time how unusual that was.

Now, as he sat there staring at the notepad, Casey remembered noticing the occasional slight flaring of her nostrils last night in the kitchen and suddenly felt embarrassed. Had she been smelling him? He wondered what he had smelled like to her. Hastily, he put the thought aside, firmly resisting the impulse to raise his arm and sniff suspiciously at his armpit. He tried to ignore the snide little voice in his mind that reminded him of the number of ways Delilah was getting to him on a personal level.

Casey was not just idly interested in these medical records. Her strange response when he asked why she didn't talk nagged at him. As a matter of fact, the more he thought about it the more certain he was that she actually could talk, but refused for reasons of her own. Or, just maybe, it was in some way connected to the water phobia, which was certainly real enough, as he had seen for himself.

Why? He retraced the word, etching it so deeply into the paper on the pad it appeared indented on the next page, and the next, a kind of shadow question that repeated itself silently through several pages until it disappeared.

* * *

Agnes Kittridge had been neither an acute or astute observer, and thanks to this fact, Delilah had both time and opportunity to sharpen her acting skills. Factually, she learned how to practice deceit, presenting a facade of obedient compliance while actively engaged in rebellion. Fortunately, Agnes Kittridge never realized that she was involved in a war from the day Delilah was delivered to Bhutu in a cage until the day she left it in a pickup truck driven by Jono Sam. Had she become aware of that fact, it is quite likely that Delilah would not have survived.

Agnes Kittridge, it must be admitted, had impeccable credentials, both scholastically and professionally. She was a large, lumpy, unattractive woman in her mid-forties, unmarried, with no close family ties. Her willingness to take assignments lasting for up to two years without leave in various out-of-the-way places around the world made her an invaluable employee for Brighton Foundation. She worked with little or no supervision, the job paid very well, and, supplemented by small monthly checks that kept her actively on-call, she did very nicely between assignments that sometimes came regularly, and sometimes had long intervals in between.

It might be said that Agnes loved her work almost as much as she loved her God. The former, she did in her own unique way, the actual methods she used often vastly different from those she described in the neat monthly progress reports she submitted to Brighton Foundation. The correctional implementer, for instance, was never mentioned in the reports and some of her other methods were neither discussed nor asked about.

As far as her love of her God was concerned, no one had ever inquired, and apparently through some bureaucratic oversight, there was no record of her ever having a psychological examination or evaluation of any kind. She had been hired years before strictly on the basis of her scholastic record and had apparently performed well, as her professional records attested. As long as she continued to produce some kind of results, no one would ever dream of inquiring into what was considered to be her private life, and most especially about her religious beliefs.

Certainly, the only ones in a position to complain about her or her methods could not. They were the feral children who were, willy-nilly, without consent or control, turned over to Miss Agnes, as she insisted on being called, for "training". By definition, a feral child is one who has been living wild with animals or as an animal. With no other reference point, they were delivered to Agnes, and for two years she was the only example of human that they encountered or interacted with.

Agnes was a religious fanatic, a zealot deeply immersed in her own fantasy world where God spoke to her daily directing her every move. As far as she was concerned, her work with feral children was a Holy Crusade. These two words were always written in huge, glowing capital letters in her mind.

The first time her God announced His presence, she was nearing the end of her last year in graduate school, and His exact words to her were indelibly engraved in her mind: "Agnes, you are My chosen one. You are My vessel and I have filled you with My Holy Spirit. Rejoice! Feel the glory of My ecstasy! You have a Mission, a Holy Crusade that you will carry out in My Name."

She was twenty-six years old when God spoke these words to her. It was nearly midnight, and her roommate was asleep. For nearly two hours, Agnes had been trying to masturbate herself to orgasm, an elusive goal she had been trying to reach for several years, ever since she read about it in a physiology textbook in High School.

It wasn't that she had any guilt feelings about it, and it wasn't that on some deep, unconscious level she really didn't want to climax. She did, and as it had so many times before without reaching that elusive goal, her body strained, nerves and muscles crying out for release. She felt like she was standing on tiptoe, stretched like a rubber band to the limits of possibility, reaching and reaching for something just a maddening fraction of an inch beyond her grasp.

She was panting, her body slick with sweat, and, no longer caring if she woke her roommate, she moaned, "Oh God, please God, oh please God!" It was then that He spoke to her, the words resounding in her head like a huge, tolling bell as her body convulsed, pulsing and throbbing in time to His words. Sometime later when her breathing had slowed to normal, she whispered into the darkness, "Thank you, God, for hearing me and allowing me to experience Your ecstasy. I will be worthy of this gift You have bestowed on me. Thy will be done."

Just before she fell asleep, Agnes decided that tomorrow she must buy a Bible and learn more about her God. She was already certain that He was her God and had given this overwhelming religious ecstasy to her alone as proof. She was also certain that as long as she did His work, He would allow her to experience this precious and glorious feeling over and over again. She was relaxed and smiling, filled with a sense of great well being as sleep took her, fully resolved to carry out any sacred mission He might give her. Her God-directed Holy Crusade began when she graduated and got the job with Brighton Foundation working with feral children.

In Agnes' mind, each and every one of the children, whom she called her "specials", was nothing more than a sub-human animal, a dirty heathen, vermin-ridden creature that must be cleansed inside and out. Then it must be civilized and brought to a state of awareness and obedience to her God and His Holy Directives as given only to her.

Over time, she developed various rituals that must be performed as soon as possible after their delivery to her. First of all- -and most important- -they must submit to the ritual of proper cleansing. This required that they be shaved; every smallest hair on their body, including eyebrows and eyelashes, must be ferreted out and removed. She did this because their body hair linked them to the animals with whom they had been living. Of course, eyelashes were the most difficult part, and she had driven the scissors into the eye of the first child, blinding him in that eye. After that, she had used tweezers to pluck out the eyelashes, a tedious and difficult process, but the results were quite satisfying to her. That was the first step.

Then, they were totally immersed in the disinfectant bath, a large tub filled with a murky, lukewarm mixture of foul-smelling chemicals designed to act as a germicide as well as an agent of sudden death for any possible lurking vermin. This cleansing process was carried out to the accompaniment of the words, "Cleanliness is next to Godliness!" loudly chanted over and over again. After this ritual had been meticulously carried out, the children were held without food or water for at least a day and night to cleanse the inside of their bodies as well. Only then did she feel they were ready to begin receiving the word of her Lord and Savior.

One of the first report entries made by Agnes Kittridge dealt with Delilah's water phobia. Still full of tranquilizers, Delilah had submitted indifferently to the shaving process, voicing only a few protesting whimpers of pain as skin was scraped off with the hair in various places on her body. She feebly attempted to get away when her eyelashes were plucked out in clumps, but all in all, she did not fight hard at all.

Agnes was taken completely unaware when, the moment she shoved the newly arrived heathen's now bald head under the smelly brew in the tub, the child erupted from the water emitting ear-splitting screams and shinnied up Agnes, climbing her like a tree. The child's shivering body came to rest, slippery and dripping, on Agnes' shoulders with both hands clenched in a death lock in her frizzy hair.

Apparently, even Agnes recognized the seriousness and intensity of the response, and she solved the problem by carrying the screaming child to the shower in her own living quarters, turning on the cold water full force, shoving her in, and holding the door shut with her shoulder. All the while, she chanted the ritual words loudly, drowning out the ear-splitting shrieks coming from the shower.

"Cleanliness is next to Godliness! Cleanliness is next to Godliness!" Agnes yelled over and over again, continuing until the screams turned into exhausted moans, and she felt a state of cleanliness acceptable to her God had been achieved.

Then, she carried the naked, dripping, still moaning child across the kitchen, down a long hall, and unceremoniously dumped her on the thin mattress of a small cot in a room near the end. After making sure the spring-loaded door latch caught firmly behind her, she clumped back down the hall, discussing the matter with her God, feeling a little put out that things hadn't proceeded in the usual way, but satisfied just the same.

Agnes didn't come back until the next morning. She was aware that the child hadn't eaten or had anything to drink since the recovery team took her, but that, too, was a necessary part of the ritual. They must be cleansed inside and out, empty vessels she would fill physically with proper food and spiritually as her God directed.

That was Delilah's first day at Brighton Foundation's Bhutu Holding Facility.

On the evening of the second day, Delilah received her name. Agnes was allowed to do this with all her specials, at least their first names, while investigations into their origins were conducted. In most instances, this name became final, a personal identity that lasted a lifetime, and all of the names chosen by Agnes were taken from the "Good Book", a fact that went unnoticed by her employers. Even had it been noted, it would have meant little to them because they dealt not with names, but with case numbers, one of which had already been assigned to Delilah.

There was, however, a difference with Delilah. She was accorded the dignity of a last name, as well. For some reason, probably connected with the shearing of what was left of her dark, still-matted hair and the traumatic bath scene that followed,

Agnes chose the name "Delilah", who had, after all, been connected with hair, and was quite a trouble-maker in her own right. At least, that was how Delilah figured it out some time later.

Agnes had a habit of talking almost continually, droning on and on. "Now I am fixing your dinner, which you will learn to eat properly. These are the clothes that you will wear every day. One must always be properly dressed. You will sleep on the cot, never on the floor. That is not proper!" This last exclamation was usually accompanied by the swish and thud of the correctional implementer, a long, supple switch, landing on Delilah's bare buttocks.

There was also a ritual to be observed in receiving the attention of the correctional implementer. Miss Agnes did not believe it had the proper intended effect when dulled by intervening layers of clothing. After being roughly shown the proper ritual position once, Delilah responded to the dreaded gesture Miss Agnes made with the switch by quickly pulling down her baggy cotton panties, lifting the hem of her shapeless shift, turning her back, bending over, and waiting.

The waiting was always the worst. Long moments would pass before Agnes would suddenly shout, "Spare the rod and spoil the child!" and deliver whatever number of stinging blows her God told her was appropriate for the infraction. She always looked up piously between blows to make sure her God was watching how zealously and well she carried out His work.

On the evening she received her name, Delilah had been standing quietly where Agnes had shoved her, numbly waiting while she wrote a few lines in the report. As usual, Agnes was talking. "Now I must give you a name," she said. "What would be a proper name for you?"

What Agnes did not know- -could not know- -was the fact that Delilah understood some of the words she said, and what she did not clearly comprehend, she was intelligent enough to try to make out from the context. She had had no less than six encounters with the correctional implementer that day, beginning with God's wrath for destroying a mattress, followed closely by more of the same for a broken potty chair, and a third time for relieving herself in the corner. The fourth time was to make sure that she understood clearly that she could not run or in any way try to avoid her just punishment. The fifth and sixth were routine chastisements to speed her education in proper table manners.

In pain from her flayed buttocks and anxious to avoid any more punishment, Delilah was paying close attention to the words spoken by Agnes. Name was a word she knew, and when she heard it, she quickly made the sign of who she was with her two forefingers. Agnes didn't respond, so Delilah held her hands up, emphatically making the sign of who she was. Auntie had told her who she was, and the sign was who she was. Auntie had never told her not to make the sign of who she was, Auntie had only told her not to speak.

For once, it was Agnes who was speechless. This savage heathen child with the strange, naked eyes and shiny bald head was standing before her making the sign of the cross, the Holy Cross! There could be no mistake! God had sent her a sign! She had been presented with a miracle and she could not question the works of her God!

After a moment, she said, "Praise the Lord! Delilah, you have a first name and a last name, as well. I will enter you in the records as Delilah Cross." And she did.

Nearly two years later, when Delilah slowly and laboriously read this for herself during one of her night prowls around the inside of Bhutu holding facility, and eight years later when Casey Lowell sat in the office at Bent Tree Farm and read it, the words were the same ones written that night by Agnes Kittridge. Her tightly written, precise words crabbing across the page gave only a small indication of the throes of religious fervor that gripped her as she wrote them:

"I have named the child Delilah Cross. Ordinarily, I would apply no last name, but she makes the sign of the cross very clearly and insistently. It should be noted that this clearly indicates early experience with a devout family, something for which we should be grateful. This matter should be looked into when convenient."

Fortunately for Delilah Cross, or perhaps it was unfortunately as things worked out, no one found it convenient to look into the matter, not until years later, and by then it was too late to change a single thing.

CHAPTER FIVE

About the time Casey was reading the reports from Bhutu for the third time, Delilah was slowly waking from a deep, restful sleep. As sometimes happens on that gentle, fuzzy edge between waking and sleeping, her thoughts drifted from subject to subject, floating as lightly and easily as a piece of fluff on a gentle breeze. She smiled sleepily and gently squeezed the soft down comforter, sliding her fingers over it, exploring the almost crisp texture of its smooth, tightly woven cover. Then she pulled it higher and tucked it under her chin, moving Teddy Bear to a more comfortable position higher against her shoulder.

She loved her bed, its softness, its warm, enveloping comfort, the sense of security it gave her. More awake now, she followed that thought, thinking about other beds she had slept in. In her first years, she had slept in a different bed nest nearly every night, some comfortable, some not, none of them ever becoming familiar enough through use to form an identity of their own. The only constant about those bed nests was the warm, comforting presence of Auntie; Delilah's memories of beds and night and sleeping in those times were sensory images of the feel, sound, and smell of Auntie.

The cot at Bhutu Holding Facility was not a bed; sleeping on the floor would have been preferable. Her bed at Hiller School, the first real bed she had ever slept in, had been comfortable, the pillow soft, the covers warm, but it never gave her the feeling she always felt in this bed, although she slept in her Hiller School bed for four years. Maybe it was just the sense of security and contentment she felt here at Bentry Farm. Maybe it was her relaxed, unstressed emotional state that allowed her to enjoy it? No, that wasn't right either.

Certainly she had been upset and tense yesterday and last night, and even this morning. It was something else. She shifted her legs and flexed her toes, telling herself that she would figure it out later.

Fully awake now, she thought, I don't care what they say, one of mankind's greatest strides forward, next to the discovery of speech, fire and tools, of course, was the invention of good, comfortable beds and warm, friendly bed covers. She grinned. Or maybe the invention of purses, belts and bowls were the world's greatest innovative discoveries. Well, maybe not purses, but the idea of containers that were good for more than one use, and a belt to hang them on so your hands were free. What good were fire and good, practical, reusable tools like a rock or a properly shaped stick if you had no way of taking them with you when you moved on? How might it have changed things had the group females possessed bags of some kind?

Suddenly she was sitting in a sunny clearing with several other group females and younglings. She had a small rounded rock in one hand and was holding a nut on a flat rock with the other. She brought the small rock down hard, missed the nut, but caught one of her fingers. Shrieking, she ran toward Auntie.

With a gasp, she was just as suddenly back in her bed. The pain in her finger was almost real, and she popped it into her mouth to wet it, then waved it to get the soothing, cooling effects of the air . . . just as Auntie had done for her on that long-ago day. Taking a deep breath, she deliberately went on with her thought. Yes, bags, belts and bowls allowed you to take your evolutionary progress with you, freeing you to invent other things . . . and you can bet that the females did most of the inventing, too. She didn't understand why she was so sure about this, but she knew it was right.

Her thoughts turned to sleep. Funny how so many everyday conversations made some reference to sleep. Sleeping well and getting a good night's sleep seemed to be a lifetime pursuit with some people, and she had had her share of restless nights and dreams plagued by nightmares she'd rather not remember.

Maybe it was thinking about beds and sleeping and nightmares that triggered it, but without warning, Delilah was reliving her first night at Bhutu Holding Facility. Somewhere, deep in her mind, a small voice complained shrilly, "No, not now!" But the pictures went on, an unreeling film in which she was sometimes reliving a memory and sometimes both the actor and an onlooker who had already read the script. No matter the viewpoint, she was unable to stop it or change it until it ran its course.

Recalling that after the ritual cleansing (it was several years before Delilah understood about that), Miss Agnes carried her naked, still dripping and moaning, down the long, narrow hall and dumped her unceremoniously on the cot in the fourth room at the end. Making sure the door latch was firmly engaged, she clumped away without a backward glance, her attention fixed on the muttered conversation she was having with her God. Paradoxically, Delilah might have found some comfort had she known that another female had once, some years before, endured that very same room and cot, had shared similar horrific circumstances – her mother. But she had no way to know that, not yet.

Delilah sat there for some time, crouched in a small, wet, shuddering, miserable ball. Her moans stopped when she landed on the cot with a teeth-jarring thump, but now she made a soft, high-pitched keening sound of distress. It grew louder, then turned into a series of explosive "uh uh uh" sounds when, after a time, with many false starts at the strangeness her fingers encountered, she explored the slick surface of her shaven head.

The big female had taken her outside! She was totally bewildered. In her mind, her hair was the outside of her, perhaps not the same outside as the rest of the group, but much like her skin, nonetheless. It had hung in filthy, matted strings to below her buttocks, serving as her protection, a shelter behind which there was a feeling of safety and security. Grooming it was a time-consuming, sometimes painful job, but Auntie didn't mind, sometimes simply biting off clumps that were too tangled or matted with leaves and other debris. Why had the big, ugly female taken her outside? What had she done with it? Did she want it for herself? That was why you took something from someone else. You took it for yourself, and the big ugly female didn't have much of her own. Yes, she reasoned, that was the reason she had taken it. That and the fact that she was bigger and stronger and could take it.

There were no grass or leaves in this place. The thin cotton mattress offered little protection. It was stiff and would not bend around her, no matter how hard she tried. She tried to get under it, but it lay directly on bare metal springs that hurt her body. After a while, she dried off, but even though it was warm in the room, she still felt cold. Involuntary shudders occasionally rippled through

126

her body, causing her to suck in her breath convulsively. She had no way of knowing that her body was reacting in its own self-protective way, trying to throw off the effects of shock, too much tranquilizer, too much adrenaline, too little blood sugar, and dehydration.

The raw spots where the skin had been abraded during the shaving process burned and stung. She rubbed her eyes, then jerked her hands away. Her eyes hurt, and the rubbing caused them to burn and sting, too. Then tears came, and the saltiness made them hurt even more. She whimpered, trying to understand why the big female had hurt her. She had not been bad. She knew she had not been bad. She had not pestered or teased. She had not made hurt until someone had made hurt on her. Her mental images of making hurt were of hitting, kicking and biting. She had not taken food. She wanted her outside. She needed her outside. And she wanted and needed Auntie.

She looked at her arms and legs. She examined her hands and feet carefully; wiggling her fingers and toes experimentally. Something was wrong with them. They did not have hurt, but they were not right. Her long, dirty nails had been clipped short, but she didn't understand that; they were not long enough and the tips were too sensitive. They felt all wrong.

She didn't understand the concept of color, but the color was wrong, too. Her arms and legs were white and sensitive, stripped

127

of the multiple brown layers of dirt that had formed an encrusted protective coating on them. Although the rain had thinned the dirt layers from time to time, lightening her color by several shades, and she could dimly remember looking this way long ago when she had been in the water, she had never perceived herself as being this color. She was, in her mind, the same color as everyone else. No one else was this color. This was a wrong color.

The thought was not quite coherent, but on some level she recognized that this was the color of the big speaking males who had taken her from the group, the ones she and Auntie had fought so hard before strange biters unaccountably made them fall asleep. It was the color of the big speaking males who had done terrible things to her in a different place. She remembered something biting her then, too, and she fell asleep again. It was also the color of the big, ugly speaking female in this place . . . except all of them also had some sort of outside. She knew this because when she had been fighting the males, several pieces of it had come off in her hands. It didn't have hurt smell, though. The hurt smell came when she bit them . . . sharp, hot, and tangy, almost like good eat. Her stomach growled. She was hungry and thirsty. She needed eat. She needed Auntie.

She stopped examining herself and looked around. She was almost overwhelmed, disoriented by the not-rightness everywhere she looked. Ruler-straight lines and sharp right angles were outside her experience. So were the flat white walls that abruptly cut off her line of sight with an almost physical impact instead of letting it slowly and gently slide away from object to object until her view was obscured by a patterned, highly- textured background of light and shadow.

No matter how she moved her head or shifted position, she could not see beyond the flat surfaces that surrounded her. Were they near or far? She could not tell. She frequently closed her eyes for several seconds to stop the visual input that made her feel dizzy. But every time she opened them, the inside of her head felt funny as she strained to find some distance reference points, so she stopped trying and focused on herself and the cot on which she sat.

She had no conception of the words bare or naked or the connotations involved, but that night she learned the feelings of complete vulnerability and defenselessness. And about confusion and fear, and, most terrible of all, the desolation of having no one when you have never before in your entire life been alone.

After a while, more in an effort to ignore the hunger pains in her stomach than from any real curiosity, she examined the mattress. She squeezed it, tugged on it, and tasted it. It smelled funny to her, with a faint lingering odor similar to the stink of the chemical bath into which she had been plunged. She lifted her arm and smelled herself. No, the long, harsh pounding of the strange, cold rain while she crouched in a miserable, screaming ball protecting her head with her arms had at least removed that terrible smell.

Clearly, the mattress wasn't edible, but she decided there was something inside of it, and set herself the task of finding out what it was.

It was harder than she anticipated. The thick canvas ticking with its blue and white stripes didn't give an inch, no matter how she pulled and pounded on it. Finally, in frustration, she used her teeth and succeeded in ripping a small hole. Encouraged by this small success, she continued to chew and tug, enlarging the hole. Finally, she worked her

finger inside and fished around, then pulled out a small wad of something white that felt good in her hand. She tasted it and decided it wasn't good to eat. Pieces of it stuck on her tongue and she had to pick them off with her fingers. She continued to pull out small pieces of mattress stuffing until there was a large pile of cotton clumps beside her, and almost half of the mattress was loose and floppy.

Feeling warmer from her exertions, she picked up a piece of the cotton and pulled at it until it became a fluffy ball. Fascinated, she made more fluffy balls from the tightly packed cotton lumps, continuing until the pleasingly soft things surrounded her. Then, she grabbed them by the handful, throwing them high in the air, smiling happily as they pelted down on her, touching her body like gentle little pats, then bouncing away.

Growing tired of this activity, she leaned back on the cotton balls and found them comfortable, something like a bed, only softer than leaves. It was close to the time for bed making. She could tell because the sun was going down. There was nothing to eat, but making a bed was something she knew how to do, something familiar in the midst of all this strangeness, something to do to take her mind away from her aching stomach. Within a few minutes she had made herself a very snug sleeping place from the now pliable mattress cover deeply layered with cotton balls, but it was still too light outside, and she wasn't ready to sleep.

She stayed where she was, thinking very hard about what had happened. After a while, she decided that this place must be the Faraway Auntie had told her about. Certainly, it wasn't the here or nearby which she could always see. And it wasn't there, either, which was also someplace she could see. She had never seen this place, so it had to be the Faraway.

Getting up, she moved to the window, keeping physical contact first with the cot and then with the wall as she moved. She knew where it was if she touched it. Her fingers fit through the one-inch squares of the steel mesh that covered the window, and she gripped it and shook it tentatively at first, then harder. The metal felt hard, like a rock, and it was solidly fixed in place. She listened and looked and sniffed, intently concentrating on picking up the slightest hint of Auntie, the group, or even something familiar. There were sounds and smells of insects, birds, trees, and other living things some distance beyond the wall, another unidentifiable thing that stopped her seeing them, but allowed her to see the sky. Those smells of living things were overlaid with a whole range of odors from close by, some of them decidedly unpleasant. They confused and frightened her. Auntie hadn't told her that Faraway didn't smell good.

Narrowing her field of focus, she began to pick out and separate other noises, nearby sounds. As she stared through the mesh squares, she located a monotonous patting sound coming from a building on the left. Although she didn't know what that strange object was, it appeared similar to the object she was inside of, and the patting sound came from inside it. Perhaps it was some strange animal locked inside a place it couldn't get out of, just like she was. She decided she didn't want to go near it because a cloud of nasty, acrid smells hung over it. Anything that smelled that bad would be dangerous. Stinks were bad, and this was a very big stink that burned her nose.

Even closer, she finally identified the irregular clumping sounds as being made by the big female. Her strangely shaped feet made that sound as she walked on this hard, slick ground.

Then she realized that the ground where she was standing was vibrating slightly with each clumping step made by the big female. The vibrations tickled the bottom of her feet and, intrigued by this phenomenon, she spent a few minutes lifting her feet and setting them down in time with the clumping sounds. She was quite caught up in this new experience, and try as she might, she couldn't make much more than a little hollow thumping sound no matter how hard she stamped her bare feet. Finally, she stopped the activity because it hurt her heels. She wondered if it hurt the big female's feet. Probably not. Her feet looked hard and unyielding like thick tree bark.

There were other sounds in the nearby where the big female was-rattles, clatters, clinks, tinkles-strange sounds that were completely unidentifiable. When they stopped, she could smell something her instincts told her was food, even though it carried a strong tang of wrongness to her slightly distended nostrils. She salivated, swallowing hard and repeatedly, welcoming the wetness in her dry throat. Her belly rumbled demandingly and clenched in a series of painful cramps.

She was very hungry and thirsty and she whined miserably, clutching her belly as the cramps tightened. She walked around the room, maintaining contact with the walls, feeling the steel mesh that also covered the top half of the door. Then, she carefully looked at the only other object in the room besides the cot, a child's potty-chair sitting by the door. She picked it up, shook it, and unable to make any sense of it, threw it against the wall. It made a very gratifying noise, so she picked it up and threw it again, her lips curling in a small, satisfied smile.

Several pieces had broken off the chair with the second impact, and the white plastic pot came to rest at her feet. She hesitantly shoved it with her foot, and it slid away. After pushing it a few more times with her foot to make sure it wouldn't attack her, she picked it up, smelled it, tasted it, and on a whim only she understood, placed it up-side-down on her bald head. She patted it. It made a hollow sound in her ears, not unpleasant, just strange. It wasn't her outside or anything like it, but it enclosed her naked head, surrounding it and touching it in a way that comforted her.

She continued around the room, still maintaining contact with the wall. After looking out the window for a time, taunted by the smell of fresh green things growing tantalizingly near outside the wall and distressed by an ever-increasing thirst, she relieved herself- -a strong-smelling scanty puddle- -in a corner of the room. She was whimpering over the pains in her stomach as she jerked and tugged the cot to a spot under the window. Being by the window was better; she could lie back and look up and out at the slowly darkening sky. The pot was uncomfortable on her head, making hurting places, so she took it off. Clutching it to her chest, she curled up in her cotton ball nest and prepared for sleep.

Had anyone been listening, they would have heard the little song she sang very softly to herself in a high, sweet, piping voice. It was the song she and Auntie had sung every night before they went to sleep for as long as she could remember. While she understood only a few of the words and her pronunciation left much to be desired, her enunciation was clear. "Baby dear, don't go there, you will get an awful scare. Teddy Bear, has his lair, under Mama's rocking chair." Then, she went to sleep.

When Miss Agnes entered the room the next morning, her education in becoming "properly" civilized began with her introduction to the correctional implementer.

* * *

Delilah-of-now moaned and jerked as the blows fell on Delilah-of-then. Turning over abruptly, she drew her knees up in a near-fetal position. She was not totally immersed now, and the part of her mind that had caused her to turn over insisted that she didn't want this, told her to get up and try to break away from these replays of yesterday, but she couldn't. They continued inexorably, the sights and sounds and smells of Bhutu washing over her, obscuring everything else.

But now the replays were different, seen from the strangely different perspective of both participant and informed spectator, actual experiences overlaid and intermingled with information about Bhutu that Delilah-of-then had not known or understood.

135

These bits of information were things that Delilah-of-now had ferreted out of Brighton Foundation computer records and archives over the last five years.

Far back in her mind, the names Hunter, Darkling, and Merlin formed, each appearing only long enough to be recognized before sliding away. They had often been with her when she prowled through Brighton computer archives. Besides detailed operating information, she found copies of old floor plans for the buildings at Bhutu, and there were several digitized pictures in the archives. Delilah had studied them, comparing the diagrams and pictures with what she remembered. She was surprised to discover that her memories were almost photographically accurate, if you considered her size and perspective when she was there.

The Brighton Foundation holding facility at Bhutu was officially number eight of the more than thirty such places they maintained in various locations around the world. It consisted of a small group of single-story buildings surrounded by a six-foot high, solid block wall fence, interrupted only by one wide locked iron gate. All vegetation around the outside of the wall for a hundred feet in every direction was kept clear, creating a kind of no-man's land in which the compound sat, floating like a heavy square raft on its pond of bare earth.

It was located at the end of a dirt road, about a mile from the village of Bhutu, and Bhutu, in turn, was linked by a poorly paved

136

road to the nearest town which boasted a small airport. This airport, scarcely more than a graded dirt strip, boasted two above ground fuel tanks and a small, unpainted wooden building with a yellow-and- green windsock mounted on the roof.

Delilah was sure about the location and color of the windsock because it had made a lasting impression on her the one time she had seen it. She remembered Jono Sam, too, because he had also made a lasting impression on her. Other than the men who took her from the group, the men who had hurt her, and Miss Agnes, Jono Sam was the only other human being she had ever seen, and he was brownish-black, almost group color.

A small Brighton Foundation plane bringing mail, of which there was little, and all of the staple food and supplies needed to keep the facility operating comfortably, visited the airport once a week. Brighton Foundation payroll records showed Jono Sam to still be a salaried employee, although other records indicated that the facility had been closed own for the last eight years. Jono Sam was the name of the Bhutu man who picked up the supplies at the airport and delivered them to the compound while she was there.

When she read his job description, Delilah thought he could be considered a very lucky man to have had such a sinecure of a job at such a high salary. Other than the weekly supply run, very little had ever been required of him. He was furnished with a pickup truck and once a month when someone was in residence, he must refill the tank for the big generator that supplied electricity to the buildings, and clear and rake the ground round the outside of the walls.

Once a month he loaded up the four trash cans sitting outside the gate and haul them away, After disposing of the trash, a simple matter of dumping it wherever convenient, he returned the empty cans to their position outside the locked gate. Other than the generator building, he had never been inside any of the buildings. Delilah was sure of that. The closest he came was when he carefully unloaded the weekly supplies on the porch outside the kitchen door.

There was a puzzling ritual involved in going in and out of the compound, one that Delilah had witnessed many times. He must drive up to the locked gate, stop, turn off the motor, and honk the horn three times, not two times, not four time, but three times. Miss Agnes had made this very clear in the tone of voice that made Delilah flinch when she used it. When he honked, Miss Agnes would go to the gate, stare at him and the pick-up truck suspiciously through the iron bars, then open the gate. After he started the motor and drove inside, he must again turn it off and wait until she had closed the gate. Only when she reached a position in front of the truck could he again start the engine, and, with her leading the way, the parade of woman and truck would slowly make its way around the front of the building to the kitchen porch on the side.

Once there, he handed her the printed manifest and any mail that might have come, and carefully unloaded the supplies under her watchful eyes as she checked off each item he placed on the porch. Once this was completed to her satisfaction, she handed him a sealed envelope that he was to give the pilot the next week.

When he left, after making a tight U-turn, the procedure was reversed, except when he was refilling the generator fuel tanks. On those occasions, after the supplies were unloaded and checked, Miss Agnes led the way from the kitchen porch, around the back of the building to the generator shed, and stood watching his every move as he emptied the cans of fuel into the tank. Then, she led him to the gate, opened it, and he was expected to leave . . . and not honk the horn in farewell, which he probably didn't feel like doing anyway.

Yes, Jono Sam knew Delilah was there. He knew this because he looked directly at her many times as she stood back out of Miss Agnes' sight, watching him through the screen door when he was unloading deliveries on the back porch. And he had also seen how quickly she scurried out of sight when Miss Agnes, following his gaze suspiciously, angrily yelled at her. He had also seen her a few other times when he drove around the building to fill the fuel tanks, standing at the mesh-covered window of her room in the back of the main building watching the truck . . . and him. After the time Miss Agnes yelled at her, he never indicated that he saw her, not in any way Miss Agnes might notice. But she knew he did because he always rolled his eyes sideways toward her as he passed the window and gave the faintest of nods.

Delilah discovered something else in the records, something that had apparently been missed in the bureaucratic paper shuffle in an office halfway around the world from Bhutu: this Jono Sam had gotten his job under false pretenses or if not that, at least by default. The man who hired him was sent to Bhutu asking for Jono Sam by name, and this Jono Sam had taken the job without making it clear that the Jono Sam the man was looking for was his father, also named Jono Sam. His father had been retired on a small pension in 1984 when Bhutu had been placed on inactive status.

Ten years later, the notation in the records was clear: "Rehire Jono Sam per A." The father would have been an extremely old man in 1994 when Jono Sam, the son, was hired. He would be even older now . . . if he were still alive. Delilah had been interested enough in Jono Sam, the father, to look up his record of employment with Brighton Foundation. She was amazed to find that he had first been recorded on the payroll in 1950, and had actually worked for them for thirty-four years until 1984, basically doing the same things his son had done while Delilah was there.

According to the dates on the old plans, Bhutu Holding Facility was completed in late 1930, and went into operation in 1931. For what purpose was not clear in the records. Delilah had a very good idea of what was involved. As far as she could tell, the Bhutu Holding Facility of her experience was exactly as it had been when it was built, with the addition of a few modern conveniences across the years.

The largest building sat in the center of the compound. There were various outbuildings, and one of them, with no visible windows and a metal door, sat, long, narrow and silent across the back, parallel with and close to the rear wall. Storage sheds, and a small garage sheltering a four-wheel drive jeep that was never driven while Delilah was there clustered around the main building in a half-circle like chicks around a broody hen. Miss Agnes had never entered the long back building, the one that was labeled "laboratory" on the old plans.

The only vegetation inside the walls was a large tree in the back corner that partially shaded the ground beneath it, and a small, carefully tended vegetable garden laid out in precise rows close to the tree. The tree and the garden were the only green things in the otherwise bare, sun-scorched earth inside the wall. Thanks to the efforts of Jono Sam, not a blade of grass could be seen in the barren, hundred-foot perimeter outside the wall. Bhutu Holding Facility sat there in stark contrast to the lush jungle that surrounded it, a small fortress designed to defend itself from the pressing urgency of growth . . . or a prison designed to conceal secrets. A prison full of dark secrets…that is how Delilah thought of it now, because that's what it was.

A deep well with a small electric pump supplied ample water, and the main building contained large, comfortable living quarters that occupied the front two-thirds of the space. In addition to a large kitchen, there was a living room with a small office set up in one corner, a bathroom, and two bedrooms. One of the bedrooms was occupied by Miss Agnes, the other, though fully furnished, was unoccupied during Delilah's two-year stay.

A long, narrow hallway separated the back one-third of the building from the living quarters. From the door in the back of the kitchen, it ran almost the full length of the building, ending at the door of a small, cement-floored, antiseptically clean bathroom. In addition to toilet and basin, a large stall shower was built into one corner. Heavy mesh screen covered the window and the overhead light fixture. There were no shelves, towel racks or hooks, no medicine cabinet or mirrors. The walls were completely bare.

Four small rooms sat side by side down the back of the building, each with a door that opened inward from the hall. Only the lower half of each door was solid. The tops were open, covered by heavy, one-inch square steel mesh, as were the windows in each room. There was one dim light in the hall and

142

bathroom, none in the rooms. The furniture in each room was identical . . . a narrow cot with a thin cotton-stuffed mattress and a child's potty-chair. There was nothing else; it was in the fourth room down the hall, the one nearest the bathroom, that Delilah had spent part of her days and most of her nights for two long, miserable years.

With an effort, Delilah fought her way back into the present, straightened her legs, and got out of bed. Were these endless flashbacks going to haunt her for the rest of her life? She wondered about this, not for the first time. Sometimes it seemed like the harder she fought them, the oftener they tormented her, worse in the past couple of months than they had ever been before. And they accomplished nothing. The endless replaying of memories and facts she had compiled about Brighton Foundation with the help of Hunter, Darkling, and Merlin, served no purpose other than to torment her, remind her of her own helplessness.

I need help, no question about it. She had read and heard enough about therapy and counseling to know that talking about the things that bothered you tended to release the pressure, somehow easing the way to being able to live with those things that could neither be forgotten nor changed. Even writing them out helped some people, but not Delilah Cross.

For a moment she stood there thinking about writing her problems out on paper. The idea was tempting, but she rejected it, not for the first time. *Forgive me, Auntie,* she thought. *I had to disobey you. I had to write in order to survive, but I have always been so careful. I ask simple questions and I give short, simple answers on my note pad. You might say my questions and answers are determined by the size of my note pad . . . and I never carry a big one.* A small smile tugged at her mouth with the thought of all her communication being determined that way. While there were very large, thick notebooks with lines that invited a veritable flood of words, there were also tiny little things scarcely big enough to express a thought.

Well, I avoid answering really probing questions, she thought, *no matter how mad they get at me. Even my answers to school essay questions are worded so carefully, keeping to the subject with no straying.* As badly as she felt, she couldn't help smiling wider when she remembered how pleased Harold Newcombe had been with what he called her brief, concise, to-the-point writing "style". Necessity certainly was the mother of her writing style, that and the danger of inadvertently saying too much should she ramble. She was sure Auntie would understand about the writing . . . but now she needed to talk to someone.

Oh sure, just walk up to Sarah and say, "Oh by the way, Sarah, while you're not doing anything important like baking cookies, would you make an appointment with the nearest shrink for me? After nearly eight years, I think I feel the urge to talk."

It sucks, she thought. At one time, this comment had been Becky and Paulie Newcombe's most favorite last word for everything from frozen pizza to taking out the trash, a remark they were careful to make only out of their parent's hearing. Impulsively she softly said it out loud, enjoying the feeling of the words rolling off of her tongue. "This whole thing sucks!"

At the same time, Casey was walking down the hall past her bedroom, his footsteps muffled by the thick carpeting. He was on his way to his room to collect his bath things and some clean clothes. He intended to take a very long, hot shower in the bathroom at the end of the hall before calling his Dad for information about Agnes Kittridge . . . and to get some badly-needed personal advice. He was not consciously aware of hearing anything, but without quite knowing why, he thought, *this whole thing sucks!*

CHAPTER SIX

Children absorb their whole culture within the first few years of their lives. Practically no conscious effort is involved, all things just are, and dozens of customs and practices dealing with personal interactions within the family and groups with whom they come in contact become indelibly imprinted. How we deal with our perceived inferiors, superiors, and peers, how we deal with strangers, and how we perceive ourselves in the overall ranking system used in our particular environment is all learned behavior although we are seldom consciously aware of it.   *From The Changelings*

Delilah finished reading this part of the article for the second time, and with a sigh, tossed the magazine into the small wastebasket beside her desk. More of the same old gobbledygook. Gobbledygook, she thought. That sounds like some sort of mushy mess a French chef would prepare from turkey. No, she corrected herself, that would be gobblerdegook. And gelatin with unidentifiable stuff in it would be wobbledegook, wouldn't it? Smiling now, quite pleased with her word game, she reached for her dictionary.

"Gobbledygook," she read. "Language characterized by circumlocution and jargon." Well, maybe it wasn't exactly gobbledygook, then. The writing was fairly clear and straightforward. No, it was just repetitious because there are only so many words you can use to say the same thing, and that's all they ever did, never coming up with a really satisfying answer to the heredity versus environment question. And how about the way a child absorbs the culture, she wondered? Doesn't their heredity control how they absorb their environment? Or how much of it they absorb? Or how what they do absorb affects them in the long run? Doesn't the random combination of genes on a molecular level make everyone's perception of reality different, just as different as they are as individuals?

That reminded her of something that had bothered her until Harold Newcombe explained it to her. It had to do with the statement that all men are created equal. She heard that statement made on a television program and it bothered her. She was aware that she was very different from the mentally retarded children at Hiller School and that she was treated differently, too. She was also aware that she was different from Harold's children, Becky and Paulie. It seemed obvious to her that none of them were created equal, so the statement made no sense at all to her.

Harold had explained the concept of all people being considered to be equal in the eyes of the law, having equal rights to equal treatment. This did not mean that they were the 'same'. That would be like comparing apples and oranges. "People are all different from each other, like apples and oranges are different, but they're still fruit."

The child Delilah sat across the desk from Harold and thought about that a while. She looked at the clock on the wall a moment, then carefully wrote her thoughts on her tablet and turned it for him to read. He had burst out laughing as he read aloud, "Am I a kind of human coconut?" It was the most different fruit she could think of, ranking above a pineapple or banana on the difference scale as she saw it.

"Delilah, I'm beginning to think you're more of a fruit salad!" he said, still laughing. She had laughed with him, understanding more from his tone than his words that he meant this as a compliment.

She sighed. She missed her talks with Harold. And no, she still had no answer to the question about heredity and environment that satisfied her. Both arguments are right and both are wrong, she thought, and neither look deeply enough into variables or consider the myriad of intangibles that influence us even before conception. And what about God? What was His position in all of this? When she thought about it now, it seemed that Harold's fruit salad analogy was more apt than he might have thought. Everyone was more of a fruit salad than they realized, and some of the fruit in the mixture was very different and exotic…especially in hers.

She had known for a long time now that it took something very special to survive Agnes Kittridge. Yes, and it was both her early environment and her unique heredity that enabled her to live two years under the complete control of that woman and remain sane . . . at least she hoped she was. And she had not only survived she had learned.

She had a thought, and fished the magazine from the wastebasket, flipped back to the article, and quickly skimmed through it again. Her eyebrows rose. There was no mention of Delilah Cross, not even indirectly, and no mention, by name, of any of the others that she knew about. She mentally went down the list, counting them on her fingers: Samuel, Rebecca, Joseph, Zachariah, Jacob, Job, and, of course, herself. Seven in all, seven wild children that she knew about, seven little feral creatures that Agnes Kittridge had called her "specials".

And how many more, she wondered, how many didn't live through it, with only a Brighton Foundation case number to mark their passage? Or maybe they didn't mark their passage. Maybe they didn't want anyone to know about the ones who died. She pushed the thought away. *Now that really is paranoiac thinking. You haven't found a single thing that even suggests something like that,* she told herself sternly.

It had taken many hours over days and weeks to find these seven names in Brighton's computer files. She knew her own case number. It was one of the seven that she picked out because they all ended in the letter A; there were also one C, an F, two M's, an R, and a V. What these letters stood for, she had no idea, but they bothered her in some way she couldn't explain.

At one time, she wondered if the A at the end of her case number had any connection to the "per A" who had ordered the rehiring of Jono Sam's father at the time Bhutu Holding Facility was reopened. It was clear in the records that after ten years of inactivity it had been reactivated in 1994, apparently just for her, then deactivated again when she was sent to Hiller School. Of course, there could have been any number of reasons, but she didn't like coincidences. Besides, why was Jono Sam, the son, still on the payroll eight years after Bhutu closed for the second time? That bothered her, too. Were they anticipating opening it again . . . and for whom? Another feral child?

Her thoughts returned to Agnes Kittridge and her "specials". If each child suffered through two years of her torture, that accounted for fourteen years. Who knew how much time there was between children? Feral children weren't common, so how long had that woman been on the Brighton Foundation payroll? This was the first time the question had occurred to her, and she could feel the small, ever- present ball of resentment and anger growing inside her, becoming hotter like a long-smoldering fire exposed to a draft.

She had no reason to believe the others had been treated any differently than she had been. "Civilizing savages" is what Miss Agnes had called it. Delilah shuddered as she remembered the tub of stinking dip and the ritual cleansing bath. Her hand rose reflexively to her head. The itch had been almost intolerable as her hair grew back in, and she had been beaten for scratching. Scratching oneself was not "proper" behavior, at least not where anyone could witness such a distasteful act. Of course, according to Miss Agnes, her God was always watching, too, noting every infraction of His rules, so it really wasn't safe to sneak one either.

And the same rule applied to belching and farting, both considered by Miss Agnes to be gross violations of her God's directives as personally given to her. Delilah could clearly remember the first time she heard Paulie emit a series of what he called "popcorn farts". They had all been sitting in the Newcombe family room watching a movie on television. During a commercial break, Paulie had gotten up to go to the bathroom, emitting a small "toot" with each step he took as he left the room.

Delilah sat in a panic, waiting for the wrath of Harold and Dee Dee to fall upon their son for this horrendous breach of propriety. Her mouth had quite literally fallen open in amazement when Harold, Dee Dee, and Becky burst into laughter, and Dee Dee, still giggling, urged him to hurry on to the bathroom before something worse happened. They call that culture shock, Delilah thought, and that's what my whole life has been for the last almost eight years . . . a series of culture shocks that began with Miss Agnes.

Miss Agnes apparently loved the sound of her own voice almost as much as she loved her God and her work. Delilah had learned to listen carefully. Somewhere in those endless monologues there were sometimes bits of information that she could use to avoid being punished, and avoiding punishment had become her prime directive during those years at Bhutu. There were no rewards for proper behavior, but not being punished ha been reward enough in itself as far as Delilah was concerned.

In one of her tirades, Miss Agnes had spoken at length about a boy named Job. She said he had boils when he was delivered to her, thus his name. Her blotchy, doughy face had twisted in disgust as she talked about how she had to scrub him. The disgusted look changed to one of satisfaction as she described how he had screamed when she poured medications over his shameful sores.

At that time, Delilah had no idea what a boil was, but she got the impression it was one of the ways God showed his anger when something displeased him. If the boy screamed, then it must have been very painful. Not screaming was one of the first lessons Miss Agnes taught her "specials". She thought about the daily pain Miss Agnes inflicted on her. She had learned not to scream . . . or even whimper. She had vowed to herself then that she would really try not to upset or displease Miss Agnes or her God. Job had done something very bad, she was sure, and God had done something even worse to him. The pain inflicted by Miss Agnes for things like belching or scratching an itch was bad, but she didn't ever want Miss Agnes' God to get mad at her and give her a boil.

Delilah sighed and flipped a page in the magazine without noticing she had done it. She had read everything she could find on feral children. Their chances of ever becoming adapted as functioning humans in human society was dependent in great part on their age at the time of becoming feral. There were learning windows for every living creature that needed more than instinctive skills to survive. There were optimal learning times, literally dozens of scarcely noticed little periods of time which, if missed, caused a lifetime of difficulties, some of them insurmountable. How many made it out of Miss Agnes' sick, twisted kindergarten with any shred of sanity left, she wondered?

Well, that was another item to add to the list of things that were assuming more and more importance in her mind, another reason to talk, especially if it granted her the satisfaction of blowing the whistle on Miss Agnes.

For a moment, she had a vivid mental picture of policemen beating a cowering Miss Agnes with correctional implementers while a small, bald Delilah, clothed in a shapeless shift, capered and danced, alternately shouting, "Spare the rod and spoil the child!" and blowing a huge whistle with all her might. The cartoonish quality of her mental picture made her smile, but she felt a kind of vicious pleasure, too. She didn't take note of the fact that she pictured herself as the child she had been, not the almost adult that she was now, or that the scene took place in the kitchen at Bhutu as it had been eight years before.

She tossed the magazine back in the wastebasket, and started across the room toward the big, old, wooden rocking chair by the window. She had come across it one day while helping Sarah put some of the winter bedding into storage in a huge, old-fashioned wardrobe in the basement. There were several pieces of very old furniture stored there, apparently unwanted remnants of some of the original farm furniture. When she recognized what was under the old quilt that covered it, Delilah was immediately drawn to it. She pulled the quilt back and gently pushed the rocker, setting it in motion. In her mind, she could hear herself and Auntie gleefully chanting, "Rocking chair, rocking chair, rocking chair," in time with its movement.

When she indicated that she would like to have it by writing, "Rocker?" on her note pad, Sarah helped her carry it to the center of the room for inspection, quite pleased that Delilah was interested in adding a personal touch to her room. She didn't comment on the fact that the rocker had, quite obviously, been custom-made for a very large person and was too big to fit tastefully into Delilah's small room. To Sarah, it meant that Delilah was settling in, marking her personal territory, nesting, so to speak, and she found this very encouraging. The rocker was in surprisingly good condition and working together they cleaned and waxed it until the old wood gleamed warmly.

On their next trip to the shopping center, they went into a fabric shop and Delilah spent nearly an hour choosing material for pads for the seat and back. She was torn between a muted rose-colored pattern that matched her room and one of vibrant, mixed-green leaves and brown vines that pleased her because it reminded her of the jungle and lush growing things.

Sarah finally settled the matter by buying some of each, telling Delilah that it would be easy to make the pads with one side of each pattern; that way they could be turned around whenever it pleased her. She assured Delilah that the greens would go well in the rose room, too. Sarah made the pads, filled them with fluffy

155

cotton batting, and quilted them by hand. They shared the job of tying them in place, and giggling, they took turns rocking to try them out, making a joke out of turning them around, trying first the rose pattern then the green leaves to see which felt and rocked the best.

That was a good memory, Delilah thought, as she reached for her friend Teddy Bear. Holding him close to her chest, she sat down, drew her knees up, resting her heels on the edge of the seat, and wrapped her arms around her knees. With her chin resting on Teddy Bear's head, she rocked, back and forth, back and forth, becoming deeply involved in her thoughts. She didn't notice that she was humming the going to sleep song in time with her rocking. For the first half of her life, she had sung the words without the slightest idea of their meaning. Now she knew what they meant and their significance to her.

It all came down to a decision about speaking. To speak or not to speak, to coin a phrase - as Paulie used to put it - that was the question. In the early morning darkness after her encounter with Casey in the kitchen, it had seemed fairly simple. Sitting here now, with the late morning sunlight pouring across the last of the blossoms on the fruit trees like golden melted butter, it didn't seem so simple at all. In fact, the stumbling blocks in her way seemed almost insurmountable; no matter what routes she took to get around them. She had very effectively put herself in a box, or rather circumstances had, but she would not admit defeat. It was like the game. In the game there was always a solution, you just had to find it, think it out, find the true way out of the maze.

After a while, she reached for the apple sitting on the small table beside her. Taking a huge, quite inelegant bite, she was struck again by how much she liked apples. It was more than the taste that she found so satisfying. The texture, the feel of it in her mouth, the smell of it, even the sound it made when she bit in and chewed, all contributed to her contentment. And, underneath these physical pleasures, apples brought back a good memory of sharing the stolen apple with Auntie.

The only thing that was as good, in her opinion, was going to Sarah's kitchen garden and eating whatever she chose from among the various vegetables growing there. The kitchen garden was Sarah's private park, the flowers red radishes, orange carrots, light green lettuce, dark green cucumbers, white and yellow squash, red tomatoes, and purple eggplant . . . hidden in the earth like little buried treasures waiting to be found.

Sarah introduced her to this particular pleasure, frequently joining her in this very healthy smörgåsbord of snacks. Delilah wasn't aware that Sarah carefully ignored her sometimes indelicate, messy attacks on a ripe, sun-warm tomato, or the way she had of stripping the husks from small ears of new corn with her teeth before she ate them. Sometimes her garden snacking was accompanied by less than polite lip-smacking and little grunts of satisfaction. Sarah ignored this, too.

Although Delilah hadn't really thought about it, she assumed that Sarah knew her whole history with Brighton Foundation, and also knew as much as anyone else did about her life before that. She didn't talk about those things to Delilah. Though she appeared to ignore Delilah's breaches of polite eating etiquette, she was fully aware that in the garden Delilah was quite naturally- -without artifice- -reenacting her early childhood, finding tasty food for herself and eating it with great gusto.

There was something else Sarah's sharp eyes saw in Delilah's garden behavior, but though she noted it, she had no way of realizing its significance. Occasionally, always while kneeling to pull a carrot or radish from its dark bed of moist, crumbly earth, Delilah would pause, staring intently at the well-worked earth as though seeing something there that didn't belong, turning her head slightly to check the surrounding rows. Each time this happened, her hand would rise to her throat, gently touching it as though it hurt. After a moment or two, never longer, she would continue with whatever she was doing.

Though Sarah didn't know it, during those pauses Delilah was suddenly filled with anxiety, living in another garden in a far different place. She was back in Bhutu Holding Facility, kneeling in the reddish earth under the big tree in the corner of the compound.

Miss Agnes intended to have a garden. Fresh vegetables nourished both the body and the soul. They were gifts from God and it was imperative that she have a garden. Besides, they were an excellent source of roughage and she was frequently bothered by severe constipation. She requested seeds and they arrived on the Brighton plane the next week with the regular shipment of supplies. Thinking ahead, she had also requested a leather dog collar for a small dog and a ten-foot leash. They also arrived with the next shipment.

On the morning she started the garden in the partial shade provided by the big tree in the back corner of the compound, Miss Agnes placed the collar around Delilah's neck and made sure it was buckled snugly without choking. She snapped the light chain leash to the ring on the collar, and fastened the other end securely to the belt around her own dumpy waist.

"Come," she said, jerking on the slack leash she had looped in her hand. Delilah's obedience training had entered a new phase.

Still chewing, Delilah got up, tossed the now-denuded apple core in the wastebasket along with the discarded magazine, and replaced Teddy Bear on her bed. She needed a shower, and maybe later she would go to the barn for a while. She had already made up her mind that she would not go back to the stream, not as long as Casey was here spying on her. Besides, she liked the barn.

159

She liked to watch the free-ranging chickens that spent the daylight hours going about their insect and seed hunting or indulging in long, obviously enjoyable dust baths. It hadn't taken long for Delilah to understand much of their inter-chicken communication, and some of it was funny.

The big red rooster was, she had decided, lazy, a braggart, a bully, and a liar. Occasionally, he would engage in a wild chase, single-mindedly pursuing some squawking hen that obviously did not crave his amorous attention. But, more often than not, he indulged in a subterfuge that Delilah considered unethical. He would strut about, then pretend to find some unbelievably luscious item of food, loudly calling to the hens to come and see and share it with him. The stupid hens never failed to hurry to him, and then he grabbed and mounted whichever one happened to take his fancy.

Delilah did not like the rooster. She had asked Sarah why they kept him. As far as she could see, the hens arranged themselves in their own carefully-ordered ranking based on intimidation, not a particularly fair system for those on the bottom rung of the pecking order, but one that seemed to work well in many species. Sarah's answer had surprised her.

"The hens like a rooster around. It fills an instinctual need, Delilah, gives them a feeling of being protected. He's supposed to keep watch for danger and give them warning. Some roosters attack people in the mistaken notion that they have evil intentions toward his hens . . . which they do sometimes. Happily, this old cock doesn't go that far, but you've heard him sound off when a hawk is around, haven't you?"

When Delilah nodded, she continued, "It's a pretty deeply-ingrained instinct because if a flock doesn't have a rooster, the dominant hen will actually try to take over. And, after all, survival of the chicken species depends on getting eggs fertilized, doesn't it?" Sarah had laughed then. "As far as that goes, most of us hens have a yearning to have a strong rooster around to guard us, even if we can't stand him sometimes, so don't be too hard on that old guy."

Delilah understood this answer, but she still didn't like the rooster. He was too full of himself, too sure of his dominance . . . and besides, he was a liar. What he needed, she thought, was for a hen to stand up to him, stare him down, dominate him, show him her power over him, teach him not to tell lies, put him in his place . . . and only then reassure him about his sexual desirability. Although she didn't consciously explore it, somewhere deep inside her, there was a sense of rightness about these feelings of how things should be . . . with people as well as chickens.

She much preferred the flock of now-wild homing pigeons. They formed monogamous pairs, tending to their sometimes-mysterious bird business and settling their just as mysterious disagreements in a quieter way. It gave her a great deal of pleasure to watch them.

Jordan had noticed her interest in the pigeons that called the old barn their home, and told her their history. Delilah liked Jordan. He was totally non-threatening and easy to be with. He always spoke directly to her, his face serious, his words carefully considered, as though what he was saying was carefully thought out in advance. She liked the way his face lit up and became animated when he talked about the greenhouse and the experimental plants he so carefully nurtured.

He once told her that she was an excellent listener, knowing when to ask questions about things she didn't understand. She had answered, writing on her note pad, "Interesting subject, want to learn." She flipped to another page and added a question, "Talk to plants?"

Jordan laughed then, and said that he was one hell of a talker when he was riding his hobbyhorse, which was most of the time. Yes, he talked to the plants, too, and so far none of them had fallen over dead from his verbal assaults . . . or his bad breath. They laughed together then, as they had so many other times since she arrived at the farm.

He was so different from Sarah and Joe that Delilah had trouble thinking of him as their son, and she marveled at the way chromosomes contributed by both parents managed to arrange themselves into totally new patterns. Yet, when she thought about it, Jordan was like them, too. Open, friendly, humorous, and easy to be around. Heredity and environment working together she wondered?

According to Jordan, the pigeons somehow managed to survive during their generations since World War I, when some patriotic Bentry raised them as part of the carrier pigeon brigade carrying messages across distant battlefields. So, he had said, they were a unique bit of pigeon history, or at least their ancestors were. At the end of the war, every last adult bird had been disposed of, and only twelve very young ones survived. They were taken to a breeder in Southern California, nearly three thousand miles away from the place of their hatching in Virginia.

One day, two months later, much to everyone's surprise, a lone pigeon returned, flying into the barn and settling itself in the now empty loft where the coops had once been. Over the next two weeks, mostly alone, but sometimes in pairs, eleven of the twelve young pigeons returned to the barn loft. There was no question as to their origin . . . they all still wore the distinctive yellow Bentry identification band on their left legs.

The word about the amazing return of the Bentry pigeons spread among the neighboring farmers, and everyone was watching for the twelfth one. Another two weeks passed and just when everyone thought it was hopeless, it came, winging low to the ground, dirty, feathers missing, and too exhausted to make it further than the stone wall beside the barn. It was a female, and she was taken in and nursed until strong enough to release; when she was, she flew directly to the loft, and home.

The Bentry family decided that these courageous, determined birds had proven their right to call Bent Tree Farm home. The money was reimbursed to the California breeder, and they were allowed to live their lives as they pleased in complete freedom. This story thrilled Delilah; she understood their terrible, driving urge to go home to that place where they were born. Yes, she thought, I'll go down to the barn after I shower and get something to eat.

By the time Delilah had collected bath things and a change of clothes, Casey was already in the shower. She heard the water running as she stepped out of her room, so she headed downstairs. She knew Sarah was already busy in the kitchen because the smell of browning meat and onions floated in the air, speaking of good things in the making for dinner. She pushed open the swinging door with one elbow, waving the other hand to get Sarah's attention. When Sarah turned with a welcoming smile, Delilah held up her things, and motioned down the hall with her head.

"Oh, sure, use the downstairs bathroom, but make it quick. I've got a yen for a little brunch. For the life of me, I can't figure out how my stomach works. Or my mind, for that matter." She turned back to the counter, talking over her shoulder as she vigorously used a wooden spoon on the contents of a large bowl. "Would you believe that smelling those onions made me hungry for French toast? And hot maple syrup?"

Delilah didn't need to be told to be quick. She was always quick in the shower, washing and rinsing and getting out in record time. Water on her body was not something she relished, not that there was anything wrong with the clear water coming from the shower head. That was like rain. It was the puddles that sometimes formed around the drains- -and the drains, themselves- -wet and dark and threatening. Yes, she was always quick in the shower and the thought of French toast and hot maple syrup made her salivate a little.

As she turned to leave the kitchen, Sarah called, "Oh, is Casey up yet?" When Delilah raised one eyebrow in response, Sarah laughed. "Okay, okay, he's up and in the shower. That's why you're down here. Us old folks ain't so quick on the up-take as you youngun's". This last was delivered in a mock old-lady quaver, and Delilah grinned widely as she let the door swing shut. Sarah's laughter followed her down the hall.

But a minute later, Sarah's face was serious and thoughtful as she added a spoonful of vanilla, a spoonful of sugar, and a good sprinkling of cinnamon to the egg mixture she used to coat the

165

bread slices. She vigorously wielded the wooden spoon a few minutes longer, the clop, clop, clopping keeping time with her thoughts. Then she turned and busied herself with cutting thick slices of day-old bread.

She knew exactly why young Doctor Lowell was here, and she was concerned about the effect his observations were going to have on Delilah. The girl had come a long way down the road toward a normal life, too far, Sarah thought, to have her progress disturbed by some young hotshot out to make a name for himself. She stopped cutting for a moment, the knife suspended in midair.

What was normal, she wondered, especially when you applied the word to Delilah? Nothing in the girl's entire life had been normal, had it? Certainly Sarah knew that there was no such thing as normal, everything was only a matter of degree, and she didn't have a clue as to what would be normal for Delilah. She chided herself for falling into the old pigeonhole trap. Delilah was one of a kind, and the answers for her were not going to be found in psychology textbooks. Delilah had to find the answers for herself, and she needed all the protection, help, and support she could get while she was doing it.

Sarah was surprised at the fierceness of her thoughts. Well, she amended grudgingly, maybe young Casey wasn't so bad, but she would have felt better if Doctor K.C. Lowell, Senior, had taken the job. Senior's qualifications and credentials were the most

166

respected in the field; it was her own request, bolstered by her personal recommendation to Amanda Brighton, that had resulted in Brighton Foundation taking the unusual step of going outside its own staff to request him for this job.

She had every intention of keeping a very close eye on Casey, though. All in all, Sarah felt that she had taken the right approach with Delilah from the very beginning, one of complete acceptance of her as she was, burdening her with no performance expectations, allowing her to learn from example, guiding with almost unnoticeable subtle pressures. It was understood that she would keep up with her college correspondence courses, but other than that, the girl was free to set her own pace, and she had been moving right along, almost visibly more relaxed and comfortable each day.

And, Sarah, thought, if she was reading the signs correctly, Delilah Cross was just about ready to break her long, self-imposed silence . . . if Casey Lowell didn't do something to upset her.

It was just about time, she thought, as she finished cutting, dipped the first slice of bread into the batter, and dropped it on the preheated griddle. First she would have a private talk with Casey this morning and set the record straight. Then, she would give it another few days, watching him carefully as he interacted with Delilah, before she called Amanda Brighton to report.

There was something upon which Sarah and Delilah agreed, even though neither knew it. While Sarah had her own computer set-up at the gatehouse and was thoroughly competent in its use, she was firmly convinced that if you wanted to keep a private matter private, you never committed it to paper . . . or cyberspace, either. Delilah felt exactly the same way.

CHAPTER SEVEN

When Casey finished drying himself after his shower, he placed the green towel on the green towel rack, smiling as he did so. The smile became a grin as he realized that the bath soap he carefully placed in the green soap dish sitting on the counter was also green. He just happened to be fond of that particular brand of soap, but it seemed somehow fitting that it should match.

The towel rack was one of six differently colored towel racks mounted to the walls on either side of the double Pullman basins. The soap dishes, too, in six matching colors were lined up neatly on the long counter. A rose-colored towel and wash cloth hung on a rose-colored rack, and a bar of rose-colored soap sat in a rose-colored dish. Casey assumed they belonged to Delilah, as they were the only people currently staying upstairs.

He felt a sudden small warm feeling as he looked at her personal things; sharing a bathroom with her gave him a sense of shared intimacy, reminding him of Carol. It had been six months since Carol moved out of the apartment they had shared for two years, a parting that left them both with very real- -if not openly admitted- -feelings of relief. They managed to remain friendly despite her periodic attempts to match him up with her unattached girlfriends.

Although he had never broached the subject of marriage to Carol, she announced that while he was good husband material, he just wasn't right for her. She needed more of a challenge, she said. The memory made him uncomfortable because the implication was that he somehow failed in the macho male department, failed to perform to her standards. What in the hell kind of challenge did she need? He had asked her that question, listened to her side step around a straight answer, and dropped the subject, but it still grated on him. He was becoming irritated, and he quickly thought about something else.

Each of the six upstairs bedrooms at Bent Tree Farm was assigned a color that carried through all of the linens. The sheets, pillow cases, bath towels, hand towels, wash cloths, and laundry bags for each room were all were the same color. Even the blankets and bedspreads were appliquéd with matching colors. As a matter of hygiene and common courtesy, everyone was expected to stick with their own assigned color. The copy of House Rules that he found on the desk in his room the day he arrived made this request, rather humorously asking that color-blind guests announce this fact so a game of musical rooms could be played until a color they did recognize was found.

Once a week, on Tuesday, if Casey remembered correctly, you were expected to strip and remake your own bed, using the clean linens stacked on the shelf in your closet. Then, you were expected to put the week's dirty linen in the laundry bag and place it outside your door. On Wednesday, it would be returned, and your only chore was to place the clean linens back on the closet shelf. Each person was responsible for their own personal laundry, either bringing enough clothing to last out their stay, or availing themselves of the well-equipped laundry room in the basement. When he stopped to think about it, the color-coding was a very neat, unobtrusive, and efficient way of handling problems that might arise with a transient population using the upstairs. They basically shared one large bathroom, even though another one was available in the office corner down the hall, and still another downstairs if it was needed.

The way mealtimes were handled was another example of efficient but unobtrusive management. Everyone was expected to take care of their own breakfast, which effectively took care of various eating preferences and waking times. Lunch had no set hours, but there was always a choice of soup, salad, sandwich material, and dessert ready and waiting between eleven and one. In addition, one of the big refrigerators held a large assortment of fruit, cheese, cold cuts, and left-overs, as well as milk, soda, and various types of bottled water. A nearby cupboard held snacks and enough quick-fix items to hold anyone over until the next mealtime, and the kitchen was open to all, day or night, contributing greatly to that informal "at home" feeling conducive to relaxation.

Dinner was the only meal when everyone was expected to sit down and eat together. This included Joe and Jordan, Sarah, Delilah, everyone in residence in the main farmhouse, and anyone using the bunkhouse at the time. The big extension leaves for the already over-sized kitchen table easily extended it to banquet size, and there were enough extra chairs in the basement storage room to adequately seat a large, floating, flexible population. The meals that Sarah dished up were really great in the hearty, home-style way one would expect on a farm.

As he stood in front of the basin shaving, Casey thought about it some more. In spite of the easy-going, relaxed atmosphere, Bent Tree was behind-the-scenes organized down to the smallest detail, and from what he had seen so far, it hummed along like a well-oiled piece of machinery. Even the farm equipment used daily by Joe and Jordan appeared to be subject to the kind of regular, methodical upkeep and maintenance more apt to be found in a much larger commercial operation.

He rinsed his face with cool water, sputtering quite unnecessarily, but somehow enjoying the sound. There was a sensitive spot on his cheek, and he leaned closer to the mirror to inspect it. Was it an incipient pimple? Without warning, his stomach tightened and a feeling of anxiety washed over him. Straightening up, he examined the feeling. Now where had that come from? Then he knew. He had just revisited his late teen-age years, a time when a pimple was a disaster of vast proportions, and the sensitive spot on his cheek had triggered it.

Putting his shaving gear in his toilet bag, he zipped it up with a decisive tug. It wasn't a pimple, and even if it had been, it was surely no disaster in his life, but he marveled at the way the mind held on to early experiences, slipping old responses into play long after the need for them had passed. This interested him, and he wondered in how many societies something as simple as a pimple could trigger anxiety and fear of courting adolescent disaster. Simple peer pressure, he decided, where breeding desirability was based on arbitrary standards of physical beauty.

This led him to consider other things. He thought of the binding of women's feet to the point of crippling them in China, a practice carried on well into this century, and to the present practices of physical mutilation in some societies, all in the pursuit of nothing more than enhanced attractiveness to the opposite sex. Stripped down to its fundamental element, the essence was an instinctive desire to increase chances of passing on genetic material. There was something disturbing in the thought that a superbly endowed, badly needed contributor to the human gene pool would fail to mate with a like contributor of the opposite sex because of something as insignificant as a pimple.

Casey grimaced at himself in the mirror. A twinge of anxiety over a possible pimple had taken him far afield, but he would like to pursue this idea further when he had the time. Then he straightened his face and looked at himself seriously. Was he good-looking? Sometimes he thought so, pleased with his boyish appearance, but most of the time, it now struck him, most of the time he wished he looked more mature, more like his Father. What's this? Insecurity? That was deserving of further consideration. Suddenly, he stuck his tongue out at himself. Not satisfied with the effect, he stuck his thumbs in his ears and waggled his fingers at himself derisively, then turned away.

As he put on his underwear and slipped on a clean pair of jeans, he returned to his previous train of thought about the farm. Nothing like this happened by chance. Even though Brighton Foundation owned and operated Bent Tree Farm for its own purposes, it took a very skilled manager to keep it running so smoothly . . . and so unobtrusively. Odd how the word unobtrusive kept recurring to him.

Casey went back to his room, and, as he put on a clean T-shirt and slid his bare feet into canvas deck shoes, he decided that none other than Sarah Clement was the mover and shaker here, doing the job subtly and well. And, it seemed to Casey, she was damned well qualified for the seemingly simple job she was doing. What really was her role at Bent Tree Farm, he wondered? There was a reason, he was sure, and there was another question for his Dad. Who was Sarah Clement? Could his Dad find out through his Brighton contacts? Not that it really mattered, but he would like to know to satisfy his own curiosity. Anomalies bothered him.

Right now, he was hungry, and it had been a long time since the coffee and cookies in the early morning dark. He glanced at the stack of folders sitting on the small desk under the window. He had carried them back to his room, not comfortable with the idea of leaving them in the office. There were no locks on the file cabinets there, and he was reluctant to leave such official records lying around unattended. He didn't feel so strongly about tidiness and left his bed unmade as he carefully closed the door behind him. Then he followed his nose and the smell of cooking down the hall.

As he approached Delilah's room, he saw the door was slightly ajar. Before his better judgment had time to do more than give an outraged squawk, he violated the cardinal House Rule of Bentry Farm, one printed in capital letters. It stated that you never entered the room of another without an explicit invitation. He did tap on the door, more of a push, really, and when it swung open, he entered, walking into the center of the room before stopping.

175

Slowly, he turned in a circle, taking in everything. How a person used their own private living space gave many clues about attitudes, interests, and even personality. He couldn't control a grin when he thought about his own 'organized disaster' method of keeping his bachelor apartment under control since Carol left. Without the weekly visits of his cleaning lady, who muttered things about pigs and other unsavory animals under her breath in Spanish the entire time she was there, he doubted that there would even be a walkway through the books, papers, magazines, clothes, and whatever else he happened to handle during the week. Ordinarily a fairly tidy, organized person, he knew he was enjoying acting out his defiance of Carol's nagging . . . something he hadn't been able to do when they were living together.

No, he thought, tidiness isn't the really important thing, although Delilah's bed was made and the room was neat. He couldn't quite bring himself to open the closet or the drawers in her bureau and dresser, but he did note the absence of make-up and perfume and the other odd fripperies he associated with female occupancy. There was none of the clutter one might associate with a teen-age girl's room, that much was apparent, and because it was uncluttered, what few things there were stood out, caught the eye.

There were three things on the polished surface of the dresser: a small, oblong case that Casey took to be a musical instrument of some kind, a small wooden statue, and a round metal medallion slightly larger than a silver dollar.

He flipped the latches and lifted the lid on the case. A pan flute rested snugly in its blue velveteen nest. He refastened the case, and picked up the medallion. It was one of those cheap souvenir coin facsimiles, machine-stamped from soft metal, and it was bent and twisted, covered with dents and nicks. Looks like it was run over by a lawnmower, he thought, turning it to read the still-legible words on the outside edge, circling the almost-obliterated outline of either a gorilla or chimpanzee in the center.

"Landon Zoo and Botanical Garden," he read aloud. Landon? Yes, Landon, Pennsylvania. Hiller School was located on the outskirts of Landon, Pennsylvania.

Putting the medallion back into its original position, he turned his attention to the statue. About three inches high, it was an extremely well-done replica of a seated ape. When he picked it up, he could see that it wasn't just any ape . . . it was the "speak no evil" monkey of the famous trio. The workmanship was skilled and finely detailed, one hand clasped over the mouth, the other resting on upraised knees in an easy, natural position. Casey didn't recognize the dark wood, but it reminded him of other carvings he had seen in the markets and bazaars in East Africa. This was not the crude, cheap tourist junk that was usually associated with the three wise monkeys, either. The absence of the other two was interesting. Ordinarily the three were a set, firmly attached to each other as a group.

He examined it more closely, turning toward the window to do so. Whoever had done this work knew his subject. The shoulders were narrower than he might have expected, the arms proportionately shorter. The eyes were expressive, gazing serenely outward, and he noticed small tufts of hair delineated on each side of the head by small ears. This was no casual representation of a chimpanzee. In fact, he decided, this was not a chimpanzee at all unless someone had deliberately made a stylized version, which he doubted. It was close, but no chimp had small ears and tufts of hair like that. A flash of recognition came and went before he could grasp it.

He carefully replaced the carving on the dresser and stepped back. The things on the dresser nagged at him. There was something he was missing and it was more than identifying the ape. It would, he knew from experience, suddenly occur to him without conscious effort. Trying to remember it would be totally counterproductive, driving the knowledge deeper under the layers of his mind. He had always marveled at the contrariness, the devious, almost mischievous way the mind played its "gotcha" tricks with memory.

There was a long bookshelf mounted on the wall over the small desk, and, with a few exceptions, the books had the worn look of frequent handling. He stepped closer to read the titles. Beginning with an excellent dictionary, they covered a wide range of topics: four college texts, two on anthropology, one on math, and one on zoology, sat in a line next to a worn, leather-bound Bible. It, in turn, rubbed covers with one of the latest computer handbooks. Further down, a thick volume of the complete works of Edgar Allen Poe was separated from a book of Walt Whitman's verses by a book discussing Darwin's theories, if the title was any indication. There were two books on genetics, a fairly new copy of Audubon's color plates, and, on the very end, a battered copy of The Wizard of Oz.

Casey grinned widely as he gently touched the cover of the Oz book, then took it from the shelf. It was still one of his all-time favorite books. A vivid memory from his childhood floated through his mind. He and his twin sister, Kaydee, read this book together before seeing the movie version. They took turns reading aloud with great dramatic flourishes and gestures as they invented new voices for each character. His Cowardly Lion was much better than Kaydee's, but her Dorothy and Toto were much more believable.

It was easy to conjure the smell of roses as he stood there holding the book. Their mother, Samantha Lowell, was a well-known author of children's books, and they were both old enough and at the same time young enough to think she might be offended to discover that they were so enthralled by a book she hadn't written. Every Sunday afternoon, they hurried to the old, over-grown rose arbor in back of the garage to find out what happened next and what strange new creatures would cross Dorothy's path.

Casey's smile became a bit dreamy. The roses had been in full bloom, their fragrance heavy in the air, the day they read the last words and somewhat sadly closed the cover. They knew there were many more books in the series, but this was their first adventure in Oz, and the two of them, placing their hands on the cover, solemnly vowed that this book would be the very first "real" book that they read aloud to their own children. So far, Kaydee had kept the vow twice, once with her son and once with her daughter. And, Casey thought, I will too, if and when I ever have any children.

He opened the cover and his face became serious as he read the words written there. "From Becky and Paulie- -Merry Christmas!" was written on the flyleaf, and underneath this inscription, in the careful, rounded script of the young, were these words: "This isn't Kansas. I miss my Auntie, too. I want to go home."

Casey took a deep breath, and carefully placed the book back on the shelf. This was more than he had bargained for, a deeply personal look into the mind and feelings of the girl Delilah had been when she finished reading that book. His memories of himself and Kaydee and this book were so warm, so good to remember that the contrast with what he had just read hurt him somewhere down deep where he lived.

Then he thought Auntie? She missed her Auntie? Delilah has an Auntie, a relative? He pushed the thought aside to join the growing list of things he was filing for later consideration and continued his scrutiny of the room.

No question that this was an eclectic selection of books indicating a wide range of interests, far more than necessary for the college courses Delilah was taking. On second thought they were not diverse, they were closely connected. Anthropology, zoology, genetics, and speciation were all crossover subjects. He should know because he had studied them all while working for his degrees. And the new computer handbook puzzled him, too. That Delilah might be more than casually interested in computers had never entered his mind. The Audubon book seems to explain her interest in the bird down at the stream, he thought, tapping it with his finger absent-mindedly.

He picked up a framed picture sitting on the desk. It was an enlarged color snapshot of a group of people, apparently taken on a camping trip. Three teen-agers, two girls and a boy, sat cross-legged on the ground. The boy was holding up a small fish, mugging shamelessly for the camera as he mimed taking a bite out of it. A man and a woman sat together on a log behind them, and, to one side, Casey could see part of a green and white tent and trees in the background.

There was a strong family resemblance between the adults and two of the youngsters. The woman was blond; one of the girls appeared to be a reddish-blond, and the man and boy both had auburn hair. Probably a couple and their children, Casey judged.

He looked at the second girl. She was looking down at her hands in her lap, and he could see a big smile on her brightly-lipsticked mouth. Her curly dark hair, not quite shoulder-length, was held back from her face on one side by a shiny barrette that reflected in the camera lens, as did the one visible earring, a big one that dangled almost to her shoulder. The two girls were dressed nearly alike in short denim cut-offs and tight-fitting knit tops that announced the bra-less status of developing breasts.

Typical teen-agers, Casey thought as he replaced the picture on the desk, probably someone Delilah knew from her time at Hiller School. He turned away from the desk, noting the battered teddy bear sitting on the bed, and the big, old-fashioned rocking chair with vivid, variegated green pads that sat by a small table near the window. Then, it struck him. The dark-haired girl in the picture was looking down . . . at a pair of dark sunglasses she was holding in her lap.

Going back to the desk, he picked the picture up again. Now

that he really looked, he could see that the dark-haired "typical teen-ager" in the picture was Delilah, a far different Delilah, one that bore no resemblance to the girl he had seen here at Bent Tree, at least not as far as her appearance was concerned.

He left the room, leaving the door ajar as he had found it. What am I dealing with here, a chameleon? A chameleon with relatives?

* * *

Paulie Newcombe introduced Delilah to computer games, and she was fascinated with them, especially the fantasy role-playing adventure games that were his favorite. Paulie was eleven when Delilah came into the lives of the Newcombe family, and he leaned toward names like "Hero" and "Falcon" and "Knight" in naming his various role-playing personas . . . he still did.

Delilah, however, had chosen one particular name, and she always used it. She was "Chameleon", and, in her mind, it was a most appropriate name for her, standing for hidden things, things there but unseen, things that were not what they appeared to be . . . secrets. At that time, she was working to perfect her third persona, the third distinct character behind whom the real Delilah could hide.

Becky Newcombe was exactly one year and three days older than Paulie, a fact she never let him forget, and she considered him a total nerd and bore. Delilah loved spending time with him, something Becky found to be totally incomprehensible. Paulie was extremely bright, and he had the knack of answering Delilah's questions in ways that were simple and understandable. No matter how apparently stupid the questions she scribbled on the little notepad she always carried with her, no matter how many times he had to explain something that was crystal clear to him, Paulie never lost patience with her.

Although Delilah didn't realize it, Paulie received as much as he gave in their relationship. Her devoted interest and her stubborn determination to learn about computers increased his own self-esteem, somewhat weakened by Becky's constant attacks, and gave him incentive to learn even more about computers so he could keep up with her questions. And he was delighted to show her all around his world of electronic circuits and microchips, and the miracles, large and small, to be found there. Even at that age, Paulie was an incipient hacker, already infected with the "must-crack-the-code" virus, though he never thought of himself that way. In his mind, it was all a big, unfolding adventure game filled with new worlds to be explored, and conquered.

Paulie never questioned Delilah's questions, never seemed to wonder why she asked them, or how she was using the information he gave her or helped her obtain. She began her first tentative forays into the private world of the Brighton Foundation computer network during her second year at Hiller School, sneaking into a terminal in the secretary's office at night. When she hit a snag, it was Paulie who found a way around it or through it or over it or under it, and if he couldn't find a way, he enlisted the help of two of his friends . . . Darkling and Merlin were their preferred game names.

In many instances, using the miracle of message services, there were as many as four young minds traveling the networks of inner space together, probing, testing, feeling their way through a complex, inter-linked series of computer data banks. Looking for and occasionally finding answers for her questions about Brighton Foundation, they did it without leaving traces of their unauthorized prowling. It was only recently that Delilah realized just what a feat the four of them had accomplished, and how risky and criminal it had been…and still was.

How to use her imagination was only one of the things Paulie taught her. She knew nothing about "let's pretend" or "what if?" and his world was filled with that kind of exploratory creativity. At the same time, he also taught her about fair and unfair, kindness, giving, friendship, loyalty . . . all those intangible things that form the threads that weave the fabric of good interpersonal relationships in our society.

In turn, Delilah taught him things about climbing trees and how to look and listen to increase awareness of his environment and what was in it. It was the tree climbing that resulted in their first shared secret. There were several big, old trees on the Hiller School property in addition to many smaller ones. One day, struck by an urge she didn't try to suppress, Delilah took off her shoes and socks and scampered up one of the bigger trees, perching on a medium-sized horizontal limb far above Paulie's head. Not to be outdone, he took off his own shoes and socks and struggled up to her, seating himself facing her in a secure position astraddle the limb with his back to the trunk.

"Ha," he said, puffing slightly from the exertion. "Thought I couldn't do it, didn't you?"

Feeling challenged and more than a little excited and playful, feelings from childhood that being in the tree brought back in a rush, Delilah stood erect on the limb, turned gracefully, and walked surely and confidently out the limb toward the end. When she got to the place where it started to bend under her weight, she bent her knees and pushed, causing the limb to spring gently up and down, balancing easily with the movement she had created. She turned again to face Paulie, and looked at him with a smug grin on her face.

Paulie's face was grim as he pushed himself erect, still braced against the trunk. After a moment, he took a deep breath and with his arms out from his sides, he took one slow step after another toward her, sometimes flailing as he fought to keep his balance on the still-moving limb. Suddenly, Delilah caught a whiff of adrenalin and fear from him. Belatedly realizing that this was no game for Paulie, she had already taken several steps back toward him when he slipped and started to fall.

Before he had time to register what was happening, Delilah was stomach-down on the limb, and Paulie found himself dangling above the ground as she held his wrist with one of her hands. Slowly, with the strength of one arm, she lifted him back up to where he could reach the limb and clamber up, then helped him scoot back to the trunk. Only after they reached the ground did the significance of what had happened register on him.

He looked at her, his eyes wide. "You saved me from falling and getting really hurt bad! You're strong," he said wonderingly, "really strong. I mean you're as strong as my Dad! Maybe even stronger!" He was silent a moment, thinking about this revelation.

Delilah pulled her notepad and pen from her pocket and wrote quickly. "Not tell,"

Paulie read her words out loud. "Not tell that I almost fell?"

When Delilah shook her head, he asked, "Not tell that you're so strong? Why not tell that? It's really great!"

Delilah wrote slowly and carefully. She printed each word, anxious that Paulie understand how important this was. "Secret! My secret. Not tell. Please."

Although it seemed longer to Delilah, it took Paulie about

thirty seconds to think about it and make his decision. "All right, Delilah. It's your secret and I won't tell. I promise." Then he laughed and added a condition. "But only if you teach me how to really climb trees like you do!"

They never spoke about it again, but Paulie had thrown her some very quizzical, meaningful glances when, following Dee Dee's and Becky's lead, Delilah handed a jar with a tight lid to him or his Dad to open. In return, she had taught him how to climb trees and feel comfortable doing it, but he never did it as well as she did.

Yes, she trusted Paulie and enjoyed playing games with him, certainly more than she enjoyed Becky's preoccupation with herself, boys, clothes, boys, make-up, and boys, but she learned from Becky, too. She learned the right hair, the right clothes, the right make-up, the right everything necessary to blend in with other young people as well as she possibly could without speaking. But then, everyone seemed to accept that handicap as long as everything else about her conformed to their idea of 'right'. Sometimes Delilah thought that Becky and her friends were as preoccupied with 'right' as Miss Agnes had been with 'proper'. The words really weren't that different, as long you understood that what is right is not necessarily proper and what is proper is not always right, something it took Delilah a while to figure out.

Using the computer, Delilah had kept in close contact with Paulie Newcombe since coming to Bent Tree Farm and, even here, the games were still on. Every Friday night, Delilah, Paulie, Darkling and Merlin met in the fantasy world of cyberspace to continue their game, the role-playing fantasy adventure they had started before she left Hiller School. The game, one of the swords and sorcerers kinds, had endless variations and permutations, and they took turns deciding which scenario they would follow.

On Friday evenings, after Sarah had finished up in the kitchen and gone back to the gatehouse, Delilah went to the kitchen and collected a plate of snacks and a big glass of milk that she carried upstairs to the office. She always used the front corner work space, and, after placing the plate and glass on a nearby shelf, she booted up the computer, tapped out a few numbers and codes, leaned back in the comfortable chair, and checked through her game notebook.

It was nice for her, she often thought, that the various people passing through Bent Tree didn't seem to be night owls. They tended to be early risers, working through the day, and going to bed early. This kept them out of the office during the night, which allowed her the freedom to use the computers as much as she wanted- -and how she wanted- -without raising any questions.

One by one, "Darkling" and "Merlin" and "Hunter", Paulie's current name of choice, would log on, each with their own few words of identification known by the other three, a kind of code designed to keep any would-be intruders out of their private game world. When it was Delilah's turn, she would type, "Chameleon here," followed by the words, "She has a secret."

CHAPTER EIGHT

The phone was picked up on the third ring. "Hello, Lowell residence." K.C. Senior's voice was a pleasant, resonant baritone and Casey thought it matched his Father's physical appearance well. Tall and tanned with a striking mane of silver hair, his kind, deep-set blue eyes were always interested and alert behind the thick lenses of his heavy-framed glasses.

"Hi Dad, me. Have I caught you at a good time? I need some background information." He paused before he continued. "And I think I need some advice. I've got a problem here that I don't quite know how to deal with, as much as I hate to admit it."

"Aha!" K.C. exclaimed in mock surprise. "Do I hear the voice of my wayward son crying out in the wilderness of Virginia?" He became serious. "It's always a good time when you call, Casey, you know that. Matter of fact, we were just talking about you. We want to ask you . . . "

He broke off, and Casey could hear his Mother's voice in the background, but couldn't quite distinguish the words. That meant

191

she was probably in the kitchen with both hands full; otherwise she would have already been on the kitchen extension. He smiled. It was so easy to picture her there in her little kingdom. As far as she was concerned, her family, the big well-equipped kitchen, and the small well-equipped office that opened off of it were the entire world she needed to be happy. Almost by osmosis, he and Kaydee had come to think of it as the center of their world as well. Unexpectedly, he felt a pang of loss, nostalgia for those almost idyllic yesterdays; for a moment, he thought he smelled the faint, sweet fragrance of roses.

K.C.'s voice sounded a little muffled. "Hang on a minute."

Casey could hear the rustling of papers in the background as his Dad shuffled through them. Cradling the phone on his shoulder, Casey swiveled the chair so he could look out the window. He was sitting in the corner office, the Kittridge file folders on the desk in front of him. He had never felt this way before that much was clear. Maybe, indirectly, becoming aware of Delilah as a person caused the change. Or beginning to understand what her childhood had been like had something to do with it. He had shared the sometimes incredibly torturous early lives of some of his other cases, feeling and hurting for them, but nothing had prepared him for the almost guilty protective feeling he was developing about Delilah. For God's sake, he thought almost angrily. I feel like I owe her an apology because I had such a wonderful childhood and that's crazy!

K.C. was back. "She said to tell you hello, and she'll pick up the phone as soon as she's through with the frosting thing she's doing." Paper rustled again, then, "Okay, son, what do you need?"

"Well, first, I need anything and everything you can find on Agnes Kittridge." He spelled the name and went on. "She was working for Brighton Foundation for sure between 1994 and 1996, and possibly much longer. She was at their Bhutu Holding Facility in Central Africa somewhere. Dad, you know how I like to work from original reports just like you do?"

"Yes." K.C.'s voice was noncommittal. Casey caught the tone. *He must have picked up on tension in my voice*, he thought.

"Well, I have the original Delilah Cross records here. I've gone over Kittridge's reports several times just to be sure, and something smells very bad. From what I read in these reports in her own handwriting, the woman was and probably still is psychotic, at least part way around the bend on a paranoiac religious trip."

K.C. didn't hesitate. He often told Casey that he trusted his diagnostic skill, and he did. "I'll take your word for it, Casey, and get right on it as soon as we hang up. Shouldn't be too hard, a couple of phone calls should do it." He chuckled. "Sometimes those old contacts come in handy." His tone was light, but his eyes had narrowed. The stress level in his son's voice had risen noticeably. There was something else bothering him, and it could only be one thing. He decided to do a little leading.

"Incidentally, what do you make of Delilah Cross? Is that young lady as puzzling and enigmatic as I've heard?"

There was a noticeable pause before Casey answered. Finally he began. "I think you know all the basic details, Dad?" The question was rhetorical because he knew that everyone in the field, including his Dad, kept up with the latest writings about her. She was too unusual, too hard to define and stuff into the proper scholarly pigeonhole. The scientific community didn't like enigmas, unsolved puzzles.

For a moment he had a vivid mental picture of a solemn group of crows standing around a pile of jigsaw puzzle pieces on an old-fashioned desk fitted with a rack of pigeonholes. From time to time, one would pick a piece out of the pile, examine it, and pass it around the group for their inspection. Then they would all mutter and argue among themselves about which pigeonhole was the proper one in which to stuff it. He frowned slightly when he thought about the word "proper". After reading Agnes Kittridge's reports, he was beginning to loathe the word.

Collecting his thoughts, he cleared his throat and continued, "Anyway, I think the water phobia is real and predates her being brought to Bhutu. I also think that she is perfectly able to talk and doesn't for reasons of her own. What those reasons are, I haven't the slightest idea, but I'm almost positive she can talk."

This time the pause was noticeably longer, and they both listened to the faint humming in the lines that connected them, the faraway rising and falling hiss sounding like voices of people speaking strange, almost-understandable languages in distant places. Neither of them felt pressured to fill the silence with words. Such easy silences had always been part of their closeness, communicating more than words could, filling both of them with a sense of togetherness and sharing.

Finally, Casey said softly, "And I think that I have a personal problem, here, Dad." He paused again, trying to think of the right words, the best way to say it.

"Go on," K.C. said. Casey was so involved in his own feelings he didn't catch the totally professional words and tone.

What the hell, Casey thought, in for a penny, in for a pound. Then he wondered where did that come from? Anyway, it was appropriate . . . and this was his Dad. He began with his arrival at Bent Tree Farm, his spying on her attempts to cross the stream, and their meeting in the kitchen. He described her nakedness the third time, and, though he hesitated over the words, feeling himself to be as naked and vulnerable before his Father as Delilah had been in front of his prying eyes and binoculars, he honestly described his feelings of sexual arousal. Even as he spoke, Casey was aware of how entwined his emotional reactions had become

195

with his objective observations, but he went on, determined to get it all out.

He outlined their accidental meeting in the kitchen at four o'clock that morning, leaving nothing out, further embarrassed by describing his feelings and unprofessional behavior out loud. Then, he said, "Dad, out of the blue, totally unplanned, I asked her why she didn't talk." He described the unusual stillness his question had evoked, and what he was sure he had seen in her eyes.

"She seems to habitually keep her eyes more or less concealed, head tipped down, lids lowered and there's something a little odd about that because her eyes are beautiful, Dad, an amazing shade of blue. And I've never seen such total awareness and intelligence, such . . . " he paused, looking for the right words, " . . . knowing and pain before in my life. I did something else," he rushed on, anxious now to get this over with. "I went in her room when she wasn't there and played Sherlock Holmes, nosing around in her personal things, and I think it's possible that she has a relative somewhere in Africa."

Again, he paused. "Dad, of all the damned books in the world, her favorite seems to be The Wizard of Oz. She plays the pan pipes, reads the Bible, has a teddy bear, a small wood carving of an ape I can't identify, and she used to dress and look like a typical teen-ager, but she doesn't now . . . and I feel guilty as hell about the whole thing!" There, it was all out. Hearing it in his own voice, he thought scathingly, how juvenile! How absolutely puerile!

It seemed like forever before his Dad responded, and Casey filled the long pause with second thoughts. Had his confession disappointed, disgusted, alienated? He knew he sounded like a guilty, sweaty-palmed adolescent confessing his sins. What did he want? Absolution? Reassurance? Would he have been better off trying to cope with it by himself? Damn it all, he thought angrily, I'm Doctor Lowell, a Doctor, a professional, respectable if not respected in this field! About the time he decided that at least he felt better for having talked about it, K.C. spoke, and his words came as a complete surprise.

"And here you had me thinking that you had some kind of real problem. Casey, in our line of work, the only time we have real trouble is when we don't see the danger, when we fail to recognize potential problems before they sneak up and take a big bite out of our ass, to put it crudely."

K.C. paused, ordering his thoughts. "As I see it, you've always used the empathetic approach to your cases, taking an active, participating role, working from the inside out instead of from the outside in, so to speak. It works for you, and very well, I might add, but in this instance you got caught off base. This young lady is, and has been from day one, a professional challenge to anyone

197

and everyone who has dealt with her personally, or even worked with the reams of material written about her. On that level alone, she is totally intriguing and probably one of the most-studied cases of her kind. Would you believe that I really wanted to take this assignment myself? From what you've told me, I wish I had."

He chuckled easily. "In my considered opinion . . . " He harrumphed noisily, and chuckled again, " . . . what you are dealing with, my boy, is the inherent professional challenge of a case that no one has been able to nail down satisfactorily. Couple that with an attractive, sexually-appealing girl who has certain characteristics that, for some reason or other, hit you precisely where you personally live . . . double whammy! Testosterone and intellect, the endless male war! As long as you recognize that you have this problem, and understand clearly that it is your problem, not hers, I think you will be okay."

As he stopped talking, K.C.'s thoughts were racing. He wondered if he had handled this satisfactorily. He felt it was much more serious than his light, easy, reassuring diagnosis might have indicated, but he didn't want his son to get any idea that his professionalism was in doubt. And he certainly didn't want to emphasize the fact that this was the kind of situation that had made or, sadly enough, destroyed other professional careers . . . and sometimes the men, themselves.

Should he advise Casey to drop the assignment? Take it over

himself? *No, wait and see*, he thought. Casey was aware of the problem. He was talking to him about it, and would continue to do so. Yes, he decided, wait and see if Casey could work it out without injuring either himself or Delilah Cross. In K.C.'s mind, neither of those options was acceptable.

They were quiet for a moment. Casey already felt better. What his Dad said made sense, and he trusted his professional integrity, not to mention his experience and wisdom.

"Thanks for that, Dad, I needed it, as you no doubt gathered. Now, here's another thing. Can you find out anything about Sarah Clement? She runs Bentry Farm for Brighton Foundation, and as far as I'm concerned she's over-qualified for the job she's doing. Her husband, Joe, handles the farming operation, and their son, Jordan, does his thing with a big greenhouse that looks new. Sarah keeps this place running like clockwork, and she seems to have developed a real, honestly warm friendly relationship with Delilah. But all you get from her is this down-home, salt-of-the-earth, just-us-folks, and Harriet Housewife bullshit. I like her, personally, but I'd like to know what's going on with her."

This time, much to his amazement, K.C. guffawed loudly. When he finally regained his composure, he said, "You know something? You've got a good nose for anomalies and it looks like you sniffed this one out right away. I've had a speaking acquaintance with Sarah Clement for nearly twenty years. That's

Doctor Sarah Clement, Casey. She was the chief staff psychologist for Brighton Foundation for several years, and Joe headed the Agronomy Department at State University. Matter of fact, I think I heard a while back that Jordan was making quite a name for himself as a research agronomist. I didn't know they had retired, but that must be why they're there."

He laughed again. "Harriet Housewife bullshit, huh? They must be having a ball with that kind of semi-retirement. You won't believe this, but it was Sarah I intended to call to find out about Agnes Kittridge. If anyone can dig up the details, she's the one who can do it."

When Casey couldn't seem to find anything to say, K.C. went on. "You know, I wondered why Delilah Cross was sent to Bent Tree Farm. I remember thinking when I heard about it that it seemed strange they should isolate her like that. Well, you can bet someone knew what they were doing when they sent her to Sarah Clement." He paused. "But how come all this secrecy? Why did they bring you in cold . . . or rather it would have been me, if I'd been available? Why bring in outsiders at all when they have a huge in-house staff? Good question, and I'm going to call Sarah and ask a few questions of my own just as soon as we hang up."

K.C.'s next words were puzzled. "I know damned good and well Sarah knows who you are, Casey, so how come she hasn't properly introduced herself? If I had taken this assignment, we would have been working together on this by now." He paused again, then said thoughtfully, "There's something odd going on here, something that doesn't quite fit, and I want to know what it is."

Casey felt subdued. "Uh, Dad, didn't you have a question for me?" He needed time to sort things out, needed to change the subject. Strange, he thought, how easily I seem to slip back into adolescence sometimes when I deal with Dad. Maybe it's because he always seems to have been there and done the things that I'm just now experiencing for myself. He's always so positive about things I'm unsure about. I wonder if I'll still feel like a kid when I'm in my fifties and he's in his eighties? He couldn't help grinning at the mental picture that evoked.

"Oh, I got so involved that I almost forgot." K.C. was apologetic.

"You certainly did," Samantha Lowell said, and Casey wondered how long she had been on the kitchen extension, and how much, if anything, she had heard. Not that he really wanted to keep secrets from her, it was just the idea that this had been a private thing, and it had been hard enough for him to share it with his Dad.

"Hi Mom," he said, and waited.

"Hi, Casey. I won't keep you long. Kaydee and the kids are planning to come down here next Monday. They've bought this huge monster of a recreational vehicle that you practically have to back up to get around a corner." After a moment's pause, "And isn't that an intriguing idea for a story?" she asked no one in particular and fell silent again.

Samantha Lowell's children's stories were very successful, unique in the way she managed to put herself in a child's mind and focus on the things that interested them, doing it in a way quite new and different. It wasn't at all unusual to find her running back and forth between the word processor in her little office and a pot of stew on the kitchen stove, but she did get distracted from time to time.

Samantha abruptly came back from wherever she had been with the huge RV, and continued as though she had never left. "Anyway, she's bringing the thing down here, just her and the children, driving it all by herself. Ray was supposed to do the driving." Her voice was slightly disapproving. "They've been planning this for a month, and she cleared all her court cases. I guess Ray tried to clear his, too," she admitted graciously, "but he can't get away right now, something technical. They both agree that it isn't worth getting a contempt citation over, so she's coming down alone with the kids, and we'll all go on a kind of slow, here-and-there scenic tour around two or three states. Your Dad will drive from here."

Casey could hear approval and satisfaction in her voice. Mom was the best, but some of her preconceived ideas about her children and her firmly held notions about what females should and should not do were positively antiquated. Casey grinned to himself and thought, and a little odd, too, especially coming from a lady who shame-shamefacedly admitted to wearing a tie-dyed skirt, a fringed white buckskin jacket, love beads, and flowers in her hair when she and K.C. got married. Both parents denied that there were any pictures of the wedding, and his Dad firmly refused to discuss how long his hair had been and what he had worn to the ceremony. But Samantha always chuckled wickedly when the subject came up, making remarks about incense, finger cymbals, and knowing where all the bodies, or at least the butts, were buried.

"Kaydee particularly wanted to know if you'd like to come along. That RV actually sleeps eight people," she marveled. "She didn't know you were on a case, and when I told her, she wondered if there would be any problem if we stopped by Bent Tree Farm to see you and spent a couple of days in the area as part of our tour. She thought that a visit to a real farm would be a special treat for the kids, and the RV has everything we need. Does that sound all right to you? I mean can you get permission for us to do that?"

"Sounds great to me, Mom. I haven't seen the kids for three or four months and the way they're growing, they've probably doubled in size by now! There's plenty of things around here to keep them busy and interested." He thought about the stream, the barn, the greenhouse, and the old school on the corner. "And there's plenty of room to park the RV and plug it in for electricity. There shouldn't be any problem at all. Joe, Sarah, and Jordan Clement are nice people; you'll like them. And, in case you didn't know it, Dad's already acquainted with the lovely Sarah," he added teasingly, and waited for a response. He didn't get one.

"Good! I'll call Kaydee right away and let her know. That way she can change her route if she needs to. Depending on when he can get away, Ray intends to meet us wherever we happen to be at the time, so she'll need to stick pretty close to the itinerary she finally decides on. Oh! Gotta run! I smell the other cake getting a little too brown. We'll call the day before we get there. Take care. Love you. Bye."

Casey smiled as his Dad spoke in a wondering voice. "Whew! That woman never slows down, does she?" Then, "I'll call Sarah right now, and while I'm at it, I'll make sure of our welcome because that RV really is a monster. Samantha wasn't exaggerating a bit. What's the number?"

Casey read it from a card he took from his wallet. The lines in the office were separate from the farm line, which rang downstairs in the kitchen with extensions in the greenhouse and the tack room in the barn. He glanced at his watch. It was only a little past ten o'clock although it felt later to him. "She ought to be downstairs in the kitchen right now. She keeps a tight schedule."

"Then, by the time you get downstairs, I'll probably be talking to her. Give me about fifteen minutes before you interrupt?"

"Sure will. Oh, before I forget, what are you going to do with His Royal Highness while you're gone?" Known affectionately as HRH, His Royal Highness was Casey's cat, a big gray, totally unflappable stray tom with regal mannerisms that clearly stated how very fortunate you were that he allowed you to stroke him and provide him with the niceties of cat life. HRH had attached himself to Casey several years before- -or vice versa- -and when they were not sharing a residence, he usually graciously deigned to share quarters with his parents.

"I've already made arrangements with Carol," K.C. responded. "And she said to tell you hello and she has a young lady she is sure is just right for your particular needs." He laughed as Casey groaned.

"She never quits, but she does have an understanding with HRH. I think he actually likes her because she won't let him bully her. Thanks Dad. I'm glad you're coming. Now, you'll get to meet Delilah for yourself and, in case I haven't told you lately, I love you guys dearly." Embarrassed by his own rush of feeling, Casey abruptly hung up.

First stop, he thought, is a quiet chat with Doctor Sarah

Clement. No, he corrected himself. First stop is the Hiller School record file on Delilah. He was hearing his own words in his mind, and he wanted to check on the results of any intelligence tests she might have had. One of the things he had seen in her strange and beautiful eyes was intelligence.

* * *

Delilah was intelligent and quick to learn, but during her first few weeks at Bhutu, the overwhelming avalanche of new information put her into sensory overload. It was too much to assimilate all at once, so, in self-defense, she simply shut down, focusing only on basic survival input. That didn't mean the new information assaulting her senses stopped, it didn't. It continued to come in and was recorded somewhere, in some fashion. But it was mostly disconnected gibberish, bits and pieces of information that formed no coherent pattern for her mind to interpret, and she was still having trouble with her distance vision when looking at a flat surface like a wall.

She functioned, learned, and began to adapt to her new surroundings, thanks in great part to the guidance and advice Auntie gave during her nighttime visits. She tried her best to understand and comply with the seemingly endless stream of orders that poured from Miss Agnes because she soon found that to do otherwise resulted in pain. Avoidance of pain is a survival instinct that runs deeper in the human brain, consciously and unconsciously, than perhaps any other instinct, and obedience to Miss Agnes avoided pain.

She learned to do things. More important, she learned not to do things. The concept of being punished for doing something was clear to her. She had received her share of blows and threats of dire consequences for doing something, for engaging in behavior unacceptable to Auntie or other members of the group. She had delivered her share of cuffs and threats when younger group members were learning the same lessons about behavior that she had learned in that crude but effective manner.

She and Auntie had talked about good and bad things. It was good to eat things that pleased the mouth, and bad to hurt or have pain. She understood this well. Bad things usually caused hurt. Good things usually caused pleasure. Picking your nose was a good thing; it made your nose feel better. Belching and farting were good things, they made your belly feel better. Scratching where it itched was a good thing; it relieved irritation of the skin. These were things that you did for yourself, not something that you did to another, so they were good things. But here, all these good things drew swift, stinging blows from the correctional implementer.

As the numbness of shock and disorientation wore off, this was the first problem that her mind actively and consciously tried to solve. Which things done and not done would avoid pain? At

207

the same time, many other fragments of information fell into place, arranging themselves into almost-comprehensible patterns.

She discovered, for example, that this object is a chair. That thing over there is also a chair. They look much the same and must stay near that thing named table in a place named kitchen. However, that thing in the room named living, though it looks different and moves back and forth, is also a chair.

This learning experience was not terribly difficult. It was similar to what Auntie taught her about things with names like tree, water, hand, foot, and biters. Chairs were more things, and Miss Agnes made it clear that she should learn these names, including any special names that might be attached to them, like kitchen chair and potty-chair . . . and rocking chair.

None of this came about in a conscious one, two, three manner; the knowledge was just there one day, or rather the realization of it was just there one night during one of Auntie's visits. She and Auntie had been softly singing the going to sleep song when she stopped suddenly and said, "Auntie! I know rocking chair! In room named living. Rocking chair! Rocking chair!"

She repeated it over and over, rocking her body back and forth. "Under Mama's rocking chair," she sang. "Rocking chair!" Auntie joined her, chanting the words, rocking back and forth, enjoying the movement, the newness of the knowing. They continued until

208

the syllables became nothing more than nonsense sounds.

Delilah also knew about "here" and "there", which helped a great deal. Auntie did not speak well, but that wasn't from a lack of intelligence or inability to articulate words. She was never taught just as she was never given a name. What she knew, she knew from listening, watching, and by speaking nightly with Delilah's Mother as she was intensively speech trained. She retained everything she learned and later taught it to Delilah.

Across the years, her attempts to teach Delilah were sometimes frustrating exercises for both of them, occasionally ending in anger and temper fits. But at other times things went well and she managed, however laboriously, to light a small fire of comprehension. Then, her feelings of satisfaction and pleasure were obvious, and when Auntie was pleased, Delilah was pleased.

On one particular occasion, she had been trying to teach Delilah the words and meanings associated with here, there, come, go, and stay. She understood them well, but trying to communicate the concept was difficult for her. They were sitting under a tree, well away from the group, and she began the lesson by saying, "We here," indicating herself, Delilah, and the tree.

Dutifully, Delilah repeated, "We here," making the same gestures.

Auntie stood, took Delilah's hand and said, "We go there." She pointed to a tree several feet away, walked to it and sat down.

"We here," she said, patting the new tree. "We not there," and she pointed to the other tree. "Here," and she patted the tree again. "There," and she pointed to the other tree.

Delilah repeated the words and gestures, but she obviously didn't understand.

Auntie tried again. "We here." She patted the tree. "We go there." Taking Delilah's hand, she led her back to the first tree and sat down. "We here. Not there." She repeated the patting and pointing gestures.

"We here, not there," Delilah said, looking from tree to tree. Patting the tree, she questioned, "Tree?"

"Tree," Auntie agreed.

"Tree here?"

"Tree here," Auntie acknowledged.

"Tree there?" Delilah pointed to the other tree.

"Tree there." Auntie rose. "We go tree there."

This time, Delilah went without prompting, and as they sat down under the tree, she took the initiative and said, "We tree here, not tree there," correctly patting and pointing.

"Yes, good," Auntie said, pleased at the progress they were making. She was quiet for some time, deep in thought about how to explain the next part. Finally, she said, "I stay here." She patted the tree. "You go there," and she poked Delilah with her finger, then pointed to the other tree. When Delilah looked puzzled and didn't move, Auntie repeated the words and gestures more emphatically.

Delilah understood an order. When Auntie spoke in that way, Delilah must obey or suffer the sometimes-painful consequences. Auntie seldom told her to do something that made no sense, but she could see no reason for this. They were fine here. They were together here. She understood what she was supposed to do, but not why. She had not yet developed the ability to even formulate the question. She did not know the word why or the importance of questioning in the development of intellectual comprehension and the acquisition of information, but her hesitation in doing Auntie's bidding was the result of wondering why, no matter how vague and unformed the question. For the first time, she was seeking reasons rather than unquestioningly doing.

"Go there!" This time it was a command that threatened immediate consequences.

Delilah went. When she reached the tree, she turned to face Auntie.

"Good!" Auntie called. "I here. You there. I stay here. You come here."

Delilah deliberately sat down with her back against the trunk of the tree. "I here. You there. I stay here." She paused, then patted the ground beside her. "Come here!" She had grasped the lesson completely. Now she was adding to it, manipulating words

211

in a clumsy attempt at humor. She was excited and pleased.

"Come here!" Auntie commanded.

"Come here!" Delilah replied, mimicking both words and tone. She was bouncing up and down in excitement at the thrill of this new experience. Then, she laughed aloud, the high, fluting sound momentarily silencing the nearby birds.

Alarmed, Auntie stood erect, straightening to her full height with her shoulders back and squared, something she very seldom did. It was a strange, new sound. She hissed softly, and her lips pulled away from her teeth. What did it mean? What was wrong? Had Delilah called a warning? She carefully scanned the surrounding area and saw nothing amiss, heard nothing strange, smelled nothing threatening.

She looked back at Delilah to see if something was wrong with her. Did she have hurt? She started to move toward her, then stopped abruptly. Auntie had just remembered. Delilah's mother had made that sound, or something very similar to it. It was a good sound, a pleasure sound. Delilah had made Mandy's pleasure sound. Auntie relaxed and gazed at Delilah who was standing quietly under the other tree.

The sound she made startled Delilah as much as it had Auntie, and Auntie's sudden alarm reaction subdued all of her playful excitement. "I come there," she said, and walked back to Auntie, not sure of her reception. She looked pleadingly at Auntie and touched her in the begging gesture, obviously worried at having done something wrong.

Auntie patted her, then held her close, rocking slightly so she would feel reassured. She quite suddenly realized that Delilah's differences were even greater than Mandy's had been. Although she was maturing much slower than the group younglings, she was almost as tall as Auntie, and under the blanket of long, matted hair and dirt, she was much more "other" in many ways than her mother had been.

Auntie was very aware of her own differences, but other than her size, which she minimized by slouching forward, the physical differences were not so readily apparent, especially when she habitually and consciously maintained a calculated distance from the older members of the group whenever possible. The young ones were more accepting, not questioning or even noticing the differences, and as they matured the differences simply did not exist in their minds.

Auntie was seven years old when she found the group, and the first year had been very hard for her. Already taller than the mature females, as tall as most of the males, she had stayed close to the group, but made no attempt to join it for several months. She had never been in a group, had never seen a group, and although their behavior frightened her, she instinctively knew that the group meant safety. She studied them, learning how they interacted with each other, how she must act in order to be accepted by them. She ate what they ate, drank what they drank, learned to make a bed as they did, slept when they did, and moved on when they did.

It took time for her digestive tract to adapt. She suffered from bouts of nausea and fevers. She took several hurting falls learning to climb trees. She learned the hard way which insects to avoid. It was not an easy time, and she often thought about going back to the safety and security of the compound. She missed Mandy and the protection of her own room, the familiarity of known things. But she was here, and the bad place was still the bad place. She talked to herself almost continually, saying words, naming things, counting her fingers and toes, repeating the numbers from one to twenty. She told herself the story of the mothers and sang the going to sleep song every night. She learned to be an intelligent, observant, thinking, speaking, surviving feral animal.

On two occasions, she watched as strange females from other groups approached and joined this one, taking their places in the ranking system by courting the favor of dominant, high-ranking group females. She watched them interact with the babes, the younglings, and the males. It took time, but she learned how it was done, and eventually made herself a place.

The fact that she was not challenging anyone for a position of dominance made her acceptance easier. The strangeness of a female who allowed no one to dominate her, but who made no attempt to dominate others, soon faded into tolerance of her presence . . . and later, the presence of Mandy and Delilah. She made some friends within the group of younger females, bonded with a few of them, and her position was established by the time Mandy arrived and Delilah was born. Mandy was not there long enough to make a lasting impression. Group younglings accepted Auntie and Delilah, making no note of the physical differences. Perhaps, on some level, they were aware that Delilah was badly handicapped. She could not climb well as they did because of her misshapen feet, but she was very strong and she did climb and swing and balance well on high branches. She often shared her food, and seldom took things from smaller younglings. She was fun to play with, always inventing games that were endlessly entertaining, exploring, trying new things . . . leading the way and teaching.

Auntie played with her lower lip as she thought about all of this. Although she wasn't aware of it, Delilah forced her to think, to reason in ways that utilized all the abilities she had, abilities that otherwise might have become lost, shriveled and atrophied in the unchallenged atmosphere of life with the group. Group life didn't require problem solving other than on a very minimal level. Life with Delilah required thought because she was always pushing the boundaries, and she had just given a hard push, taking

the lesson Auntie was laboriously teaching into another
dimension.

Auntie grunted. "Hungry," she said. "Find good eat." She felt
uncomfortable and anxious. Anxiety made her stomach hurt, and
it always felt better if she put food in it and followed with a good
nap. "No more speak," she ordered as she turned to go the trees
where the group was feeding.

Delilah obediently followed. She thought about the strange
sound she had made, and touched her throat. It had come from
here and out of her mouth like speak or any other sound, but it
had come from someplace else, too, a place inside her head. The
words had made it happen, she decided, and it was a new game
she could play with words. She was suddenly anxious to learn
more words. But the sound that came with the new game had
startled her and alarmed Auntie. She must be careful not to make
that sound again.

Satisfied, she followed Auntie, leaning forward, allowing her
arms to hang loosely from her shoulders. She spread her legs
slightly, and walked with the slightly pigeon-toed gait that was
the way to walk. After a few steps, she stopped. This was the way
to walk but, for some reason, it didn't feel quite right. She
straightened her back and raised her head, squaring her shoulders
and letting her arms fall to her sides. This was how Auntie had
stood a few minutes ago. This was how group members stood

when they were displaying, challenging, or looking around for danger. Sometimes when they walked on a high, flat tree limb they stood this way, but not when they walked on the ground unless they were carrying something in both hands.

After a moment, she brought her legs together, noticing how easily they touched each other, even at the knees, and the way her misshapen feet pointed straight ahead. Intrigued by the way her whole body felt and the slight difference in perspective caused by the change in the position of her head, she took a few steps forward. It felt strange, different, but not bad. She stopped again, caught up in her first conscious realization of her difference, not only from the group, but also from Auntie . . . Auntie with whom she so closely identified. Then, as Auntie half-turned and grunted a hurry-up sound, Delilah slouched forward and followed her, arms dangling, rocking slightly from side to side, noticing for the first time that her own knuckles never touched the ground as Auntie's occasionally did.

That is how Delilah learned about here, there, come, go, and stay, words that stood her in good stead in avoiding at least some of the beatings so happily administered by Miss Agnes. Miss Agnes also taught her sit, stand, lie down, be still, fetch, give, and quiet. All of these commands she obeyed. There was only one that she refused to obey . . . no matter how often she was beaten or how harshly Miss Agnes insisted that she speak, she never did.

217

It wasn't until she got to Hiller School that Delilah discovered these were common words, commands known and obeyed by most well-trained dogs.

Then there was the matter of time. The concept of time is difficult for any child to comprehend. They have fully operational body clocks that notify them when to eat and when to sleep, when to wake, and when it's time for other bodily functions to take place. The body regulates not the conscious mind. Man is the only living creature that arbitrarily sets time parameters for himself and his activities and insists that his children live within them, whether those parameters happen to fit their own personal preferences and biorhythms or not.

Miss Agnes spoke often about time. It was always time for something . . . time to eat, time to sleep, time to water her garden, time to take out the trash. Delilah correctly figured out that time was connected with doing something. She also understood that God frequently told Miss Agnes what to do, and presumably what time to do it. But she incorrectly made an assumption based on accurate observation and insufficient information.

A large, round, battery-operated clock hung on the wall in the kitchen. It fascinated Delilah. She could hear the small, regular thuds it made as the minute hand traveled its prescribed distance, and the more subtle whir and click of the hour hand making its rounds. While quieter, these clock sounds were, in their regularity

218

and cadence, similar to the sounds coming from the building out in back, but the clock emitted no particular smell that she could detect.

Miss Agnes always looked upward at the clock before announcing it was time for something. She would turn around, or even walk from another room to do so. She also looked upward at the same angle when she spoke to God or when He spoke to her.

Based on these quite accurate observations, it is no wonder that, for more than two years, Delilah thought the clock was Heaven, and that God, whose other name was Time, lived in it. A while later, after daily exposure to Miss Agnes' fire and brimstone brand of religion, she decided that if the clock was Heaven and God lived there, then the bad-smelling building out in back was hell, and the beast confined there was the Devil himself.

CHAPTER NINE

Over a period of time, Delilah came to understand how important Auntie's visits had been during that first chaotic year at Bhutu. Without them, she would have probably become completely psychotic . . . a screaming maniac, or completely withdrawn and lost in an isolated world of autism. Auntie's visits brought with them a sense of reality and reason in a world gone mad. Auntie's explanations, possible only because she could speak, helped Delilah understand what had happened, what was happening, and, above all, why it was happening. It is always the not knowing that causes the greatest amount of fear-induced stress, the inability to cope, the reversion from thought-directed actions to reflex reactions to stimulus on an instinctual level. Auntie helped her to understand, to know what was happening.

Bhutu Holding Facility was just exactly that, a place where subjects, as they were called, were held for various periods of time until they were taken somewhere else. There was still nothing in Delilah's mind that could logically make any distinction between prison, jail, and holding facility. All were places where you were held against your will, a place that took away your freedom.

Auntie's first visit came on the fifth night of Delilah's captivity. She was sleeping with the cot under the window where she could lie back and still see out, feel the fresh night breeze as she went to sleep. She understood that it was forbidden to have the cot under the window. It must stay in the stuffy dark corner and she must sleep on it, not on the floor. She had dragged it to this position the first night and the following morning one beating she received was for having done so. Delilah's first lesson in surviving the civilizing process was how to be a sneak, and she learned the lesson very well.

The big, ugly female made much noise when she arose in the morning. Delilah could hear her very clearly; she awakened at the first sound, usually a harsh, hawking, snorting sound the female made clearing her throat and nose. By the time she came clumping down the hall to Delilah's room, the cot was always back in the corner and Delilah was lying still and straight, breathing softly with her back to the door. She was never found out, and this was the first of several small victories that she enjoyed in her war with Agnes Kittridge.

It was this victory, too, that raised the first questions in Delilah's mind about Miss Agnes' God. If He was, as Miss Agnes said, everywhere, and if, as she said, He saw everything, then He was here in this room watching everything Delilah did. He knew that she was moving the cot under the window every night and back to the corner every morning. He also knew all about Auntie's nighttime visits. This led her to more conclusions. Either He really didn't care about these things or Miss Agnes was lying. On the other hand, maybe He was saving up these nightly sins and would, sometime later, visit some terrible punishment on her, maybe even banish her to hell, that bad-smelling building out in back where the Devil lived.

Or, and she liked this explanation best of all, He slept at night just like Miss Agnes. Delilah decided He probably slept in the clock on the wall in the kitchen; or maybe He slept in Miss Agnes' room because He was her God, and Delilah sometimes heard her loudly calling out to him at night. Whatever the reason, He never told Miss Agnes about her various nightly transgressions. To be safe, just before she went to sleep each night, she thanked Him for not telling.

Earlier on the evening of Auntie's first visit, Delilah sat in the center of the cot for a long time looking out at the compound and at the dark, shadowy tops of the trees that she could see beyond the wall. She found that if she focused her eyes just right, the squares in the mesh disappeared almost magically, and she told herself she could climb right out the window and run free, run back home to the group and Auntie. Eventually, she curled up and fell into a restless sleep, only to waken suddenly to the knowledge that Auntie was coming.

She sat up quickly, locking her fingers in the mesh, looking and listening. Then there were small scuffling sounds and Auntie was there, quietly shoving a wooden packing case up against the wall under the window. Climbing up on it, Auntie settled herself with a satisfied grunt. Although the window was low enough to see through while standing, sitting was more comfortable.

"I here," she said softly, leaning into the mesh. Inside the room Delilah quickly scooted over against her, feeling the comforting exchange of body warmth so familiar to them both.

Delilah made little "Uh, uh, uh," sounds of distress. "Afraid," she whimpered. "Home," she pleaded. "Afraid!" Her voice rose, and Auntie quickly hushed her.

"Look," Auntie said. "Good eat!" She held up the fruit she had been carrying. Tearing off small chunks, she pushed them through the mesh into Delilah's waiting mouth pressed close to the mesh. The fruit was juicy and sweet, and Delilah licked the sweetness from Auntie's fingers, lapping at any stray juice that ran down the mesh, making sure nothing dropped on the cot to leave guilty traces that might be seen or attract flies. She had already learned about flies. The big ugly female and her God didn't like flies.

For a while, they sat silently, fingers touching in silent

communion, content just to be together. Then Delilah spoke. "Home now?" She locked her fingers in the mesh, shaking it. She was sure Auntie could pull it loose and free her. "Home?" She made a pleading gesture, and leaned her head against the mesh.

Auntie stuck her finger through one of the squares, rubbing it on the rough stubble that had appeared on Delilah's shaven head. "Where outside?" she asked. "Outside gone!"

"She took it!" Delilah moaned.

"Come back," Auntie observed, rubbing the bristles gently, fascinated by the strange way they felt against her finger. Delilah had not been aware of this, and, in fact, had avoided touching her head since being beaten for scratching. She put her hand up, and they both rubbed, thoughtfully exploring this new tactile sensation.

After a moment, Auntie began what was probably the longest speech she had ever made before. She went slowly, searching for words, occasionally substituting gestures when she couldn't find one to express her meaning, and her meaning was clear to Delilah. There could be no going home. She must stay here in this terrible place. And all because she was different.

Delilah knew she was different. Auntie was different, too, but not as different as she was. Auntie could be part of the group, she could go back. Delilah could not, especially now. "Other know," Auntie said. "Come. Get. Kill."

She gave a deep, grunting moan. "I hurt. You hurt. We not same." She touched her finger to her cheek, then stuck it through the mesh. Delilah licked the offered finger, tasting the salty moisture. She touched her own cheek where tears, silent and desperate, slid downward, and offered her finger to Auntie, who in turn tasted.

"This cry," Auntie said, "this hurt." She pressed her face to the mesh and Delilah did the same, their eyes locked, breathing each other's breath in the way of the group.

After a while, Auntie launched into the story she had told Delilah every night she could remember, a ritual of just before the time to sleep. It calmed Delilah, and as she listened, the words took on new meaning for her, and she came to understand that she would stay here because Auntie told her she must.

"How find?" she asked.

"Know here," Auntie answered. The words came slowly, with many pauses. "There," she gestured to the next room down, "there come from Mother. There," she pointed to the room further down, "there your Mandy Mother come from Mother. Mother same. Mother die. Know here. Bad place!" She pointed to the long, windowless building sitting to the rear. Her grimace was so ferocious, so out of character, Delilah drew back. "There bad bad." Auntie touched her shoulder, then closed her arms protectively around her stomach. "There make hurt."

225

That this was a bad place, the bad place of all Auntie's stories, hit Delilah like a blow. She must stay here? In this bad place? "Oh, oh, oh . . . " Her sounds of anguish threatened to rise to howls.

Auntie hushed her, making small soothing sounds. "Here not same. Wait. Learn. I come. Teach me." She paused, thinking. "No, not same. Bad other males not here."

That reassured Delilah somewhat. It was still the two of them. Auntie was there, on the outside while she was on the inside, but just the same, it was the two of them the way it had always been. And she was sure that if things got too bad, Auntie would find a way to take her back home. That was the tiny fixed hope that kept her going for the next year, that and the visits Auntie' made at least once a week.

The visits followed a pattern. Auntie always brought her something good to eat . . . a deliciously sweet fruit, a handful of big, white, wiggling grubs, or some crisp, fresh greens. First, Auntie would feed her, and after all guilty traces of the treats had been cleaned up, they would sit in silence for a while, bodies leaning into each other through the mesh, fingers touching, enjoying the physical closeness. After that, they would talk.

Delilah did most of the talking, telling Auntie what had happened since their last time together, what she had learned, heard, seen . . . and endured. Auntie always listened intently, stopping her from time to time to ask the meaning of a word or a more detailed description of some object. Although she had taught Delilah to speak, the child's vocabulary was growing at an astounding rate. Her mind was a sponge that soaked up every sound and syllable, making connections along pathways that had been there ready and waiting.

As the year went on, she tended to forget that Auntie didn't have as many words as she did. But Auntie, too, was learning, augmenting her early information, things she had forgotten. She gave the best advice she could, mostly common sense admonitions.

Delilah was having a very difficult time with speaking . . . or rather not speaking. Auntie was firm and quite unshakable on that subject. Delilah should never speak one word to anyone except Auntie. Should Delilah forget this for one moment, she would be endangering Auntie and the group. Just as they had never spoken words where anyone in the group could hear, and held most of their whispered conversations at night when the others were sleeping, so must Delilah continue, no matter the circumstances or how much she wished to speak.

It was in the sixth month of the first year that Delilah discovered what writing was, making the connection between the spoken word, the scribbled marks Miss Agnes made on pieces of paper, and the marks that marched, row upon row, in the things filled with paper called "books". The orderliness and precision of these marks in books pleased Delilah, making patterns for her eyes to follow. Sometimes she thought that if she looked at them long enough, she would be able to see the picture they made. She was sure they made a picture of something.

Miss Agnes used several children's picture books to teach her "specials" the names of things when, she often said disgustedly, the little savages had enough intelligence to learn anything at all. She had not really worked with Delilah before because it was obvious that no matter what she did, Delilah was not going to even attempt to say words. But the books were helpful in teaching them to understand the names of things, so she periodically gave Delilah a cursory lesson using the picture books to show her what things were.

On the day of Delilah's epiphany, Miss Agnes had been none-too-patiently showing her a picture of a table printed in a child's picture dictionary. "Table," she said, tapping the kitchen table at which they were seated for this lesson. She had no way of knowing that Delilah was familiar with this method of teaching . . . it was the way Auntie taught her, and she was watching very carefully.

Miss Agnes pointed to the picture in the book. "Table," she said, not noticing that she pointed to the printed word underneath the picture rather than at the picture itself.

"Chair," she said, pointing first to the empty chair across from Delilah, then at the picture, again not touching the picture itself, but the word printed underneath.

Delilah could see that the pictures looked like the two things Miss Agnes had pointed out, that each object was different; she could also see that the little black marks underneath the pictures were different, too. She slid her eyes over the other pictures on the page. A plate, a knife, a bed, all things she already recognized, all things, but different. Each set of black marks underneath the pictures was different. No, she decided, same but not same like the things were same but not same. They were words that spoke on paper, words that said the names of things so the eyes could hear like she heard Miss Agnes talking with her ears! The little black things were the names of things!

Caught up in her marvelous discovery, the correctional implementer came down on her hand with a whishing snap before she could react. Perhaps it was just as well she didn't try to pull her hand away, she thought, the rapidly rising red welt bringing tears to her eyes. Any efforts to escape usually resulted in even harder, more painful blows.

"Pay attention!" Miss Agnes shouted, looking upward to see if her God had witnessed this infraction when she was trying so hard to teach this heathen. Apparently satisfied that it was duly noted in God's record book, she quickly continued the lesson.

"Point to the table! Point to the chair! Point to the picture of the table! Point to the picture of the chair!" She was only slightly mollified when Delilah unhesitatingly and correctly pointed to each one.

As she sat on the cot that evening, it dawned on Delilah that the book Miss Agnes held in her hands every evening, the "Good Book" she called it, was filled with words. She was not talking to the book as Delilah had thought, the book was talking to Miss Agnes' eyes, and she was speaking the words her eyes heard. With this new awareness came other discoveries no less important. She, too, could learn to read . . . and write! Then, she thought, I can speak! The words on paper will speak for me!

When she told Auntie about this, Auntie was quiet for a long time. Finally, she said, "Learn read, no write."

"Why?" Delilah asked, "Why no write?" By this time, she not only knew the word, she understood that it was used to acquire information. Miss Agnes had taught her that. She knew Delilah wouldn't answer, but the question flew from her mouth several times a day anyway. "Why did you do that?" followed by a sharp blow from the correctional implementer was a daily routine for Delilah.

Again, Auntie was quiet for a long time as she reasoned out her objection and searched for the words to express it. "Write same talk. Write talk on paper. Read, learn, not talk. Other read your write talk. Not good. Not write."

Those were her final words on the subject, and, as always, Delilah obeyed. She had always done exactly what Auntie told her to do and not done what Auntie told her not to do. It was the way. She would not speak and she would not write, but she would learn to read . . . and write. Auntie had not said she should not learn how to do it, just that she should not do it.

The lessons she was learning in survival did not include any training in scruples or honesty in her dealings with others. Delilah never had a thought about the moral dishonesty of this decision and the fact that she never again mentioned writing to Auntie. For her, it was a logically reached conclusion and she deliberately avoided the subject from then on even though she spent many hours learning the letters and carefully tracing out their shapes with her finger.

She felt no guilt about anything she did because she had no sense of rightness or wrongness in her actions or the actions of others. At this point, she was simply operating on the attraction/repulsion system . . . lack of pain and feelings of pleasure attracted, encouraging repetition, and pain repulsed, causing avoidance.

In much the same way, she felt nothing but pleasure and satisfaction when she obeyed Auntie's order and refused to write

231

for Miss Agnes. It became a kind of game, and she enjoyed playing games. She would sit staring blankly at the paper or chewing on the pencil, accepting the inevitable beating such behavior elicited. In the process, she learned to accept pain under some circumstances as necessary in order to achieve a goal. And the fact that it worked served to reinforce the concept.

Before long Miss Agnes stopped trying, assuming that Delilah's inability to write was somehow linked to her muteness, and it really wasn't worth the effort. Her job, after all, was to instill the basics of civilized behavior and an awareness of and devotion to her God. And, she thought, the little heathen was learning to read and was becoming very good at following the instructions she printed out for her on scraps of paper. Certainly, no one could ask for more, but she looked upward for her God's approval, just to be sure. Of course, He approved. He always approved.

The first time Delilah brought good eat to share with Auntie, something whose name word was "apple", it was because of something she had learned. Every evening, when Miss Agnes escorted her down the long hall, they went first to the bathroom where Delilah was expected to relieve herself before going to bed. Delilah always cooperated in this endeavor whole-heartedly because Miss Agnes didn't tolerate what she called "nasty accidents", and although the small potty-chair was there, she also

232

frowned on its use.

After washing her hands and drying them on the small towel Miss Agnes carried tucked under her belt, she waited while Miss Agnes opened the thing whose name word was "door" by turning something on the door. Delilah did not yet know the word for doorknob. She did know that there was nothing on the inside of the door, and she logically concluded that it was the knob that controlled its opening and closing.

For several days she watched carefully, noting how the latch moved in when Miss Agnes turned the knob, and out again when she released it. Quite casually, she explored the hole in the door jamb and pushed the rectangular metal latching tongue in and out with her finger. She decided that the thing came out of the hole when the knob was turned, and went into the hole when the knob was released. It took a leap of creative thinking, but she finally figured it out. If the latch couldn't go in the hole, the door could be tugged open from the inside by pulling on the mesh on the top half.

Within a week, she had solved the problem. When Miss Agnes' back was turned, Delilah tore a label from a can of condensed milk and put it, wadded in a small ball, in the pocket of her shift. She thought, correctly as it turned out, that the best time to stick the wadded paper in the latch hole was on the way out in the morning. That way, she was behind Miss Agnes as she led the way to the bathroom for the morning activities, and Delilah was expected to pull the door closed.

In the evenings, she was expected to enter her room after Miss Agnes opened it. Miss Agnes wouldn't notice it wasn't actually latched when she opened it because the knob turned as before, and she had long since stopped giving it a precautionary tug before she clumped away down the hall at night. It was just wasted effort, and she was tired at night. Then, when she was ready to go to sleep, all Delilah had to do was remove the wadded up paper and Miss Agnes would find the door properly latched the next morning when she was usually more alert.

From that time on, Delilah was free within the building at night, free to roam, explore . . . and steal food. She did this nearly every night, sometimes sharing tidbits like an apple or orange or hard biscuit with Auntie on those nights she came to visit. Sometimes it was very messy and she had to bite off pieces of apple and break the biscuits into pieces small enough to shove through the one inch squares of the window mesh.

One night, when she was fairly sure Auntie would come, Delilah brought a jar of peanut butter back to her room. Auntie thought it was delicious, and ate almost half of the jar. Making all kinds of funny faces, smacking her lips, unable to speak while her tongue worked to get the peanut butter off of the roof of her mouth, Auntie made the begging gesture, indicating that Delilah should scoop out more with her finger and shove it through the mesh. It was fun, like a new game they both enjoyed. Cleaning up the mesh with their tongues was fun, too.

On another night, she asked Auntie about God. "What God?" Auntie asked, and Delilah tried her best to explain how Miss Agnes spoke to someone all the time, someone Delilah could not see, smell, hear, taste, or touch although He was everywhere and saw everything. He also lived in or was the clock. After a half-hour of fumbling attempts to make Auntie understand, Auntie finally settled the matter to her own-if not Delilah's-satisfaction.

She looked all around, she sniffed, reached out as if feeling for something, strained her neck upward, turning her head as though listening, and finally smacked her lips as though tasting. "No God here," she announced. "No God there." She pointed inside the room. "No God there." She pointed beyond the compound wall. "Maybe with ugly female, but no God here."

Toward the end of the year, Auntie had to stop her frequently, asking for explanations. Finally, she had to ask her to speak more slowly and use smaller words. The night this happened they gazed at each other for a long moment in silence, deep in their own thoughts. The weak moonlight washed across Delilah's face, highlighting its smooth whiteness. The mesh between them suddenly became a barrier that left Auntie sitting in darkness, creating a wall between them that they both felt somewhere deep inside.

"Not same." There was sadness in Auntie's voice.

"No," Delilah said desperately. "I am me. Same. Me!"

"Not same," Auntie insisted. "Not smell same," and she leaned close to the mesh, sniffing. "Eat," she gestured, "not same. Too much . . . " She paused, searching for the word, grimaced in frustration, then brightened, " . . . too much water wash," she finished triumphantly.

Delilah dropped her head, inhaling her own odor. Then she leaned closer to the mesh, sniffing Auntie, who obligingly raised her arm and pushed against the mesh. Such a good smell, Delilah thought, such a familiar smell, a mingled smell of Auntie and group, something they had shared as long as she could remember, the "us" smell that distinguished them from all others.

With rising dismay, she sniffed herself again. Auntie was right! She did smell different. Then she whimpered as she realized that she smelled almost like Miss Agnes. All Auntie and group smells were gone, stripping her of her identity, her belonging.

"More not same," Auntie continued, ignoring Delilah's distressed whimper. "Not walk same. More high, more . . . "Again she looked for a word, couldn't find it, and substituted a gesture, making a straight, perpendicular line with her hand.

Delilah didn't need the word, she knew exactly what Auntie

236

meant. It was the thing that had earned her the most beatings, the most serious lesson in the long list of lessons that Miss Agnes beat into her. She heard the words like a litany in her head.

"Stand up straight! Shoulders back! Arms at sides! Head up! Eyes down! Don't hunch your shoulders! Don't scuttle! Don't shuffle! Down on the heel! Up on the toe! One straight step at a time! Heel! Toe! Heel! Toe! Straight, straight, straight!"

It was painful, sometimes agonizing, and endless. For almost three months, she had stood at attention every day, marching up and down the kitchen, back and forth, back and forth, while Miss Agnes beat time with the correctional implementer. Sometimes she sat ramrod-straight in a kitchen chair for two hours at a time, each small relaxation of muscles or shift in position greeted with a stinging blow righteously wielded by a dedicated Miss Agnes. She was still required to repeat the drills at least twice a week.

Anger washed through her. She was not the same. She would never be the same again, and she knew it, just as Auntie did. She had learned too many things. She had endured too many things. She had also learned to cheat and lie . . . and hate, though she didn't yet know those words.

She stood up on the cot and grasped the mesh, furiously shaking it, tugging with all her strength. It bent inward slightly and one of the fasteners in the top corner popped loose with a ripping sound. That was something else she had learned. She was

237

very strong and fast, much stronger and faster than the ugly female. She could hurt the ugly female. But Auntie said that was another secret, another thing she must never use or even show. No "other" must ever know she was stronger than they were. This was a secret of the Mothers, too, one that must be kept because terrible things happened otherwise.

"Help!" she demanded, pulling on the mesh again. "Go home now!"

"Sh, sh, sh," Auntie said anxiously, and she began to speak of the things she had impressed on Delilah from the time she was old enough to understand. Always keep the secrets. Never speak. To do so would bring harm to Auntie and the group. Then she told the story of all the before mothers, and the story of Delilah's mother, a story she had whispered to Delilah every night just before time to sleep.

She sang the going-to-sleep song, the words clear, most of the meaning obscured by lack of knowledge, but the tune pleasing to the ear as always, and Delilah, calm now, resigned, joined her. They repeated the final words several times, rocking back and forth, but there was no joy in them.

Finally, Auntie touched her upper left chest, just under her shoulder for a moment, then made the sign, the sign of who she was. Delilah made it, too, because it was also her sign, the sign of who she was. She touched beneath her own left shoulder, too, although, unlike Auntie, the skin there was smooth and unblemished . . . she had no scars there at all.

After this night, Auntie came to visit only a few more times. Then, sometime after the beginning of the second year, she didn't come any more. As the weeks went by, Delilah became more and more anxious. She spent many nights crouched on the cot by the window, clutching a jar of peanut butter to her chest like a talisman, waiting, hoping in some dim way that the peanut butter would bring Auntie to her. Sometimes, she called, not in words, but with meaning clear. "Auntie, where are you? I am here. I am alone and afraid. Please come, Auntie!"

Once or twice she thought she heard Auntie answer from somewhere in the distance, but she didn't come. Delilah's plaintive calls blended in with the night sounds of other jungle creatures and drifted away into the dark. After a while, she understood that Auntie was not coming and she was alone here in the bad place. What was infinitely worse was the knowledge that she could leave this place whenever she chose. On any night she could pull the screen off of her window or simply walk out the kitchen door, climb over the wall and be free to go home. But she could not because Auntie had forbidden it.

The next time she saw Auntie, it was three years later in a place very far from Bhutu. They came close enough to recognize each other, touch, and speak a few words, that was all. That was

239

when Delilah's heart was broken, when the hurt came to live in her eyes.

CHAPTER TEN

Casey had heard of Hiller School. Just about everyone in this narrow specialty had at one time or another. K.C. had done an evaluation of one of their students a few years back and he held the facility in high regard, generous in his praise because of their staff and the methods they used with their special students. Although it had operated for many years, new techniques and innovations were continually being tried out and incorporated when they proved successful. In a way it was an experimental approach involving careful evaluation of each youngster, and the design of individual teaching methods for each special need. The classes were very small, the teacher to student ratio seldom higher than one-to-five. In many instances when necessary, the teaching was one-on-one.

While they seldom had more than twenty students at one time, usually six or seven as residents and the rest as day students, their success rate was very high. Their teaching and preparation of the mentally-retarded and learning dysfunctional youngsters to be mainstreamed into regular schools or, in some cases to live on their own or in group homes as they reached adulthood, was nearly one-hundred percent successful, something to be proud of.

Casey wondered who had made the decision to send Delilah there . . . and why. It would be interesting to find out because these decisions were not casually made, as he had just discovered about her being sent to Bent Tree Farm. Sarah Clement had been in place waiting for her, of that he was sure, though he had nothing concrete upon which to base his feelings. He simply couldn't believe it was all just a happy coincidence, and it bothered him. He couldn't help thinking that a school for the mentally-retarded didn't seem quite right for a special case like Delilah, and four years was a long time to spend in that atmosphere, regardless of the quality of the teaching.

When he opened the first Hiller folder, he found a school brochure on top of the reports. As he looked at the color pictures, he idly considered the fact that the Brighton Foundation powers-that-be seemed to have a special fondness for using restored and renovated older places, historically significant places representative of their era, well worth preserving while being used for modern purposes.

Hiller School had been a private residence, a showplace mansion in the late eighteen hundreds, and still sat gracefully on it's five acres of landscaped grounds. The structural changes that had been made to create classrooms, a small infirmary, a large dining room, kitchen, and quarters for the small live-in staff, were not apparent from the outside. There were already more bedrooms on the second floor than were actually needed for those students who were better served by living on the premises.

The large, comfortable-looking house that had been built for the school director and his family was placed unobtrusively in the back left corner of the grounds. The landscaping had apparently been carefully designed with shrubbery planted on rolling mounds of boulder-strewn earth and trees that screened the house from the main building, giving it complete privacy from the school. Casey could see gravel paths leading to the fully equipped playground area behind the main building near what had probably been the old carriage house and stable.

Very nice set-up, Casey thought, then turned his full attention to the records. He saw that the first item under the brochure was another one of those Brighton Foundation release forms. Package delivery slip, he thought with a surge of irritation. When he picked it up he could see it wasn't an original and wondered why as he set it aside and quickly scanned the other sheets, looking for intelligence test results. These records were thorough, detailed and professional; it was going to take time to follow Delilah Cross through the next four years of her life.

* * *

Delilah didn't remember her arrival at Hiller School in Landon, Pennsylvania. She was weak, nearly comatose, and barely able to stand in defiance of the hunger, dehydration, and repeated doses of tranquilizers that pulled her body toward the ground with an almost physical force and whirled her mind to the edge of unconsciousness. She had spent most of the trip in this condition, alternating between brief periods of hazy awareness and deep, dreamless sleep.

She did remember the ride from Bhutu Holding Facility, and her tranquilizer-muted feeling of excitement at seeing, hearing, and smelling so many new things. And she remembered her feeling of disappointment that the truck moved so fast she couldn't take them all in. The feel of the breeze in her face as they traveled was an exhilarating thing once she lost her fear of the truck and the jouncing, bouncing motion as it traveled down the dirt roads. She remembered the smoother ride and the sound the tires made on the roughly-paved main road, and the interest she felt when she saw the thing waving on the roof of the shed building where they stopped and got out of the truck.

It was alive, she was sure. It was a bird, she thought, tied to the roof like she had been tied to the kitchen chair last night. She touched her neck. The collar had rubbed raw spots as she struggled to find some relieving slack in the chain leash that bound her to the chair. Yes, she had decided, it was trying to fly away, but it was no more successful in escaping than she had been. She remembered all these things. And she still had the small, carved ape figure that Jono Sam had pushed into her hand when Miss Agnes was busy talking to the man inside the shed building.

Jono Sam did not fully understand the impulse that caused him to take the figurine from his Father's work table as he left his house to pick up the big, ugly woman and the child and take them to the air strip. He was vaguely aware that he chose that particular one because his hand automatically moved to it. Why, he didn't know, but it felt right. His Father could always make another one and he felt something was required, some small parting gift to the child so that she would know he was aware of her, an acknowledgment of her existence. He didn't know why his few glimpses of her caused this feeling in him, but it was there. When the big, ugly woman told him to stay with the child while she went inside the building, he gently touched the child's shoulder and pushed the figurine into her hand.

Though she didn't understand many of the words he spoke because his way of speaking words was different from Auntie and Miss Agnes, Delilah understood from his gestures that she should put it in the pocket of her baggy shift dress. She knew she must not let Miss Agnes know she had it. She nodded, looked at the figurine a moment, rubbing her fingers gently over the smooth surface, then gazed upward into his kind, smiling face. He smelled good. Slowly and hesitantly, as though she had to think the proper muscles into smile shape, she smiled back as she shoved the figure deep into her pocket.

That day, the day Jono Sam would always remember, his breath caught in his throat as he looked down into her upturned face. Those eyes, he thought. His father had spoken about eyes the color of the sky that held nothing but cold reflections. But her eyes were deep pools of unknowable depth. An old soul . . . yes, one of the ancient ones. But no matter what his father had said about that color, there was no evil in the eyes of this child. She speaks with those eyes, he thought, she is full of knowing. Though he prided himself on being a modern man and did not follow the old religions born deep in the jungle, he was filled with awe, as though he had somehow been granted a special privilege. He knew it had been the right thing to give her the figurine and, although he never spoke to anyone of this moment, he would never forget it or her.

And Delilah remembered Jono Sam, too. She remembered him because of the ape figure, his smell, and his smile. It was the first time she had ever smiled, moving her mouth into something other than a grimace. Yes, she remembered him because it was her last memory of her country, and because, in that one brief moment of sharing, she began the process of learning that all humans were

246

not like Miss Agnes. Jono Sam had no way of knowing how good Delilah was with secrets and she could not tell him. Then, the moment was gone. Miss Agnes was back, insisting she swallow some pills with a small sip of water from a paper cup, and Jono Sam turned away.

The pills were effective and she slept most of the time, roused barely enough to walk, half-supported by Miss Agnes, through various airports, terminals and official checkpoints. She was only dimly aware of the loud announcements and hurrying crowds, returning to drug-induced darkness during the sometimes-lengthy waits for connecting flights. Miss Agnes ignored the curious looks and questioning glances from other travelers, and those who might have asked her questions about the poorly-dressed, sleeping child did not, turning away when they encountered her coldly challenging, intimidating stare. On those occasions when the tranquilizers wore off and Delilah began to show signs of returning awareness, Miss Agnes promptly fumbled in her large, well-stuffed purse for another pill, insisting that Delilah swallow it with the first small sip before allowing her a little more of the water she so desperately craved.

Only one minor incident marred the trip for Miss Agnes, and that had been easily handled. On the first leg of the trip, she had hauled the nearly comatose child to the small plane lavatory and seated her on the small commode, hoping she would urinate, thus avoiding any messy accidents in her seat. As Miss Agnes turned away to wash her hands, the child had slipped far enough down into the commode to allow the water to touch her buttocks. As she struggled up out of the darkness, attempting to get away from the water, she had grabbed the flushing mechanism. The roar of the flushing and the sounds of rushing water were enough to bring screams of fear and caused a short-lived attempt to get away. Miss Agnes simply grabbed her, covered her mouth with one hand, and held her until she relaxed and went back to sleep.

Delilah's only memories of that trip were dim, scarcely more than blurred feelings of intense thirst, feverish longing for water, and an illusive memory of something bad happening in the lavatory of an airplane. She would never know that this was all part of God's plan for the trip.

God wanted the trip to be as easy as possible for Miss Agnes. Miss Agnes was positive about this. He had very clearly told her so. She knew that managing the child on the long, tiring trip would be nearly impossible if the child was awake, and even worse if she was allowed to eat and drink, thus requiring trips to the bathroom. She had encountered this problem with her first "special", and although that trip had been a relatively short one, it had been anything but pleasant. She was still disgusted with the memory. Until that time, she had no idea just how much urine and feces could be expelled in three hours by a small, screaming body that had forgotten all of her careful toilet training.

From then on, starting the day before the trip, she simply withheld food and water for the duration and kept them nearly unconscious with tranquilizers while en route. This allowed her to enjoy the trip, happy in her anticipation of soon being snug and content in her own little home until her God once again called her to do His glorious work.

There were seldom any questions about the condition of the children when they arrived at their destinations. When there were, Miss Agnes easily answered them with vague comments about fear-induced stomach upsets and the necessity for tranquilizers to spare them the ordeal and stress of the trip. Certainly her God seemed to have no problem with this explanation, and eventually she came to believe it herself.

It was, therefore, a rude awakening for Miss Agnes when her reception in Landon, Pennsylvania jerked her quickly and unpleasantly from her mood of smug complacency over a job well done. They had arrived about ten o'clock at night on a commuter flight from Chicago, and were to be met at the Landon Municipal Airport by a Brighton Foundation car and driver for the trip to Hiller School. As she stood looking around, steadying Delilah with a firm grip on her shoulder, the driver, who apparently had no problem picking them out of the crowd, walked up to them. Although his only words to her were a clipped, "Hiller School," the casually dressed, auburn haired man had frowned at the sight of a slumping, unsteady Delilah in her shapeless shift and sandals. Behind the lenses of his glasses, his hazel eyes were cold, narrowed with disapproval as he stared at Miss Agnes.

Then, without another word, he removed his jacket and wrapped it around Delilah, none-too-gently removing Miss Agnes' fingers from Delilah's shoulder as he did so. In one smooth motion, he picked the child up and turned toward the exit doors. He walked quickly and was outside of the terminal before Miss Agnes, quite outraged at his preemptory behavior, managed to collect herself. She grabbed her carry-on bag and hurried out behind him. Her protests were lost in the cold wind that whistled across the parking lot, and she was chilled and out of breath by the time she reached the car. The man, who had already placed Delilah's limp body in the back seat and closed the door, stood waiting for her, leaning against the car with his arms folded.

"How dare you?" she sputtered. "I'm going to report you for such rude behavior!" Her eyes bulged and the purplish-red nests of veins on her cheeks seemed to writhe in agitation. "Who are you, anyway?"

"My name is Harold Newcombe. I'm the director of Hiller School, and I want to know what is wrong with this child. Is she ill? Why is she comatose? I want the answers now so I can call on ahead for a doctor!" He turned and opened the front door of the car. "Get in. It is, after all, the month of November and it will probably snow tonight, something you seem to have overlooked when you dressed the child."

He started around the front of the car, then turned back, intending to ask about Delilah's luggage. The words went unspoken when he saw Miss Agnes gazing raptly upward, her lips moving as she had a hurried conversation with her God. Apparently, she received an acceptable answer, because, as he watched, she nodded her head vigorously and climbed into the front seat of the car, slamming the door with unnecessary force.

With no effort to disguise a disgusted snort, Harold Newcombe climbed in the car, started the motor, and in a short time the heater was providing a flow of welcome warm air. He turned to Miss Agnes as he picked up the car phone from the center console. She was busy fitting her bag on the floorboard in front of her seat, and he waited until she straightened up before he spoke. He had decided it was better to have this discussion while the car was parked so he could concentrate fully on their conversation.

"All right, it's late, but I'm going to call our pediatrician, Doctor Howard, and ask him to meet us at the school. If you don't mind, Miss Kittridge, it would certainly help if you would provide some information about the child's condition." Although he was very angry, he managed to keep his words and tone

251

neutral and business-like. He could report this whole thing later and had every intention of doing so. But right now, he needed information.

"Oh," he added, "and would you give me the baggage check for the child's luggage? I think it would be best to pick it up later because I want Doctor Howard to see her as soon as possible." Without wondering how he knew, he was sure the child had no luggage.

Without further prompting, Miss Agnes went into her practiced explanation of a "bit of tranquilizer" and "upset stomach" and "stress and anxiety" that had served her so well in the past.

He listened without interrupting, and when she appeared to have finished, he asked, "When was the last time she had food and water?"

After a bit of flustered mumbling, she admitted it had been the full length of the trip, nearly three days, which she explained was a result of nausea and vomiting. She neglected to say, however, that Delilah had also been deprived of food and water the day before they left Bhutu Holding Facility. She also failed to mention that Delilah had put up such a fuss about it, she had to use the collar and leash to secure her to a chair, and vigorously apply the correctional implementer several times to keep the child still and quiet.

Miss Agnes paused for a moment. Then, because she habitually filled silences with the sound of her own voice-was, in fact, unable to control the compulsion-added an afterthought that caused him to clench his teeth. Had she been looking, she would have seen the small, rhythmical twitching of a muscle in his cheek.

"Oh, and she doesn't have any luggage. Why should she? Like all of these little heathen savages, she was naked in a cage when they delivered her." Her face mirrored the disgust in her voice as she finished. "She didn't bring anything with her to Bhutu except a lot of filth and vermin."

Again she paused, glancing at him in expectation of receiving if not a sympathetic response, at least an understanding nod, neither of which she got. Unable to be quiet, her voice rose, righteous self-congratulation apparent in every word. "I saw to it she was properly cleansed, properly fed, and properly covered. I trained her in appropriate civilized behavior while she was in my care. Now it's your job to see to her while she's here. Yes," she concluded with a pious upward glance, "I have done my Christian duty by Delilah Cross, and now you must do yours."

When this information was met with nothing more than an outraged, disbelieving sound of disgust from the other side of the front seat, she quickly glanced upward to see if her God had noted this man's reprehensible behavior. Apparently He had noted it and

253

had given her some instructions. She nodded and quickly fumbled in her purse, pulled out a small sheaf of papers and thrust them at Harold.

"Here are all the documents, and I would appreciate it if you would sign this release right here." Her stubby finger, still showing a dark ring of embedded dirt under the nail, a lingering memento from her Bhutu garden, pointed to a space on one of the sheets. When he took the papers, she closed her purse and shifted her carry-on bag from the floor at her feet to her lap.

Without comment, Harold turned on the overhead light and flipped through the papers. What she wanted him to sign was a delivery slip, that, among other things, stated that she had delivered Delilah Cross, Feral Child, to Hiller School. It said nothing about the child's condition at the time of delivery, and he once again pierced her with a long icy stare as he thought about it.

Miss Agnes shifted uneasily in the seat, looking out the window, fidgeting with her purse, rubbing her face, uncomfortable under his gaze. She didn't like the silence, needed to fill it, opened her mouth several times and almost spoke, then closed it firmly with a small smacking sound. Finally, he took a pen from the dashboard and affixed his signature, the date, and time of day, deciding that the sooner this woman was officially out of it, the better for all concerned. He regretted the fact that she would have to be an overnight guest at Hiller School before her flight out, which he assumed was scheduled for the next day. By nature a gentle man, he felt an urge to inflict serious physical damage on this woman, a feeling that surprised him with its intensity.

Without a word, Miss Agnes reached over and pulled the signed receipt from his fingers, leaving the rest of the papers behind. Then she opened the door and got out of the car with a breathy grunt as she stood up under the weight of the carry-on bag. The heavy thunk of the slamming door cut off whatever he had intended to say, and he sat there in amazement as she stomped off, watching until she entered the terminal. When her lumpy figure was out of sight, he shook his head in disbelief, then heaved a sigh of relief at being rid of her. He quickly made a couple of phone calls, checked on Delilah, making sure his jacket was tucked closely around her, and drove away through the night toward Hiller School.

He needed a copy of that release form for his records, and he would request one with the report he intended to file in the morning, along with the strongest, most urgent, harshly-worded complaint that he could formulate. No, a complaint was not enough, he thought as he drove through the quiet streets of Landon. The woman was sick. He would demand that Brighton Foundation begin an immediate investigation and evaluation of Agnes Kittridge. It was imperative that she should not be assigned to another case, of that he was sure.

Within an hour after their arrival at Hiller School, Delilah had been undressed, examined, bathed, dressed in a hospital gown, and hooked up to an IV bottle. There was considerable horrified and irate discussion between Harold, Doctor Howard, and Nurse Ruth Romer, who lived at the school, about the raw, abraded marks on her neck and the fading scars of older such abrasions. The still-livid stripes criss-crossing her lower back, buttocks, and upper thighs testified to recent beatings, and faint scars clearly indicated that the skin had frequently been broken in various places as the result of similar beatings. The three of them agreed that the marks on her neck were made by some form of restraint, probably a collar, and the other marks came from beatings administered over a period of time, including recently.

Harold Newcombe was an intelligent, thoughtful, quiet man in his late forties, a devoted family man who enjoyed working with children. He was professionally well-qualified for his position as Director of Hiller School, and his calm, reserved manner was balanced by a keen sense of humor; he was well-liked by employees and students alike. But it was an angry, upset man who yelled, "God damn it!" and threw copies of Delilah's records from Bhutu half-way across his office in disgust after looking for but not finding any mention in Agnes Kittridge's reports that such treatment had ever been necessary or used. As far as he was concerned, there was no conceivable situation that could possibly require abuse of a child.

As he calmed down, it occurred to him that it was fortunate that Agnes Kittridge had gone on her way. Considering my reaction to her in the car, if she had been here when we looked at that child's body, he wondered, would I have been able to control myself? Would I? The question disturbed him, opening up a hidden door in his emotions that led to places he hadn't known existed, dark places full of primal protective instincts. It made him uncomfortable, and he put the thoughts aside.

After Delilah had been unhooked from the IV and antiseptic salve applied to the abrasions on her neck, Nurse Romer gently lifted her and offered her orange juice by holding it to her parched mouth, and spilling a few drops on her lips. Delilah greedily drank it without opening her eyes or actually waking up any more than necessary to swallow. Then she carried the limp child upstairs to the room already prepared and waiting and tucked her in. Doctor Howard felt she had been heavily dosed with tranquilizers, but she was sufficiently hydrated now, and needed to sleep it out until she woke up on her own. When she went back downstairs to tidy up the small infirmary, she found the ape figurine as she was preparing to throw Delilah's old clothing into the trash. The finely-carved statue of the speak-no-evil ape was apparently the child's only personal possession, and, after a moment spent admiring the detailed craftsmanship, she smiled and walked back upstairs to Delilah's room and placed it carefully in the center of the dresser.

Delilah woke nearly ten hours later. She did so with a start and the immediate realization that she was in bad trouble. She had wet the bed, and was, in fact, still peeing. It took a hard, conscious effort to contract the appropriate sphincter muscles and stop the warm flow. There was a large soppy area under her buttocks that she knew was soaking into the mattress and her dress was wet to the shoulders. She could literally feel the skin on her lower back, buttocks, and upper thighs crawl in an almost primal effort to become thicker, stiffen into armor to protect against the pain of the beating she knew was coming.

As she lifted the covers and swung her legs over the side of the bed, the urine reek made her eyes water, and she blew hard through her nose to clear it as she stood up and stepped away from the bed. It was not until she tried to remove her dress that she realized it was not her dress, but some sort of thing open in the back and tied behind her neck in such a way that she could not lift it over her head. After a few painful efforts, she understood that she could not get it over her head, and that her frantic efforts were only hurting her neck, tearing the crusts from the raw places.

Her eyes frantically darted here and there, unable to fix on anything familiar. This was not her room, it was someplace else and she had no idea of where she was or how she got here. Where was the shed with the bird tied to the roof? Where was Miss Agnes? Where was the black man who smelled good, who gave her the piece of wood that looked like a tiny Auntie, the black man who made that strange thing with his mouth that made her feel good? Panic rose in her, washing over her in a wave. Her knees felt strange, like they would not hold her up. She was panting, taking short, gasping breaths that sounded loud in her ears.

Suddenly, she heard Auntie's voice, almost as clearly as if she were standing nearby. "Not know what do, not do." Yes, she thought, not do. She took a deep breath, and turned slowly, examining her surroundings.

A room colored what she recognized as blue. A bed, not like her cot with its thin mattress, a bed like the one used by Miss Agnes, with things she recognized as blankets, whose other name was bed covers. She didn't realize that her finger, with a will of its own, was slowly tracing the letters B-E-D on her thigh.

She shivered. Her body felt uncomfortable all over, not right. She stared in amazement at the small bumps standing up on her arm, and touched the small hurting place where it bent. It was red and looked like a big biter had found her. She wondered how it had happened. She would hear and feel a big biter, even if she was asleep. She did not remember. Her belly rumbled. She was hungry, but there was no smell of food in the strange-smelling air.

She shivered again, and continued to look around her. A chair, not like any other she had seen, but a chair. It was colored white. Again, unnoticed, her finger traced the letters C-H-A-I-R. There was a window and something she recognized as curtains like Miss Agnes had in her rooms. The light coming in from the window did not look right, there was something wrong with it, but she decided she would see out later.

A thing sat against one wall, a thing she recognized as a dresser, like the brown one Miss Agnes kept her clothes in, but not the same. It was smaller and colored white like the chair. There was something sitting on it, something that triggered memory, and she stepped closer and picked it up. She recognized this. It was the piece of wood that looked like Auntie. The man had given it to her. She was unaware that the corners of her mouth turned up at the memory. She gently traced the carved features with her fingers, wondering for a moment how it had been done. She had no doubt that it was a made thing, like the pictures of people and animals in the books that Miss Agnes had let her look at, but not the same. For a moment, the brightly-colored label on a can of peas appeared in her mind, and she could almost hear the faint buzzing of flies.

She was thinking about that when she raised her head and saw herself in the large, white-framed mirror hung low, at child's height, over the dresser. She did not actually see herself because she had never seen herself before. In her mind, if she ever thought about it at all, she looked like Auntie and the other group members. What she saw in the mirror was something that looked like a small Miss Agnes standing in a window behind the dresser.

She grunted in surprise, her eyes fixed on the figure. Her nostrils flared, trying to pick up a scent. There was nothing other than the still strong reek of her own urine, but the figure also flared its nostrils, obviously trying to get her scent. The figure had on a strange dress and it looked wet. There were red stains on the neckline, and she could see red sore places on the neck.

She thought about the sore places on her neck, and raised her hand to touch them. The strange figure did the same. Delilah looked down at the wetness on her fingers. It was red. She stretched her hand out toward the figure, watching as its red-stained fingers reached toward her. She touched the coldness of the mirror, leaving a red stain there. So did the figure. It was then that she screamed, a long, drawn-out ululation that began with a series of uh, uh, uh, sounds and ended with a loud, whistling, despairing shriek that hurt her throat. The sound seemed to bounce off of the walls, and brought an immediate response in the form of Nurse Ruth Romer, who rushed in the door making soothing noises.

Nurse Romer quickly tossed the stack of clothes she was

carrying on the dresser and dropped to her knees beside the screaming child. Ignoring the wet gown and the strong urine smell, she grasped Delilah firmly in a warm, enveloping hug that brought an almost immediate cessation of the screams, turning them first into sobs, and then, finally, into gulping, quivering snuffles. All the while, Nurse Romer kept up a crooning stream of comforting words. "Poor baby, it's all right. You're just scared and cold. It's all right, you don't have to be afraid of anything." She didn't know how much of what she was saying was understood, but she knew from experience, the meaning was clear to the most disturbed, upset child.

As Delilah stopped shaking, Nurse Romer's fingers were busy untying the knots in the back of the gown. She slid it off and tossed it to one side without missing a word. "My goodness, child, with a full liter pumped in your arm and a big glass of orange juice, it's no wonder your poor little bladder couldn't handle it, what with you so sleepy. And I wanted to be here when you woke up 'cause I knew it would all be strange. I just left for a few minutes to get you some clothes. See, there on the bureau, all those new, pretty clothes? They're all for you."

She loosened one arm from the hug, and pointed, noting that Delilah's eyes followed the gesture, fixing on the stack of clothes. Okay, she thought, so far, so good. Now to get her to the bathroom, cleaned up, and dressed. Carefully, carefully, she told herself, remembering the warning she had been given about the child's water phobia.

The Doctor returned very early that morning, and Harold Newcombe had come in with him. After briefly checking the still-sleeping child, the three of them had gone downstairs and had a brief consultation, deciding on the best way to handle Delilah for the next few days. Apparently, they had all missed some sleep over the child, shocked by her condition and the abuse she had obviously suffered. After warning Nurse Romer about the water phobia, the two men gave her a few instructions that were, in deference to her recognized expertise with children, more suggestions than orders, and left her to it.

She felt badly that she had not been there when the child awoke, but that couldn't be helped now. And she would stay with her every waking minute for the next few days, easing the way from where Delilah had been to where she was now. As she caught a glimpse of the now-open sores on Delilah's neck, she added a small prayer that the child's new life would be a far happier one for her than the one before had been.

"Okay, Delilah, first we need to get you washed up a little bit to get some of this pee off of you. Then we need to get you dressed and get you something to eat. You're cold, I know, and I'll bet you're hungry, aren't you? And, you know what else? I'll bet you still have to go to the bathroom, don't you?" She smiled, stood up, and turned to pick out a bathrobe and a set of underwear from the stack of clothes on the dresser. She didn't see that Delilah nodded her head very deliberately two times in response to her questions. Yes, she was hungry, and yes, she needed to go to the bathroom. She also didn't see that the corners of Delilah's mouth turned up ever so slightly at the corners in response to her smile.

But she did see the panic building in the child's eyes as she turned back to her. Wide and wild looking, those amazing blue eyes were switching rapidly back and forth between her and her image in the mirror. "Oh," she said, her voice still a low, crooning singsong, "you discovered the mirror, didn't you? That's what gave you such a fright, isn't it? Isn't that an amazing thing, to be able to see yourself in the mirror? And you can see me, too, can't you? Look! See what I'm doing?" She smiled widely, and waved at herself. "No, there aren't two of me, just this one real me."

She moved away from the mirror and patted Delilah's shoulder. "It's like a picture, don't you see? A picture of you that moves when you do and does everything that you do . . . but only when you stand in front of it." Taking Delilah's shoulder, she asked, "Wouldn't you like to see yourself? We can stand here together and see what we look like." With a bit more gentle coaxing, Delilah stepped in front of the mirror, leaning slightly against Nurse Romer for reassurance. After one glance at the smiling reflection of Nurse Romer, she stared at herself. She moved her hand, then shifted her shoulders. Yes, the reflected Delilah did the same. Nurse Romer had on clothes, but she was naked.

Now she knew the truth. Somewhere, sometime since she had been taken from the group, she had been changed. Miss Agnes had taken away her hair, her color, and her group smell. Now her identity, the internally perceived sameness with Auntie that had persisted in spite of those changes, had been taken away, too. She didn't know who that was in the mirror, but she did know that it wasn't who she was at all.

There were two things about Nurse Romer that made an impression that lasted long after Delilah left Hiller School. One was her hug. Nurse Romer was a hugger. It was the first time Delilah had been hugged, experienced that warm, enclosed, secure comfort of total body contact, since she had been taken from the group. The other thing was her good smell. Nurse Romer simply smelled good, much in the same way the man who had given her the ape figurine at the airport in Bhutu smelled good, even though she knew that they didn't smell the same at all. And that was as far as she ever defined it. Nurse Romer became her first human friend; Harold Newcombe, who also smelled good, became her second in this strange new world, a place Delilah would always think of as Auntie's Faraway just as she knew

265

Bhutu Holding Facility was the bad bad place.

CHAPTER ELEVEN

Casey pushed himself back from the desk and raised his arms in a hard upper-body stretch. He could feel the muscles across the top of his shoulders tighten up even more than they were before, then relax as he slowly lowered his arms and consciously let his shoulders droop. That's a bad habit, he thought. It sneaked up on him while he was in college and it just wouldn't go away. When he consciously thought about it, he maintained good working posture. But when he became intensely focused on what he was doing, he tended to crouch forward as if by doing so he could coax more meaning from the work he was doing.

Well, there it is, he thought with a feeling of satisfaction. He leaned back in the chair and locked his hands behind his head as he stared at the stack of Hiller School folders on the desk in front of him. He'd found it, the anomaly that leaped from the pages of Delilah's scholastic records. He'd been sure it would be there.

When she arrived at Hiller School, the first battery of tests found that she was performing just as Agnes Kittridge had described, reading and responding to simple verbal and written commands, displaying the comprehension level of a slow second-grader in those areas. There were huge gaps in her knowledge of simple objects like buttons, zippers, laces, buckles, stairs, and music. In fact, she had little if any comprehension of most of the things children in developed countries incorporate into their information base between the ages of birth and five. He smiled when he read the comment that this was, of course, quite consistent with children from some aboriginal tribes in undeveloped countries. Yes, he thought, one might say Delilah had come from an undeveloped country, all right, and a tribe so primitive the use of tools was rudimentary, a use for fire had not been discovered- -and written language had not yet been invented.

Apparently, according to these early, concise, business-like reports, she had learned at a phenomenal rate. In a surprisingly short period of time, their various intelligence tests found her to be performing far above their expectations except in two areas. She did not speak or make any attempt to do so, and when given a pencil or crayon and shown repeatedly how to hold it and use it, she appeared to mentally shut down, "turn off" was the phrase used in the report. While she knew all of the basic colors and could match the crayon colors to the color blocks, she refused to hold the crayon or pencil properly or attempt to make marks with them even in coloring books. A little further on it was also noted that she apparently enjoyed chewing up crayons and spitting them out, so much so that she was denied access to crayons for an indefinite period of time. This state of affairs continued for about three months after her arrival at Hiller School. Then, quite suddenly, seemingly overnight, Delilah was writing with a skill congruent with her reading ability.

There was a brief report of this miraculous occurrence. According to Harold Newcombe, it was his opinion that she had been quite able to write all along, but had, for reasons unknown to anyone but herself, refused to do so. He further noted that he had furnished her with a ballpoint pen and note pad and encouraged her to use it to ask and answer questions. She seemed excited and pleased by this idea, he wrote, and asked as many questions as her vocabulary allowed, paying close attention to the answers. She increased her working vocabulary quickly, but did not give more than minimal answers to questions put to her, even when it was apparent that she understood the questions and could answer them at length if she chose. He also noted that her habit of chewing up crayons stopped when she began to write. She did very well coloring in color books, staying carefully within the lines and using true-to-life color choices in her pictures.

Director Newcombe had concluded this report with an opinion, much like the one Casey had recently written to the effect that he felt she should not be pressured on this subject, but allowed to continue at her own pace.

According to subsequent reports, it was shortly after this that Director Newcombe requested and promptly received permission to take Delilah to his home, introduce her to his wife and children, and include her whenever possible as part of the family in their group activities. It was his opinion that while living and interacting with the mentally disadvantaged Hiller School students was a beneficial learning experience for her, it was most important that she also encounter and interact with an average family in a normal family environment. Apparently, whenever possible, she had been included in and interacted with Director Newcombe's family for the rest of the time she was at Hiller School.

Casey closed the folder, picked up the stack of files, and took them back to his room. He'd found what he was looking for, and perhaps a little more, come to think of it. Certainly the question he had about the photograph in Delilah's room was answered. He was sure that the people with her were members of the Newcombe family and she seemed very much a part of the group, too. He liked Harold Newcombe. Based on his reports, the man appeared to be intelligent, sensitive, and obviously looking out for Delilah's best interests.

What, he wondered, caused some people to treat Delilah as somehow special? It was obvious that Harold Newcombe felt that way. And Sarah Clement certainly seemed to have taken her under her capacious, motherly wing. It was far more than her history, which was unique, he thought. It was something inherent in Delilah, herself, something that demanded respect while calling out unexpected protective instincts. He was uncomfortably aware of his own feelings on that subject.

Maybe it was her personality? No, it went far deeper than that. She's controlled, intense, driven, distinctly individual, with a strong character . . . and at the same time completely vulnerable. He thought again of his feelings about her, trying to gauge them objectively, and failing. With a shrug, he decided that his Dad had more than enough time to talk to Sarah. Time for him to go down and make a few waves of his own, and maybe pick up a few more pieces of the Delilah Cross puzzle.

* * *

Harold Newcombe was the second friend Delilah made at Hiller School. Actually, he was the first, even before Nurse Romer, but she had no memory of her arrival and didn't know that he had quite literally taken her out of Agnes Kittridge's hands at the Landon airport. She had been at the school for three months, gradually adapting to this new life with Nurse Romer's loving help, when she had her first conversation with Harold Newcombe. It was her first conversation of any kind since last speaking aloud with Auntie, and her feelings were confused; fear, excitement, and guilt were all mixed up with a compelling desire to ask questions, find out things, to know. While his words were spoken aloud and hers were laboriously printed on a lined school tablet with many misspelled words and pauses as she searched her limited vocabulary for words to express her meaning, it was still a conversation, an exchange of information, the first of many between them.

It might not have happened at all, or at least not so soon, had it not been for a series of events that brought them together late at night in a small classroom, the one on the first floor in the front corner closest to the driveway.

Harold's reason for being there was simple. When he pulled in the driveway on his way home from a meeting that had dragged on and on, he saw the light in the classroom and went to investigate. He was tired, the meeting had been a boring waste of time, and he was irritated at having to detour into the main building to turn off the light. Someone, he thought, would get a reprimand in the morning; then he smiled to himself, knowing full and well that by morning the reprimand would have turned into a gentle reminder . . . if he mentioned it at all. He was still smiling as he pushed the half-open door of the classroom fully open, his hand automatically reaching for the light switch before he looked around the room and saw the small, night-gowned figure standing at the blackboard. A paper towel was spread on one of the front desks, and on it sat a jar of peanut butter and a half-eaten apple. A spoon was stuck in the peanut butter jar.

Delilah's reason for being there was also straightforward, but how she got there was more complex. It began when she discovered that most of the interior doors of Hiller School, including the bedroom and classroom doors, were never locked. She was, in effect, free to come and go as she pleased, any time she pleased. Within a week of her arrival she had prowled and explored every easily accessible corner of the large, two-story building, stopping in the kitchen for a snack on every trip.

There were four other live-in students with separate rooms like hers. As was customary in these late nineteenth-century mansions, the entire second floor was devoted to bedrooms. Ten of them, five on each side, lined the hall that ran the length of the building, one of which had been converted into a large bathroom. Another served as a linen storage room, and a third belonged to Nurse Romer. An electronic system incorporating the standard call buttons and monitoring equipment found in hospitals had been installed. The call buttons activated a light over the student's door and a buzzer and light in the attendant's room.

The students understood the rule about wandering around at night and were very good about staying in their rooms. The attendant was usually only awakened for urgent trips to the bathroom or an occasional stint of soothing nightmare-induced fears. Of course, Delilah understood the rules, too, but she was too accustomed to prowling at night to change her ways, especially with all these rooms to explore and all the strange and wonderful new things to investigate . . . like the blackboards, for instance.

The night Harold Newcombe found her she had a piece of chalk in one hand and an eraser in the other. Clearly printed on the board were the words, "I can read words. I can rite words." She was concentrating so hard, she didn't hear him coming, and after one abortive motion to erase the words, she realized it was too late, and turned to face him.

After a moment he said, "Well, Delilah, I see that you know how to write as well as how to read."

It was a statement, not a question, but she nodded anyway. No use denying it, she was caught, and she shivered thinking of the beating that was sure to come. Even though no one had hit her, or even yelled at her since she had been here at Auntie's Faraway, which was also named Hiller School, this was a very bad thing deserving swift punishment. She eyed the long wooden pointer that leaned in the corner by the blackboard. It was the only thing she had seen here that even vaguely looked like a correctional implementer, and she knew that being beaten with it would hurt badly.

"Why don't you erase that, Delilah? It's late, and we both

should be in bed. You and I will talk about this in the morning, is that all right with you?" Harold Newcombe's voice was gentle.

For the first time since he had entered the room, Delilah raised her eyes to his face, searching his expression for anger or some indication that his gentle words and tone were a way of playing with her, getting her off-guard before he hit her. Miss Agnes had often played that vicious little game with her, but she could usually tell by the sickly-sour smell coming from Miss Agnes that the beating was coming regardless of her words.

She could smell nothing like that coming from Director Newcombe, so she turned and carefully erased the words she had written and placed the chalk and eraser in the tray beneath the blackboard. She picked up the peanut butter and the remains of the apple and Harold put the paper towel in the wastebasket. They walked to the door in silence and Harold turned out the light.

Side by side, they walked past the stairs and turned into the semi-darkness of the kitchen. He turned on the light and waited by the door as she found the lid to the peanut butter jar, laboriously screwed it on, and nimbly climbed up on the counter to return the jar to the cupboard. After placing the spoon carefully in the sink, she deposited the partially eaten apple in the trash basket beneath, and walked back to him. Harold had not failed to note her familiarity with the location of things in the kitchen. She's been here before, he thought, restraining the urge to smile at the mental picture of her small night-gowned figure slipping here and there throughout the building on what had apparently been frequent exploration trips.

He turned out the light, closed the door behind them, and together they went back down the hall. He walked with her up the stairs to her room, slowing his steps as he noticed the effort she made to take the steps, one with each foot, just as he did. His hand was warm and non-threatening on her shoulder.

Outside her room, he said, "Go to bed now, Delilah". His voice was still gentle. He smiled. "And stay in bed this time, all right?" He gave her shoulder a final pat and said, "I'll see you in the morning after breakfast. Goodnight."

Delilah nodded, gazing at him for a moment. Then she closed her door and climbed into bed. Just before she went to sleep, she thought about how he smelled. It was an odor that she associated with settled, sexually satisfied adult males in the group, a secure, non-threatening, comfortable smell, and she thought that meant everything would be all right. As she relaxed, her senses were filled with images of humid warmth, sun-dappled leaves, group sounds, and she could almost feel the comfort of Auntie's body close beside her as she slipped into a deep, dreamless sleep.

Sleep did not come as easily for Harold as it had for Delilah. His mind was full and busy. There was excitement at having accidentally made a discovery of some magnitude, finding the key that could, if carefully used, begin to unlock the doors to secret rooms in Delilah's mind. And there was anxiety that it be used carefully, with no clumsy slips that might drive her back into her prior refusal to communicate . . . even in writing.

Self-imposed. Her refusal to write except in secret was self-imposed and required deliberately carrying out a deceptive charade over time. Subterfuge. He remembered the problem with the pencils and crayons, and the easy way she had held the chalk. Why would Delilah feel it necessary? The question led him directly back to Agnes Kittridge. The collar marks on Delilah's neck had, for the most part, faded into faint, brownish traces, but one deeper abrasion on the right side would leave a small permanent scar. And what kind of scars that collar and other abuses had left in her mind was something at which he could only guess. Deeper than the physical ones, of that he was sure. But why not write? Was it somehow linked to the not speaking? He had no answers.

As much as he wanted to question Delilah about her time at Bhutu and the treatment that she received at the hands of Agnes Kittridge, Harold realized that for the time being the subject should not be approached directly. One step at a time, he thought, going gently and carefully.

He sighed tiredly and turned over, snuggling against the comforting warmth of his wife, Dee Dee, adjusting his own

277

breathing to the slow, peaceful rise and fall of hers. He offered a silent "Thank You, God", appreciating just how fortunate he was to have two normal, healthy, bright children and a wife like Dee Dee, always there, always loyal, always supporting and nurturing. His last thoughts before falling into a restless, dream-filled sleep were about Delilah's strangely beautiful and disturbing eyes, and his decision to let her take the lead in her own way, at her own pace, an approach that ultimately proved to be exactly the right one.

He was waiting in his office the next morning when Nurse Romer brought Delilah in. His eyes met Nurse Romer's over the child's head, and he nodded reassuringly in response to her questioning glance. Satisfied that all was well, she patted Delilah's shoulder and urged her to a seat in the chair across the desk from Harold; then she left the room, leaving the door standing open as was customary whenever an adult was alone with a Hiller student.

Delilah was relaxed, quite sure everything was all right, and she looked around the room with interest. She hadn't been in here before because Harold customarily kept the door locked when he wasn't in the office, a fact she knew because she had tried the door several different times on her nightly prowls. The first thing she noticed was the predominately masculine smell of the room, indicating to her that this was his territory, a place occupied almost exclusively by him. Although it wasn't as strongly defined as the sometimes rank, musky-urine smells marking the special places of dominant group males, she understood clearly that this man was the dominant male here at Auntie's Faraway and she was fortunate that his smell transmitted acceptance with no overtones of sexual desire.

Auntie had taught her early, and repeated the lesson often. Sexual contacts other than the obligatory but token sexual meeting, greeting, eating gestures, and those used to diffuse group tensions must be avoided at all costs, no matter how she, herself, might feel about it. Auntie had taught by example, staying far away from the group males during those times when the need to mate was strong in her, enduring and withstanding the battle between her body and her mind. Even when the need was at its highest peak, Auntie never showed the swelling or displayed a driving urgency to mate the way the other females did. Her time of need didn't last as long either. That was part of her difference from the group.

Delilah had learned this lesson well. She didn't clearly understand why this must be so except that it had to do with having babes, and they must never have babes. She liked babes, but she never questioned Auntie's often-repeated order about it. She had disobeyed Auntie's order about writing and the man had caught her, but nothing bad had happened. She knew she was going to speak more words on paper, but she would be very careful.

All these things went through her mind almost unnoticed as she inspected the room carefully, seeing many new things she had no name for, becoming aware for the first time that she could now find out, ask questions by writing them. She was excited as she finally turned her attention back to Harold. He had waited patiently, watching as she examined the room, seeing her intense interest and growing excitement.

"I have something for you, Delilah," he said, and pushed a lined tablet and a bright pink ballpoint pen across the desk to her. She looked at them, then at him, hesitating. Did he mean she was to take them? She wasn't sure.

"Here, let me show you." He took the pen and clicked it several times, showing her how the tip went in and out when you pushed the button at the top. Then, he clicked it again, and with the tip out, wrote two words on the cover of the tablet, slowly printing them in large, block letters, saying each letter as he did so.

"There, see?" He turned the tablet toward her. "That is your name, Delilah Cross. This is your tablet and this is your pen." He offered the pen, holding it out to her. "This is a ballpoint pen, a pink, ballpoint pen. It does not have an eraser, so you must write carefully. The tablet and pen are yours, Delilah," he repeated.

She stood up and took it from him, clicking the point in and out several times, the sound distinct and sharp in the quiet room. This was a pen, he had said, a ballpoint pen. It was not like the pencils the students used. It was like the one Miss Agnes wrote with, only a different color. Miss Agnes had never tried to get her to write with a pen. She was not allowed to touch Miss Agnes' pen. But he said this was her pen, her own pen. And this was her tablet. He said so, and put her name on it.

Slowly and carefully she opened the tablet to the first page, clean and white, the empty lines marching neatly across the page. She looked from the tablet to him just as he glanced at the wood-cased battery-operated clock mounted on the wall beside his desk. Following his gaze, her eyes focused on the clock.

Harold looked at her just in time to see her freeze, become absolutely motionless as she stared at the clock. Something about her stillness disturbed him. She didn't appear to be breathing. Delilah?" It was a question, and it was not until he repeated it, louder this time, "Delilah?" that she relaxed and looked at him, the intensity and depth of feeling in her eyes clear, but incomprehensible to him. "What is it, Delilah?" There was concern in his voice.

With no hesitation now, she wrote her first question on the first line of her new tablet with her new ballpoint pen. There were only three letters in the word and those letters were uneven and ragged, drawn rather than written. It was very different from tracing letters on her leg as she had before. It was different from writing on the blackboard, and it gave her a feeling of satisfaction like nothing else she had ever experienced. She was suddenly aware that what she had written would still be there when she closed the cover and opened it again. It was like a book, a book that she had made.

The question mark she drew at the end of the word she printed straggled across two lines, but the question was legible and clear. Harold read it when she turned the tablet back toward him.

"God?"

He looked at her, shocked beyond words. His mind raced. Of all the possible questions she might have asked, this was the last one he would have expected. Was she asking if the clock was God? Was she asking if time was God? Did she actually mean God or was she simply confusing words? What did she mean? What was she asking? He thought again of the stillness of her body, the intensity of her gaze as she looked at the clock. It wasn't a casual question, it was important to her, and he had the terrible feeling that their whole relationship from this point on would be based on his ability to give her the correct answer.

She waited, returning his gaze calmly. He wondered if his confusion was showing on his face. He tried to maintain an outward semblance of composure as she carefully directed his attention to the clock, pointing to it emphatically, then at the word she had written. Again, she waited, gazing at him expectantly.

He looked at the word on the tablet. It crouched there like a small, vicious, black animal sprawled waiting on the page, the "G" its head, the "o" its body, the "d" leaning toward the question mark that draped itself across the lines like a tail. He stared at it for a long moment, fully aware that some part of his mind wouldn't be surprised in the least if the tail moved, sinuously rearranging itself to a more comfortable position across the lines as if it, too, waited for his answer.

"The clock is not God, Delilah. It is only a clock, a thing made to measure time just as your pen is a thing made to write with and your tablet is a thing made to write on." Harold had chosen his words carefully and spoke slowly and clearly. "Do you understand that?"

After a moment, she wrote again, and turned the tablet for him to read. "Lik chair?"

He read the words out loud, then answered. "Yes, Delilah, like a chair is a thing made to sit on." He thought a moment, then pulled up the cuff of his sleeve to show her the watch on his wrist. "This is a watch." He took his own pen and wrote the words clock and watch on her tablet. "Both are things made to tell us what time it is. They are things, not God. Do you understand?"

Delilah looked at the words on the tablet, at his watch, and

283

finally at the clock. Then she wrote, forming the letters carefully. "Tiim note God?"

Harold smiled. "No, Delilah, time is not God, either." He was pleased at the way this was going. She was grasping everything, quickly carrying the exchange forward, and seeking further information. It was then that a moment of enlightenment washed over Harold. Agnes Kittridge, he thought. Agnes Kittridge had a religious fixation. He had seen her talking to God at the airport. It couldn't be anything else that prompted these questions. He suddenly felt sick, and knew he had to do something or say something here and now to begin undoing what he could only guess had been done to the mind of this child.

"Delilah, I am going to talk a lot now. Maybe you will not understand everything that I say, but please try hard, all right?" When she nodded, he continued slowly, choosing his words carefully, taking a calculated risk.

"Agnes Kittridge is sick, very sick inside of her head." He paused when he saw the change in Delilah's face. Her eyelids lowered, her head tipped downward, and all animation disappeared from her expression. "It's all right, Delilah, she is gone and will never hurt you again. You will never see her again." He emphasized the words, repeating, "You will never see her again. Do you understand?"

Harold found he was holding his breath, releasing it only when she nodded and looked up at him, once again revealing her eyes though her face remained still.

"I don't know what she told you about God, Delilah, but whatever she told you is wrong. There is much to say about God, and we will talk about it as much as you want to, but it will take time." Harold chuckled and deliberately looked first at his watch and then at the clock. "We will have lots of time to talk about anything you want to talk about, but first you must learn more words. Do you understand that you need more words?"

Her eyes had followed his as he mentioned time, looking first at his watch and then at the clock. He had answered her first question satisfactorily, allaying fears about the possible reappearance of Miss Agnes in the bargain. God was not the clock and God was not time; she was fairly sure now that He didn't live in the clock, either. This man was right. She needed many more words to ask all the questions racing through her mind. She picked up the pen and wrote on the tablet, "Mor word yes," and smiled at his chuckle when he read the words. It was a small smile, a bare upward curving of her lips . . . but it was a smile.

That first question- -and his answer- -opened the dialogue that continued between Harold and Delilah for nearly four years. It was a deeply satisfying, provocative, sometimes intensely frustrating learning experience for them both. It was a dialogue that grew in sophistication and complexity at a rate that amazed and he was sometimes left him breathless by the speed of her comprehension, the scope of her quest for information, her accurate and often brilliant leaps of logic . . . and her sheer intelligence.

Sometime after the second year, Harold Newcombe began to sense something sitting there in her mind like a silent, skillfully-camouflaged back-seat driver giving directions, steering their conversations toward unstated destinations. He shrugged the feeling off most of the time, but occasionally he thought he caught glimpses of another Delilah, a shadow Delilah who could speak, who was concealing more than she revealed, and who was driven by motives and following agendas toward goals known only to her.

CHAPTER TWELVE

Like all great explorers and adventurers, Jamie Prentiss was possessed of more than his share of imagination. As the oldest he was, of course, always the leader and most of the time his little sister, Laurie, had no problem with being his trusty sidekick, his merry band, or even his faithful dog if that was what he required. She did however, on occasion, refuse to play the role he imperiously assigned, such as the time he wanted to tie her to a tree, gallop around her on his imaginary Indian pony, and shoot at her with his home-made bow and arrows.

But most of the time she went along agreeably because his invented games were always fun, and sometimes she got to be a maiden fair or a beautiful princess in need of rescue. She loved the damsel in distress roles because they didn't require much more than lady-like cries for help, and rapturous pretend-tearful thank-you's when he rescued her from dragons or horrible villains.

After a while, Jamie had tired of exploring the barn and stepped outside the smaller door opposite from the large, open

287

roll-back doors through which they had entered. Laurie followed as he drifted toward the holding pond, her attention quickly caught by the mallard ducks drifting here and there across the dark water.

"Oh listen, Jamie! The ducks are talking!" She watched a moment, then asked, "Why are they different colors?"

Pleased that she should ask, and even more pleased that he knew at least part of the answer, he explained. "The men ducks are the bright-colored ones and the women ducks are just plain old brown." Seeing her brows knit, he knew from experience that she was getting ready to ask why that was.

Because he didn't know why, he quickly headed her off at the pass. "Hey, look! There are babies out there! See 'em? They're right by that big clump of stuff in the middle. See? See the brown mama duck with 'em?"

Laurie stood on her tiptoes and shaded her eyes with her hand. The sun was bright and reflected off the water, dazzling to the eyes as a small breeze ruffled ripples and waves. "I can't see them," she said disappointedly. "Oh, I wish I could!" After another moment, she said accusingly, "Jamie, you're just making it up! There aren't really any babies out there! You're teasing me and Mama said you weren't supposed to do that any more." Tears filled her eyes. "I'm going to go tell Mama. That's a mean thing to do." She half-turned back toward the barn, her lower lip thrust out in a pout.

"Wait, Laurie!" Jamie was challenged. There were baby ducks out there and he could prove it. "Look, Laurie, there really are baby ducks out there. Just help me find something to use as a raft, and I'll take you out there and show them to you, real close!" He hadn't even had the idea until the words came out of his mouth, but when he thought about it, it seemed like a truly marvelous idea. It was another great adventure in the making, far better than any he had imagined before because they were actually going to do it, not just play pretend about it.

Laurie quickly turned back. She could hear the ring of sincerity in his voice, and within a very short time, they were back in the barn, finding and discarding various pieces of scrap lumber for the raft. Their voices rose from time to time as they disagreed on what would work and what wouldn't, or exclaimed happily over a perfect piece of raft material. When Jamie found a small roll of wire just right to bind their boards together, he cried, "Eureka!" He didn't know what that meant, but it seemed appropriate for such a discovery.

Behind the house, just up the small rise from the barn, Sarah and Kaydee Lowell Prentiss were deep in a discussion about the kitchen garden. Squatting down from time to time to inspect various vegetables, picking a little of this and that to go in the lunch salad, they agreed on the fact that organically-grown vegetables were far superior to any other kind, but Sarah pointed out, quite seriously, that the experiments with genetically-engineered hydroponically-grown vegetables going on in the greenhouse just might, in the foreseeable future, go a long way to alleviating world hunger.

Kaydee nodded her head in agreement, then laughed as she carefully removed a large worm from one of the summer squash plants that sprawled across the end of the neatly-spaced rows. "Too bad we have such a cultural prejudice against these little creepy-crawlies. This guy is a neatly-packaged bundle of protein if I ever saw one." She giggled as she dropped it in the small pail Sarah used for this purpose. The free-ranging chickens would happily benefit from it's addition to their diet, converting it in their own way to truly chemical-free, wholesome eggs.

Kaydee paused to listen, her practiced Mother's ears tuned to her children's broadcast frequency. Yes, they were still in the barn, and although she couldn't make out their words, she heard nothing unusual in the rise and fall of their voices as they disagreed about something. Satisfied that all was well, she turned her attention back to Sarah and the garden.

"You know, Sarah, this place is beautiful and we really do appreciate your interrupting your routine to let us visit. It's a real learning experience for the kids, and for me, too, I guess. I've never actually stayed on a farm, never even thought about it, for that matter." Kaydee's tone was serious. "I don't know what I expected, but this place feels like . . . ", she hesitated, looking for a word. "It feels somehow right, like this is how people should live."

Suddenly embarrassed by her words, Kaydee finished in a rush, "Not that I'd do very well as a farm wife, too citified, you know." With a quick change of subjects, she asked, "Where are Dad and Casey? I know Mom is down by the brook absorbing detail and background that will wind up in one of her stories sooner or later." She glanced at Sarah questioningly. "And where's Delilah?"

Kaydee was curious about the mysterious Delilah Cross, the reason her brother was here at Bent Tree Farm. She had casually read a few articles about her in the past, but the oddly attractive, self-possessed young lady she had met last night, and briefly seen again this morning at breakfast, was not in the least what she had expected. She didn't know for sure just what she had expected, but Delilah wasn't it.

Sarah's smile was understanding. She could hear all the questions in Kaydee's voice, and appreciated the discretion that prevented their being asked. She really liked Kaydee; her down-to-earth openness and easy manner were free of any pretensions, and Sarah wondered how she appeared in the courtroom. This tanned, wholesome-looking young woman with the smear of garden dirt on her chin and faded baseball cap on her head, looking far younger than her thirty-two years, was a respected lawyer, holding her own with her husband in a very successful civil law practice.

Casey loved her dearly and was very proud of her, that much Sarah had picked up when they discussed his family's proposed visit. And she thought she had answered his questions about her role here at the farm and her reasons for not waving her credentials at him, answered them at least well enough to put his mind at ease without going into any details. She felt a little guilty about the small dance with the truth she had done when K.C. called, but that had gone fairly well, too. She liked K.C., which was, after all why she had asked for him as an outside consultant.

Then Sarah's grin widened. As far as that went, she thought, she liked the whole Lowell family. They had arrived the evening before with K.C. at the wheel. The RV was a very long one, and he had to back up once to get it through the gate into the driveway, and twice more to get it backed in parallel to the bunkhouse. Joe and Jordan had rigged up an electrical connection from the bunkhouse and in short order everything was hooked up and operating.

It was getting dark by the time they finished and the Lowells were road weary, so after brief introductions and a quick guided tour of the vehicle for Delilah, Casey, and the Clement family, they had all gone up to the farmhouse for dinner, saving the exploration of the farm for this morning.

"Well, we seem to be able to account for everyone except Delilah. Jordan, is giving the Lowell men, Senior and Junior, a guided tour of the greenhouse and all the marvels and wonders contained therein." Sarah chuckled. "That should take at least an hour because Jordan is, I hate to admit, somewhat obsessive about the subject." She paused, looking thoughtful.

"As for Delilah, she is either upstairs working on her correspondence courses, or somewhere on the farm doing 'her thing'. Oh, and Joe is running the cultivator through the soybean field. There, that accounts for all of us, I think," she finished.

Sarah was deliberately teasing, and when Kaydee responded with a puzzled frown, she relented and said, "Delilah doesn't require watching. She is quite her own person and free to come and go as she pleases. She is extremely intelligent, on her way to becoming very well-educated, and her only problems are the fact that she doesn't speak and she has a water phobia which, incidentally, concerns only herself. You've seen the notepad she carries?"

In response to Kaydee's nod, she concluded, "You really ought to have a conversation with her and find out for yourself firsthand." Sarah's smile was a little guilty. "I didn't mean to lecture you, Kaydee, but I have to admit I've become very fond of the girl, and I get a little over-protective sometimes. It seems like she's been treated like a side-show freak for a long time and that really angers me. We treat Delilah like the normal person she is, and I hope you will, too."

When Kaydee nodded understandingly, Sarah looked at the garden and said, "We'd better get busy and pick the rest of the salad, don't you think?" and led the way toward the clump of carefully-staked tomato plants drooping under their red burdens.

After a moment of listening to the children's voices still audible in the barn, Kaydee followed her, exclaiming over the size of the tomatoes on the heavily-laden vines, thinking that she would certainly talk to Delilah at the first opportunity. Sarah's small lecture had only served to increase her curiosity, especially when she sensed something slightly amiss in her brother's manner, a certain reserve that she had never before felt between them. She had the feeling that he was hiding something from her, and after meeting the girl, she was pretty sure that whatever it was, it involved Delilah.

In the barn, obsessive about and Laurie eventually found two medium-wide boards short enough for them to handle, but long enough, in Jamie's opinion, to float their combined weight. Laurie carried one board and he carried the other, along with the wire. They stopped by the edge of the pond, and with Laurie's willing but inept help, Jamie laboriously wired the boards together.

"It's not very big," Laurie said doubtfully. "Will it hold us up out of the water?"

"Sure," Jamie replied confidently. "See, we'll just sit on it with me in front and you in back like it was one of those big surf boards you see on TV. Our feet will hang in the water, but who cares about that? Won't hurt our tennies, and we can paddle and steer with our hands." He examined his creation with pride and enthusiasm. "And we can get up real close to the ducks, too."

This last was enough to quiet any qualms Laurie had about this adventure. She really did want to see those baby ducks, and maybe even touch one, she thought excitedly. Besides, if anything happened, they could both swim, at least enough to get back to shore, couldn't they? She looked out to where the clump of reeds and grass pushed up above the surface of the water. It really wasn't very far, she told herself.

After a bit of splashing and several false starts, Jamie had them balanced on the boards. He said in his best hero's voice, "I'm Captain Jim. I'll steer and paddle. You're the crew, and you keep your balance," he ordered. "And keep a weather eye out for whales and sharks and pirates!" he added as an afterthought.

"Aye aye, Sir," Laurie said meekly, holding tightly to his waist and adjusting her balance as he bent forward and began to paddle, leaning slightly first to the right, then to the left as he alternated hands. She obediently looked for whales and sharks and pirates.

That, she hoped, was at least as good as 'keeping a weather eye out', which she did not know how to do. She decided to wait until later to ask about it, and relaxed into the pleasure of the ride. This was their best adventure, the very best, she thought.

Suddenly, Jamie gave a hard push with both hands and straightened up as the raft slid smoothly forward, then lost momentum. "All hands quiet, now!" he muttered. "Crew, look over my shoulder. Target dead ahead!"

Laurie heard them before she saw them; the low muttering of the mallard hen and the high 'wheep-wheep' of the ducklings as they discussed whatever ducks talk about filled her with excited anticipation. In the background, she could hear the quiet, rasping, almost-whispered comments of the male as he joined the conversation. Then she saw them, and, without thought, turned loose of Jamie's waist, and clapped her hands in delight.

The hen was sitting on the slightly elevated bank of tangled roots, small twigs and other debris out of which the clumps of reeds and grass grew. Her half-dozen black and yellow ducklings were clustered around her. They had obviously just come out of the water, and the ducklings were grooming themselves, rubbing their small bills on the oil glands near their tails and industriously spreading the oil thus obtained over their bodies, paying particular attention to their chests and the tiny stubs of down-covered wings where someday feathers would grow. They looked somehow quite ludicrous as they performed this ritual that was so vital to their survival as waterfowl.

The raft's approach had been quiet, and, if noted, had not been considered a danger, but at the sound of Laurie's hands coming together, the reaction of the ducks was swift and unexpected. As her frantically wheeping ducklings scattered in all directions, the hen burst forcefully from the hummock and attacked, squawking loudly as her wings beat at Jamie's unprotected face and shoulders. He threw up his arms, yelling in alarm, and lost his balance, taking Laurie with him as he fell into the water with a splash and went under. When he came up, he grabbed for the raft, hanging on tightly.

Unexpected as the attack and dunking were, Jamie wasn't really upset. They were   good swimmers, both of them. The water, though murky, wasn't really cold at all and Captain Jim hadn't lost his ship even though attacked and dunked by a flying monster that could well have been a small dragon. With a grin, he looked around for his crew. His grin faded. She wasn't there. "Laurie," he called, scanning the water all around the raft. She wasn't there!

He panicked then. "Laurie!" he screamed, kicking his feet wildly, turning the raft in circles. Where was she? He couldn't think. Then he saw her just as her head broke water near the hummock. She took a great gurgling breath, her eyes wide in desperation, and went under again before he could speak.

Without actually thinking, Jamie pushed the raft to the spot near the hummock where Laurie had come up. He took a deep breath and slipped under the water. There she was. He could see she was doubled over, reaching below her. What was she doing? The water wasn't very deep, not much over his head. He tugged on her arm, attempting to pull her up. She turned toward him, and came up with him, but only until her head barely broke the surface of the water. After a gasping breath, he yelled, "Here, hang on to the raft!"

"Can't!" she cried, her face contorted with fear. "Tangled!" She went under again, and this time, Jamie went with her, following her right leg down with his hands. Grasping her ankle, he tugged, then pulled hard. He could feel her hands pounding on his back as her small ankle seemed to stretch in the joint. He needed a breath, so he went up again, pulling her up by the arm.

"It's your shoelace," he shouted at her as she hung on to him, desperately gulping air. "Take off your shoe!" he yelled in her ear.

Again, he went down with her. This time, he felt around carefully. Yes, it was the shoelace. The round plastic butterfly decoration attached to the end of it was tangled in a wad of roots. As she pulled, the bow part of the lace came untied, but now each tug only served to tightened the wet lace in the eyelets of the shoe, making it impossible to get her foot out.

Jamie tried with all his might, pulling her downward to loosen the lace, fumbling and tugging, trying to loosen it enough to get her foot out of the shoe, then trying to pull the ornament from the weedy tangle of roots. He stopped only when he ran out of air or when Laurie pounded on his back to tell him that she must have air. She was exhausted now, limply allowing him to support her head barely above water with one arm as he clung to the raft with the other. He lost count of the number of times they had gone under, but it seemed like an awful lot.

He was tired, too, and tears streamed from his eyes as he looked toward shore. Then he yelled for help. Over and over again he called as loud as he could until his voice was only a hoarse croak, but he never loosened his grip on Laurie. He knew he could swim to shore himself, but what would happen to his sister before he could find help and get back? In a dazed sort of way, he thought, I'm Captain Jim and I will save my crew!

He was nearing the end of his endurance, the strain of supporting Laurie against the downward pull on her leg becoming harder and harder, when Delilah reached them.

"Shoe," he croaked, looking up at her. "Tangled." That was all he could manage. She seemed to understand, and before he could say anything else, she ducked under the water. He felt the downward pull of Laurie's weight on his arm ease, and a moment later she reappeared, standing beside him with Laurie cradled in her arms. She motioned her head toward the raft, raising her eyebrows questioningly.

"Yes, I'll hang on," he said. Then he looked at Laurie, who had begun to sob tiredly. She only has one shoe on, he thought. Mom will be mad about that. Those are new shoes. He was aware of Delilah moving away toward the edge of the pond with her burden.

Suddenly, he grinned. Then he giggled wildly. Laurie had almost been drowned by a butterfly! Oh, what a good joke! "A butterfly," he said aloud, then burst into tears, deep racking sobs that shook his body.

Delilah was more than half-way to the bank when, without warning, before her mind could register that it was happening, she was there, in that other place, in that other time.

It was hot and humid that day, more so than usual, the air heavy with the kind of steamy, enervating heat that often followed the time of rain. In the late afternoon, they had drifted out of the shade of the trees in two's and three's and lined up on the narrow beach edge of the small river to drink. The water was murky with silt washed down by the rain, but it was drinkable enough because the now-gentle backwash of the river's current kept most of the floating debris near the center as it drifted past. Small branches and limbs, clotted wads of leaves, and clumps of dead reeds left ripples and small wakes behind them, and the usual heavy swampy odor had been replaced by a fresher, cleaner smell as a result of the rain's house-cleaning activities.

Only Delilah actually went into the water, splashing along the sandy bottom that she could feel but not see until the water rose nearly to her armpits. She was a sturdy child of five or six, larger than any of her peers, and, unlike the rest of the group, who would venture no closer to the water than necessary to slake their thirst, she liked the water, liked the feel of it on her body as she splashed and played.

She had discovered this new game several months before, and after a while the elders stopped putting up a fuss about it . . . except Auntie, of course. Auntie always paced up and down the bank, grunting and muttering anxiously to herself until Delilah was out of the water and once more safely beside her.

The elders would not allow any of the other younglings to join her in the water although she could see they weren't afraid and wanted to join her in this game just as they did in all the other games she invented. But anyone who tried was unceremoniously pulled back and loudly scolded. The elders plainly felt that the water was bad, but no one, not even Auntie, had indicated a reason for this.

The first time she took the babe into the water with her was quite by accident. She had been trusted to carry and cuddle the babe since shortly after its birth, and no one noticed that she was still carrying it one day when she happily waded into a small stream that ran beside the route they were traveling. She only became aware of it when the babe shifted its position, inching higher and clinging a bit tighter to her neck. It had shown no fear or discomfort, only interest in this new experience and, feeling both guilty and delighted, Delilah did it several more times, playing splashing games which the babe clearly enjoyed.

On this particular day, however, the first time Delilah had ever gone into the river, someone noticed that she had the babe in the water and raised the alarm. Everyone screamed at her, even Auntie. Delilah was confused by this. She expected the others to be upset, but Auntie watched her closely whenever she was in the water. She had never put up a fuss about the babe the other times. Delilah had taken this lack of response as tacit permission, another secret they shared as they did so many others.

The screaming and threats continued as she waded back to shore. The mother roughly pulled the babe away, and gave Delilah a shove that sent her sprawling on her backside in the mud of the bank. She cuddled her babe protectively as she glared at a thoroughly intimidated Delilah for a moment, then turned to walk away.

The whole thing would have- -should have- -ended there, but it didn't because the babe had different ideas. Feeling that it was being deprived of a very enjoyable play-time, it set up an almost hysterical outcry, holding its arms out to Delilah, who had just gotten to her feet, then twisting and squirming, trying to free itself from its mother's arms.

Finding that this didn't work, it bit hard, drawing blood, and when the confining arms loosened, it slipped to the ground, scampered quickly to the water's edge, and, without hesitation, plunged in. Momentum carried it out several feet before it sank in water well over its head. Coming up almost immediately, it screamed and thrashed wildly before going under again.

The whole group rushed to the edge of the water, wailing their fear and distress. Some of them grabbed sticks and branches, screaming as they beat them on the bank or splashed them in the water near the bank, but no one entered the water.

Only Delilah kept on going, and she reached the babe when it surfaced again. Grabbing it by both arms, she was making soothing sounds as she started to lift it up to the usual position against her chest. Without warning, she was struck a powerful blow under the water and knocked backwards and under, still holding on to one of the babe's arms. She had lost her grip on the other one when she was hit.

The crocodile had been drifting lazily downstream in the middle of a clump of debris. It wasn't particularly hungry, but food was food. It chose its target, and the few ripples it made in its diagonal approach went unnoticed in the thrashing disturbances made by the struggling babe and Delilah's run through the shallows. Ignoring the splashing near the bank, it closed its jaws on the babe's body, jerked, and struck Delilah with its tail as it turned away.

When Delilah's head broke water, she was gasping for breath and her eyes were water-blurred as she scrambled for footing. She had no idea what had happened. She did not even glimpse the crocodile. She only knew that her legs hurt badly, something under the water had hit her, she still had hold of the babe, and she better get to shore as quickly as possible. She limped back to shore with all the speed she could muster.

The strangely silent group was waiting for her, and she went straight to the babe's mother. It was only when she raised the babe to hand it to her that Delilah saw that all she held so tightly was the babe's arm, delicate blood vessels still leaking blood, shreds and strings of muscle and tendon hanging from the small knob of white bone where it had been ripped from the shoulder socket.

She stared at what was left of the babe, unable to comprehend. In a daze, she wondered where the rest of the babe had gone, and, not knowing what else to do, she offered the pitiful remnant to the mother.

Taking the small arm from her, the mother raised the small, lifeless hand to her nose and sniffed, the sound snuffling loud in the silence. She keened softly for a moment, rocking back and forth, then erupted, screaming her anguish so violently the others stepped back, leaving her and Delilah in a small cleared space. Delilah was numb with shock and non-comprehension, seeing and hearing nothing . . . until the first blow fell.

The Delilah of now shuddered, some small part of her mind trying vainly to escape reliving the blows that she had received with that lifeless little arm in that faraway then.

The mother pounded and pounded, hitting again and again, raining blows on her head and shoulders. Delilah had made no effort to protect herself. The blows made a sickening sound as the fragile bones of the arm shattered and crunched against her sturdier skull. Finally, there were only liquid, mushy splats that left gobs and smears of jelly-like gore smeared in her hair, clinging to her face, oozing down her chest and shoulders.

When Delilah fell to her knees under the rain of blows, Auntie intervened. Rising to her full, intimidating height, she stepped between them. She growled deep in her chest, and her lips pulled back in a threatening grimace as she gestured to the mother that it was enough, the punishment fit the crime, let be or suffer the consequences.

The mother, silent now, energy spent, held the small blob of tissue and skin to her chest. The small hand still dangled and, as she turned away, it swung back and forth against the breasts it had clutched to nurse just a short time before. She looked down and moaned, a tortured sound that went beyond sadness and loss.

Auntie pulled Delilah to her feet, leading her toward the river bank. Scooping up a handful of water, she attempted to wash Delilah's face, only to be met with frantic screams of terror at the first touch of water. Making soothing sounds, she used leaves and grass to wipe away the worst of the mess, and led the child away from the water, following the others back into the shelter of the trees.

The group, along with the mother carrying her small, sad burden, moved far away from that place before seeking a sleeping place. The sounds of the her sorrow and Delilah's soft, keening wails of pain and terror echoed through the darkness far into the night.

Suddenly, Delilah was back in the present, thinking, as she had so many times before after one of these flashback episodes, thank God, that's over! This had been a bad one; she could still hear her sobs and feel the wetness of her body.

Slowly, one bit of information at a time came into focus. First, she became aware of the weight of the child she held clutched to her chest. It was far heavier than she remembered the weight of the babe. Then she understood that it was the child's sobs she heard; she felt each convulsive breath against her chest and stomach. She saw that the child was wet, that she was wet, wet all over. She could feel the droplets of water running down her face, dripping from her chin.

Delilah narrowed her eyes because the sun seemed very bright, then realized she had lost her dark glasses somewhere. She saw that a slimy piece of pond weed hung in the child's blond hair, stared at it for a moment, then looked down at the water that rose to her hips. The child's feet and lower legs dangled in the water. One foot was bare, the other wore a sneaker. The sneaker was blue, with a bright yellow plastic medallion attached to the lace. A butterfly was etched into the medallion's surface.

Realization hit her, the impact on her mind as sharp and hard as the blow from the crocodile so many years before. She staggered, then caught her balance, feeling the mucky ooze of the pond bottom, invisible through the dark water, squish between her toes and settle on the tops of her feet, completely covering her sandals. Terror unlike anything she had ever before experienced, not even in the worst of her nightmares, threatened to overwhelm her.

This was real. It was real, not her imagination, not a dream or a memory. She was holding a little girl. The little girl's name was Laurie Prentiss and she wore one blue sneaker with a yellow butterfly on the lace. And she, Delilah, was standing hip-deep in the murky water of the holding pond . . . and she could not move.

Delilah screamed, or at least she tried. It felt like her throat was caught in a vise that clamped it so tightly she could scarcely breathe. She tried again and all that came out was a rasping whisper. Finally, straining so hard the cords on her neck stood out with the effort, and her throat felt like it had stretched beyond its limits, she screamed, "Auntieee!" She took a great gasping breath. "Danger!" "Help meeee!"

Click! Suddenly, there were two Delilahs. One had just frantically screamed for help, frozen somewhere between the past and the present. The other was somehow calm, methodically assessing the situation.

The calm Delilah could hear splashing behind her and the shouts of Jamie as he, too, began to cry for help again, frightened by her scream. He was all right, still clinging to the makeshift raft. She could hear the distressed quacking of the mother duck and the high peeping of the scattered ducklings as they hurried to her. Overhead, she could hear the whir of wings as the other mallards that had taken to the air in fright, circled low trying to locate the danger.

The calm Delilah spoke in her head. "That was wrong. You called Auntie for help. Auntie is not here. You called in group language. No one understood. Now, call for help. You need help. Call for help the right way!"

Click! There were no longer two Delilahs, just one, but that one was thinking, even though locked in the grip of a terror so deep and unrelenting she could not physically move. Taking another deep, ragged breath, she screamed the words so loudly that she could hear them echo from the high barn walls.

"Saraaah! Caseyeee! Help meee!"

CHAPTER THIRTEEN

With the exception of Joe Clement, everyone on Bent Tree Farm heard Delilah both times she screamed for help. Joe was cultivating a field in the far northeast corner of the farm, and missed out on all the excitement. He did see Delilah running at top speed across the far end of the next field over going toward the barn, and marveled to himself at her speed and the way she jumped a fence without breaking stride. But Delilah often ran simply because she liked to run, and he thought nothing more of it.

Sarah and Kaydee had just reached the back porch with their baskets of vegetables when the first scream came. The high-pitched, ululating wail that was partly a piercing whistle brought them up short, raising the hair on the backs of their necks as they tried to identify a sound that neither of them had ever heard before, but recognized as one that clearly and urgently demanded immediate attention. Kaydee hastily put her basket on the step and started toward the barn, ever conscious of the children and correctly locating the ungodly sound as coming from the general direction of the place she assumed they were playing. She belatedly realized that it had been some time since she had heard their voices, and her fast walk changed to a quick trot. Sarah was right behind her, thinking that some farm animal was in terrible trouble, although she couldn't imagine what animal it might be. She knew a child couldn't have made that awful sound, but whoever- -or whatever- -had made it needed help.

They were side by side as they entered the barn through the wide double doors, and when Kaydee called the children, her voice was high and strident with anxiety. It echoed back in the emptiness, and the only response was the startled cluck of a hen that had been dozing on her nest, and the low, questioning sound of the pigeons high overhead.

"Oh my God, Sarah! The pond!" Kaydee's face twisted in anguish, and they both ran toward the smaller open door on the backside of the barn. Just as they reached the door, the second scream for help came, this time clearly from a female. Without stopping to analyze it, Kaydee and Sarah later agreed that they both thought it was Samantha Lowell; neither of them thought it might be Delilah.

Samantha went out shortly after breakfast with the avowed intention of " . . . finding fantastic story ideas under every bush, behind every tree, and floating in little leaf boats down at the

311

brook." No, it never entered their minds that it was Delilah, not until they had a clear view of the pond and grasped what was happening.

It was different with the Lowell men. They were just leaving the greenhouse with Jordan, deeply involved in a discussion about the possible long-term effects of genetically altering vegetables to produce their own insect killers. The way those residual toxins might contaminate both livestock and the humans eating them as they traveled up and down the food chain was important, and one of the experiments in which Jordan was currently engaged. Both K.C. and Casey, after a moment of shocked disbelief at hearing that sound at this time in this place, immediately recognized the first scream for what it was, an ape's shriek of danger and fear, and they both knew it was Delilah.

All three men reacted immediately, but Casey was faster. He rounded the corner of the barn just as the second scream for help came, this time in clearly understandable words. Splashing through the water, scarcely aware of the thick mud at the bottom of the pond pulling at his feet with every step, he reached Delilah and took the sobbing child from her shaking arms. As he did, Jordan swam past him toward the clump of reeds at the center of the pond. The water was just deep enough for an adult to swim, and as it deepened toward the center, swimming was far easier and faster than wading and fighting the muddy bottom all the way. He reached Jamie quickly, but it took a bit of soothing reassurance to convince him to release his death grip on the raft. The return trip was slower, but Jamie cooperated, following Jordan's quiet instructions to relax and let him do the work.

Casey was reluctant to leave Delilah standing there alone, so he waited, his eyes on Delilah as he talked soothingly to Laurie until K.C. splashed up beside him. Her sobs had dwindled to tired sniffles by the time he handed her to K.C., and he heard her murmur brokenly, "Grandpa, I lost my new tennie 'n Mama's going to be awful mad at me," as K.C. turned toward shore where Kaydee and Sarah were anxiously waiting.

When Casey turned back to Delilah, he saw that the shaking that started in her arms now enveloped her whole body; her eyes were becoming dull and unfocused in her pale face, and he was already moving to catch her when her knees buckled. He swung her up in his arms, noticing with one part of his mind that she weighed more than he thought, probably due to heavier bone structure, and, with quite another part that her body felt solid and warm and feminine against him through the wetness of their clothes. He could feel the tremors rippling through her convulsing her arm and leg muscles. He tightened his hold, pressing her firmly against him as he moved through the shallower water, trying to give comfort with the contact, to reassure her that everything was all right, that she was safe.

313

Jordan, carrying the hiccuping but no longer tearful Jamie, went past him, joining the women and K.C. on the bank. Casey moved slowly toward them with his heavier burden. After calling a question about Delilah's condition, and receiving a nod in reply, K.C., carrying Laurie, Jordan, with a supporting arm around Jamie, accompanied by Kaydee and a limping Samantha, started off for the house.

Samantha arrived on the scene last, out of breath and disheveled, her silver-white hair hanging in wisps around her ears and stuck in wet ringlets on her sweating forehead. She had been down by the brook and without thinking took the most direct line to reach the pond. Her knee was bruised and skinned, and she had lost her wide-brimmed hat along the way, both casualties occurring when she clambered over the old stone wall at the end of the barn. Later that afternoon when she retraced her steps at a much slower, limping pace, she found her hat by the wall, its crown crushed by her feet as she dropped from the wall to the ground beyond. Looking at it sadly, she thought about how old she was, how frightening the betrayal of her aging body. Somehow, perhaps because she lived so much of her internal life in the realm of children with her writing, she had not faced the reality that the years were marching on. It was a much younger person who chose the direct, cross-country run, not the sixty year old woman who should have taken the longer but safer roundabout way back up the path to the farmhouse and through the barn.

Peter Pan you ain't, she thought ruefully. Refusing to give in to this mood, she walked down to the pond to talk to the ducks and see what they had to say about all the excitement. Certainly, they had an interesting story to tell, of that she was sure. She was only slightly favoring her knee as she walked from the wall to the pond.

Sarah quickly made sure Laurie was all right aside from being scared and tired from her long struggle to keep her head above water, and assured herself that Jamie, too, was physically none the worse for wear. Then, she stood waiting as Casey took the last few squishing steps up the bank with his burden.

"She's out like a light," she said, then asked, "Hurt or fainted?" She was walking close beside Casey, her hand on Delilah's shoulder, and her almost clinical words belied the anxiety she was feeling.

Casey could hear the worry in her voice, and answered her as reassuringly as possible, considering that he was very worried himself. "I don't know for sure, Sarah. Physically, I don't think anything really happened to her other than getting wet. It's what's going on emotionally and psychologically that's bothering me."

Then it finally soaked into his awareness. "My God, Sarah! She went into murky water that was almost up to her chin! Look at her! Her hair is soaking wet. That means she was under the water, too. And she can't swim . . . " He broke off, still trying to absorb the situation. "She called you, Sarah, and she called me. Just as clear as a bell, she called us. She can talk!"

They were walking quickly now, and Sarah, who had moved slightly into the lead, dropped to keep step with him. "Casey," she asked quietly, "what was that terrible noise that she made first? I have never heard anything like that in my life. It gives me the shivers just to think about it."

Before he could answer, Delilah moaned and stirred in his arms. Her eyelids fluttered slightly and she whimpered, making small "uh, uh, uh," sounds. He had to shift his hold as she curled up slightly with her hand gripping the front of his shirt. He walked faster, anxious to reach the house and get her cleaned up and into bed. Although Sarah didn't know it, he recognized that those small sounds were definitely ape-like, and her continued unconsciousness was beginning to worry him. Fainting under the circumstances was a fine protective measure for stress and emotional overload, but if it continued too long, it became another matter entirely.

"Sarah," his voice carried a warning, "Delilah has been very seriously traumatized. You realize that don't you?"

"Yes, I do know," she answered. The timbre of her voice changed and her delivery became precise and authoritative. "It's pretty clear her instinct to save the children was strong enough to override her survival instinct and force her into the water. That's a very deep and basic instinct, particularly in us females, one that can take precedence over our prime directive of survival. Going into the water was traumatic enough to cause her to freeze because, for her, it meant her own survival was at stake. Unsolvable dilemma for her."

Casey glanced at her as she paused, thinking I was right all along. This woman's got a mind like a steel trap. She's the mover and shaker at Bent Tree Farm, for sure.

"Did you see that she didn't actually freeze until the children were no longer in urgent danger?" Sarah was speaking rapidly now, her mind totally engaged. "Laurie could make it to the bank without too much trouble, and Jamie was safe enough for the time being hanging on the raft. She got Laurie out of the deep water before she actually became aware of what she considered to be her own dangerous position. She answered one instinctual demand before the other kicked in, and that one in turn was far stronger than her self-imposed ban on speaking." She paused again, looking at Casey. "You know, I've been convinced for a long time that her water phobia was survival instinct at work because something very bad happened to her. There's certainly nothing irrational about that, as far as I'm concerned. And her not talking? That is something she consciously decided to do or not to

317

do for reasons of her own."

They were just passing the garden, and Sarah suddenly remembered something she had observed. She thought about the way Delilah occasionally became quiet in the garden, her body tensely still, her quick gesture to her throat, the almost surreptitious glances around. Right now isn't the time to go into it, she thought, but it certainly needs further examination. She was firmly convinced that nothing Delilah did, no matter how inexplicable it might seem to an observer, was in no way irrational. There were reasons for everything she did, and this realization was just coming full bloom into Sarah's mind. The knowledge had been there all along like a nondescript little plant, unobtrusively waiting to burst into vibrant, attention-grabbing color.

"Well, one thing we know for sure," she continued, "Delilah Cross can talk when she feels it necessary to do so. Yes, she's been traumatized." Her voice was thoughtful. After a moment she added, "She's really very strong, Casey, and that can make a big difference."

They were going up the back steps as she spoke, and Casey turned to face her. He grinned hugely. "Well, Doctor Sarah Clement, it is very nice to finally meet you. I do believe I'm going to like you just as much as I like your alter-ego, Sarah Harriet Housewife, and I would say that Delilah will have the best care three well-qualified psychiatrists can provide."

Everyone was in the kitchen, all talking at once. Their voices rose and fell, the children's higher, exited tones soaring in counterpoint over the lower adult tones. They all fell silent when Sarah led the way into the kitchen followed by Casey carrying the still-dripping, comatose Delilah.

Laurie broke the silence first. "What's wrong with her? Is she drownded? Did she get all drownded saving us?" Her treble voice broke as she turned on Jamie. "Look what you done!" she shrieked. "It's all your fault! Delilah had to save us and she's drownded! And I lost my brand new shoe-oo-oo . . . ." She broke into deep, convulsive sobs. Jamie's shamefaced muttered denials were unintelligible.

"Laurie!" Sarah's voice demanded immediate attention. "Look at me, Laurie!" When Laurie turned a miserable, tear-stained face toward her, Sarah said, "Delilah is not dead. She is not drownded, she is just very tired and needs to rest. She is not dead, do you understand?"

Her deliberate use of Laurie's word brought smiles to the adult faces, and those smiles served to further convince Laurie. She nodded slowly, and the sobs stopped. Over her head, Kaydee mouthed a "thank you" to Sarah, and exchanged glances with Samantha. Without a word, they began to herd the children out of the kitchen. Before she let the swinging door close, Samantha said quietly, "We'll take them down the bunkhouse and get them showered and cleaned up. A little nap might be a good idea, too."

"Wait a minute," Sarah ordered. "Take something for them to eat and drink. Their blood sugar must be low. They spent a lot of energy out there." Samantha nodded agreement, and Sarah quickly loaded a tray with fruit, cookies, and a pitcher of milk. "There's dishes in the bunkhouse nook." She thought about the strained look on Samantha's face. And get yourself a hot cuppa something too, with lots of sugar."

After Samantha left, it was quiet in the kitchen for a moment; only the gentle dying swish of the swinging door and the small plopping sounds of water dripping from Delilah's muddy sandals breaking the stillness. Then Jordan, who had been standing quietly to one side, asked, "Is Delilah going to be all right? Is she hurt?"

His question served to break the inertia that seemed to be affecting them all. "Good Lord," Sarah exclaimed. "What's wrong with us? No, Jordan, she isn't hurt, but she's had a bad shock." She looked at him, love evident in her expression. "Get yourself down to the gatehouse and get cleaned up. We can handle things here." As he turned to leave, she added, "Oh, and go tell Joe that you Clement men are on your own for lunch." He nodded agreement over his shoulder as he left.

Sarah looked at Casey, then at K.C. who had been sitting

quietly at the table watching and listening, apparently deep in thought. "Gentlemen, don't you think it would be a good idea to get Delilah cleaned up and into bed?" She chuckled, a pleasant sound coming from deep in her chest. "You don't seem to mind standing there holding her, Casey, but if you'll carry her down the hall to the bathroom, I think between K.C. and me, we can get her in and out of the shower real quick. She doesn't need any more water on her than absolutely necessary right now." She sniffed loudly, exaggerating the sound. "If you don't mind me saying so, that pond water stinks, and you could do with a clean-up yourself, Casey. By the time you take care of that, we'll be ready for you to help us get her upstairs to her room."

As he turned toward the door to the hall, Casey could feel the blood rising up his neck, flooding into his face, making his cheeks burn. His ears felt on fire. He had never felt such embarrassment, and the small grin he saw on K.C.'s face didn't help matters at all. Sarah had, very unerringly, nailed him. He knew it, she knew it, and K.C. knew it. In a strange, benumbed way, he had been quite content to just stand there and hold Delilah, just hold her. He knew he would never be able to live this failure down because he wouldn't ever let himself forget it. He had a patient, a comatose patient who needed immediate attention, and he just stood there like a bemused ass.

And that damned Sarah! As flustered as he was, he couldn't

help noticing her quick change from professional analyst on the pack porch to the down-home folksiness in the kitchen. As she and K.C. followed him down the hall, he also noted that Sarah had, very neatly, removed him from any part in the bathing of Delilah. My God, he thought hopelessly, am I that transparent and that unprofessional? Am I so obviously personally involved that they feel it ethically unsuitable for me to see her naked? See her naked again, was the thought that, quite unbidden, came next.

Casey's self-recriminations were abruptly halted in the bathroom. As he shifted Delilah to K.C.'s arms, she stirred restlessly. The sounds came again, "Uh, uh, uh." They weren't as loud as before, and Sarah quickly turned the shower on to a gentle lukewarm spray. She removed Delilah's sandals, dumping them unceremoniously on the floor as he went out the door. He was moving very slowly, and he was only halfway up the stairs when he heard Delilah again. He wheeled, taking the steps two at a time, and trotted down the hall to the bathroom.

"Crocodile!" "The babe!" "Auntie!" "Help me!" The shouted words were clear, separated by several shallow, panting breaths. Her voice was raspy with strain. Like the words she screamed from the pond, they were painful and agonized. Casey's stomach clenched, tensing in gut-deep response as he came up to the still-open bathroom door. In retrospect, the scene had comic overtones, but no one was laughing. Casey took it in at a glance, struggling to understand what he was seeing. No, he thought, I understand what I'm seeing, I just don't understand what it means.

Both Sarah and Delilah were standing in the tub under the shower. Delilah was naked, her hands clutching Sarah's shoulders, her eyes locked on Sarah's eyes with wild intensity as the water poured down over them both like a gentle, lukewarm rain. Sarah, fully clothed including her shoes, had her hands on Delilah's cheeks. Their faces were so close that their noses were almost touching as she returned Delilah's gaze. Her head was gently nodding, her body gently rocking, the small motion transmitted to Delilah through her hands on Sarah's shoulders.

Suddenly, Delilah lifted her head, glancing up at the shower as though becoming aware of the water flowing down over her body for the first time. Returning her gaze to Sarah, she said clearly, "Cleanliness is next to Godliness." Her voice was different, harsh and strident, someone else's voice, and she shivered violently. "Spare the rod and spoil the child!" This last was a shout.

K.C. was sitting on the closed toilet seat, intent on the low, almost singsong chant of words he was speaking to Delilah. No, Casey corrected himself. He's talking to Sarah, telling her what to say and do. It was when he focused on the words, the sounds he was making, that Casey finally understood. He eased himself to a squatting position with his back against the door jamb, intent on the drama being acted out in this most unlikely of all places, but perhaps the only place in the world it could have happened.

"Sarah, see if you can ease her down to a sitting position. Get the water off and ease her down. Sit down with her, and keep making small grunts and sympathetic sounds. Hold her eyes with yours and keep the close face position if you can." K.C.'s voice was gentle, smooth, almost hypnotic, and he continued without a break as Sarah followed his instructions. She struggled a bit as she tried to find sitting room for her ample bulk and Delilah's more compact form within the confines of the tub. "She needs to feel your breath, to smell your love, Sarah. Put your arm around her shoulders and pull her in very close. She needs the body contact. Now, put both arms around her and see if you can ease her head down against your chest. That's right. That's good. Keep making sounds. She hears them, hears your heartbeat and breathing.

Delilah was quiet, almost passive, making no further sounds after the last almost vindictive biblical reference, and as Casey shifted a bit to ease the strain on his knees, he saw that she had both arms around Sarah, snuggling close as Sarah continued to mutter small sounds. Sarah's hands were moving now, smoothing Delilah's hair, removing the hairpins, teasing the tangles out with her fingers. K.C. was quiet as Sarah worked with Delilah. "Is she resisting at all?" he asked, and allowed himself a small, satisfied grin when Sarah shook her head. He turned to look at his son, as though just now noticing his presence.

"Bonobo," Casey said softly. In response to K.C.'s questioning look, he repeated. "Bonobo," he said, thinking of the small wooden statue on Delilah's dresser, the flute, and the battered medallion. "Pan pan paniscus, not chimpanzee." He said it quietly, almost whispering. K.C. nodded in understanding and turned back to the tub.

Thoughts rushed at Casey almost too fast to understand. Pan pan paniscus, the Latin name for Bonobo apes, Pan flute. The disfigured medallion from the Landon Zoo. The carved wooden figure that was not right for a chimpanzee. All three so carefully placed on the otherwise empty dresser. Each one had meaning, significance. They meant that Delilah knew exactly who she had spent the first years of her life with, and had, apparently known it for some years. It also meant that what everyone had assumed were the time-dimmed, half-remembered memories of her past life were, in fact, very much a part of her present. And Auntie? Auntie was real, he was sure of that now.

K.C. took a large bath towel from the rack and stood with his back to the door. Sarah and Delilah were also standing now, preparing to leave the tub. Sarah, her wet clothes plastered to her body, her shoes squishing, but still muttering soothing sounds, wrapped the towel around Delilah. She glanced at Casey, who was still squatting by the door, and jerked her head to indicate he should leave. He did, but stopped on the landing, leaning over the rail to see the hall. He felt guilty doing it, but he couldn't help himself.

K.C. came out of the bathroom first, and glanced at the stairs. When he saw Casey leaning over the banister, he grinned, gave him a triumphant 'thumbs up' sign, and mouthed the word "later" before turning and going out the front door. Then, Sarah and Delilah came out. Casey's eyes widened at the picture they made as they slowly moved down the hall toward the stairs.

They were still very close together, each with an arm around the other, their free arms reaching across their bodies, holding them close in a tight, circular embrace. Delilah's right leg was pressed tightly to Sarah's left leg, and as though they had practiced this method of walking for years, they came down the hall like some strange two-headed, three-legged creature. Both center legs moved in unison, coordinating with the outer legs with no apparent thought. No matter how strange this method of locomotion looked, they were making smooth if slow progress down the hall.

Casey went on up the stairs and down the hall to his room, stopping to kick off his mucky sneakers before he went inside. He would have to do some clean-up work as well. No doubt he left tracks everywhere he had walked since leaving the pond, and he never even thought to remove them. Grabbing clean clothes, looking forward to ridding himself of the swampy smell that seemed to get stronger when he thought about it, he went into the bathroom.

He didn't enjoy that shower much. He was too busy castigating himself. He was disgusted with what he had become . . . a sneaking, peeking, eavesdropping adolescent. How could he presume to have a place with true professionals like his dad and Sarah Clement? He had just witnessed a marvelous feat of professional teamwork. K.C.'s knowledge and experience coupled with Sarah's insight, understanding and ability to empathize, both of them working together in a focused, intensely concentrated manner had probably saved Delilah's sanity. Certainly they had had brought her back from the brink of . . . what? He didn't know, but it was bad, a very bad place.

And himself? Doctor K.C. Lowell, Jr.? In his mind he saw the picture of a dumpy, wet, rocking, grunting Sarah as she crouched in the bathtub being an ape mother for Delilah. That was professionalism of the highest caliber, a level of performance he could never hope to reach.

"Shit!" he said, the word bouncing back at him from the shower walls. "Shit, shit, shit!" The echoes became a jeering chorus. No, he didn't think much of himself at all, and he could just imagine what K.C. and Sarah must be thinking about his miserable performance. He made up his mind. As soon as they got together to talk, he would officially withdraw from the case, and leave the field to the professionals. As far as he was concerned, Delilah deserved the best . . . and he just wasn't it.

CHAPTER FOURTEEN

As Casey got dressed, his thoughts were full of all the alternative actions he might have taken in this affair. His lip curled in derision at the word. Affair? Was that what was motivating him? Did he want an affair with this girl-woman? He tried to be fair with himself for a moment. Sex? Yes, the idea was intriguing, exciting, but it was more than that. Sex in and of itself - the act and fantasies about the act - had been an ever present companion since his early adolescence where nothing more than a passing thought could trigger a reaction. Certainly he was more controlled and deliberate now, consciously picking and choosing the time, the place, and the partner.

The memory of himself and Carol, slathered with whipped cream, mock wrestling on pink satin sheets came unbidden to mind causing him to grin. He amended his earlier thought. Sometimes he was more controlled and deliberate. Yes, sex was great, but he never lacked for partners and he couldn't believe that his sexual urges had gone so far out of control as to destroy all of his professional training and objectivity just like that. No, it was something else, something about Delilah herself that triggered his downward slide into the total mindless idiocy he had displayed this morning.

Maybe its chemistry, he thought tiredly, as he gathered up his smelly, wet clothes from the bathroom floor. In the hall, he gingerly added the mud-coated deck shoes to the load and trekked downstairs to the basement laundry room. He rinsed them all in the big sink, using a stiff brush to remove the mud from his shoes, then put them in a washing machine with a good amount of detergent. After turning it on, he went upstairs to the kitchen, the rhythmical thumping of the shoes against the sides of the tub keeping time with his steps.

He stood before the open door of the big refrigerator examining its contents, then decided that he wasn't hungry. Breakfast was sitting heavy in his stomach, and he just wanted a good, hot, sweet cup of coffee. He busied himself putting the big coffee maker to work. He was standing there staring at it without seeing it as gurgling water changed to steam, back to water again, then made its journey through the coffee grounds, emerging as a dark, fragrant brew, when his Dad came in.

"Hi, Casey," K.C. said as he crossed the kitchen. He sniffed loudly. "I must say you smell better than you did a while ago." He chuckled and added, "No, you don't necessarily smell better, you just don't smell period."

"You know what?" Casey asked as he turned around. "Even though I know exactly how and why a coffee maker works, I'm always amazed that it actually does work. The guy who figured this out must have been a real coffee lover, don't you think?" He turned back, reaching for a cup.

"Want a cup?" The words were addressed to the cupboard shelves. Mentally he kicked himself for being a coward. Why hadn't he asked about Delilah? He felt off base, flustered in much the same way he had been the morning Delilah found him sitting in the dark kitchen. What in the hell is wrong with me? I need the services of a shrink worse than she does.

K.C. said something to him, but Casey missed it, preoccupied with his inner monologue. "Sorry, Dad. What did you say?"

"I said that I'd wait for Sarah. Delilah's sleeping and probably will be for a couple of hours. Sarah will be back as soon as she showers and changes clothes." He glanced at his watch. "Shouldn't be more than a few minutes now, so I'll wait and have the coffee then." He felt awkward, and decided that his son's obvious tension was catching. "Smells really good, doesn't it?"

They were sitting silently at the big table engrossed in their own thoughts, when Sarah bustled in. She filled the room with pleasant chatter, reporting that all was well with the children, and they were presently napping in the RV under Kaydee's watchful eye.

"Did you know Samantha skinned and bruised her knee coming over the stone wall?" she asked. In response to their suddenly concerned attention, she added, "It's nothing serious, but she'll be limping a bit for a few days. She's incorrigible, you know. After she ate a bit and drank a cup of tea, she took off to look for her hat. Seems she lost it somewhere along the way."

Sarah paused, frowning slightly. "Come to think of it, she really made good time cross-country all the way from the brook stepping-stones to the pond. Lord knows I'd be dead of a heart attack or stroke if I tried something like that!" She glanced down at her rounded belly and laughed. "Guess I'm in pretty good shape, at that . . . for the shape I'm in." Her laugh was genuine. There wasn't a self-conscious bone in her body, and her self-acceptance was apparent.

The Lowell men, husband and son, looked at each other. "That's my Mom," the son agreed, laughing aloud at the same time the husband asked, "Are you sure she's all right, Sarah? She doesn't like to admit it when she's hurt . . . a bit of age-denial going on there."

The son looked at his father, amazed at what he had said. This was a highly personal comment, one that went deep into family relationships, a private matter that he had never mentioned to his son. Age-denial? His mother? The forever-young pixie? How old is she, he asked himself, shocked by the answer. Sixty! His Mom was sixty years old! How had he managed to avoid that fact? He was just as guilty of denial as she was if what his Dad said was true, and he had no reason to doubt it. And his Dad was sixty-three! He stared down at his coffee cup. This is really my day, he thought . . . lousy professional, lousy son. His sense of failure deepened.

"No, it's minor, K.C.," Sarah reassured him. "I looked at it; and it's just a skinned place and a bruise on the side of the knee-cap." As they talked, Sarah had been busy, making sandwiches, heating left-over soup, setting the table, no motion wasted, her body moving as quickly and efficiently as her mind. Something was going on here, she knew for sure. Just what it was she didn't know, but the tension was palpable, apparently coming from Casey, whose hangdog expression was difficult to ignore. So she kept talking.

"Well, K.C., I've been waiting for you to ask me what happened to my lovely, shapely, youthful body in the last few years. What's the matter, too polite?" She turned from the stove, her grin crinkling the corners of her eyes. "There's a story behind it, you know, want to hear it?"

When they both turned to look at her expectantly, she thought, Aha! Gottcha! "I can do it in one word. For professionals like you guys that should be enough." She paused, then said, "Bulimia."

The surprise was clear on the faces of both men. "True," she continued. "Typical case, just a fairly late onset." Her face became serious. "It took years, lots of help and support from everyone around me. For that I give eternal thanks to my dear Joe and the Brighton Foundation. Without them, my pleasingly plump, happy self would probably not be here preparing this delicious repast for you. End of story." Both her tone and facial expression said she meant it . . . end of story.

Casey wondered why she had decided to unburden herself with this personal confession now. K.C. didn't wonder . . . he knew why. Sarah was responding to his personal remark about Samantha, letting them know that there was a level of trust here that went far beyond the professional. The smile K.C. gave her was warm and understanding, as personally reassuring as a hug, a reply that spoke to her louder than any words.

As she sat down, Casey, still enmeshed in his own problem, couldn't wait any longer. Without looking up, he said, "I'm removing myself from this case. I resign, and I'll submit my resignation by FAX to Brighton Foundation this afternoon. I don't think I need to give you explanations because it should be very clear as to why." After a moment, he finished, "And I'd like to apologize to you both for my miserable performance today. I am totally embarrassed and ashamed, especially after watching your professional teamwork."

"I won't say it's ill-advised," K.C. said slowly. "I won't even say that I think it's hasty and not well thought out." He looked across the table at his son. His serious expression was made somewhat comical by the big yellow dollop of mustard on his chin, unnoticed residue from the thick roast beef sandwich he held in both hands.

"What I am saying," he continued after pausing to swallow, "is that all three of us," his glance included Sarah, who sat in her accustomed place methodically spooning thick potato soup from the bowl in front of her, "all three of us," he repeated for emphasis, "have quite unexpectedly found ourselves in a place none of us have ever been before, not professionally, or personally either for that matter."

Sarah nodded her agreement, pointedly using her paper napkin. Feeling less constrained to be polite, Casey said, "Wipe your chin, Dad. Unless you'd like some catsup for your nose?

With exaggerated dignity and aplomb, K.C. unfolded his napkin with a rustling flourish and wiped away the offending yellow blob. He examined the results, and remarked with a grin, "Don't tell Samantha, but this is the best sandwich I've ever eaten. Sarah, be sure and give my compliments to the chef."

This brief exchange relieved some of the tension they had all been feeling since Casey made his unexpected announcement, and Sarah followed with, "Look, young man, if you think what

335

we did was the carefully thought out work of professionals, you've got another thing coming. No one knew what to do. We simply played it by ear, particularly me. If anyone knew what he was doing, it was your Father." She glanced at K.C..

He took it up from there. "And if I hadn't spent time in Africa researching apes, I wouldn't have had a clue as to what was needed there in the bathroom. When I recognized the sounds she was making, it was the only thing I could think of that might help her. The girl was somewhere back in her past. Reassuring and comforting her the way it probably had been done then . . . well, I made a guess, and we were lucky that I guessed correctly. At least I hope I did."

He paused, then snorted. "Professional my ass! Casey, you've got it all wrong. And something else," he turned to Sarah, "while you were busy doing such a remarkable job of being an ape mother, did you hear Casey correctly identify the species?"

Startled, Sarah put her cup on the table with a thump. "What? What do you mean species? I thought she was with chimpanzees. You mean she wasn't?"

For the first time since the episode in the bathroom, Casey's face brightened. The sincerity of their admission of acting on guesswork, and their complete lack of condemnation or indication of disappointment in his behavior had gone a long way to reassure him.

"No, Sarah," he said eagerly, "she wasn't with chimpanzees, she was with Bonobo apes, a very distinctly different species. For a long time, they were just called pygmy chimpanzees, though comparatively they aren't pygmies; no one paid much attention to them. Then, much later, they were actually identified as a separate species, one that we still don't know too much about other than the fact that they're more intelligent, closer to humans in anatomy, and more human in many ways than other species of apes. And would you believe that they share at least 98% of our human genetic make-up? Definitely our closest relatives."

Casey grinned happily and his voice was filled with enthusiasm as he continued. "Some of our most learned and respected Primatologists think the bonobo apes might be a close counterpart to Ramapithecus or a precursor of Australopithecus, both viable options as the stem of good old Hominidae!"

Time, Casey thought, to admit another failure. "Sarah, remember that little wooden carving on her dresser?"

K.C. looked puzzled, but Casey didn't stop to explain. "Sarah, I went into her room." Casey could feel the heat begin to rise in his face. "Let's face it, I was snooping, and that was one of the things I noticed. It bothered me. It wasn't until I put it together with the close eye contact there in the bathroom and that high, shrill, whistling note in her first call for help, that I realized it was bonobo, not chimpanzee. That carving is a very well-executed replica of a bonobo ape, obviously done by someone who knows them very well."

He paused, thinking about the carving, then turned to K.C.. "It's the speak no evil ape of the trio, Dad, very appropriate for Delilah, don't you think? I wonder where the other two are? Does anyone know where she got it? And what wood carver would be that familiar with the bonobos? That bothers me somehow."

The question was addressed to Sarah, and when she shook her head, K.C. remarked, "That whistling sound should have tipped me off, too. Very distinctive once you've heard it before."

"There's more," Casey spoke again. "Sarah, what else does she keep on her dresser, very carefully placed?"

Sarah thought a moment. "Her pan flute and a battered medallion. That's all. She never leaves anything else sitting there. Do you think those things mean something, too?"

"Think about this a minute, Sarah." Casey was grinning again. "Pan pan paniscus is the species designation for bonobo apes." He paused, watching her face as the meaning and the attendant connotation became clear to her.

"My God!" The words exploded out of her mouth. "Pan flute! She not only knows, she's made a kind of secret joke, or it's a symbol and the dresser is her altar . . . or maybe both!"

K.C. had been listening closely, his forehead wrinkled in concentration. "And the medallion, Casey? What is it? Where does it fit?"

"That, I'm not sure of," Casey answered. "It's pretty beat up, but it's either a gorilla or a chimpanzee on one of those cheap medallion souvenirs, and it came from the Zoo and Botanical Garden in Landon, Pennsylvania. That takes us straight back to Hiller School, doesn't it? Do we agree that we should talk to Harold Newcombe as soon as possible? I've been going through their files and I have some other questions for Mr. Newcombe."

Casey didn't notice that he had rejoined the team, or the fact that Sarah and his Dad exchanged pleased glances as he did so. He was too involved with following his own thoughts. "There's something else strange here. That voice she used to say 'Cleanliness is next to Godliness' and 'Spare the rod and spoil the child' was eerie. Gave me goose flesh." K.C. nodded in agreement, his face thoughtful. Just as Casey opened his mouth to say something else, Sarah spoke up.

"Oh, this is off the subject, but while I think of it," she said, glancing at K.C., "I made a couple of calls to Brighton headquarters. I was pretty sure that the woman you asked me about, Agnes Kittridge, doesn't work for them any more, and hasn't for the last seven or eight years." A frown touched her face, deepening the small creases in her forehead as she continued.

"But there was something a little odd about it. The first person I talked to did a tap-dance around the subject, so I thanked her nicely and called a very old friend who is still active in Brighton affairs, and who shall remain nameless." Her grin was almost wicked, as she finished. "Anyway, this friend was quite agreeable to a little off-the-record detective work. I should be hearing from them any time now."

She got up to clear the dishes from the table, missing the puzzled, questioning glance K.C. exchanged with his son. Sarah sounded positive that Agnes Kittridge wasn't a Brighton employee now, and hadn't been during the time Delilah was at Bhutu. Obviously, she hadn't seen Delilah's records or the more than two dozen reports signed by Agnes Kittridge over that two year period of time. K.C. gave a warning shake of his head as Casey opened his mouth to speak, and Casey continued smoothly.

"Oh, there's something else, too. It's about this 'Auntie' person she called to for help." Sarah and his Dad both nodded. They'd caught that, too. "Well, I'm not proud of my prowling, but I looked at her books. One of them had something written inside the cover, something about wanting to go home, and missing her 'Auntie'."

They sat there a long time in silence after that, evaluating all of this new and puzzling information. Finally, Casey asked, "Sarah, I heard you singing upstairs. And I thought I heard Delilah singing, too. Did I imagine that?"

"No," she answered thoughtfully, "you didn't imagine it. In

fact, it was very strange, gave me a compelling feeling to tell the truth. I got her into the old sweats she sleeps in and into bed. She was hanging on to her teddy bear for dear life, and I tucked her in and sat down beside her, talking about anything that came to mind. Then, I noticed she was humming, a strange kind of little tune, and I told her how sweet it sounded. She started to sing the words, and it was a little nursery rhyme kind of song about a baby, a rocking chair, and a teddy bear. The words were simple, and after a while, I sang it with her because she seemed to expect it . . . then she went to sleep. And there was a smile on her face."

Sarah was silent a moment, frowning slightly. Finally, she said, "More symbolism, I think. Her teddy bear, which is named Teddy Bear with capital letters, seems to be her most treasured possession, and she was very excited about getting that old rocking chair up to her room, too. They're both connected to that little song in some way, I think." She sighed. "So many things have been sitting there, right out in the open. It's almost like she desperately wants someone to unravel the puzzle, isn't it?"

"No, I don't think so, Sarah." K.C.'s words were slow, thoughtful. "Nothing that happened today was planned, and these small things we see now had no apparent importance, or even relevance to the situation as it was, at least not in the way anyone would notice . . . except my very observant and perceptive son, that is. No, I think these things were all her way of . . . " He stopped abruptly, grinned at Casey, and pushed back his chair and stood up. "Is there any coffee left? I think I could use another cup."

Sarah was aware that he had decided to keep his opinion to himself and wondered why. What private thoughts did he have about Delilah? Casey didn't seem to notice at all, and Sarah caught a brief glimpse of the narrow path full of pitfalls and traps that K.C. was traveling in his relationship with his son.

As he walked across the kitchen, K.C. asked over his shoulder, "How long do you think she'll sleep, Sarah?"

Sarah looked at her watch. "Not too much longer. I'll go up in a few minutes." She grinned. "I'll sit and rock in the rocking chair. Maybe I'll get some sort of inspirational insight on how we should handle this." Then she frowned. "I wonder just where in time she'll be when she wakes up?"

"Hopefully in the present," K.C. answered. "What we saw was a kind of reenactment, a reliving of whatever it was that caused the water phobia in the first place. From what we heard, it was something bad, very bad. Then the water in the shower triggered some other traumatic event."

"Yes," Sarah agreed, then shuddered. "A crocodile . . . and a baby . . . " Her voice drifted into silence.

"Well, what do you think? Shall we just play it by ear?" K.C. waited for their nods, then concluded, "And no questions, either.

We'll play follow-the-leader and let Delilah take the lead in her own way at her own speed."

Casey was struck by how their decision, quite independently reached, reflected the way Harold Newcombe had handled Delilah, and the way he, too, had decided that letting her take her own road to wherever she was going was the best way for her. He frowned. There was no question in his mind now. Delilah was exerting a powerful but subtle, almost subliminal influence on everyone around her. What was it? How was it done? He had no answers and he pushed the thought away, shoving it far back in his mind as though it was dangerous to even think about. But it sat there, ticking away like a small but deadly bomb.

K.C. was at the counter pouring coffee when Samantha came in the back door, the battered sun hat in her hand. He turned to her and asked, "Are you all right, dear? Sarah said you'd skinned and bruised your knee."

Samantha leaned into him as he put a comforting arm around her shoulders. His face softened as he looked down into her face, and reading her need, attuned to every subtle nuance of her behavior, K.C. tightened his grip, pulling her even closer to him.

If her son hadn't been watching closely, looking for the sixty-year-old woman he now realized was walking around in his mother's body, he would have missed this moment of wordless, intimate communication between his parents, just as he would

343

have missed seeing the lines of weariness that appeared on her face and the momentary droop of her shoulders. He saw them, and he also saw it when, as if catching herself, she squared her shoulders, smiled brightly and laughed, waving the hat like some bedraggled battle flag. Once again she was the Mom person he had, until now, accepted as a timeless, permanent reality in his life.

How long, he wondered, is it going to take my mind to grow up like my body did?

* * *

Delilah slowly floated up out of a deep, dreamless sleep. The awakening was easy, and her first dim awareness was of how warm and relaxed her body felt. When she opened her eyes, her first thought was that she had slept very late because the light in her room was not the usual early morning sunlight. Then, a small repetitive sound caught her attention. After a moment she recognized it as the low swish-and-creak of her rocking chair going back and forth. How strange, she thought drowsily. It must be my friend Teddy Bear rocking himself, and drifted away, almost but not quite asleep again.

After a few minutes or so, she came back to fuller awareness. The rocking chair sounds were still there, and she smiled as she tightened her grasp on Teddy Bear. After only a moment, she realized that if she was holding him, it could not be him in the rocking chair, and this was followed immediately by the realization that Teddy Bear could not rock himself. Someone else was in the room, and as her attention focused she could hear the gentle rise and fall of breathing and caught a small whiff of Sarah's talcum powder.

Curious but unalarmed, she carefully raised herself up on her elbow and saw Sarah sitting in the rocking chair. She was gazing out the window, her face calm and reposed as she kept the rocker in motion with gentle pushes of her feet. She didn't notice the movement or hear the small rustling of the bedclothes as Delilah took a quick look and lowered herself back into a prone position. How strange, Delilah thought. Why would Sarah be sitting in her room rocking? As if the question was the key that opened a closed, watertight door, memory came flooding back in a rush that almost swept her away. It was murky and dark like the water in the pond, swirling in oily ripples as though disturbed by the passage of some huge, predatory reptilian monster just under the surface.

It took all her will power then, and the sharp, piercing pain as her teeth clamped on her lower lip, to maintain her silence. Why she felt it necessary to remain silent, she didn't know, particularly after the full memory of the events at the pond and her cries for help filled her mind. It became easier as she examined the facts, and the tension slowly eased. She was all right, that much was

345

evident. And the children were all right, at least she thought so. She frowned at the uncertainty. There were gaps, big gaps in her memory.

In her mind, Delilah slowly and carefully retraced her steps. She had been one field over from where Joe was cultivating the soybeans. She had heard Jamie calling for help. She had run to the pond, seen Jamie clutching the boards of the makeshift raft as he called for help. Then she had seen Laurie's head slip under the water. And she had run into the pond . . . into the pond. She felt goose flesh rising on her arms and tried to ignore it. It's over now, she told herself, no danger, no monsters. She forced herself to continue remembering. She had freed Laurie's foot, leaving the shoe tangled in the underwater roots. A blue shoe with a yellow butterfly attached to the lace. The butterfly medallion hung before her mind's eye like a small sun, filling her vision. She jerked her mind away from it, suddenly afraid that if she looked at it too long she would be blinded, or, like the butterfly etched on its surface, be stuck there forever in mute, burning agony.

Go on, go on, she told herself. You got through it, you're here, you're safe. She took a deep breath, exhaling slowly and quietly. She must finish this before she could deal with the present, and Sarah's presence was the present. As she realized that one part of her mind found the two words, present and presence, quite cleverly put together, the strained lines of tension on her face began to relax. So did the muscles in her body. She was handling it.

All right, she had carried the sobbing, dripping Laurie into waist-deep water. And then she had panicked, trapped in the murky river water of the past, and Laurie had become the babe. Her stomach knotted in a cramp, but she forced herself to finish the thought honestly . . . what was left of the babe. And then she had called for help because some part of her realized that she could no longer move, more deeply mired in the horror of the past reality than the oozing pond mud of the present.

And then? After that? She struggled to remember anything past that point. There was nothing more. Nothing. How she got from the pond to her bed was a total blank. She sniffed quietly. There was no trace of pond smell on her and she was in her sweats. That meant someone had undressed her, bathed her, and put them on her. And there was Sarah quietly rocking by the window. At least that small mystery was cleared up. Sarah had bathed her and put her to bed, and now she was waiting for her to wake up.

So, Delilah thought, I blacked out, totally went away, fainted, passed out. She busied her mind with finding synonyms rather than giving in to the rising worry about that period of blankness, and what might have happened. After a moment, she came up with another synonym that brought a faint smile . . . swooned.

Nothing happened, she reassured herself, thinking of the fainting people she had read about in books, seen on television and in movies.

Up to this point, she had refused to address the problem she had created for herself by calling for help. That part she remembered clearly. In her panic she had screamed out the group call for danger and help. Then, in response to the prompting of some calm inner voice, she had called out for Sarah and Casey. Obviously, they had heard her, so where did she go from here?

The dilemma she had been wrestling with over the need to speak to accomplish her mission, and the way to begin speaking without stirring up too much consternation, causing too many uncomfortable questions, seemed to be resolved, taken out of her hands quite by accident. No, she thought with amusement, not taken out of my hands, taken out of my mouth.

Of course, I could simply pretend to be as amazed as everyone else by this miracle of trauma-induced power to articulate. She smiled at the lovely pomposity of the words, but she didn't think she could get away with that. Or she could simply remain silent, leaving them to wonder and invent theories to explain it.

When she really examined her feelings, other than the small nagging worry over the blank time, she was full of anticipation and a kind of satisfaction that the decision to speak had been made for her. And, she concluded as she turned over, making sure the covers rustled loudly this time, I'll just follow their lead and react the way they want me to. That chameleon-like method of adopting protective coloration had worked well for her so far.

Sarah's voice was cheerful. "Oh, you're awake, Delilah. How are you feeling? You look rested. Hungry, too, I'll bet. You missed lunch, not that it was anything special."

She paused a moment, looking out the window as she stood up. "You know, this rocking chair and that view are a great combination. Peaceful and restful. My Grandma had one of these old rockers. While I was sitting here I realized how right she was when she used to tell me that rocking chairs were good for the soul." With a sigh, as though reluctant to part with the moment, or face the next one, Sarah turned to face Delilah. "Well, young lady, are you ready to get dressed and go off in search of food?"

Delilah sat up on the edge of the bed and looked at Sarah questioningly. She was wondering whether or not she should answer, suddenly unsure of herself. There were no clues as to what was expected in Sarah's words. She had no way of knowing that Sarah was just as unsure of herself, but for different reasons. Her noncommittal questions and statements were designed to elicit meaningful responses from Delilah, something she could use to gauge Delilah's current mental and emotional state. Without appearing to, she studied Delilah's face, hoping to get some clue about what was going on in her mind. Other than a faint up-turn of her lips, the smallest beginning of a smile, there was nothing. Come on, come on, she thought, say something Delilah.

Delilah stood up, took a deep breath, and raised her arms high above her head in a luxurious stretch. By the time she lowered her arms, she had made up her mind. Something she had been aware of subliminally had finally consciously registered. Sarah was anxious and upset in spite of her calm, non-committal facade. The faintly acrid odor she was emitting with her perspiration was one Delilah connected with anxiety.

She's worried about me, Delilah thought, and with the thought she acted. Faintly, in the back of her mind, Auntie's voice whispered, "Not do, not do," but she ignored it. She walked up close and raised her eyes, wide-open and sincere, to meet Sarah's. At the same time, she gripped Sarah's shoulders with both hands. Sarah didn't move, deeply shaken by the similarity between Delilah's present position and the one that she had assumed in the downstairs bathroom only hours before. It took a moment for her to realize that Delilah was speaking to her, and another to realize what she was saying.

"Sarah." Delilah said softly, her voice husky, hoarse from strained vocal chords. "I'm fine, Sarah, and hungry as a bear." She chuckled and Sarah could feel the little puffs of breath on her face. "And I need to find a tree before I embarrass us both."

Sarah enveloped her in a hug that spoke louder than any words she could have said, and Delilah returned it with a feeling of pleasure so intense tears came to her eyes. Finally, reluctantly, she pulled away. "Bathroom," she said.

She started toward the door, then turned back. "French toast?" she asked. "With hot maple syrup?" She touched her throat. "Hurts. Too much yelling." She was smiling as she walked down the hall and closed the bathroom door behind her.

Sarah stood there for several seconds, happiness and surprise playing tag across her plump face. Then, she collected herself and left the room thinking that she, too, would like some French toast. She was also thinking that Delilah had very neatly taken control of the follow-the-leader game, leaving the three professionals to follow wherever she chose to lead them.

On her way down to the kitchen, Sarah stuck her head in the door of the office at the end of the hall, waving her hand to catch Casey's attention. When he looked up from the folder he was studying, she said softly, "Come on downstairs. Delilah wants some French toast," and started down the stairs, leaving his surprised questions hanging in the air unanswered.

In the bathroom, Delilah remembered something. The remark about the bear in the woods was something Paulie Newcombe had said on one of the family's summer camping trips, crude enough to draw a reprimand from Dee Dee. Strange, Delilah thought, that

351

of all the things I could have said, Paulie's silly attempt at bathroom humor was the first thing out of my mouth.

But maybe not so strange, she concluded, as she rinsed her face. She wanted to talk to Paulie. Yes, Paulie. She had always wanted to talk to Paulie. She could remember so many times the temptation to do so had been so great it took an almost physical effort to keep from confiding in him, to turn and walk away instead of pouring out her heart to him. Yes, I really want to talk to Paulie, she thought, and Harold, too.

CHAPTER FIFTEEN

Failing to answer his questions, Casey firmly checked an impulse to follow Sarah down to the kitchen and throttle her to pay for his frustration. Instead, he picked up the phone and called the bunkhouse thinking if the kids were napping in the RV, then his Dad and Mom would probably be in the bunkhouse. The number was taped on one corner of the desk, apparently for the use of anyone in the office wanting to save a walk to the bunkhouse in order to talk to someone there. Convenient, he thought, and mentally thanked the person who had thought to do it, even if it was probably laziness rather than consideration that prompted it.

He guessed right, and K.C. answered on the second ring. "Dad, she's awake and up." He paused, fighting his irritation at Sarah's cute way of telling him nothing. "As far as I can tell, considering the look on Sarah's face, the way she announced that Delilah wanted some French toast, and bounced off down the stairs, everything seems to be all right. Any advice on how to handle this for right now? I mean should we all avoid the kitchen, all descend on the kitchen, what?"

He stopped, suddenly aware he had been spitting out the words, giving K.C. no opportunity to answer. He caught a movement out of the corner of his eye, and swiveled in the chair in time to catch a glimpse of Delilah as she crossed the landing and went out of sight. "She just went downstairs, Dad."

K.C. laughed. "I'm just as excited as you are, and now that you mention it, French toast sounds good to me, too. How does it sound to you?" He laughed again. Casey could hear his Mom's voice in the background, and caught something about just eating a big roast beef sandwich and getting fat as a pig.

K.C. continued. "I've already coached Samantha and Kaydee on how they should handle this, and Kaydee will brief the kids when they wake up. I'm pretty sure that Sarah has already talked to Joe and Jordan about it. The scenario plays out casual. We certainly can't pretend nothing happened, but until we see where she is for ourselves, it's follow her lead all the way, okay? Act natural, and save a place for me at the table, will you?"

Casey couldn't help laughing as he hung up. Leave it to his Dad, he thought affectionately. All the irritation and tenseness were gone, replaced by anticipation. It reminded him of the way he used to feel as a kid before he and his Dad set out on one of their monthly jaunts. Just the two Lowell men off in search of adventure was Samantha's way of putting it. Maybe I'm not such a failure after all, he told himself, successfully ignoring the small nagging voice in the back of his mind that told him hearing Delilah's real speaking voice was a big part of his anticipation.

Grabbing the folders from the desk, he hurried down the hall and put them in his room. As he did, he heard Sarah call his name, and something about if he wanted French toast while the syrup was hot, he'd better get it in gear. So he did, surprised at the rumbling sounds coming from his stomach and the realization that he was hungry, really hungry, for the first time since this morning.

* * *

Two days later, on Friday night, Delilah quietly closed the bedroom door behind her and went down to the kitchen. There had been no sound in the house for more than an hour, so she assumed that Casey had bedded down for the night. He's probably tired out, she thought. They're all probably tired out from waiting for me to babble like an idiot, spilling out the story of my life in a rush, making up for all the silent years, answering all the unasked questions that sat poorly-concealed on their faces.

No, she told herself, it isn't going to be like that at all. There was a specific goal that she intended to reach, and each step had to be thought out carefully. With that in mind, she limited herself to monosyllabic answers in response to the oh-so-casual questions about how she felt, and isn't it a beautiful day? The years of self-discipline, of saying nothing when she felt like screaming out words - or epithets - made it easy for her.

They were walking on eggs around her; that much became clear when she asked Sarah what had happened after she blacked out. Actually, she had simply asked, "What happened?" and Sarah had understood exactly what she wanted to know. They were alone in the kitchen after dinner, Delilah squatting in front of the dishwasher, handing the dishes up to Sarah as she put them in the cupboard.

"You fainted when you realized what had happened, that you were waist-deep in muddy water," Sarah recited. "You screamed for help. Do you remember that?" Oh, Delilah thought, there's the first direct important question anyone has actually asked me. She looked up at Sarah and nodded.

"Well, we all heard you, everyone but Joe, that is, and converged on the pond. Jordan went after Jamie, Casey took Laurie from you, handed her to K.C., and caught you as you collapsed. He carried you back to the house." Sarah paused, seeming somehow reluctant to continue.

Delilah waited. Nitty-gritty time, she thought, one part of her mind marveling at the seemingly endless store of cliches, colloquialisms and nonsense syllables that seemed to be in permanent residence there. Finally, Sarah seemed to make up her mind, and finished quickly. "K.C. and I got you into the downstairs shower and did a quick job of sluicing off the pond goop. I walked you upstairs, got you into your sweats and into bed."

She put her hand on Delilah's shoulder and squeezed. "Would you believe it was like dressing a big, life-size doll?" she asked. "Your eyes were open but you were limber, and when I rolled you around in bed and covered you up, you reached for Teddy Bear, snuggled him under your chin, and went right to sleep." She stopped talking, her hand still gripping Delilah's shoulder. It remained there as Delilah stood up.

Sarah wouldn't lie to her, Delilah was sure of that, but she was avoiding something, leaving something out. Sarah was anxious, leaving slight pauses between the words in certain places as though waiting for some response, some indication that her words had triggered her memory of the events. They hadn't.

"Blank," Delilah answered the unspoken question, shaking her head. She couldn't tell if the expression on Sarah's face was disappointment or relief.

She was still puzzling over that expression when, working as quickly and efficiently as Sarah, she assembled a variety of snacks on a tray, poured a glass of milk, and started back upstairs. No use worrying about it, she told herself, as she went to the front corner workspace in the office. Either she would remember it all for herself or it would eventually come out. Most people, she had learned, weren't nearly as good at keeping secrets as she was.

She had asked Sarah one other question. "Senior?" she had asked. "Psychiatrist?" Delilah was not surprised at the answer, but Sarah's reaction was completely unexpected. Her look of surprise had quickly changed to a big smile, almost as if they were conspirators and Delilah had come up a brilliant answer to a thorny problem.

"Sure is," she had answered, and laughed out loud. "And one of the very best, too!"

"Out-numbered," Delilah had commented, making a sad face, then giggling as Sarah burst out with what could only be described as a guffaw followed by several hoots and snorts, as she tried to get her breath. Delilah didn't realize that Sarah's laughter was an over-reaction, that her comment hadn't been that funny, that there was something else on Sarah's mind. They finished up in the kitchen, and Sarah gave her a big, warm hug before she left for the gatehouse, obviously satisfied that everything was all right with Delilah.

Time enough for that later, Delilah thought, and within a few minutes she had booted up the computer, entered her game name, Chameleon, and the words "She has a secret."

Munching on a mouthful of peanuts, she sat back and waited for the others to log on. She opened her game notebook, looking at the map, a replica of the one that appeared on each of their computer monitors during the game. It was precisely and carefully plotted on graph paper, each filled-in square denoting an area already explored, each blank an unknown mystery. She was surprised at how many squares the four of them had filled during their adventures together.

She checked over her solution to the puzzle that had ended last week's game. Darkling was especially good at inventing intriguing traps involving numbers; it had taken her more than an hour to figure out that if his instructions were followed as given, Chameleon and anyone else who followed them literally would wind up dead or badly injured in a deep pit. The answer, she was sure, was to take one step forward, three sideways and stop, ignoring all of Darkling's other instructions.

During the time the four of them had played the game, the level of sophistication of the tricks, traps, and evil creatures to be battled, avoided, or otherwise circumvented, had kept pace with their own mental maturation, becoming more complex and convoluted as time went on. There had been a slow, subtle shift from their earlier swashbuckling blood-and-gore derring-do to intricate reasoning problems that must be solved before the characters could progress. While Darkling was especially good at inventing puzzles involving numbers, it gave her great satisfaction that her own word contributions using synonyms,

359

homonyms, alliteration, and puns that often led the unwary into dead ends, had earned her the cyber game title of "Master of Misdirection".

Words, she thought. All these years, I made up for not saying them by acquiring them, accumulating them, hoarding and playing with them in my mind. For a moment, she slipped backward in time, back to Bhutu Holding Facility and the child she had been, the child tracing out words on her thigh with her finger.

The warning tone from her computer console brought her attention back to the present. One after the other Merlin, Darkling, and Hunter announced their presence at the cyberspace game board. In their imaginations it was not a game board, it was a world, an endless series of underground caverns, grottoes and dungeons full of half-seen monsters, mazes, traps and dangerous pitfalls. All of the obstacles must be overcome to reach the treasure vaults hidden somewhere in the depths of the labyrinth. Only recently had it struck Delilah how the game seemed to parallel her own struggle to survive and reach the goal she had set for herself.

After a moment's hesitation, Delilah quickly typed a message that she knew would immediately jar the others out of their usual anticipatory game mood.

"Hunter," she wrote, "he who has a witch for a sister, are you receiving?" Paulie's identifying code words always amused her. The war between him and Becky had never reached a truce stage and probably never would. They were too different.

It took a few moments, then the words ticked across her monitor screen, as they did on each of the other three. "Name and code?" She grinned. Paulie was cautious.

"Chameleon. She has a secret." She waited a moment, then typed, "Hunter, are you in your room at home and is your private phone plugged in?"

This time, the response took longer, and she could almost see the three of them puzzling over this very unusual break in their carefully maintained impersonal game relationship.

Since Delilah left Hiller School and came to Bent Tree Farm nearly two years before, she and Paulie had maintained close contact, talking frequently via computer mail, discussing anything and everything that currently interested them. From hot-air ballooning to religion, nothing was sacred. And they learned things in the process, not only about themselves, but also about subjects that would not otherwise have come to their attention, a kind of on-going educational process that benefited them both.

While researching through computer libraries for information about the effects of radiation on sperm and potency, a subject that had caused Paulie some anxiety when a broken leg required several X-rays, Delilah found a great deal of related information.

Not only could radiation in sufficient amounts cause sterility, but in lower amounts it could cause subtle changes in genetic material leading to mutations, many of them viable, a subject in which she was very interested.

In turn, while looking for information about God for Delilah, a subject with which, in his opinion, she seemed overly-preoccupied, Paulie was amazed to discover how man, particularly in Western civilization, had changed from bowing to a pantheon of gods, ones that needed to be appeased on every imaginable occasion, to the idea of one deity. That concept took thousands of years to take firm root and flourish, often planted on the sites where other, older gods had once been worshiped by skin-clad savages.

In Paulie's view, even the one God as described in the Old Testament appeared to be a carnivore, finding grace in Abel's meat offerings while spurning Cain's fruit of the soil, and many bible chapters seemed to be devoted to the preparation of meat exactly to God's taste. Paulie felt sympathy for poor Job, too. The game God had played with him was vicious and sadistic in his opinion. Furthermore, exactly whom had Cain found to mate with if the only humans were Adam and Eve and their children? Lillith from the land of Nod? Created elsewhere by God but not disclosed? And even after the idea of one God was accepted, wars were fought over the proper method of worship, bloody struggles that involved powerful kings and kingdoms, wars that continued right into the present.

The world was on fire with religious wars, not about the existence of God, but often about the way he should to be worshiped, as interpreted by mere humans. Delilah hadn't believed him at first when he told her about the "Shoe Button War". He had found the information under religious oddities, and he finally convinced her to read it for herself.

In that instance, in the late nineteen hundreds, a church had actually come to physical blows between parishioners over whether or not God approved of women wearing shoes that buttoned rather than laced. The schism ran so deep, two different churches were formed as a result, each group firmly convinced that they had correctly interpreted God's wishes about women's shoes. Currently, one church denomination was still deeply involved in the shoe war, only this time it was over whether or not women's open-toed shoes were lewd, lascivious, and immoral. Feeling quite profound and sophisticated, he and Delilah had agreed that there was nothing sexy about open-toed shoes or female toes, unless, of course, one happened to have a foot or shoe fetish...a subject they also explored at great length.

Yes, Paulie had learned things while doing research for Delilah, things that caused him to wonder and probe, questioning things most people simply took for granted as being true because someone else said it. He had remarked facetiously to Delilah in one of his letters that she had been lucky to escape the religious war currently going on right in the Newcombe household.

At that time, according to Paulie, Becky was worshiping the great Prom God and believed that the proper attire for doing so consisted of a scrap of cloth that scarcely covered her body. Dee Dee, while accepting the Prom God's contribution to the emotional well being of her daughter, was a devout worshiper of the Propriety God. She insisted that the proper attire for worship should conceal certain portions of Becky's anatomy from public gaze. Harold refused to comment other than mumbling half-audible prayers to his own Peace and Quiet God. And Paulie? He had silently implored his Computer God to transport him away from it all . . . without crashing. Delilah smiled as she remembered. This was sort of a dirty trick to pull on Paulie, but she wanted to sneak up behind him when he wasn't looking and yell, "Boo!"

When words finally appeared on her monitor, they came from Merlin, not Hunter. "Merlin, the precocious alchemist," he identified himself. "Hunter, take care. Demons often lurk in the shadows waiting to pounce on the unwary. This may be a trespasser with evil intent. Demand further identification."

Delilah read the words, feeling a surge of affection for Merlin. Right in character, she thought, the wary Merlin who made his way carefully, avoiding tricks and traps skillfully, ever concerned for the well-being of his fellow travelers in the game. They had never met each other. While she and Darkling had probably seen each other around, but never met or knew who the other was in person, from the very beginning of the game, they agreed that anonymity was the rule. No real names, no identities other than those they chose to conceal or reveal in their game role characters. While Paulie knew each player personally and they knew he was Hunter, the others were simply Merlin, Darkling, and Chameleon to each other.

Following Merlin's lead, Darkling added his thoughts, also staying in character. "This shadow world is ours, and ours alone. Intruders are not welcome here. Hunter, pose a riddle, a conundrum that only the true Chameleon could properly answer."

After a pause, Paulie's words appeared on their monitors. "There was a young lady who went to a zoo. By a tree that evening, what did she do?"

Not bad, Delilah thought. In fact, it was very good. No one in the entire world knew about that incident except herself and Paulie. "Very good, Hunter," she typed quickly. "She pounded and pounded until she was tired. Then the young man pounded as though inspired." Poor poetry, she thought, but the answer is clear.

"Yes to both your questions," was his response. Merlin and

Darkling remained silent.

She could feel them waiting for her answer with almost palpable attention. Now, she was unsure. The game mood was disrupted for her, and she was sure the others felt the same way. And she wanted to talk to Paulie, speak to him, and answer, at least in part, the questions he would ask.

"Chameleon has shed her skin and changed her colors." She, too, stayed in character. "With deepest apologies to her fellow adventurers, she begs permission to leave these caverns dark and deep to seek a private audience with the mighty Hunter on his mundane speaking instrument."

"Granted." The answers came one after the other, and one by one they logged off.

Without clearing her screen, Delilah gave a tension-relieving sigh, picked up the phone, took her small telephone directory from the pocket of her jeans, and punched out the numbers of Paulie's private line. As she did so, it struck her how strange it might look to others that she should keep a telephone book. So many little details, so many things to keep track of in maintaining her deception. Her thoughts about how many other small details she might have overlooked were abruptly halted by Paulie's voice.

He answered on the first ring. "Delilah?" His tone was disbelieving. "Is that really you, Delilah?"

For a moment she was unable to answer, taken off-guard by

his voice. It no longer had the breaking uncertainty she remembered. It was smooth and deep, sounding much like his Father's voice, not at all what she expected. Then she realized that it would be even harder for him because he had never heard her voice at all.

"Yes, Paulie." She paused, swallowing the lump that had, for some reason, appeared in her throat. "It's me." Her voice had returned to its usual high, melodic tone, the strain-induced hoarseness dissipating in a day, but now her throat ached, and she felt like crying. Instead, she chuckled. "Paulie, do you realize that this is the first time I've ever talked on a telephone?" She laughed again, this time more easily. "Are you properly impressed that my first call is to you?"

"I'm impressed, amazed, and astounded," he answered, taking his cue from her, keeping it light and easy. "But I'm more impressed with myself at this moment."

"And why would that be?" she asked.

"That would be, dear Chameleon because you sound exactly the way I have imagined you would for all these years." He paused. "I'm not going to ask because I know you'll tell me in your own way in your own time. But, Jesus, Delilah, do you realize what a shock this is?" He rushed on. "I've got to ask. How long have you been able to talk? Did it just suddenly happen? Like did you just wake up one morning talking?"

When the rush of questions stopped, Delilah realized that she had to give him some answers. He deserved it. She thought of his endless patience with her notepad scribbles, the care he took to answer her questions, sometimes over and over again until he was sure that she understood his answers. She had kept many things from him, but she had never lied to him, probably because he never asked, simply accepting her without question. He was the one person in the world that she felt deserved an honest answer, so she gave it to him.

"Paulie, I'm not going into the details right now. That's something I want to talk to you about face-to-face. But Paulie, I've always been able to talk. There were just reasons . . . ", her voice trailed off. She could hear Auntie's voice whispering, "Not speak, not speak."

Delilah cleared her throat, and finished the sentence. "There were good reasons why I didn't talk. And when it's time, you'll understand all those reasons, Paulie. I'll make very sure you do. Until then, will you just trust me?"

His answer was prompt. "Delilah, I've always trusted you, and always will. Not to worry, I'm always here for you, I think you know that." There was no doubting his sincerity.

"Thank you, Paulie." She was near tears. "I'll be calling you again soon." She managed a small chuckle, and shifted into game talk. "There be things afoot, mighty Hunter, things that will require the combined art and magic of all our brave warriors. Will you make them aware that the call to battle will soon come? Bespeak them clear that the dragon beast we stalk is well armored, wily, and possessed of much venom. A single misstep will mean imprisonment in dungeons deep, and perhaps the risks be too great to think upon, even for the bravest of warriors and most skillful of magicians."

"Aye, Chameleon," he answered, "I'll rally the troops and await the call." Then, in his normal voice, he asked a question that really surprised her. "Time to do some really big-time computer hacking, huh?"

When she didn't respond, he continued, "Come on, Delilah, I think I was about twelve when it dawned on me that you were after something - or someone - connected with Brighton Foundation. But I still don't know what or who, or even why. Maybe now you'll fill in some of the blanks?"

"Yes." Her voice was serious, "I think it's just about time." After a moment she continued. "I don't think I've ever told you how much your friendship has meant to me, Paulie, or how many things you have helped me understand about living in this world. There was only one other that was there for me like that, who tried to help me make some sense out of the madness that surrounded me." Her voice broke on a sob.

"Damn!" The word exploded out of her mouth, shocking them

both. "If I'd known that talking would make me cry, I'd probably kept my mouth closed." She sniffled loudly. "Talk to you soon, and thank you, again, Paulie."

"Before you hang up, Delilah," Paulie said, his voice suspiciously hoarse and uneven, "I've got to tell you something. Do you realize that this is only the second time I've ever known you to cry? Not once, over all these years, have I ever seen a tear, except that evening we did the pounding."

He fell silent, and she could hear him take a deep breath before he continued. "After we pounded that damned medallion, I went home and cried myself to sleep. Do you know why? Because I bought it for you, Delilah, and I was so proud about that. And when I saw you doing your best to destroy it, I was hurt in a way that only a little boy can be hurt. And then, I thought, when I saw you were crying, it hurts her, too, so I sat down and helped you."

There was a long silence before she answered. "I never realized, Paulie. Something really terrible happened to me that day. It wasn't just the bite, it was something more, something much worse. I can't talk about it now, but I promise you I will, someday. I still have the medallion, you know. It sits on my dresser with my pan flute and the wooden ape figurine. Remember that?"

When he said that he did, she continued, consumed with the need to somehow make up for the hurt she had given him,

370

"Remember how excited we were when we finally figured it out?"

He was regaining some of his normal enthusiasm. "Bonobo," he answered.

"Yes, bonobo," she affirmed. "That was quite a piece of detective work for a couple of kids, don't you agree?" She laughed, pleased that she had managed to cheer him up, then said, "I'll call again, soon. I want to talk to the rest of the family, too, but later on. Don't tell them yet, Paulie. I want to surprise them, okay?"

"You got it," he answered. Then, almost embarrassed, he said, "Delilah, you've got the most beautiful voice I've ever heard. Worth waiting for. Bye." He hung up without waiting for her response.

She slowly hung up and sat there looking at the phone, loving Paulie for simply being himself. Then she came alert. Swinging the chair around, she found herself facing Casey. He was leaning against the jamb of the open office door, arms folded across his chest, and he had, from all appearances, been standing there for quite some time.

Delilah was torn. Fear about what he might have heard of her conversation and how he might interpret it, and righteous anger that he should dare to so openly invade her privacy warred within her. Righteous anger, fueled by the nagging resentment of his spying on her at the brook, won.

She stood up to face him. "Well, look who's here," she said, her voice dripping with loathing, the treble tones almost humming with anger. "Tell me, Doctor Casey Lowell, Junior, does Brighton Foundation pay you overtime for night work like this?" Her tone was scathing, years of resentment riding each clearly enunciated word. "I imagine they do because lurking around like some foul-smelling, eavesdropping fungus must take a special kind of talent."

She slammed the half-full glass of milk down on the tray, spilling some of it on the small plate of cookies, picked up the tray and started toward the door. As she went past him, she asked, "By the way, do they furnish the binoculars you use in your spy work, or do you have to furnish your own?"

Unable to stop herself now that the dam had, in effect, burst, she turned back to pick up her game book. "Tell me, Doctor Casey Lowell, Junior, why didn't you write in your little report that Delilah Cross was naked the last time you spied on her at the brook? Certainly that fact must have all sorts of deep psychological implications that Brighton Foundation would want to know about!"

She stood there looking straight at him, her eyes blazing. A memory of the incident in the kitchen came to her, the pheromone odor of sexual arousal. "Or is spying on naked girls your special private sexual fetish? Is that why you were sitting in a dark kitchen at four o'clock in the morning?" With that parting shot, she went down the stairs, her heels stomping hard on each step as though punctuating her angry thoughts.

Casey's first thought was that he had just been taken down, and taken down very royally, by a woman. By an adult female, not a girl. The thought chased itself around his mind. His second thought was a sense of wonder at the extent of her vocabulary and her use of it. For someone who had been mute for at least eight years since childhood, she used her voice extremely well, insult after insult precisely spoken with exactly the right tonal quality to emphasize their intended meaning. He found he was sweating as he went down the hall to his room and closed the door.

He had spent most of the evening in the bunkhouse with his family, laughing, talking, and playing with the children. Then, when Kaydee announced their bedtime and Samantha retired to her ever-present notebook, he and his Dad went for a long, leisurely walk around the farm, enjoying the evening cool and the feeling of being far from urban bustle and noise. They sat on the bank by the stream in companionable silence listening to the murmuring of flowing water for a while. Then crossed it on the stepping stones, and followed the path across the field to the stile.

As they paused there, Casey took the opportunity to ask a question that had been bothering him. "Dad, what is going on with Sarah and this Agnes Kittridge thing? If she had any knowledge of Delilah's files, she would know Kittridge worked for Brighton during that time period. I mean, wasn't she still working for them at their headquarters then? And there are no reports filed from here, at least none that I was given. That really bothers me because it's obvious that Brighton hasn't forgotten about Delilah or I wouldn't be here."

K.C.'s frown was etched into his face by shadows cast by the moonlight. "I wish I knew, Casey. I don't think Sarah is lying, or even intending to deceive about this. She's just too openly honest in her conviction that Kittridge wasn't working for Brighton at that time. For the life of me, I can't imagine what makes her so sure about it."

He took off his glasses, rubbed his eyes, and sighed deeply as he replaced them. "We could simply confront her, Casey, just hand her the Bhutu Holding Facility record folders and let her read them for herself, but I'm reluctant to slap her down like that. It's not really urgent right now, and she seems to be using her mysterious Brighton friend to get information. What do you think? Shall we just wait a bit?"

Casey nodded. As usual, he thought, K.C. was right and it didn't seem urgent enough to confront Sarah with right now. "Fine with me, Dad," he said, and they climbed over the stile and strolled up Palmer Road toward the farm.

On their way back up the driveway, they saw the light upstairs in the office. After saying good night to his Dad by the bunkhouse, Casey continued on to the farmhouse. When he came upstairs, it was his intention to turn off the office light, and he stuck his head around the door just as Delilah was punching up a number on the desk phone.

The idea that he was spying on her hadn't entered his mind. He was surprised that she was going to talk to someone on the telephone, and felt a compelling need to know who she was calling, and why. He hadn't thought beyond satisfying that curiosity. Indeed, he made no attempt to conceal his presence, standing there like some brainless oaf with his ears flapping. His own self-loathing exceeded anything Delilah might be feeling, he was sure of that.

Now, he was straddling the uncomfortable horns of that beast called dilemma. Regret that he had violated her privacy again, sparking her obvious and well-justified anger, vied with intense interest in the strange content of her conversation with someone named Paulie, who, judging from her comment about the rest of the family, was Harold Newcombe's son. She had been on the computer just before the call, and when he thought about it, he realized that she had not shut it down when she made her angry exit.

He went back to the office to turn it off, and saw the words on the screen. On three separate lines were the words, "Granted."

"Granted." "Granted." Those three words kept him awake for hours as he tried vainly to fit them into her conversation with Paulie. What had been granted . . . and by whom?

Delilah had always been able to talk. That's what she said. One theory fully substantiated. And even though she and Paulie seemed to share a long-standing relationship that had apparently gone unnoticed, even by Paulie's father, the news had been a surprise to him.

Casey marveled at the self-control and discipline that Delilah had exercised, beginning when she was only eight years old. Incredible, he thought. And there were good reasons for her silence, she had said that, reasons that she wanted to discuss face-to-face with Paulie. A twinge of something he refused to identify brought vertical frown lines to his forehead.

Judging from her end of the conversation, this was not a resumption of a childhood relationship that had ended when she left Hiller School. It was too relaxed and easy, in spite of the obvious emotional impact it was having. Probably been keeping in touch by mail, he thought. He could check that out with Sarah easily enough, he thought, then stopped himself. Delilah's mail was none of his business.

Another theory was substantiated, too. The medallion, Casey thought. Paulie knew all about it. It's on my dresser, she had said, mentioning the other two things that sat there. He puzzled over her statement about something very bad happening on that particular day, something worse than being bitten, something that Paulie didn't know about. And it hadn't been run over by a lawnmower, they had pounded it . . . together. The twinge of something returned.

And the bonobo figure. Paulie knew all about that, too. Apparently the two of them had worked together to discover the exact species of ape it represented, and had done it when they were quite young. The small inner twinge that he refused to acknowledge grew stronger than before.

Then there was that strange mode of speech she had gone into, almost a parody of old English style. Apparently, Paulie understood the style and content, and, for a moment, Casey was disturbed by the implication that there were other people involved in what almost sounded like a conspiracy to commit a crime.

The thought made him smile. Talk about becoming paranoid, he thought. Delilah and Paulie were just teenagers, and because he was discovering such depth and complexity in the private, heretofore concealed life of the much observed, closely-scrutinized Delilah Cross, did not mean every small thing had some portentous hidden meaning.

He came to the final thing on his mental list, and frowned. Who was the other person who had helped Delilah? It was not Paulie's father, Harold Newcombe, and it wasn't Sarah, either. She had spoken sadly, in the past tense. That shadow figure, someone named Auntie?

It wasn't until he was almost asleep that the import of her parting shots registered on him. She had been reading his reports! That realization kept him awake for another hour. When he did sleep, it was restless, disturbed by dreams of being faced with the task of capturing dozens of laughing Delilahs, each different, each dissolving and slipping away as he tried with all his might to catch her.

CHAPTER SIXTEEN

Delilah called Paulie on Saturday afternoon and spoke to him briefly. Now, a few hours later, she sat at the computer in the corner office space waiting for Merlin, Darkling, and Hunter to log on. She closed the main office door to the hall when she came in, hoping that if Doctor Big Ears Casey Lowell, Junior was lurking about, he would get the message and go away. Since she had so clearly stated her opinion of him and his spying activities, he had kept his distance, but he was watching her all the time. She could feel it. He was aware of her . . . just as she was aware of him.

Lurking, she thought, watching. No, not really descriptive of his present behavior. Actually, he avoided looking at her and maintained a respectable physical distance between them, even at the dinner table when everyone gathered for their communal evening meal. His family had been friendly and open, including her in the laughing banter that seemed to be their normal dinner table conversation. She liked them and they all seemed to fit right in with the Clement family, too; the two groups merged and melded with no sign of awkwardness or fencing for position. Everyone seemed assured of their particular place, meeting as equals. This thought caused Delilah to frown. What was her place? She was not a blood member of either group and she certainly wasn't an equal. The question disturbed her and she didn't pursue it any farther.

K.C. didn't give any indication that he was exercising his professional skills or even observing her, either. That was good because she liked him very much. His thoughtful way of speaking and his soft, soothing voice pleased her, as did the easy way he interacted with the two children. Elder statesman, she thought. She had recently run across that term and wondered about it. Older, wiser, dominant male was how she defined it for herself now.

But something had been nagging at her like an annoying gnat, coming back again and again to pester. With an agile mental snap, she caught it. Casey's behavior reminded her in a way of how Sammy Truesdale acted after she had forcibly removed him from the bathroom at Hiller School. She smiled. It was not a nice smile, but before she could follow the thought, the computer demanded her attention with a soft warning ding-ding.

One by one, Merlin, Darkling, and Hunter logged on, and she wasted no time, immediately beginning to type, using their habitual game language. It seemed easier that way, distanced from herself and assuming the Chameleon persona. In a way, it would be easier for all of them, making the transition from fantasy to fact seem almost natural in its progression.

She smiled as she typed the first sentence. To a casual observer, it would have appeared to be a continuation of the fantasy adventure that they had played for more than two years, a new plot, perhaps, but merely an elaboration of their already existing, carefully-woven shadow world.

"Here, then, speaks Chameleon, she who has a secret. There be strange things afoot, comrades, and she wishes to enlist your aid in a new, exciting, and mayhap dangerous quest. Are all willing to consider this proposal that will halt our present endeavor for the nonce?"

The "Ayes" came quickly, and she continued. "Then hear ye this tale, and hear ye it well, for the path we must follow is dark and treacherous, full of pitfalls for the unwary. Capture by enemies will result in unspeakable indignities and agonies too hideous to contemplate. Understand ye well, comrades, the dangers be many, often lurking in unsuspected places." She paused a moment, thinking, then continued, this time using the story-telling style often used to set the scene for video game players. "Here, then, is the story of the captives:

'In days gone by, deep in a jungle far away from civilization, lived a people in peace and tranquility. They were an innocent people, who, if they thought about it at all, identified themselves only as the group. They were happy and content with their primitive lot, having never known anything else, and life proceeded through the generations undisturbed for a very long time. They had no written records or verbal history, so the length of time is unknown.

Then, a bad thing happened. They were discovered by outsiders, whom they thought of as them, the others, those who are different from us of the group. Not warlike by nature and having no weapons, group members were helpless to do anything except wave their arms, shake branches, yell empty threats . . . and flee. The others soon captured several of them and carried them away into captivity. They only took females, forcing some of them to leave their babes and younglings behind. Many of the babes died because of this, and there was great mourning in the group.

These others had prepared a very special prison for their captives; it was not more than two days travel by foot from the home of the group, but that was much farther than any of them had ever traveled. Because they had no conception of the meaning of prison or captivity, they made no attempt at rescue.'"

Delilah stopped again. She realized that she had to go carefully, giving enough information but not too much and she was finding it difficult. This was going directly out on the line to her friends with no chance to rewrite, and she was becoming tense. Of the three people reading this as she wrote, only Paulie knew her background, and she could almost feel him sitting on the edge of his chair, his mind working furiously as he added things together.

Taking a deep breath, she went on. "'There were only a few of the others, and it is most likely there was only one in charge who hired a few people to help him. What they were doing to their captives was kept a secret, known only to themselves and perhaps one or two others living in another country far away. It was these others in another country who gave the orders, supplied the money, furnished the necessary supplies, and made this thing possible. That much is known. Perhaps they received reports . . . and perhaps they didn't. That fact is unknown . . . solving the riddle of those reports is a vital part of this quest.

Many years went by. Some of the captives died- -or were killed- -in that special prison. From time to time, more members of the group were captured to replace them. It is believed that many generations of these captives existed, but it is not known how many. Then something happened.
No more group members were taken for a time. All of the captives in that prison had died or been killed . . . except two. They were the last, and they were sisters. The older one managed

to escape and make her way back to the group. She learned about the group and their general location from her mother, who had, in turn, learned it from her mother, and so on back through the generations. They had guarded and held on to a belief in group, and home, and freedom that had become only hearsay during all the years and generations of their captivity.

It was very hard for the one who escaped. There had been many changes during the generations of isolated captivity, and she wasn't the same as the group any more. But she persevered, adapted, and learned their ways, even fighting when it became necessary, and finally they accepted her into the group as one of them.'"

This time, the pause was longer before Delilah continued. What to say? What not to say? How to say enough . . . but not too much? Finally, she went on.

"'The last living captive mourned for her older sister. She was alone and very afraid. For two long years she thought about escape, feeling more frightened and desperate every day, afraid to leave the security of her captivity, afraid of what would happen to the babe she was carrying if she didn't. Finally, she made the decision to leave, and she had to kill her captor in order to do so. Perhaps it was easy because he had grown old and complacent across the years he had run this secret, terrible prison. That this was not the same other as in the beginning, but one who had taken his place, is known. It was he that she killed. His name is not known . . . and that, too, is part of the quest.'"

Delilah leaned back in her chair, aware of a slight headache beginning at the base of her skull. Muscles, she thought. I'm strained to the breaking point. Even my teeth hurt from clenching them. She raised her arms and massaged the back of her neck, feeling the muscles relax. Taking a sip of milk, she continued, thinking that there wasn't much farther to go. She had come this far, and she could finish it, this tale of innocence betrayed, durance vile, anguish, a captive mother, and finally murder. It was the very dream stuff from which they wove their fantasy worlds, was it not? What, she wondered, were Darkling and Merlin and Hunter thinking now?

"'She who had killed was heavy with child and she was injured in the struggle with the other. It took her a long time to find the group because they moved from place to place in their territory. She got lost, she did not know how to find food, and sometimes, in her hunger, she ate bad things that made her sick. Finally, she could go no further. It was dark and she sat under a tree, crying and calling out for her sister. It was then that fortune smiled . . . or perhaps God finally took pity on her. That is not known.'"

The words she had just written sat on her monitor screen accusingly. Where had that come from? Was that what she really thought? Certainly, she had actively pursued the concept of God

385

since, in her innocence, she reasoned out that the God of Miss Agnes lived in the clock . . . or was the clock. The last four words she had written struck her. "That is not known." Who did know? She pushed the questions aside and went back to the story.

"'The sister heard her cry and came to her. The sister took care of her, protected her, and found her food, but she did not survive. She died less than a four months after her babe was born. The name of this last captive was Mandy. That is known.'"

Delilah stopped again, unable to go on. Mandy, she thought. Finally, I have written your name. You will be remembered. They will carry on the battle long after these written words have disappeared into the static-filled blackness of electronic space.

"'The sister took Mandy's babe as her own, raising it and teaching it all the things it should know about the present . . . and the past.'" Delilah took a deep breath. Up to this point, her whole story could easily be dismissed as a fanciful, somewhat dramatic game tale; what she would say next brought it into reality, the here and now. "That, then, comrades, is the tale of the past, bygone years. But wait, there is more . . . the story is not yet ended.

'A long, peaceful time went by, perhaps as much as ten years. Then, the others came back to this far away place, found the group, and captured Mandy's babe, who was now a youngling. What happened to this youngling is not known.

Two years after that, they came again, this time capturing the sister of Mandy. They took her back to their country and placed her with others from different groups, all of them held in one place together. There, she had a babe of her own, perhaps to relieve the loneliness she felt at the loss of her sister's child whom she had loved dearly. This is known. They were last seen, mother and babe, four years ago. This is known. The place is also known.

Now heed this carefully, because it is important. The sister of Mandy, the last survivor of that terrible time of captivity, has an identifying mark, one that was used to permanently identify certain of the captives, and by this mark you will know her from all others.

This thing was done by the other who was killed by Mandy. He used acid to brand them, slowly drawing letters one by one high on the left side of their chests close to their shoulders. They were fully awake, strapped down on a table when this was done, and they screamed and writhed in agony, helpless to do more. The scars of that acid burning are distinctive and deep, deep as pain, deep as a lifetime. The sister of Mandy has four X's, all in a neat row, burned into the flesh near her left shoulder. That is known.'

So, now the tale of the captive generations is ended, but where it ends, the quest begins. It is twofold. The first part is to find the sister of Mandy and her babe, who is now a youngling. They are surely still captives who have suffered great wrongs through no fault of their own. The second part is more complex, following a twisted, well-concealed trail backward through time for perhaps a half a century or more to find those truly responsible for this outrage. Yes, one of the others who actually did these things is long dead at the hands of one he abused, and rightfully so. But those shadowy figures in the background, those others who supported and enabled and protected, deserve to face justice also, deserve to be exposed for who they are and what they did . . . and, perhaps, are still doing in some other part of the world.

Hearing all this, my fellow warriors, do you now wish travel along with me? My quest is not for the faint of heart, nor is it a matter of bold battle. There are no dragons here, at least not those who can be slain by sword in honest confrontation. Rather, it requires the patience of a spider, detecting prey in the smallest vibration of web. The swiftness and lightness of foot of a practiced thief, and the cunning and wit of a wily magician to cast spells of invisibility so no one can say where they traveled or why . . . these are the qualities needed here. Understand well before you commit to this new adventure that the price of discovery could be higher than you might expect or be willing to pay. And now the story is done . . . or has it just begun?"

Delilah sighed as she leaned back in her chair, her hands dropping limply into her lap. She was finished, and as she waited she wondered anxiously if she had said too much. Or too little?

The responses came quickly, and Delilah smiled in relief as they came up on her monitor screen. How could she have doubted them?

From Darkling: "Bravo, Chameleon! At last, a righteous quest worthy of my skill!"

From Merlin: "You tell a compelling tale of good and evil, Chameleon. There can be no greater quest than righting a wrong of this magnitude!"

From Hunter: "Chameleon has, indeed, shed her skin and wrapped herself in rainbows! Behold, fellow warriors, and rejoice in the wonder of her true colors! Let the game begin. Evil-doers await our attention!"

"Thank you, comrades," Delilah typed quickly. "My tasks have become many and varied. The need for concealment is great. With permission of the mighty Hunter, I request that all things concerning our quest be cleared through him. Agreed?"

Had Casey seen the monitor, he might have spent another restless night wondering at the three words that appeared one after the other on separate lines. "Agreed." "Agreed." "Agreed." And well he might have wondered who had agreed . . . and to what.

After she logged off and shut down the computer, Delilah sat back and waited. She was tired, her shoulders climbing toward her ears with strain. She was full of doubts. It had been very hard to tiptoe around the truth like that. How many of the things she had avoided saying-or lied about-would Paulie pick up on or read between the lines?

She didn't have long to wait. She was sure he would call and he did, apparently just as sure that she would wait for his call.

"Hi, Paulie," she said tiredly in a low voice.

Without preliminary niceties, Paulie plunged right in. "That's what happened at the zoo, isn't it? You found her, didn't you?" They were statements, not questions, and he went right on. "What I want to know is why did she bite you? She did bite you, didn't she?" This time it was a question, and he waited for her answer.

"Yes, she bit me, not that young male I pointed out. And yes, I was protecting her. Paulie, have you any idea how unexpected that meeting was? Neither of us was prepared for it, and we both made mistakes, bad ones." She rubbed the faint scar on her wrist, as she had many times before, a visible sign, a talisman.

He waited, saying nothing, so she continued. "I rushed her, went right up to the bars and called to her. She knew it was me, finally, and came to me. I looked different and I smelled different, a lot different, but she recognized me, and she was frightened." Paulie still said nothing. "We hadn't seen each other in three years. This is a confidence, Paulie, only for you ears, okay?" Without waiting, she went on, taking his assurance of silence for granted.

"Those two years at the Bhutu Holding Facility were pure hell for me. Paulie, Agnes Kittridge was totally insane, but I had no way of knowing that. I had nothing to judge by. Other than the two men who caught me and the three men who examined me before I was taken to Bhutu, she was the first human I had ever seen . . . as far as I remembered," she added carefully.

"What is her name, Delilah?" Paulie asked, his voice gentle, careful not to disturb or disrupt the delicacy of the moment. "What is the name of this ape mother you love so much?"

"She was called No Name, Paulie. She was never given a name, just branded with four X's. I called her Auntie." Delilah felt guilty at not telling him the whole truth, but she was walking a very narrow line, now, and determined to protect the secret at all costs. She had violated enough of Auntie's confidence in her, but she consoled herself with the thought that, in the end, the benefits for Auntie and her babe would far outweigh the betrayal.

"Anyway, she was the only mother I knew. That whole first year in Bhutu she came to visit me at night, sitting on a box outside my window. Just the fact that she found me there, came to that place where she had spent five years in captivity, the place where she was born and branded, came in spite of her obvious fear of the place . . . that was mother love, Paulie. Bhutu was the place, the bad place of her nightmares, the place of the captivity. But after a year she didn't come any more. I like to think she was still close, and sometimes when I called, I thought I heard her answer, but she didn't come any more."

Her voice broke, but she went on, "She brought me good things to eat. Sometimes it was a piece of fruit, and we would have to lick it off our hands and the steel mesh that covered the window to keep me from running away. It's hot there, and things like that attracts flies. Then, we would just lean against each other through the mesh, satisfied to be together."

Her voice became fainter, musing. "There were so many different kinds of flies. Miss Agnes hated flies. She made me official fly-killer and that's when I learned how many different kinds there are. She had a quota of how many flies I had to kill every day. She had a little can, you see, and I had to put all the flies I killed in that little can so she could count them every evening when she put them in the trash."

"She counted the flies?" Paulie's voice was full of a kind of amazed wonder.

When she continued, it was with a kind of lightness that caused Paulie to frown because it was so inappropriate for the sick insanity of what she was describing.

"At first, I didn't know how to count. She knew that, but it didn't seem to matter. For a long time, I wondered how she came up with the number of flies I had to kill every day. It was thirty-three, and it was only after I had been at Hiller School a while that I found out that twice thirty-three is sixty-six, the number of the beast from the Bible. Remember when we talked about that, Paulie? You thought it was dumb of me to be so interested in things like that. Well, now you know why. I was trying to find answers, some kind of logic in what went on there at Bhutu."

Paulie remembered all right, and he had to fight a growing feeling of unreality as she continued to rationally connect different pieces of her past, creating a picture that he didn't want to look at but couldn't avoid.

"When I finally figured it out I laughed, but I really wanted to cry. It wasn't funny. I had to have exactly thirty-three flies in that little can every day. Anything but thirty-three dead flies got me a beating with her correctional implementer, and I learned to count in a hurry . . . all day long every day I killed and counted flies. Sometimes I killed more, but I learned to hide their little squashed fly bodies and add them to the can when I ran short on my quota. I really learned to be a good sneak, Paulie. And that can, I can still see it in my mind, just as clear now as it was then. It was a pea can."

Her giggle was as unexpected as it was jarring. "That's cute," she said. "Properly stated, it was a can that had contained peas, not a can into which one peed, nor a was it a type of nut that southerners call 'pecans'. No, it's the label I remember. I would look at it and wonder how the peas got into the can, and how many peas had been in the can, and how such a beautifully

393

colored, realistic picture of peas got on the can in the first place. The picture was much prettier and brighter than the peas were. I noticed that and wondered what had happened to them in the can. Isn't it strange how a child's mind works?" she asked, then went on without waiting for an answer.

"Miss Agnes never knew I hid flies. She never knew about the nighttime visits or the way I prowled around the building at night, either. There were lots of things she never knew because her God didn't tell her. I used to wonder about that, too. I mean why He didn't tell her. I think she would have beaten me to death if she had known." Delilah's voice trailed off, leaving only the faint humming sound on the lines that connected them.

Then, "Do you know I still can't help following flies with my eyes? I try to guess where they will land, and how long they will stay when they do. Most of the time I'm right, too. I learned a lot of things about flies, what they like best to eat, where they like to sit to sleep. Did you know they make a kind of a half-loop when they land on the ceiling?" She paused, thinking about flies. Paulie could think of nothing to say.

"They learn, too. I chased one particular fly for a week, a big black one. He was loud and not very fast, but every time I got just close enough to swat him, he'd zip away, just out of my reach. You see, in the daytime when Miss Agnes wasn't right there with me, she kept me on a leash that snapped into a ring she screwed

394

into the wall, and that fly seemed to know just how far it reached. I think he was enjoying the whole thing. They do enjoy things, you know. Finally, he found a little blob of jelly on the table and settled down to a fly-feast. I waited patiently until he was so busy eating he forgot to watch for me, and I splatted him good." She chuckled.

"But," she concluded sadly, "I splatted him too loud and too hard. I woke Miss Agnes up from her nap and that was bad. She beat me good, and wouldn't let me fish him out of the jelly and put him in the pea can. I never did get to count him."

Paulie had been figuratively holding his breath, knowing he was hearing things not really meant for his ears, things that she didn't realize she was saying out loud. He remembered the strange little girl Delilah had been when they first met as children nearly six years ago. She had come directly from that place, that hellhole, he thought. And the things she was saying now were the things that she had never said but carried inside herself because she would not talk and would not write them. He shuddered, feeling the pain deep inside himself, not only shocked but physically nauseated at the insanity and horror she was describing in such a matter-of-fact way. He suddenly wished for his Father. His Father would know how to handle this, how to cope with it without harming Delilah.

Then, Delilah was speaking again, resuming the story as

though she had never digressed, as though the madness and brutality she had just described, the flies, the leash, the insane woman who had beaten her had never existed.

"Her coming to see me there, in that place, kept me in touch with reality, and even at that, I don't really know why I didn't go completely crazy. Or maybe I am. Sometimes it's hard to tell," she added thoughtfully.

This time the silence was long, but not uncomfortable.

"At first at the zoo," Delilah finally continued, "at first, she was so glad to see me, as glad as I was to see her. Then, I think she realized that I was a human, and she was afraid that I would draw attention to her, cause someone to take a closer look, endanger her babe. She is unique, Paulie, one of the last two captives, the last branded one."

Delilah stopped. Go carefully here, she thought. Bend the truth. "Anyway, she grimaced at me, threatened, telling me to go away. I didn't, I held on to her hand through the bars with both of mine, pulling at her. You know I'm strong, Paulie, and she bit me so she could get away. And then I ran, crying, hurt beyond anything you could imagine. I had, beyond all odds found my friend, my mother, and she rejected me. Now do you understand why I was pounding that medallion? I was trying, as a child would, to pound away the hurt by destroying it.

I'm glad I didn't because in some strange way that medallion became one of the symbols of my quest . . . and that's when I got so really interested in computers. I figured out that someone, I didn't know who, was responsible for what had happened to me and to her. And I was right, too. Agnes Kittridge was one of Brighton Foundation's valuable and trusted employees. So that's where I started."

She was back in the present now, and she was through talking, at least about the past. Paulie, though full of misgivings and sick with hurt for her, managed to keep it light. "Do you know what I think? Huh? I think, considering your neat tale on the computer, that you have found out one whole hell of a lot about this. One thing for sure, the three mighty computer hackers are going to find out the rest, and in damned short order, too."

He paused, thinking, then continued, "And do you know where we'll start?"

Delilah was relieved that he had smoothly moved on, not asking any of the questions that he probably had on his mind. She realized that she had done a lot of talking, but the words had just come out of their own accord. As she was discovering, sometimes uncomfortably, words couldn't be erased like a misspelled word on her notepad. "No, where?" she asked. She felt drained. All she wanted to do now was curl up in bed with her friend, Teddy Bear.

"We'll go right smack into Brighton Foundation's archives. I know they've got archives, all big organizations do. And Brighton isn't just a big one, Delilah, it's an old one. From what I've heard Dad say, they've been around forever. That kind thrives on records of every kind, filing, cross-filing, and re-cross-filing, leaving trails as broad as highways. And I don't think there will be any security firewalls on the information we're looking for, not the way we'll approach it."

She could hear enthusiasm bubbling in his voice. "I know you're tired, Delilah, but will you answer me a couple of questions? We can't just go barging in asking for information on feral children."

They both winced at the words, but he went on quickly. "And I don't think we should approach Bhutu Holding Facility directly either. What part of Africa, Delilah, and how did you get supplies? They probably used the same system when you were there that they did in prior years because it was already in place, just like they used Bhutu for you because it was already there."

"That's an easy one, Paulie. It's in Zaire and a small plane came in at a town not too far from Bhutu once a week at the same small place I flew out of when I came to Hiller School. Then, a man named Jono Sam picked the supplies up there and brought them to the facility in a truck." She chuckled, thinking of that strange parade, of Miss Agnes' measured steps as she led the truck in and out of the compound.

"He drove a blue pickup the same color as the cars Brighton

uses, and I only know his name because I found him in the Brighton personnel files. He's still on the Brighton payroll, by the way, and his father, who is also named Jono Sam, had the same job before him starting back in the thirties. Jono Sam, the son, gave me the carved bonobo figure at that airport the day I left." Why do I keep throwing out these little nuggets of information? Then she went on, too brain-tired to work at solving any more puzzles. "Miss Agnes gave him her list and whatever mail she had going out, and he gave it to the pilot the next week. It was a regular routine."

"Bingo!" Paulie almost shouted it out. "Airplanes use fuel and file flight plans . . . and pilots are on payrolls. That's more than enough for starters." He thought a minute, then asked, "One other thing, this man who was killed. Do you know how long ago that was? If he was a Brighton man, there has to be a record somewhere. I don't expect a full page obituary or anything, because the operation was obviously hush-hush, but there has to be some record of a field death like that in their records."

It took Delilah a little longer, but the answer came quickly enough. "It was probably about nineteen or twenty years ago, give or take a little. That would make it somewhere around 1982." After a moment, she added, "Sometime during the summer months."

Paulie was surprised at the certainty in her voice and the fact that she had narrowed it down to a three-month period, but he gave no indication. "That means whatever had been going on there could have started as early as, what, at least forty years before that, in the early 1940's, and probably before that." He whistled softly. "That's a great start, Delilah. I'll assemble the troops tomorrow, make battle plans, and mount the attack. On tiptoe, of course, " he added.

She joined in as he laughed, and they said good night, both of them aware that they were fully committed and might land in a great deal of trouble if they were caught. Though unvoiced, they were both having the same second thoughts, not about the quest but about the wisdom, or even fairness of involving Darkling and Merlin. They were long-time friends of Paulie's, and Darkling had dated Becky for a while. But neither of them had even a vague idea of what a famous-or infamous-person their Chameleon was, or how personally important this was to her.

Or maybe, after tonight, they did. The thought buzzed through her head like a clever fly, refusing to land so she could swat it. It was still there when she went to sleep, but at least she didn't dream, and her rest was peaceful.

CHAPTER SEVENTEEN

Delilah dreamed about the zoo that night. The colors, sounds and smells were vivid and clear, not dreamlike in any way. Like so many of her dreams about the past, the day at the zoo was a reliving of the event in her sleep. Sometimes she wondered if they were really dreams at all or if she was really asleep because she was always dimly aware that some part of herself was awake and watching, had been there before, and knew the inevitable outcome.

This outing was something special; Paulie and Becky talked of nothing else for a week. This was not unusual for Paulie, but extraordinary for Becky. She usually managed to sustain concentrated interest only in herself, clothes, and boys. Delilah was excited about it, too. They were going to the Landon Zoo to see something special, crossbred lion and tiger cubs on display for the first time.

"Tigons and Ligers and Bears, Oh my!" Paulie had said, growling and grimacing horribly.

As they were noisily taking their usual places in the family station wagon, Harold Newcombe, concerned and thoughtful, always aware of her background when others tended to forget it, touched Delilah's shoulder. "Are you sure that you understood what a zoo actually is, that it's a place where animals from all over the world are kept in captivity so people can see them and learn about them?" She nodded. Then he asked if she knew there were chimpanzees and other apes there, and would this bother her.

That question caused her to look up quickly, seeking eye contact with him. This was the first time he had ever directly referred to her early years, the years before Miss Agnes. She saw only concern for her in his eyes, and her hand automatically rose to touch his where it still rested on her shoulder. It was the group reassuring gesture, almost a stroking movement, but he was not aware of its significance and she was not consciously aware of having made it.

She couldn't answer this with a simple shake of her head because it was two separate questions. Harold often played this kind of game with her. She grinned at him and wrote, "Yes!" and "No!" underlining both words for emphasis. She had seen television shows about zoos and read everything she could find about them; she had watched the parts devoted to primates very carefully. They were captives much in the same way she had been at Bhutu, and still was if that meant being forced to be some place you didn't want to be doing things you didn't want to do with no choice in the matter. But the apes seemed fairly content and Delilah saw no one resembling Miss Agnes anywhere around, so she assumed that they were cared for and not beaten or otherwise abused.

Yes, Delilah thought, she understood about zoos. That confidence lasted until they reached the zoo, parked the car and were walking toward the entrance. Then, in one nearly overwhelming wave, the sounds and smells assaulted her senses. They were walking in a group, Becky, Paulie and Delilah in front, Harold and Dee Dee close behind. When she stopped, Dee Dee, who was saying something to Harold about ticket prices, bumped into her.

"Oh, are you all right?" Dee Dee was immediately all motherly concern, her hands fluttering from place to place like small birds as she touched Delilah here and there checking for damage.

Harold was watching Delilah's face. It had gone pale and he could see small beads of perspiration on her upper lip. Placing a comforting hand on her shoulder, he asked, "Is this going to be too much for you? Do you want to postpone this visit to another time? We can always come back another time, you know, or I can leave Dee Dee, Paulie, and Becky here, take you home, and come back easily enough."

He waited, watching the rise and fall of her chest and the

flaring of her nostrils as she fought for control. Slowly, the color returned to her face, and she shook her head.

"Are you sure, Delilah?" She nodded and managed a weak smile.

For once, Becky and Paulie said nothing though both of their faces registered concern. Delilah understood, and widened her smile to reassure them both. "No, I won't spoil the trip," the smile said to Becky, and, "Yes, I'm okay," was its message to Paulie, Dee Dee and Harold.

Harold purchased the tickets, led the way through the turnstile, then paused just inside. "Okay, group, what will it be? Souvenirs first or last, eat now or later?"

Delilah was surprised that they planned to eat in the zoo. The thought hadn't occurred to her, but she dutifully raised her hand to vote with Dee Dee, Becky, and Paulie when they chose souvenirs first, eat later, and they turned toward the gift shops just inside the entrance. It was a relief to Delilah to be inside. The sounds and smells of the animals were over-ridden by people voices and mixed store odors of scented candles and one she associated with new clothing coming from racks of brightly decorated T-shirts. As she followed the group around the store, a rack sitting on a counter caught her eye. It was filled with what at first she took to be coins. On closer inspection, she could see that while they looked like big silver coins, they were imprinted with the zoo name and pictures of various animals. There was one, in particular, that she took from the rack and inspected closely. The animal in the center was a chimpanzee, and around the outer edge, forming a circular frame, was embossed "Landon Zoo and Botanical Garden."

"Do you like that one, Delilah?" She was startled. She had been so engrossed in the medallion that she hadn't been aware of Paulie coming up behind her, but she saw that he wasn't engaged in a stalking game.

"Let me buy it for you," he said. "Oh, look at that!" He picked up a different one. "Here's a Tigon. I want this one."

He took both to the cash register and paid for them, proudly handing the small plastic bag containing the chimpanzee to her, as he pocketed the one he had chosen. "I think they're both neat, don't you? Maybe I'll start a collection. Hey, that's a good idea. I've already got one from the carnival and another one from the flea market."

Delilah nodded and smiled her thanks. Paulie was a good friend, she thought, not for the first time, and an honest person, too. Unlike Becky and some of the other people she had met, his smell always matched his words and facial expressions.

She was thinking hard, trying to prepare herself for the onslaught outside, as they all stood waiting for Becky to make up her mind which T-shirt design she wanted. "Oh, Mom, can't I have both of them?" Becky asked. When Dee Dee said no, Becky pouted prettily and turned to Harold. "Please, Daddy?"

Paulie groaned, and then, twisting his face into a mocking pout, said in a quavering falsetto voice, "Oh, please, Daddy, can't I have two medallions?"

Harold, struggling with a grin, shook his head at Paulie, and said, "Becky, that hasn't worked since you were five years old and I'm continually amazed that you keep on trying. Now pick a T-shirt and get it over with, or we'll leave and you won't even get one."

In a remarkably short time, Becky made her choice, and they were back outside. Delilah was better prepared now; as they walked along, she could distinguish several varieties of birds and animals fairly close to them, but the odors weren't overwhelming because she expected them. They were coming to the reptile house, no mistaking that particular musty-acrid odor, but there was another dank, swampy smell coming from somewhere behind the building. It made her very uncomfortable, reluctant to go any closer. No one questioned it when Delilah indicated that she would rather wait outside while the others went through the reptile exhibit. After all, lots of people had an aversion to snakes.

As she sat on a bench near the reptile house entrance, sharing it with an elderly couple, she couldn't help grinning to herself. What would these people think if she told them that from time to time in her early life she had thoroughly enjoyed eating the raw bits and pieces of snake she managed to coax from one of the group members? Her nose told her that several antelope species were quartered nearby, too. She wondered if there were any small Bush bucks there. She had eaten raw bits and pieces of them, too. At the time though, their name, like so many other food names she learned from Auntie, was simply "good eat." She enjoyed their meat even more than snake.

She realized she was hungry and the nearness and the smell of what had been "good eat" not so long before was causing these uncivilized thoughts. Civilized, she thought, a good, solid, Miss Agnes word. I wonder if I will ever fit the meaning of that word deep down inside where the real me lives? She had another thought. Did regular people have these reactions, too? Did this elderly couple feel something, however dim and not consciously realized? Is that why they were busily eating from the bag of peanuts they shared, jaws working in unison as though they had practiced chewing together for a long time? Did their old instincts tell them that food was nearby, thus triggering hunger? Is that why everyone seemed to be eating?

She looked around. Most of the people walking past her held some sort of food, were actually eating something as they walked, or gave off the strong odor of just having eaten something. Even small children in strollers seemed to be busy with their bottles or poking bits of food in their mouths. Delilah was still engrossed in exploring this idea when the Newcombes came out of the snake house, blinking in the sunlight as their eyes adjusted from the dimness inside.

"Boy, am I ever hungry," Paulie said, echoed by Becky's, "Me, too," which she immediately followed with a demand for a hamburger, fries, and a cold drink from the nearest refreshment stand.

"What are you grinning about?" Harold asked Delilah. She shrugged, then pulled her notepad and pencil from the small tote bag slung over her shoulder. She didn't like to carry purses or bags, but the new jeans that Becky insisted fit her "just right" were too tight to put anything in the pockets. It's dumb to sew on pockets if you can't use them, she thought, as she wrote, "I'm hungry, too," and then, "everyone is eating." She gestured to the people in their area. Indeed, all of them seemed to be eating or drinking something. She touched her stomach, which had just rumbled loudly, and wrote, "Why is everyone so hungry?"

"That's a darned good question, Delilah," Harold answered, his eyes narrowing a little as he thought about it. Her questions were always good ones, he realized, and never casually asked. "Now that you mention it, we always seem to eat our way through these visits to the zoo."

He turned to Dee Dee. "Did you ever notice how many

refreshment stands there are? There are two full-service restaurants here, too, and all of them are always busy. Why do you think that is, Dee Dee?"

Dee Dee puzzled over this for a moment, then said, "Maybe it's all the walking in the fresh air?" As usual, when asked for her opinion, what started as a statement underwent a metamorphosis in mid-sentence, rising to a question mark at the end. "Oh well, shall we get something to eat now?"

Without further discussion, they joined the line of people waiting at the nearest concession stand, and in a surprisingly short time stood holding their containers of food and drink, looking for a place to sit down and eat. Every available place was already occupied, so, after a minute or two spent waiting hopefully for someone to get up and leave, Harold suggested they walk down to the Botanical Garden. It wasn't as busy as the areas near the concession stands, he explained for Delilah's benefit, and they should be able to find benches where they could sit and eat in pleasant surroundings.

He looked at them over his glasses. "That is, if no one's in danger of dying of starvation on the way." It wasn't a question and there were no objections as he turned and led the way, walking briskly down a wide, graveled path between the trees.

The Landon Zoo was a showplace, a state-of-the-art creation that gave the illusion of a completely natural setting for both animals and people. The various animal enclosures were spacious, and few bars were visible except in those exhibits where visitors were allowed to get a closer view of the animals. Both sides of the paths between areas were heavily planted with trees, shrubs, and flowers, and followed the gently rolling contours of the land. The entrance to the gardens lay at the end of the path at a T-intersection. Signs to either side announced "Large Carnivores" to the left, and "Primates" to the right, which delighted Paulie.

"Hey, this is just where we want to be! The tigons will be with the large carnivores!"

As Paulie led the way into the botanical gardens at a trot, a lion roared angrily, the sound echoing as it tapered off to an irritated coughing rumble. The breeze was coming from that direction, and Delilah, bringing up the rear, shivered slightly at the mingled smells of raw sexual readiness and frustration that it carried. She didn't have to see them to understand the anger and frustration of the male lion at being unable to reach the estrus-reeking, ready female calling urgently from the enclosure next to him.

They found two benches near the entrance, and quickly consumed their lunches, dropping their containers in a nearby trash can with some good-natured joking about litterbugs and what their size and color might be. Then, Paulie hurried on ahead, and the others followed. Delilah, bringing up the rear of the

Newcombe family parade, paused just outside the entrance as the others disappeared from view around a bend in the path to the left. She had half-turned to follow them when the breeze changed, coming now from the direction of the primate exhibit.

She stood very still for a moment, trying to understand. Mixed in with other, half-familiar odors and sounds, she smelled and heard group. It was definitely group, but not her group . . . or was it? Without hesitation, she turned and ran to the right, toward the primate exhibit, following the curve of the path around to the entrance. She paused, taking a deep breath, waiting for her heart to stop pounding before she walked through the entrance. This is impossible, her mind told her, this is a mistake . . . then she went in.

The various apes were separated according to species, housed in large enclosures with tree trunks and limbs for climbing, heavy ropes for swinging, shelves and ledges for sitting, and buckets and balls and other things for playing. Open doors led to inside quarters. There were perpendicular bars separating the apes from the visitors, with an additional waist high horizontal bar running the length of each area to indicate that people shouldn't approach any closer.

The now strong group smell was coming from around a corner, and as she came closer her nostrils flared, sorting out individuals, while her ears isolated sounds. Pre-puberty female, a stranger.

Male youngling, a stranger. Adult female, a stranger. Older adult female, familiar. Babe, a stranger? Babe, not stranger. Female . . . familiar? Her heart thudded hard then seemed to turn into a stone lump in her throat. Auntie! Auntie was here!

Delilah ran around the corner, trying to take in everyone and everything at once. "Auntie," she called. "I'm here!" Fortunately, there were no people in this area; most of the visitors were congregated around an enclosure around the corner near the entrance where keepers were bringing in food for the chimpanzees. Later, Delilah realized that even if there had been people there it would have made no difference to her at that moment. Nothing meant anything except reaching Auntie.

And there she was, slowly approaching the bars that separated them. Delilah saw that she was carrying a babe, the babe who carried both its own and Auntie's smell. Quickly ducking under the horizontal railing and moving close to the bars, Delilah leaned into them, holding out her hands, tears running down her cheeks. For just a moment, Auntie hesitated, and Delilah made the sign of who she was. Then Auntie closed the distance, taking Delilah's hand, pressing close until their shoulders touched between the bars.

"It you," Auntie said softly, leaning forward until their faces were only inches apart, their eyes locked in silent communication, sharing breath in the group way. "Yes, it you."

The babe stirred, and Delilah gazed into its eyes. After a long, intense look, it gently touched her face. "Who?" it asked. "Who this?"

"Babe speaks?" Delilah asked, not quite understanding why she should be surprised. Then, the questions came. "How did you get here? What happened? Why are you in this zoo?" She would have continued but Auntie stopped her.

"Slow," she commanded. "I tell. Quiet. Listen." The quiet orders had the intended effect. Delilah calmed herself, taking time to glance around. They were still alone, although she could hear voices somewhere around the corner.

"Four not rain other come. Hide. Come again, hurt here." Auntie pointed to her thigh. "Sleep, wake, fight, more hurt, sleep, wake, here."

Delilah understood. "How long here?" she asked.

Auntie thought a moment. "Not know, rain, go inside." She patted the babe who had been listening intently. "You gone. Need. Get babe. Babe speak." Her forehead wrinkled. "Not speak? You not speak secret?"

"No," Delilah whispered. "Not speak secret. Need to get you out of here." The voices were getting closer, and Delilah knew someone would come around the corner any minute and she shouldn't be so close to the bars. "I'll come back soon. Get you and babe out of here!" Her voice was desperate, her need for

413

Auntie overwhelming in its intensity. "Get you out!"

"No!" The fierceness of Auntie's voice was chilling. "No!" she repeated. "Go now! Not come back. Not come back. Go!"

Delilah was shocked. Why was Auntie acting this way? Couldn't she see Delilah needed her? "No," her voice rose. "No, not go!"

The people were just around the corner when Auntie said one more time, "Go, not come back!" Her lips drew back exposing her teeth and she hissed loudly, her actions immediately imitated by the babe.

Delilah heard the babe say "Go!" just before Auntie barked a shrill, metallic danger call that brought an immediate response from the others. In the confusion of screams, threatening, jumping, and posturing, Auntie looked deep into Delilah's eyes, gave her hand a comforting squeeze, then raised it to her mouth. Before Delilah realized what was happening, Auntie had bitten her just above her left wrist, bitten her hard enough and deep enough to immediately draw blood.

As she jerked back away from the bars, Delilah looked at her bleeding wrist, unable to believe what Auntie had done. At the same time, Auntie backed away, too, losing herself and the babe in the noisy confusion of the group just as the first people hurried around the corner to see what was causing all the excitement.

For a moment longer, Delilah stood there, her eyes fixed on a rectangular plaque attached to a small stone pillar. "Bonobo Apes," she read, "Pan pan paniscus." Then, she ducked under the horizontal bar and ran.

The blood had almost stopped dripping from her wrist when Harold Newcombe found her in the botanical garden, huddled in a miserable ball on the bench where they had eaten their lunch. After some primary first aid and a temporary bandage applied by zoo medical personnel, he explained that she would have to go back to the primate exhibit and point out the ape that had bitten her. When she shook her head "No," he insisted. They had to isolate the animal for a while to make sure it hadn't transmitted rabies or some other disease through the bite, nothing more.

When Harold, in the company of several keepers and a zoo official, led Delilah back around the corner to the bonobo exhibit, she carefully avoided looking directly at Auntie, who sat quietly in a far corner holding her babe protectively against her chest as she watched Delilah. After a moment, Delilah pointed out the young male as the culprit. She felt no guilt about blaming it on him. Harold had said no harm would come to him . . . and she had to protect Auntie and the babe, didn't she?

Only after the others turned to leave did Delilah look directly at Auntie and see that she was making the sign of who they were. Tears came again as she made the sign of who they were in response, then turned and walked away, knowing that she would never come back to this place . . . could never come back no matter how much she might want to or need to.

After a trip to the hospital emergency room for a thorough cleansing of her wound, a more substantial bandage, and a painful tetanus booster shot, they went home. As the subdued group of zoo-goers got out of the station wagon in the driveway of the Newcombe's house, Harold announced in a "there will be no nonsense about it" voice that it would be an early bedtime for everyone. After a round of comforting pats and quiet good nights, Delilah trudged off toward the main building.

When Paulie took out the trash just before dusk that evening, he became curious about the strange noises he heard coming from the back corner of the Hiller School grounds. Following the sounds, he found Delilah sitting on the ground under one of the big trees. She had placed the chimpanzee medallion on a flat rock and was methodically pounding it with another. Tears were pouring down her face, mucous was dripping unnoticed from her nose, and she made small grunting, agonized moaning sounds with each blow she struck.

Paulie stood there watching for a minute or two, then turned and started to walk away. After a few steps he turned back, and without a word sat down in the dirt close beside her. After a while, the blows became slower and less forceful; finally Delilah just sat there holding the rock, staring down at the scarred and

416

battered medallion. The hurtful sounds had stopped, but tears were still running down her cheeks and dripping off of her chin. As though she had just become aware of them, she wiped her face and nose on the neat bandage that enclosed her left wrist, leaving it considerably worse for the wear.

Paulie reached over and gently took the stone from her hand. He looked at her, waiting until the intensity of his gaze caught her attention, as he knew it would. When she looked at him, he smiled. Delilah didn't notice that there were tears in his eyes, too. Then he began pounding the medallion, not stopping until it was nearly dark and her crying was done.

When Delilah woke up the next morning, it took her a moment to realize that she was not in her little white room at Hiller School, she was in her little rose room at Bent Tree Farm. There was no bandage on her left wrist, just a crescent-shaped silver scar . . . but there were tears on her cheeks, her pillow was damp, and Teddy Bear's face was wet as though he, too, had been mourning, sharing the pain of her loss.

CHAPTER EIGHTEEN

Something strange was happening to Sarah Clement. She could not remember the last time she felt indecisive about anything. Her days were filled with decisions large and small and always had been. She wasn't prone to second-guessing herself; the push-pull of emotions she was feeling now was both unwelcome and somehow threatening in a way she couldn't define.

She sat in an easy chair in the den of the gatehouse. Her feet were propped on an ottoman upholstered in fabric that matched the chair, neither of them matching anything else in the room. This room, the family room, as Joe insisted on calling it, was warm, inviting, and casual, a room that demanded nothing of you that you didn't want to do.

Television was there for watching, bookcases were filled for reading, and the sofa was there for napping. The worn and mismatched furniture, a collection of old favorites reflecting the individual tastes of herself, Joe, and Jordan, blended together comfortably. All in all, it was a room well suited for its intended purpose, Sarah thought, looking around. Strange how the big communal rooms of our tribal ancestors, places where every aspect of life from birth to death took place in the presence of others, have changed with the advent of efficient heating, lighting, and plumbing… and our need for privacy right along with it.

This thought led her to the consideration of the compartmentalization of our lives by rooms. Bedrooms clearly state their purpose, none-too-subtly demanding that you lie down, change clothes, sleep, or go somewhere else. Kitchens are for cooking and eating, temporary gathering places gradually falling into disuse, and bathrooms state their requirements, not encouraging dawdling. She pursued the idea a bit further, wondering if anyone had ever done any research on the subject, particularly as it related to the psychological effects of anomie, feeling alone and isolated from your own society, your own group, your own family. Even more important, had any of those people she had met ever experienced such isolation and alienation to the point of wreaking havoc in their personal lives?

Invariably, Sarah's thoughts continued and turned to Delilah and how such factors had played a defining role in the formation of Delilah's behavior and character. She took a deep breath. Okay, Sarah, she told herself, you've avoided it long enough. Pick up the phone and call Amanda. Either tell her the whole story about the pond and Delilah talking, or edit it down to something you feel comfortable with. There, she thought, is the problem . . . why do I feel so uncomfortable?

The feeling had slowly been taking shape, developing an ever more palpable form of its own over the last few months. Part of her success in life had come from an ability to think logically, forming conclusions based on reason rather than emotion, and she had been feeling an odd reluctance to talk to Amanda about Delilah. The last time she had talked to Amanda had been the unusual occasion of Casey Lowell's hiring with the stated reason of evaluating Delilah's status in her development. Casey had been an outsider and Sarah felt a bit stumped why Amanda had been so relentless in bringing Casey into the situation. When she looked for reasons, it came down to something in Amanda's voice when she asked about Delilah. There was a discordant note, almost as if there was something vital she urgently needed to hear, needed to know, and she was reaching for it over the telephone lines that connected them, grasping for it, then hanging up, both relieved and disappointed when it didn't come. It made Sarah uneasy and she could not say exactly why.

She owed Amanda Brighton a great deal, both professionally and personally. The fact that Delilah was now speaking, the strange circumstances that had brought it about, the way she partially revealed the cause of her water phobia . . . all this information should be given to Amanda immediately.

Yes, she owed Amanda, really owed her, perhaps even her life.

Through the three agonizing years it had taken to fight her way through the worst of the bulimia, Amanda kept her on the Brighton Foundation payroll, kept her on the job, making it clear that she was confident in Sarah's ability to do her job while fighting this tenacious disease. To the best of her ability she had reciprocated, working hard and long at her job of in-house psychiatric counselor for Brighton employees.

Through all those years, her contacts with Amanda had been on the phone, casual "how are you and the family getting on?" calls, with an occasional direct query about an employee Sarah was counseling. It was only within the last few months that Sarah realized with a distinctly uncomfortable feeling that the information she was giving Amanda during those casual, friendly calls had more often than not violated doctor-patient confidentiality. Somehow, there was now something disturbing in the tone of their conversations which made Sarah question if she really knew the actual reasons why Amanda wanted the information or what she was doing with it. And she had been reluctant to ask.

Sarah had timed her retirement to coincide with Joe's retirement from the University's Agriculture Department. A few months before, during one of Amanda's phone calls, Sarah had mentioned their plans to take lump-sum retirement benefits and buy a small farm, gladly swapping the noisy reality of urban living for a "howdy neighbor" rural atmosphere. That way, they could also furnish Jordan with the place he needed to continue his plant research, setting up a small greenhouse and lab, with land enough for experimental crops.

Sarah had been very open with her dreams of seeing that her grandchildren, when they came, had a place, a home place, where trees and fields and animals were as real as the cow dung in which they were sure to step. Amanda laughed when Sarah voiced these thoughts, the sound dry and raspy, reminding Sarah of autumn-dried leaves crackling beneath your feet. She remembered thinking that she had never heard Amanda laugh before. Her laugh was at odds with her soft, cultured speaking voice, and Sarah could almost imagine that they came from two different people.

It was three months after she revealed her retirement dreams that Amanda called with her proposition. Simply put, Sarah and Joe would take over operation of Bent Tree Farm, both of them on the Brighton Foundation payroll for a period of five years. The farm was almost ready to become fully operational, having only partially utilized its full potential. Sarah and Joe would have full authority to run it as they saw fit, providing a private, quiet place for various Brighton employees and grant recipients to work on individual projects undisturbed.

Then Amanda added, quite casually, that there was already a

large, new greenhouse and fully equipped experimental lab at Bent Tree, something that young Jordan should find interesting. Oh, and in addition to the extensive remodeling of the main house and barn, the gatehouse had been enlarged and modernized, turning it into a very comfortable family home. It had taken Sarah, Joe, and Jordan a week and a trip to Bent Tree Farm to accept the offer.

And it was nearly a year later when Amanda called to discuss Delilah Cross and the necessity of finding a place for her when she left Hiller School. The farm was running smoothly and the Clement family was busy and happy, completely satisfied with the new life-style. What a happy coincidence, Amanda said, that Sarah, of all people, just happened to be at Bent Tree Farm, the perfect place for the child to spend the next four years.

Of course, Amanda realized that it would be a terrible imposition. Sarah would be called on to keep a semi-professional eye on the child, but it wasn't a matter of treating the child, so Sarah would have no professional duties requiring that she research her files or anything like that. And her salary would increase, of course. Delilah was quite stable and intelligent, and she was a ward of Brighton Foundation. They paid for all her expenses, so it was understood that she should want for nothing. If Sarah would, from time to time, Amanda said, just give her a call to let her know how the child was doing, no further reports would be needed, certainly no time-consuming written reports of any kind.

It was then, in a very off-hand manner, Amanda had added that there had been some high-level discussions about closing down some of the Brighton facilities within the next five years, Bent Tree Farm among the ones being considered for closure. Should that happen, she would arrange for Sarah and Joe to buy it if they chose, and at a very good price, too.

That was the second time that Sarah heard her laugh, a chuckle that seemed to ooze down the lines and crawl into Sarah's head, causing her to jerk the receiver away from her ear, not sure why she did it. Interference on the telephone lines, she told herself, that's all. She put the receiver back to her ear and told Amanda how lucky Delilah was to have such a caring person looking out for her interests. After the slightest of pauses, Sarah agreed that Bent Tree Farm was the ideal place for the child to spend the next four years until she reached maturity at eighteen.

It was a little while later that she realized that Amanda Brighton had, in a roundabout way, offered the Clement family a kind of security few people could look forward to, and the prospect of owning Bent Tree Farm provided fuel for more than a few daydreams. It was only recently that Sarah began to wonder if it had been more a matter of presenting a tasty carrot on a stick to a donkey with tunnel vision than a genuine promise of future security.

So, two years ago, Delilah had come to Bent Tree Farm and Sarah had done her job, watching and reporting to Amanda. Sarah liked this strange, non-speaking girl on sight, feeling a kind of protective affinity for her that grew over time. When she thought about it now, Sarah realized that her desire to protect Delilah began on the day of her arrival. She even knew the exact moment it happened . . . when Delilah brought the bread and butter to her nose, and took a deep, appreciative sniff before looking around as though she had committed some offense for which she would be punished.

Sarah sighed and got up from her chair. When she analyzed it, her feelings for Delilah were like her feelings for Jordan . . . motherly. In her own way, she was just as emotionally involved as young Casey, but his feelings of attraction for an underage girl who was his patient were totally unacceptable, professionally and personally. A whole different problem.

She walked aimlessly around the room, affectionately patting Joe's old recliner and straightening a pillow on Jordan's beloved old sofa as she went by. She stopped at the window and stood looking out to where the moonlight made the stone wall along Palmer Road dimly visible. Then she realized she had made a circle around the room, not looking at the table by her chair where the telephone sat reflecting back the light from the lamp beside it.

It was getting late, she thought. Soon it would be too late to call, and the matter could be postponed until tomorrow. She chided herself for the feeling of relief the thought gave her, but her thoughts continued without her conscious direction. Old people needed their sleep, didn't they? Then she wondered how old Amanda Brighton actually was. She went back to her chair and sat down, refusing to look at the phone that squatted there. It looks like a malevolent toad, she thought. Or her conscience made manifest. No matter the reason, she didn't want to look at it.

How old is Amanda? Sarah busied her mind with putting together what facts she knew, comments of her co-workers at Brighton, rumors, and it all added up to what? As nearly as she could determine, no one she knew had ever seen Amanda Brighton. All her own contacts had been by telephone, and they had gone on for nearly ten years, but that wasn't enough. Surely she knew more than that.

Sarah concentrated on Brighton Foundation. It was founded by Amanda's husband, Albert. Her forehead wrinkled in thought as she searched for a date. In the very early thirties, of that she was sure. Now, what else did she know? They had a son in his fifties who died in an accident not too long after she had gone to work at Brighton, and Albert Brighton died a few months later. That was about eighteen years ago. She frowned, engrossed in her mental detective work.

She did remember Albert Brighton's memorial service. The foundation had closed down for a week of mourning, and all employees, while not ordered to, were strongly urged to attend the service. In a sudden flash of memory, she saw Amanda Brighton, a slender figure standing ramrod straight in the family pew. So Sarah had seen her . . . but not really. Amanda had been wearing a hat with a heavy black veil that obscured her face, making her features impossible to discern. That's odd, Sarah thought. She had the distinct impression that Amanda Brighton was quite alone in the pew. Weren't there any relatives? No friends?

She was sure her memory was right. At a time when friends and relatives would have normally put in an appearance, Amanda Brighton was alone in the pew, but in the row behind her sat several white-haired men in black suits. Sarah remembered thinking at the time that they looked like a row of stiff-backed crows perched on a fence, and as they were filing out, she caught the sounds of their voices as they quietly spoke to Amanda . . . some foreign language, German, she thought.

Now then, Sarah thought. To have a son in his fifties, Amanda must have been in her seventies when her son was killed and her husband died, and that was . . . that was, her mind almost refused to add up the numbers. That was nearly twenty years ago! Sarah leaned back and closed her eyes. Ninety years old, at least! Amanda Brighton was in her nineties! Unbelievable was the only word in Sarah's mind, and it seemed such a limp little word, wilted and ineffective, not coming close to expressing what she was feeling at this moment. No, she told herself, I'm not prejudiced about older people. I'm not! But common sense and experience says that the mind inevitably loses something in the aging process, just as the body does. The olden days tend to assume greater clarity and reality, sometimes replacing the present entirely for periods of time.

More than ninety years old! The number buzzed in her head like an angry bee. Still completely controlling a huge, complex organization, no doubt through an agreeably complacent Board of Directors, who, in turn, controlled all the top decision makers. How many Brighton employees had the slightest idea that a shadowy, aged, matriarch was pulling the strings, making decisions behind the scenes, accountable to no one?

I sure as hell didn't, Sarah thought, letting her breath out with an explosive whistle, and I dealt with her directly all these years. The memory of Amanda standing alone in the pew and the black-suited German-speaking men behind her kept coming back. There was no one with her then, no one nearby except those men. And there was no reason to think there was anyone with her now. My God! She could be completely senile, or deep into senile dementia, or living in some yesterday . . . and no one would know. All she had to do was pick up the phone and make 'suggestions'. Her name was enough to extract instant obedience. Yes, her name and the favors she had handed out so slyly.

The shame Sarah had been feeling as she worked out her part in this charade was slowly replaced by anger. The realization that she had been manipulated, hooked by her bout of bulimia, grateful for the bounty received, and blind to the small violations of ethics and morality - even her pride at being singled out for attention by such an important and powerful person - these were the things that fueled her anger. Weaknesses, those were what Amanda used, unerringly going for the most vulnerably frail parts of the human psyche.

How many other loyal Brighton employees made private telephone reports, Sarah wondered? Surely, hers wouldn't be missed. She looked directly at the telephone now, knowing she wouldn't be placing a call to Amanda tonight, and not until she figured out just what role she had already played and was expected to continue playing in the life of Delilah Cross. That Delilah was the target she didn't doubt, and her gut level instincts told her that more than ever before, now that she was talking, Delilah needed protection.

"Hey lady, are you going to sit there and stare at the phone all night?"

Sarah was startled, and with a small gasp, she turned quickly to face Joe. He was standing in the doorway, a pot in one hand

and a pitcher of milk in the other, his pajamas rumpled and his hair looking well slept-in.

He grinned, then pulled a sad face, his lower lip pouting like a petulant child. "I woke up," he whined, "and found myself all alone in bed. There was nobody where your body was supposed to be, so here I am." He grinned again, the affection clearly visible in his eyes.

"How about some hot cocoa and togetherness? Sure cure for I-can't-sleep-itis, as you well know." He squinted his eyes thoughtfully. "If you don't hurry up, I'll make the cocoa myself, and as you also know very well, I always let the milk boil and the cocoa gets that film all over the top."

"Well, seeing as how you put it that way, Prince Charming, invitation accepted," Sarah replied, grinning at this man with whom she had shared all of the important things in her life, good and bad. Their change in life-style since coming to the farm had improved their relationship, making a close, solid marriage even better as they shared the daily routines instead of separating to pursue their individual careers. Jordan, too, had displayed his satisfaction at the way this family-style living had worked out. He had been living on his own since his college days, and the idea of going back to being the son in the house of his parents was distasteful because he valued his freedom, particularly where female friends were concerned. Sensing his reluctance, Joe and

Sarah discussed this privately, deciding how they would handle it.

As sometimes happens, the stereotypical image Jordan formed of his parents simply did not exist, and he was pleasantly surprised to find they both treated him as an independent adult, free to come and go as he pleased without comment or advice unless he asked for it. He had a private entrance to his bedroom from the porch, and his own private bath. If he had an occasional overnight guest, the subject was discreetly ignored.

Bent Tree Farm has been good for all of us, Sarah thought, as she made the cocoa and served it in the over-sized brown mugs she kept especially for this purpose. She sighed as she sat down across from Joe. For the first time in a long time, she was filled with misgivings and uncertainty about their future, and she didn't like the feeling at all. As she sat there sipping cocoa, she could hear the word "outnumbered" in her mind. It seemed a lot longer, but it had only been a few hours since Delilah said it, and at the time she was more outnumbered than she knew. Now the odds were even because, Sarah realized, whatever the consequences, she was firmly on Delilah's side.

* * *

On Saturday morning, Sarah and Delilah were baking bread. Sarah had slept badly and gotten up early. Too restless to stay in the gatehouse, she went up to the main house and started coffee. Then, feeling the need for company, she went upstairs and tapped

431

on Delilah's door, pretending to need help with a spur-of-the-moment baking project. They started early and the loaves that were now in the big oven were announcing themselves to everyone within smelling distance.

A little later, K.C. and Casey drifted into the kitchen, drawn by the olfactory announcement, and were sitting at the table drinking coffee while they waited for the first loaf to emerge. Sarah had promised that the first loaf- -or loaves- -were to be eaten fresh from the oven. Plates, knives, butter, a big pot of honey, and various jars of jam and marmalade already sat on the table. As she put the first crusty-brown loaf on the table in front of them, she announced that fresh bread didn't slice well. "Just forget your manners, dive in and hack off a piece because there are plenty of napkins."

She and Delilah joined the men at the table, and for a few minutes they engaged in a ritual nearly as old as mankind, the breaking of bread together. The silence was broken only by small sounds of crusty bread being cut into manageable chunks, the small unavoidable sounds of chewing, and an occasional hum of whole-hearted enjoyment.

They were working on the second loaf when Kaydee pushed through the swinging door, announcing, "I smell something heavenly!" Sarah's mouth was full, so she waved invitingly and patted the chair beside her where Kaydee joined the chewing and humming group.

The third loaf was on the table when Samantha and the children came in the back door. "Oh, marvelous!" Samantha said. "Freshly-baked bread." She glanced at the group at the table, and reached for plates and knives, the invitation to join clear, if unspoken.

"It smells good," Jamie said, "like a bakery. But it's just plain old bread and butter. Nobody eats plain old bread and butter."

"We're eating it, and we're bread experts," K.C. said. "We're eating it because it's the best thing we ever tasted, so sit yourself down and have a piece with honey." He glanced at Sarah, who nodded. "And if you really and truly don't like it, then you can just wait until this afternoon when the cinnamon rolls are ready." He pointed to the counter. "See, they're sitting right over there waiting their turn in the oven."

It took no more persuasion, and when the adults sat back with contented sighs to enjoy their coffee, Jamie and Laurie were still busily eating bread and butter and honey with only an occasional glance at the waiting trays of cinnamon rolls.

"Thank you, Sarah, that was a special treat," Kaydee said. "And you, too, Delilah." She smiled warmly at Delilah, who returned the smile with a wide one of her own, responding to the open, honest style that seemed to be a part of Kaydee's personality.

Kaydee turned back to Sarah. "I just got a call from James. He's flying into the regional airport this afternoon, and I was wondering if I could borrow a car to go pick him up? I know we intended to leave here in the morning, but we had no idea James would be able to clear his calendar so quickly." Again, she turned to Delilah, easily and naturally including her as an integral part of the group.

"In case you didn't know, James is an attorney, too. We have a joint practice that usually keeps us both busy, but we share the work very well. He's an excellent trial lawyer and I'm a demon on case law and research, so I do my part of the work, then he does his. Usually, we manage to coordinate our vacations, but this case he just finished was hard-fought." She made a face, then grinned. "It's a sad but true fact of life that when an individual takes on a big corporation, the big guy has the time, the money, and the legal talent to drag it out forever."

There was a knowing chorus of agreement from the table. "Anyway, we were lucky this time," Kaydee continued. "The senior company executive was fighting us tooth and nail to avoid paying our client damages, but he died quite suddenly." Her face puckered in a frown. "That doesn't sound right. We weren't glad the man died, but we were darned glad that the man who took over was anxious to settle the matter out of court in an amount we considered fair to our client."

Kaydee turned to Sarah. "I know it must be an imposition to have such a big family group hanging around, but I really would like James to have one day on the farm. Then we can get on our way bright and early Monday morning."

Casey started to say something about using his car, but she blithely interrupted. "Mom and the kids want to go along, and your little scooter isn't big enough for all of us and James, and his luggage, too." She laughed. "Which, if I know him will consist of one overstuffed carry-on bag."

Sarah was agreeable and went to the key board beside the back door. "Here you go, Kaydee. These are the Rover keys. It's an easy driver with plenty of room for everyone, including James and his luggage, or lack of it." She laughed. "You know, I like James already. It's always been my motto that he who travels light creates little washing."

She turned to take the last two loaves of bread from the oven, replacing them with trays of cinnamon buns. "I don't suppose anyone is interested in lunch? Or is that a rhetorical question?" There was a concert of groans from the group at the table. "I'll take that as a vote of disinterest. Joe and Jordan can pig out on the last loaves of bread for their lunch, and the cinnamon rolls are dessert for tonight."

There was a small flurry of good-byes and hugs as they left, and the kitchen suddenly seemed very quiet; the sound of voices, car doors closing, and the Rover's engine were clearly audible. No one spoke until it turned from the driveway into Palmer Road, and its sound drifted away.

When Delilah spoke, it was so unexpected that Sarah, K.C. and Casey turned in unison to look at her, not sure they had heard her correctly. She repeated her question. "I wonder if I could have a moment of your time?" Their assent to this strangely formal request was quickly given, and she made a second request.

"It may seem silly, but would all three of you sit on one side of the table so I can face you?"

Sarah took the tray of cinnamon buns from the oven as Casey moved around the table to sit by his Dad. When she came back, she sat beside Casey, watching with unconcealed curiosity as Delilah took a seat on the opposite side of the table facing them squarely.

Sarah and K.C. were privately marveling at the pure soprano sound of her voice. Neither of them had actually heard her speak entire sentences yet, and the clarity and precision of her enunciation struck them both. Casey felt somewhat differently. He had heard her speak-at length-both to Paulie Newcombe and to himself, and he felt a pang of anxiety about what he was almost sure was coming. He had not told K.C. about his great eavesdropping caper, but he had a feeling Delilah was going to do just that. He studied his hands intently, waiting for the ax to fall on his unprotected neck, almost welcoming it.

Delilah sat there a moment, gazing at each of them in turn. Her head was up and she made no effort to conceal her eyes. In a half-aware way, K.C. and Sarah realized that she was deliberately revealing her eyes for them to read however they chose. Whether this stemmed from defiance or from a desire to be clearly understood, neither of them knew. They did know that the impact of those startling eyes was almost physical, speaking almost as loudly as her voice.

"I sat you there like that for a very selfish, childish reason," she began. "I don't know how many times I've sat in this position before, but every time the people across from me were the lord high inquisitors and I was the uncivilized heathen." She made no attempt to conceal the bitterness in her voice. "I want you all to understand that the situation has changed. I am no longer a child, a feral child, but I feel like I am still being treated like one." She looked at Sarah. "I don't mean to include you in that, Sarah. I want you here as my friend, do you mind?"

Numbly, Sarah shook her head. What was happening here? Delilah had taken charge, her words revealing an assured clear-thinking adult. Then it dawned on her that no one had ever really known what Delilah thought. Without speech, nothing about her private thoughts and feelings had ever been clearly visible. Easily misconstrued facial expressions and body language and a few words scribbled on a note pad led to easy assumptions. It didn't enter her mind that she had, with her caring, her affection, and her acceptance of Delilah's individuality and independence, helped to create the young lady sitting opposite her. Had she thought about it, she might have felt a sense of pride and accomplishment, a feeling of satisfaction at a job well done. But she didn't think about it because she was too full of anger and guilt about being manipulated by Amanda Brighton.

Casey still sat with his head down, staring at his hands. She knows I'm squirming, he thought. She knows it. The thought was enough to mobilize him. He raised his head and looked at her squarely, and said, "Before we go any further here, Delilah, I owe you a couple of apologies, first for spying on you at the brook, and again for listening to your private telephone conversation." He didn't wait for an answer. "And I think you owe me an apology for reading private files and reports without permission." There, he thought, you've got the ball, Miss Cross, now run with it. "Oh, and one other thing. I furnish my own binoculars." He wanted to say more about sexual fetishes, but closed his mouth. That was just too personal to mention in front of his Dad and Sarah. And he didn't mention prowling in her room.

K.C. and Sarah both turned to look at him, puzzled and curious. He ignored them, continuing to look straight into Delilah's eyes, confronting her.

Delilah laughed, the sound pleasant and easy, cutting through the tension like a knife. "Apology accepted and given," she said, leaning back in her chair as she continued. "I'll go first because there is very little you don't already know about me. I have always been able to talk. I didn't for personal reasons which I will not discuss, so it's no use asking. I had intended to pick my own time and place, but the matter picked its own time, as you know." She took a deep breath before she continued.

"As for the water phobia, it is rooted in a horrible incident that happened when I was quite young. I was standing in waist-deep muddy water holding a babe when a crocodile grabbed the babe, knocking me down and under with its tail. No one came to help me. They were afraid, so I had to get out of the water by myself, holding the babe's arm. That was all that was left of it, you see. The crocodile ripped the rest of it away. I was severely punished. The mother beat me with the babe's bloody arm. Beat me, and beat me, and beat me. After that I never went in the water again, because I couldn't."

Delilah's calm, factual delivery was belied by the strain in her voice, and there was horror on all of their faces even though the scene in the shower had begun to prepare them for the horrors of her life. This was worse, far worse than anything they had imagined.

After a moment, she continued. "I know it's a question you all have. No, I have no childhood memories of anything other than being with the apes, and they were bonobos, not chimpanzees." She looked at Casey. "Many of those reports are wrong, incomplete, or totally falsified." Her ears picked up the unconscious breath they all took in unison. Now what caused that?

Still wondering about it, Delilah concluded. "I have questions, but one in particular I want answered. Who knew that Agnes Kittridge was a psychotic religious fanatic? If it wasn't known, why wasn't it, and is she still on the Brighton Foundation payroll?" These were safe questions, she was sure, logical questions from one who had been abused.

Delilah didn't notice that Sarah's face turned almost white at the mention of Agnes Kittridge because she was looking at the Lowells whose nods indicated that they would find out for her. "These are my last questions for now. Doctor Senior, are you here as part of evaluating me, or is it just a coincidence? I know your son is doing an evaluation, but will someone tell me why it's being done, and why now? Is there some special significance?"

"Coincidence, Delilah," K.C. answered briefly. "Not involved." Which is not exactly the truth, he thought. I am involved with Casey.

"Don't know what the purpose is," Casey said, "and the timing seems a little wrong to me, too. Too early."

440

For the first time since she sat down, Delilah lowered her eyes and asked the most important question of all, easing it out like an afterthought. "Something else I've wondered about. Does anyone really know how old I am?" No one answered her. There was a bit more conversation, but Delilah got no more answers.

When it was over Sarah went back to the gatehouse, sick at heart and deeply thankful that she had not called Amanda Brighton. If it was in her power, she would never speak to her again, but the battle was just beginning. Delilah was involved, her family was involved, and she realized Joe and Jordan would have to be told the whole story right away, all of it. At least she knew the enemy, she thought, as she walked heavily into the family room and dropped into her chair. The enemy was Brighton Foundation, and Amanda Brighton, an ancient, unspeakably evil crone.

Sarah sat there for a long time thinking about evil. Agnes Kittridge! Oh my God! Amanda Brighton had arranged for Delilah to spend two years alone with Agnes Kittridge!

CHAPTER NINETEEN

James Prentiss did not look like a successful attorney. In fact, he didn't look like an attorney at all, successful or otherwise. That's assuming there is some stereotypical pattern to which they conform, one to which they must adhere in order to match the image television has created in nearly everyone's mind, at least in America. Of course in England they wore strange little wigs perched on their heads which would alter perceptual expectations. The thought that James Prentiss didn't look like an attorney was usually the first one to cross the minds of nearly everyone meeting him for the first time. The four permanent residents of Bent Tree Farm were no exception to this quite typical reaction.

When the Rover pulled in the driveway, it was met by a kind of welcoming committee, the members all coming together on their way to somewhere else. Joe was coming from the barn after bedding the animals down for the night, looking forward to a long, hot shower, dinner, and an evening in front of the television set. Jordan left the greenhouse, satisfied that his precious plants were safe until morning, thinking about a pleasant evening of food, drink, laughter - and perhaps more - with the young lady veterinarian from Centerville he had been dating for the last six months. Sarah and Delilah had just seated themselves on the steps of the big front porch, as they often did in the late afternoon, allowing dinner to stew in its own juices, as Sarah put it. The two

Lowell men were just coming up from the stream where they had been sitting on the bank deep in conversation for the last hour.

They all stood together as Kaydee, still driving, pulled into the parking area across from the farmhouse and jumped out. Samantha exited more slowly from the other side, still favoring her bruised knee. Everyone stood waiting until James, deep in conversation with the children sitting on either side of him in the back seat, finally looked up. Realizing that they had arrived, he struggled out, a laughing child still clinging to each side like some strange, wiggling, giggling growths.

Laughing and feigning imminent collapse, he managed to free himself and turned to face the waiting audience. The first thing you noticed about James was his size. He was big, big in the way football players are big, but well proportioned without the appearance of bulk or extra pounds. He had on a pair of faded jeans, well-worn jogging shoes without socks, and a T-shirt that said, in bright red letters, "God Save Us, To hell With The Queen!" His smile was big and genuine, the deep crinkle lines around his eyes attesting to the fact he used it often, and the upturned lips and humor-filled eyes added to the impression of a big, easy-going, relaxed, happy man.

He enveloped his father-in-law in a bear-hug, exchanged friendly shoulder punches with Casey, and carefully acknowledged the round of introductions to Delilah, Joe, Jordan, and Sarah, repeating each of their names and maintaining eye contact as he exchanged firm handshakes with each of them.

Sarah thought, yes, while this man doesn't look the part he could certainly sway a jury because he exudes friendly sincerity and charm in a way quite unexpected in so big a man. James looked comically puzzled at the children's laughter as he pulled his luggage from the rear of the Rover . . . one bulging, straining-at-the-zippers carry-on bag. Sarah immediately liked him, and it had nothing to do with the minimal washing the one over-stuffed bag implied. It was something almost subliminal that she felt in the way he looked at and touched his children that told her he was a good father.

Delilah shared her opinion about James although for different reasons. His smell said, here I am, mature, settled male, friendly, approachable, non-threatening. Come as close as you like, it's safe.

As he shook her hand, his face sobered as he said, "Thank you, Delilah Cross. Kaydee, Samantha, and the kids told me all about the great pond adventure and rescue. We owe you." Then, still holding her hand, his face crinkled into a huge smile and he quite deliberately looked her up and down, exaggerating his head movements and rolling his eyes as he did so.

Everyone watched with interest, not knowing what was coming next. "That is very strange," he said. "Have you by any chance shrunk in the last couple of days?" When she shook her head, he said, looking around, "From the way I got the story, the heroic rescue of our wayward children was carried out by some huge, bigger-than-life person, as big as me maybe, or at the least a hefty Amazon type! Why you're just a petite little pee-wee, aren't you?"

The laughter was general, and Jamie pounced on the words. "Petite little pee-wee! Petite little pee-wee!"

After a moment, Laurie joined in, repeating the words a couple of times. Then she asked, her round little face serious, "Jamie, what's a peetie pee-wee? It sounds like a bird. Is it a bird?" The question was enough to silence him because he didn't know the answer, and the laughing group dissolved as they moved off to tend to their own affairs, every one except Jordan promising that they wouldn't be late for dinner.

* * *

Earlier that Saturday afternoon while Sarah sat in the gatehouse engrossed in a guilt-inspired search through the past, Delilah placed a brief phone call to Paulie. The Lowells, Senior and Junior, had taken a roundabout stroll that eventually brought them to the stream, and, in unspoken agreement, they seated themselves on the bank in the dappled shade. During the last week summer had settled in, not yet too oppressive, but hot enough to make the shade and the gentle, cooling effect of

445

running water welcome. It was a while before either of them spoke. Then K.C. broke the silence, speaking quietly as though loathe to interrupt the sound of the stream.

"I don't intend this as any kind of a test question, Casey, but I'm curious to know if you picked up on the same things I did, sort of verifying my own impressions." He blew out his breath in a long, slow exhalation. "I don't know about you, but I feel like I just walked into the middle of a movie. I have certain clues as to the beginning, I am watching action going on in the middle, and I am wondering where in the hell it's going to end."

"That makes me feel a little better, but not much." Casey picked up a small stone, examined it carefully then tossed it in the stream. "Okay, here goes. I'll give it to you more or less in the order it happened as I saw it, and what I thought at the time." He turned to look at K.C.. "I do not come out smelling like a rose, Dad, but there's no use dwelling on it, is there?"

"You know about the first part, so I won't go over it again. Delilah just verified what I picked up in the records about Agnes Kittridge, and, incidentally, Sarah hasn't come up with anything about her, even using her contacts. I get the distinct feeling that someone is intent on concealing information about Agnes, including where the body's buried, even. Or maybe I'm just being paranoid about it."

K.C. grunted noncommittally, then said, "The tonal quality of

446

Delilah's voice when she asked about her, and the fact that it was one of only three questions she asked, struck me as odd. Something very bad happened to Delilah during those two years with Agnes Kittridge, that's for sure, and unless I'm badly mistaken, Delilah wants revenge of some sort." His voice drifted off a moment, then he said, "Revenge? Not on Kittridge necessarily, but on whoever was responsible for Kittridge being there, that's where she placed the emphasis." He glanced at Casey. "Sorry for interrupting, go ahead."

"I agree with you about that, Dad. I keep thinking about that "Cleanliness is next to godliness" outburst in the shower. That had to be Kittridge, but unless Delilah decides to talk about those two years, and I hope she does talk about it to someone, it's just guesswork. She was very positive about the psychotic religious fanatic part though, wasn't she? At least I seem to have pegged that part right." He stopped, not expecting an answer.

"Are you going to explain that very strange interchange about apologies, Casey?"

Casey sighed and picked up another small rock, rolling it between his fingers. "Yes, but it's not easy to keep admitting that I'm an ass." After a moment in which the stone landed in the stream with a small plopping sound, he described his eavesdropping on Delilah's telephone conversation. He described the impressions he had gotten of a close, long-term relationship with Paulie Newcombe that began when she first arrived at Hiller School and continued on to the present. "She quite literally verified our assumptions about the objects on her dresser being symbols, but symbols of what I can't figure out for sure."

He thought a moment, then said, "Something traumatic seems to have happened at the Landon Zoo. Paulie seemed to know that an animal had bitten her, which is traumatic enough, but she said that something else happened that day, something much worse than the bite, something Paulie did not know about, but she would tell him about later."

K.C. waited patiently as Casey picked up another small rock and looked it carefully as though the words he was about to speak were etched on its surface in microscopic script. Finally, still studying the stone, he described the ensuing tongue-lashing from Delilah, sparing himself no humiliating detail. He was completely surprised when K.C. laughed heartily and honestly.

"Got exactly what you deserved, didn't you son? Not to worry, she doesn't seem to be harboring any hard feelings . . . or she's a lot better at hiding her feelings than I thought." He paused to brush an exploring ant from his sleeve. "And she's damned good at that, too, but there's something else. Did you get the feeling that the whole thing this afternoon was choreographed, very carefully calculated to give us answers to questions that were obvious while eliciting very specific information from us in return?"

Casey thought a moment. "Well, she didn't have much planning time for it because no one knew about James' unexpected arrival. But she put us on the defensive immediately with her seating arrangement. Wasn't that a neat way of literally turning the tables on us, putting us in the bad guy inquisitor role? What did she ask? About Agnes Kittridge, about why we were there, and does anyone really know how old she is, isn't that about it?"

"That's about the way I read it, and the table-turning was really very good strategy, although she explained it quite easily. If we did anything except quietly follow her lead, we immediately joined the ranks of inquisitors she had so neatly set up for us." There was a grudging tone of admiration in K.C.'s voice. "I wonder if she plays chess?" He didn't expect an answer.

There was a long silence. The leaves above them rustled quietly, stirred by a light breeze, and the gurgling murmur of the stream suddenly sounded louder as they once again became aware of the sounds around them.

This time it was Casey who broke the silence. "Well, I think I told you that she was very intelligent, and you told me she was an enigma. I told you that I thought there was something very strange about how her whole case was handled, more so than any simple bureaucratic fumbling would explain." He turned to face K.C.. "What do you think, now that you've had a real opportunity

449

to interact with Delilah Cross?"

The answer was a long time coming, and when it did, Casey grunted in surprise at his Dad's words. "First, son, I think your gut-reactions are functioning properly, and your glands are not running away with your brain. Delilah Cross is not a sixteen-year-old girl. She is a woman grown and probably at least eighteen years old. She knows her true age, I'm sure of that. She dropped her eyes and there was a kind of coyness in her voice, a sound of 'I know something you don't know' that I've heard before. I think the question was rhetorical and she only wanted to find out how we came up with our estimate, and make us admit that it is only an estimate based on a hurried examination by an irritated doctor whom she had just bitten."

He paused, thinking, a deep furrow creasing his forehead. He took off his glasses, idly polishing them on his pants leg. The ultra-violet protection of the lenses had created lighter-colored shadow glasses on his otherwise tanned face, making it look somehow vulnerable and exposed.

Casey waited. There was more, he knew, not that what he had just heard wasn't enough food for thought to require a lot of digesting time. He recognized his Dad's movements, designed more to create a pattern for his thoughts than to clean the lenses of his glasses. For as long as he could remember, his Dad had engaged in this near-ritualized maneuver when following a half-formed theory, giving it time to assume a form that allowed him to express it in words.

There were more surprises in his next words. "This girl, or rather young woman, is, without a doubt, the most intelligent and complex person I have ever encountered. For whatever reasons, and I'm sure she has them, she is at once both devious and naive." He paused, ordering his thoughts before he continued.

"Being naive is to be expected, considering the fact that her actual life experience has been very limited, but the deviousness is something else. The refusing to speak, then admitting that she intended to do so at some other time of her own choosing is a display of both. Perhaps it was a method of controlling a situation over which she had no control by exercising an extraordinary amount of self-control over herself. In effect, she had a secret and it gave her a kind of power over the people who were controlling her." K.C. paused and shifted position, brushing ineffectively at a small iridescent fly that seemed to be enamored with its reflection in his glasses.

"And I think it became a kind of game that she enjoyed playing because she always won by saying nothing. The almost smug way she threw out bonobo and said the reports were wrong indicates that she gets satisfaction from knowing things that others don't think she knows . . . reading reports about herself, for example. Yes, secrets are important to her."

451

He took a moment, rubbing his ankle saying, "I think some little critter bit me," then went on. "The blackout she had was real and will probably not be remembered. No question that the water phobia is real. So is that stark and appalling story of the crocodile and the babe. But that raises another question. Certainly, no one helped her because apes generally won't go in the water, but then, what was she doing in the water in the first place? And carrying a babe? I believe her when she says she doesn't remember anything except being with apes, and that means she should have acquired their dislike of going in water through simple imprinting. So many unanswered questions."

When K.C. stopped talking, he looked at his son for a long moment. Emotionally involved, all right, he thought, but he's still an observant professional. Then he continued. "She's been the exclusive property of Brighton Foundation for close to eight years. During that time, every minute of her days and nights - and years - has been spent under one form of observation or another. And the only indication we have of any truly uncivilized behavior comes from Agnes Kittridge and that only indirectly. If I understood you correctly, Casey, Kittridge only reported that certain things had been taught, but she made no direct observational comments about Delilah's actual behavior, other than commenting about the water phobia and her making the sign of the cross."

K.C. waited for Casey's nod before he went on. "The reports from Hiller School all indicate ignorance and illiteracy but nothing not easily found in children living in many isolated parts of the world. Do you agree?"

"Yes," Casey agreed. "I remember thinking that she came from a place so isolated that the use of fire hadn't been an everyday function, and the things she didn't know or understand seemed consistent with a feral background."

It was K.C.'s turn to nod agreement. "All right, he said, let's look at this from a scientific point of view for a minute." The small fly was back at his glasses, this time vigorously trying to mate with its reflection. "Can't get a much closer viewpoint than that," he laughed, and brushed the fly away again. "You know the extremely low percentage rate of successful feral child adaptation into society. Actually, two or three years living alone with animals of any kind, especially at a very young age, leaves an imprinting pattern nearly impossible to erase, at least by any method currently in use. Yet, here we have the mysterious Delilah Cross, who, I do believe, lived with animals as an animal for eight to ten years, more than half of her life, and who says she remembers no prior human contact."

K.C. reached over and tapped Casey's leg to emphasize his point. "Tell me son, based on her performance this afternoon, how could this possibly have been a feral child? And if she truly was, and all the documentation says she was, what were her early imprinting patterns? What made her different, what is allowing her to - or driving her to - accomplish things that the scientific community agrees are impossible?"

Casey could not answer. His Dad's analysis was correct, of course, and Casey understood that he himself had yet to acquire these many years of experience, both clinical and in the field, which his father could now access so easily. As Casey watched silently, not knowing how to formulate a reply, K.C. pulled up his pant leg and scratched his ankle thoughtfully, bending over awkwardly to examine the little red spot just becoming visible.

"Yep, the damned little critter got me. Strange how you don't know they're there until they decide to bite. I remember once being out in the field on some study or other and standing directly on the entrance to an ant's nest without noticing. Had on shorts, too, and didn't even feel the damned things moving all over my legs until they decided to bite. It's an amazing thing how they all bite at the same time, and I don't believe the theory that the bite signal is transmitted by pheromones in the air. It happens too fast, and besides, which one makes the decision and tells all the others? There are so many things we don't know for sure, things we just have to make educated guesses about . . . which brings us right back to Delilah Cross, doesn't it?"

Giving his ankle a pat, he pulled up his sock, and straightened up, looking at Casey as he asked, "Overload?"

"Yes and no," his son replied. "Something else just struck me. About Sarah, did you notice how she reacted when Delilah talked about Agnes Kittridge? I actually felt her flinch. And, when you think about it, she's in a very tight place, you know. I didn't push it, but I have the strangest feeling that she was put in place here just for the purpose of overseeing Delilah and Delilah doesn't seem to have an inkling about it. They really care about each other, and I wonder how Delilah will react when she finds out?"

"That will have to take care of itself, Casey. We aren't going to tell Delilah, or make any waves in that direction because, as I see it, Delilah is walking a psychological tightrope right now. She relies on Sarah more than you might think. Their interaction is much like mother and daughter at this point, and Sarah is very good for her stability. I think we agreed to let her lead the way in her own direction at her own pace, and I still feel that way."

"Dad, there's something else. You just reminded me of it." Casey's voice was low, his tone almost tentative. "I'm the first to admit that like it or not I'm emotionally involved." He stopped, reluctant to voice his thoughts, then forged on. "I don't like it one bit, but I can't seem to control it. But you aren't involved with Delilah in any way, other than what little you've seen of her." When K.C. made a choked snorting noise, he laughed, and added, "Well, not so little considering the bathtub episode, but I think

455

you know what I mean. Have you noticed that everyone around her seems to feel very protective about her? At first I thought it was just me, part of my problem, but I found it in almost the same words in Harold Newcombe's reports from Hiller School, Sarah as much as said it, and now you are saying the same thing. Can you explain what's happening?"

K.C. spent some time gazing around, up at the trees, following the run of the stream, and finally turned to face Casey. "Well, for one thing, you were right about her eyes. They are very unusual, strange and beautiful. And she uses them like weapons, at least that is my impression. I have to be honest, and I'll have to check this out with Samantha and Kaydee to get an honest female reaction, but when she is focused on me, I feel slightly disappointed when she turns away or lowers her lids. I don't know if this is a typical masculine response, but I don't think so, Casey."

His face was thoughtful as he continued. "I've read some research papers about dominance potential in both animals and humans that suggest some individuals seem to be born dominant, regardless of their expected rank or status in the group to which they belong. Perhaps it's a form of magnetism that speaks in a language we humans don't yet understand but react to instinctively, but there is for sure something noticeable enough in effect to be remarked on. How many times have you heard or read the terms born leader or Alpha male and female?"

Casey nodded his agreement, and K.C. finished his thought. "That might be what is going on with Delilah. Certainly, it deserves a lot more attention to how others are reacting to her. Fascinating, absolutely fascinating."

His last words were said more to himself than to Casey, but Casey nodded his agreement vehemently anyway as the import became clear in his mind. Maybe his poor performance had some explanation beyond runaway testosterone, lack of self-control, and unprofessional behavior after all. He found the thought very comforting.

* * *

In the gatehouse, Sarah was wondering about how Delilah would react when she found out about her duplicity, dreading the moment when it came out, sick with the knowing that it would have to. The realization that she had been carefully maneuvered into this position sat like a rock in her stomach, making her nauseous in ways that were not physical. Bitterly, she said the name out loud. "Agnes Kittridge."

It hung in the air like a bad smell, refusing to go away. Oh yes, she remembered Agnes Kittridge. She had several discouraging sessions with her, about, if she remembered correctly, about nine years ago. Certainly, it was well before Delilah Cross was found in the jungle and taken to Bhutu Holding Facility.

457

Sarah's diagnosis of Agnes Kittridge had been acute psychosis with full-blown delusions fixated on God. Her recommendation had been that Kittridge be permanently suspended from her job and hospitalized, both to be done immediately. Her prognosis had been based on experience and case history. In her opinion, while Agnes Kittridge could still function in the real world, her condition was long-standing and progressive, and would eventually result in complete withdrawal into her delusional world. Sarah had filed her reports with the head of the department, Doctor Quillan, an older psychiatrist whose position she later assumed when he retired. She had thought no more about the matter, and it had been, perhaps, a month before Amanda called her. As she sat there in her chair, Sarah's upper lip curled, expressing the contempt she felt for Amanda . . . and for herself.

It had all been so smoothly and gently done. After inquiring about Sarah and her family, congratulating her about Joe acquiring permanent tenure at the college, and a few moments of inconsequential chat, she remarked that the Agnes Kittridge matter had been taken care of and the case was closed. Sarah could just send all her Kittridge records to Doctor Quillan, who would see that they went into the permanently closed-records file. And that's what Sarah did.

Yes, Sarah thought, the matter had been taken care of all right. There was no connection with the Kittridge matter when Doctor

Quillan retired two months later and, over the heads of several other equally qualified people, Sarah was elevated to his position. No, there was no connection at all, was there? The matter had been taken care of and she had been paid off handsomely for her part in the affair, no matter how innocently she had done it. Now she knew why her recent queries about the present whereabouts of Agnes Kittridge had gotten such a run-around, and why there had been no return call from Amanda Brighton.

Sarah clasped her arms over her ample bosom, trying to hug away the pain. What had she been thinking? She simply had not connected K.C.'s request for information about Kittridge with Delilah. The thought hadn't entered her mind. As far as she had been concerned, it should have been a simple matter to find out if Kittridge was still alive, and if so, in what mental hospital she currently resided. Such a simple thing.

Sarah's face sagged tiredly as she suddenly realized why Amanda had insisted that her position here at Bent Tree Farm, as it related to Delilah, was that of 'unprofessional caretaker', a glorified baby-sitter who made occasional verbal reports on the phone. Of course. If her position had been professional, she would have immediately requested Delilah's records just as Casey had, records that would have contained all the reports made by Agnes Kittridge.

So Kittridge had stayed on the Brighton Foundation payroll,

and had been sent to Bhutu to live with Delilah Cross in completely unsupervised isolation for two years, free to do whatever her delusional mind directed. As Sarah remembered the lumpy face, dumpy body, the protruding, not-quite-sane eyes, a part of her mind was filled with a kind of horrified wonder. How had Delilah had managed to survive it with any part of her mind intact? What had she told Casey as he carried Delilah up from the pond? Delilah's strong, that's what she had said. Yes, she was strong, stronger than she had known at the time.

"My God," Sarah cried aloud, "Why?" These words seemed to hang in the air long after they were wrung from her, echoing and reverberating in her mind with each step as she got up and slowly walked the seemingly endless driveway up to the farmhouse to start dinner. And face Delilah without drawing attention to how truly terrible she felt.

CHAPTER TWENTY

Dinner turned into a festive affair, filled with laughter and good-natured banter. If Sarah seemed preoccupied and unusually quiet, no one noticed, except Jordan, who hadn't expected to be there at all. Earlier, when the group in the driveway separated and went in different directions, she had stopped him and asked, as a favor to her, if he would stay home this evening because there were some matters she needed to discuss with him and Joe.

He had agreed at once. In the first place, she never interfered with his private life or any plans he might have, and she knew about his plans for this evening. In the second place, he felt a pang of concern at the serious, almost distraught expression on her face. As he watched her during dinner, his concern deepened. It was something serious, he decided, and judging by Joe's relaxed participation in the general confusion of conversation, his Dad wasn't aware of it.

The after-dinner clean up became more of a party than a chore. Everyone pitched in, milling about, getting in each other's way, laughing, joking, and in general contributing more to the confusion than the cleaning effort but a great deal to the feeling of relaxed good humor and friendliness. Before too long, Sarah shooed them all out, pleading a long day, suggesting that a good night's sleep would be an asset for the busy day tomorrow.

The Lowell and Prentiss families left for the bunkhouse and the RV, their thanks and good night's filling the kitchen with a lingering feeling of warmth. Sarah smiled tiredly as she looked at the last cinnamon roll sitting on the plate. After a moment, she picked it up and tossed it to Delilah, who had just turned toward her. When Delilah caught it deftly, a puzzled look on her face, she said, "Bedtime snack for you. It looks so lonely sitting there."

She sighed, the exhalation loud in the room. "We're lucky that no budding Nobel Prize winners from Brighton were scheduled for this week. I can just see their frowns of disapproval at all the hustle and bustle and noise, can't you? But look out on Monday because scheduling called a little while ago. Some young genius from somewhere or other suddenly requires our bucolic atmosphere of peace and quiet."

She frowned. A disquieting thought had just occurred to her, but she set it aside for the moment, finishing, "But it was really nice to have the house full, wasn't it? It's always seemed to me that this place cries out for generations under its roof."

She smiled then, her customary good humor showing.

"Delilah, I do believe we have just set a world's record for the disappearance of a double-sized baking effort! There's not even a breadcrumb left. Unless you want to engage in another early morning session of dough-pounding aerobics, which I don't, we'll just rely on the bounty of old Mother Freezer tomorrow."

Delilah groaned dramatically, placing the back of the hand holding the cinnamon roll against her forehead in an exaggerated silent movie gesture of despair. When the smiling Clement family turned to leave, they all felt a faint jolt of surprise at hearing her voice, the unexpected sound of it, the unmistakable affection in the "Good night, sleep well," that she sang after them.

They walked silently to the gatehouse, each involved with their own thoughts and, still without speaking, arranged themselves in their customary places in the family room. Sarah didn't pause or hesitate. She plunged right in, beginning with a request that they not interrupt her, that they just listen very carefully evaluating everything she said because it was important that they form their own conclusions about what she was going to tell them.

Neither Joe nor Jordan had ever heard this strained tone in her voice; they sat quietly, waiting for the worst, whatever it was. They both felt a sense of dread, and the thought of cancer or some other deadly disease hovered like a noxious cloud that they tried to avoid, to dissipate by refusing to take a deep breath of it or otherwise acknowledge its presence in their minds. They were surprised and more than a little relieved when Sarah began at the beginning, going back to the time when she first went to work for Brighton Foundation. No matter what it was, it couldn't be as bad as what they had been dreading. But as she talked on, her quiet, sometimes almost inaudible recital of facts began to take on a horrible life of its own.

After a while, Joe began to feel as though Sarah was carefully describing a huge venomous reptile of a kind they had never before seen for themselves. Beginning at the tail, she described the beautiful scales, the fascinating curves and loops into which it so easily coiled itself, and the way it had slowly, subtly, hypnotically woven itself through her life . . . and the lives of her husband and son. In his mind Joe could see how the tightening coils had gone almost unnoticed in their in sly gentleness, their light, stroking touches pleasant, becoming welcome after a while as they seductively promised even greater pleasures in exchange for . . . Joe stopped himself there, thinking no matter what, his Sarah, this woman he so dearly treasured, was not about to exchange her integrity and goodness for simple security, no matter how much they all loved Bent Tree Farm.

He started to interrupt her to say this, but Sarah wasn't finished, and she stopped him with a tired wave of her hand. She had not been easy on herself, on the part she played, and was, she thought, still expected to play. "I want to go back to this person, this Agnes Kittridge." She almost spat the words, the anger in her voice viciously out of place in this relaxed warm haven of a room.

"I want you both to clearly understand what happened there. With full knowledge of Kittridge's insanity, the certain inevitability of her slide into a state where only she and her conception of God lived and interacted, Amanda Brighton deliberately sent Agnes Kittridge to Bhutu Holding Facility. Then she condemned Delilah to two years of solitary confinement with her, an innocent, helpless, feral child completely subject to the whims of her psychotic delusions."

Sarah stopped and looked down at her hands. She had not noticed before but now she saw that they were clenched so tightly that the nails were cutting into the flesh of her palms. She deliberately loosened them before she continued. "There could have been no reason for Amanda Brighton to do this other than to destroy the child, perhaps even cause her death. But at the very least it was almost certain that her mind would be warped beyond all hope of recovery. It was a deliberate act."

The anguish in Sarah's voice was soul-deep and searing. Joe and Jordan both moved forward in their seats, preparing to get up and go to her, but again she waved them back, continuing, determined to finish it before she gave way to the tears that filled her eyes. If I cry, she thought, I might never stop because I could

465

have done something, followed up on it, done something.

She pushed the thought away. "I've been reporting to Amanda about Delilah by phone for almost two years now, not very often though, because there hasn't been much going on to report. Then, young Doctor Lowell arrived on the scene to do an evaluation, basically to determine if Delilah has the skills and adaptability to live on her own. I wondered about this being done now, because it seems to be at least a year or more too early. Eighteen is usually considered the age of emancipation, and it seems unwarranted now."

Her small chuckle drew equally small encouraging smiles from her husband and son. "You should know that his being here is all my fault. When the subject of evaluation came up, I insisted that someone outside of Brighton Foundation staff do it. Amanda went along with that, probably because she couldn't come up with a reasonable excuse, at least not one she thought I'd swallow as easily as I swallowed everything else she fed me."

Her smile disappeared at the self-condemnation in her voice, almost as if someone else had said the words. "Anyway, I asked for K.C. because I knew him and respected his judgment. As you know, he was busy, and young Lochinvar came galloping up at full tilt." They all smiled at this. Casey's infatuation with Delilah was obvious to anyone within shouting distance.

Sarah's voice sounded very tired and defeated as she told them that she was probably violating confidential material by discussing all this with them, but it was a little late in her career as betrayer of professional matters to worry about it now. Joe frowned. It was one thing to get into a mess, but he didn't like the way she was beating herself to death over it. He wanted to say something, but she was going on, so he held his tongue. I'll be quiet, but just for the time being, he thought grimly.

"Apparently young Casey had no intention of being a rubber stamp for anyone and he started by insisting on the original records, going right back to the beginning with Delilah. And there it was, two years of reports from Bhutu all made by Agnes Kittridge. I just found this out this afternoon - seems such a long time ago - when Delilah asked us about Kittridge. When I think of it, Casey's insistence on original records instead of computer print-outs must have sent a few warning pulses back along the Brighton grapevine, too."

She thought a moment. "Then, he called his Dad with some questions about some of the things that didn't seem to right to him, things about Agnes Kittridge and Delilah's two years at Bhutu. At the time, he didn't know my background, but his Dad filled him in, and called me as the obvious person who might find out about Agnes Kittridge for them. When K.C. called me asking about her, it never entered my mind that it could possibly have anything to do with Delilah. I assumed he was following up on something else connected with his own professional interests in the field . . . he is well known for his meticulous research. So I just picked up the phone and called Brighton Foundation."

Sarah paused, then said, "I can't believe I could have been so stupid. When I didn't get answers there, I blithely called Amanda, the absolutely worst thing I could have done. I haven't had a return call from her, but now we suddenly have an unexpected, unscheduled visitor due on Monday." She looked at them questioningly. "I don't want to sound paranoid, but I'm at the point now where anything out of the ordinary looks suspicious to me."

This time, the pause was very long, and she looked at each of them before continuing. "I know that what I am going to tell you now is clearly a violation of professional ethics, but I'm at the point now that I need help, and I think Delilah needs help, too. You can only help me - and her - if you know it all. But it goes no further than this room, do you both understand?"

Their agreement was quick and reassuring, and she closed her eyes a moment, grateful that these two best-loved men were in her life, standing beside her like strong granite pillars in this dismal bog of misery. Quickly then, she told them what had happened during the time Delilah was blacked out, and described in detail the strange meeting she had conducted in the kitchen that afternoon, including her questions about Agnes Kittridge. She was almost finished, but there was one more thing, something she still could not come to terms with. "I think you should know something I find very shocking and hard to deal with. Amanda Brighton is more than ninety years old. I figured it out and I am sure."

As he absorbed the significance of this, Joe let his breath in a long, low whistle, and Jordan grunted, "Oh boy!"

Then, Jordan cleared his throat. "Mom, did you report anything about Delilah talking? I mean has there been any contact other than you inquiring about the Kittridge woman?"

She shook her head, then explained her reluctance, the way she had felt about the urgency, the greedy way Amanda had probed at her for information, somehow always maneuvering her way around to questions about Delilah talking.

Jordan nodded as though this verified something he had been thinking. "As I understand it, Delilah was found seven or eight years ago, and that old bat would have been in her early eighties at least even then, probably lapsing into some form of senility . . . or even senile dementia, right?"

"But," Sarah began, "she's still running . . . "

Joe interrupted without apology. "I suggest we take a break. Let's adjourn this family meeting to the kitchen, and continue it over hot cocoa." He stood up, went to Sarah and pulled her up from her chair. He enveloped her in a hug, kissed her on the cheek, and turned her toward the door, patting her butt firmly as he did so. "We've got a lot to discuss, and a plan to make, because I've got a feeling this Clement family is going on a snake hunt."

"Yeah, I agree," Jordan said thoughtfully, then asked, "Mom, where do the Doctors Lowell stand in this? Any ideas? I think it would be a very good idea to locate and identify all the snakes in the neighborhood." His voice took on an angry tone. "We sure as hell know who the old mama viper is . . . and where she keeps her den."

Sarah assured them that the Lowells were concerned only with Delilah's welfare and neither of them was Amanda's man. She explained that Casey was ready to cancel his contract with Brighton Foundation because of his emotional involvement, and K.C. had no Brighton connection whatsoever, nor had he ever had.

Their discussion went on for another hour, and two things became clear. No matter what the outcome, there were no second thoughts about saying good-bye to Bent Tree Farm, and no one could come up with any idea as to why Amanda Brighton apparently hated Delilah badly enough to go to the lengths she had to destroy her. As far as they knew, she had never even seen Delilah.

And they were all in agreement that a long, frank discussion with both the Doctors Lowell should take place after breakfast the next morning, but about the wisdom of including Delilah in such a discussion, they were still undecided as they went to bed.

* * *

Breakfast the next morning was slightly more subdued than dinner had been, but the children were in high spirits. At Sarah's prompting, Delilah agreed to take them to the barn and tell them the story of the Bentry pigeons. She ran back up to her room and returned with her pan flute, in order, she said, to show them the strange way some of the pigeons responded to it. Samantha and Kaydee confessed to an overwhelming desire to increase her audience, and James volunteered to go along as a trusty steed for the children.

"More a beast of burden, like a donkey," he laughed over his shoulder as he went out the back door, carrying Laurie in his arms with Jamie attached to his back like a limpet on a rock.

Suddenly, the sound of the pan flute drifted back, a dancing, happy tune keeping time with their steps to the barn. When the Lowell father and son stood up from the table with the intention of following the general exodus, smilingly intrigued with Delilah's display of playfulness, Sarah quietly asked them to stay. They seated themselves again, joining Joe and Jordan who were still sitting in their places regarding the coffee cups on the table in front of them with serious interest.   After filling all the empty cups, uncharacteristically fluttering a bit over the refilling of the

471

creamer and sugar bowl, Sarah seated herself, suddenly at a loss of where or how to begin what amounted to a baring of her soul.

Joe cleared his throat, and took the matter out of her hands. He began at the beginning just as Sarah had the night before, followed the story down through the years, and, in a surprisingly short time, arrived right here, at this table, in the present. He concluded with their suspicions about the short notice they had received about tomorrow's arrival, and how it seemed to fit the pattern of Amanda Brighton's style of manipulation.

A part of Sarah's mind was lost in admiration as she listened. Oh, she thought, Joe's good all right! Sometimes it was easy to forget the years he had spent in the classroom, defining and re-defining, clarifying points for the students in his class, using short, accurate sentences that were easy to remember and translate into notes. That side of him seemed to get lost in the easy-going, laid-back, quietly thoughtful, sly-humored man who shared her bed, and her life.

When he finished speaking, it was quiet for a moment, then Jordan began. There was nothing smooth or professional about either his method of delivery or his words.

"I'm mad," he said, "mad with a cold, deep anger at what has been done to my Mother and to Delilah. She says," he nodded his head toward Sarah, "she says that you two are definitely not Amanda Brighton's puppets. Well, let me say this right up front I

472

hope you aren't, because if I ever find out that either of you have engaged in any kind of double-dealing in this whole thing, I am going to take it very personally."

He paused, his gaze going from Casey to K.C. and back. They both returned his gaze steadily. Then, K.C. spoke. "I understand you completely, Jordan, and I would expect that under circumstances like these my son would feel exactly the same way. In fact," he put his hand on Casey's shoulder, "I should be very sadly disappointed in him if he did not."

Casey started to say something, taking a deep preparatory breath, but Jordan interrupted. "There's something else that you should understand clearly. My Mother loves Delilah like her own daughter. My Father loves Delilah like his own daughter. And I love Delilah like my own sister. She's been hurt enough, and I am very proud that because of my Mother's skill, and caring, and love, Delilah has come to no harm here with us at Bent Tree Farm. And while you may think I'm just being dramatic, please hear me well." He paused a moment, then finished, his voice vibrating with the intensity of his feelings. "I will not let anyone hurt either of them again."

If Sarah had been surprised at Joe's presentation of the situation, she was dumbfounded now. Her quiet, studious, plant-preoccupied son had these feelings? This young man who was so intent on maintaining his own independence? I'm a psychiatrist, she told herself, and I don't know my own son? Where in the world had this depth of loyalty and love been hiding? How could I have missed it?

For the moment, Casey found he had nothing to say. All of his suspicions about the way Delilah had been handled had been confirmed. And, just as important, his feeling about the way Delilah influenced the people around her had been given a solid boost. He stood up and put out his hand to Joe and Jordan in turn. After a firm, eye-engaged handshake with each of them, he strode around the table, pulled Sarah from her chair in a way reminiscent of what Joe had done last night, and gave her a big, hard hug and a kiss on the cheek. He looked startled when both Joe and Jordan burst out laughing.

Sarah laughed, too, as she disengaged herself and stepped back. "Joe did pretty much the same thing with me last night, Casey, but he also patted my butt. I don't think you should get that carried away, at least not with everyone watching."

Casey resumed his seat amidst the tension-relieving laughter, and they all became serious again. "Dad," he said, "is there any possible way you can stay on here a little longer? I know you've got editorial deadlines on your book, and the family expects you to leave with them in the morning, but I think we need you here for a while."

K.C. grunted thoughtfully. "As I see it, we have to talk to

Delilah right away. My opinion is," he looked around the table, "that Delilah is far more mature than we give her credit for. Think about what she said about Agnes Kittridge, the tone of her voice when she asked those questions. I think she's as angry as you are, Jordan, and if I'm right, she has already targeted Brighton Foundation as the enemy. But I don't think she even knows Amanda Brighton exists. When we talk to her that much will have to remain among the five of us, at least for the time being."

He stopped, removed his glasses, looked at them a moment, then put them back on. "As I told Casey, it's my opinion that Delilah is walking a mental and emotional tightrope right now. Her whole life since she was taken out of the jungle has been a matter of self-control, a game of secrets. The secret of being able to talk was revealed by circumstance, not through her choice, and she seems to have handled that well enough. But how much stress she can take without cracking completely, I don't know. We had best all keep her blackout in mind."

Their faces were serious as he looked at Sarah. "This is hard, Sarah. She doesn't know you're a psychiatrist, and she doesn't know of your connection with Brighton Foundation other than as she found you all, low-level employees that have given her love and acceptance. I don't think she should be presented with the truth just yet. Do you all agree?"

He glanced at Casey. "There's no problem with me staying on

here. I'll simply make the time up somewhere else, and now that James is here to help with the driving, they can go right on touring." He grinned happily. "Samantha is very understanding, and if I hint that perhaps our son needs some assistance, she'll be more than happy about my staying on."

Then he frowned, the furrows cutting deep into his forehead. "But what about the one coming tomorrow? They know you're here, son, but there isn't supposed to be anyone else hanging around."

Joe, who had been sitting quietly all this time, suddenly chuckled. "Well, Doctor Lowell, if you don't mind assuming a disgraceful disguise as a farmhand, riding around on the tractor with me once in a while, and making calculated appearances from time-to-time carrying a shovel or some other such uncouth thing, I think we can make you disappear right in front of their collective noses."

After the chuckles subsided, they could hear the sounds of voices coming toward the house, and they all stood up in preparation for leaving before the others arrived. Story hour was over, and Sarah spoke up at last, speaking softly and quickly.

"One last thing, the most important thing. I can see that we've got to talk to Delilah this afternoon. We can't take the slightest chance that she speaks where this Brighton person might overhear her. I don't know why it's important to her, but I have the sickest feeling that this is exactly what that old snake Amanda Brighton has been waiting so long to hear . . . that Delilah Cross is talking."

CHAPTER TWENTY ONE

Delilah had discovered a new game, at least that's how it felt to her. Telling the story of the Bentry pigeons had turned into an exciting adventure for her, although her audience wasn't aware of it. Hearing the sound of her own voice speaking and echoing back from the high roof of the barn, experimenting with modulation and tone to increase the effectiveness of her words, and stopping from time to time to play a bit of melody on her flute- -inventing the sound of birds flying, the sadness of home loss, the joy of reunion- -all had given her more pleasure than she could remember ever having experienced before. And her audience was both attentive and appreciative.

When they all trouped in from the barn, they found Sarah busy setting various lunch and snack materials out on the kitchen counter. Amid their loud and sincere praises of Delilah's story telling and flute playing abilities, Sarah managed to insert the suggestion of a picnic down by the brook, adding that wading in the shallow stream under the watchful eyes of the grown-ups might be a fun thing for the children to do, and certainly a much safer water sport than rafting on the pond. There were chuckles from the adults and enthusiastic cries of agreement from the children.

"Not only that," she added, "if you take blankets, of which there are several I keep around for just that purpose, taking a nap in the shade by the stream is just about the nicest thing I know."

"And just how would you know that, Sarah?" James was laughing as he asked. "Been sneaking away, have you?"

Before she could answer, K.C. strolled through the swinging door from the hall. "Well, and how was the story hour? We heard some lovely sounds coming from the barn." He smiled in Delilah's direction, then scooped Laurie up, holding her high before arranging her comfortably against his chest.

"Glad to see you're still with us, my dear. I could have sworn the Pied Piper himself was luring you and Jamie away to the dark and dismal cave where he keeps all the stolen children."

Laurie's face was serious. "Oh, Grandpa, don't tease. Delilah told us all about the Bentry pigeons. And I nearly cried 'cause it was so sad."

"But it ended happy ever after, just like it was s'posed to," Jamie commented. "I didn't cry, but Laurie really did, I saw her."

Laurie wiggled herself down to the floor, the better to confront him. "Well, Mr. Smarty, I don't care if you saw me. I'm not 'shamed of crying when something's sad, like you are. I saw real tears coming out of your eyes, too. And you got a runny nose. You wiped the snot on your sleeve!"

She turned to Kaydee, her tone becoming righteous and indignant. "He did Mama, he truly did! He wiped his nose right on his sleeve, and if you look you can see it's all yucky with boogers!"

The speed with which Jamie stuck the offending arm behind his back caused all the adults to struggle with smiles, and Jamie quickly changed the subject, something he was having to do with increasing frequency lately. He used to win every confrontation with Laurie, but since she started school his victories were becoming fewer, and this skirmish had been a total disaster.

"Hey, Grandpa, we're going to have a picnic down by the stream!" he announced importantly. "Are you coming along?"

"I don't think so, Jamie," K.C. answered, "but I'm sure your Grandma wants to." He looked across the kitchen. "Samantha, could I talk to you a minute?" She looked at him quizzically, but limped across the kitchen without saying anything, and they left through the swinging door toward the front of the house. Whatever they discussed, it didn't take long, and they were back before the two large picnic baskets were packed.

The picnickers went out the back door and down the steps, following the path toward the stepping stone crossing. Delilah had stayed behind in response to Sarah's restraining hand on her arm, and turned to help set the table. Her movements were smoothly and efficiently coordinated with Sarah's as they performed a kind of ageless homey ballet around the kitchen.

Delilah had a puzzled look on her face as she tried to sort out the mixed impressions she was receiving. There was something not quite right, but she didn't know what, why, or from whom the signals of unease were coming.

"Oh," Sarah said, as she placed a huge bowl of potato salad on the table, and turned back to the counter where a plate of cold cuts, pickles, and olives waited. "Please set places for six, Delilah. Everyone not picnicking will be in for lunch in a few minutes."

They had gathered around the table, Joe, Jordan, Casey, K.C., Sarah, and Delilah, all in their accustomed places, and it wasn't until they finished eating and the coffee was poured that Delilah understood at least some of the subtle messages she had been receiving.

K.C. began. "Delilah, I don't want you to feel defensive, or get the idea that we're somehow ganging up on you, but there are some questions that only you can answer. We're in a situation here that requires straight answers from all of us." His gesture included everyone at the table, and Delilah looked at Joe and Jordan, obviously wondering how they came to be included.

K.C. did not explain, but continued, "I think that, as a matter of fact, we intend to answer more questions for you than ask them." He paused, his face at once kind and serious. "What we want is for you to listen carefully to what we have to say, and then answer our questions. I want you to know right up front that we all agree, all of us sitting here, that you are far more adult and able to cope than anyone ever gave you credit for."

Delilah looked at Sarah, the question plain on her face. The sense of anxiety- -that was the only way she could define it- -was apparent now, coming from all of them. It's catching, she thought, as she felt her own stomach muscles involuntarily tighten.

To her surprise, it was Sarah who spoke first. Her surprise deepened as Sarah described, in graphic detail, what had happened during the period of her blackout after the pond episode. She left nothing out, including the conclusions they had drawn, and Delilah felt a rising sense of dismay at how much she had inadvertently revealed, how much these people actually knew. She lowered her eyes, fastening them on her hands carefully folded on the table in front of her.

Then, Casey began, taking his time. It was painful for him, that much was clear as he explained how he had gotten the job of evaluating her quite by default, the spying on her, the careful reading of her records, the peculiar things he had noted there, the prowling through her room, and his calling K. C. for assistance. His face reddened as he flatly stated that he had been ready to resign when he realized that his emotional involvement was interfering with his professional objectivity.

His face flaming, Casey turned to face Delilah, and at the movement, she raised her eyes to his. The expression on her face was unreadable to everyone sitting at the table, but it soon became clear that she did not intend to drop her eyes from Casey's, no matter how long it took to win this particular battle of wills. She didn't know why it was important that she dominate and assert control. She just knew it was.

The flush left Casey's face as the moments ticked by. For some reason he didn't understand, it felt like his very masculinity was being challenged by this girl suddenly become woman, and he realized that Delilah was consciously challenging him, trying to dominate him, make him look away and thus acknowledge her power and ability to control him. The thoughts took form in the back of his mind, disjointed but clear. It's a game. Asserting dominance, using her eyes like weapons.

This was followed by a sudden flashing thought that shook him to the center of his being, giving the lie to everything he had ever believed about himself. He wanted to look away, admit his inferiority, submit and be dominated by her. He was ready to look down then, and he wondered if she read his thoughts, or smelled them rising from him like a smoky cloud . . . and discovered he didn't care. At that moment, he saw the awareness in her eyes, the slightest hint of softening in her expression. She knew.

Across the table, Jordan took a deep breath and looked away from them. Perhaps because he was a young male like Casey, he was more sensitive, more receptive and alert to the nuances and subtle signals sent out almost unconsciously by approachable females. Although Delilah was sitting perfectly still, her face expressionless, not looking at him, Jordan could almost physically feel the aura of powerful sensuality emanating from her and understood that come what may, Casey had just surrendered to her. In some mixed-up way, he felt both relief that the strange, compelling attraction Delilah was manifesting so clearly was not aimed at him, and a sense of loss and envy that her attention was focused on Casey and not himself.

K.C. had been thinking his own thoughts as he watched the power struggle going on between his son and Delilah. He, too, was aware of the almost palpable aura surrounding Delilah, and when he became aware of Casey's capitulation, he was suddenly filled with misgivings for his son.

At that moment, Joe cleared his throat loudly. The sound served to disrupt the silence that had become more embarrassing the longer it went on. It didn't take a genius to see what was happening between these two, Joe thought, and now wasn't the time or place for them to settle the issue. Delilah and Casey both looked toward him at the same time.

"Jordan and I don't have a lot to contribute here, Delilah. We're here because we love our Sarah, and we feel like you're part of our family. In our opinion, there's something going on that we don't like, and whether you approve of it or not, girl, we're closing family ranks around you."

Before Delilah could react to this totally unexpected announcement, K.C. spoke. "We do need some answers, Delilah, and it's up to you to decide whether or not you want to trust us. Considering what we do know, and what we've been able to assume from that, it's clear that you have trusted no one." He sighed sadly and shook his head before he said, "And rightly so, as far as I can see."

There were nods of agreement from around the table as he continued, "Delilah, please don't resent the fact that we have all discussed you behind your back. It was, I assure you, done in your own best interests."

Delilah spoke for the first time, her tone of voice unexpectedly sarcastic and jeering. "Of all the ways it's been said to me over the last eight years, that's the neatest way of putting it I've heard!" She looked around the table at them, at their shocked faces, and burst into laughter, the sound full of anger and anguish.

After a moment, her face straightened. "No," she said quietly, "you wouldn't know, would you? Everything was always done for my own good; those were the words used when a doctor, yes, a

485

doctor, molested me on the examining table just after I got to Hiller School. And those were the words they spoke to me after discussing me in my presence like I was a piece of furniture . . . or maybe a strange, surrealistic picture hanging on the wall." She paused, then added, "Or maybe an animal, a weird, unpredictable, dangerous animal."

She stopped, out of breath from the force of her feelings. Like a volcano that has finally found a weak spot in the cool outer crust, a fountain of rocks and lava from the depths of her soul was threatening to erupt. No one spoke. They looked at her with compassion and concern, but she didn't notice, and she was beyond caring. Her pain was palpable, her words pushing at them, abrading, hurting them nearly as much as they hurt her.

"I had just come from the Holy Church of Miss Agnes Kittridge, you see, where daily, for two years, those exact words were part of the ritual beatings as she sacrificed my child-body on the altar of her insane God."

There was a moan of anguish from Sarah, and tears trickled down the sides of her nose. Joe looked at her questioningly, and she gave him a slight shake of her head, trying to smile to reassure him.

Delilah dropped her head onto her hands as they lay on the table in front of her. Her voice was muffled, but the words were clear. "You wouldn't know about this either, would you?

Certainly, it wasn't in any of the records I read, and I read them all. I learned to read a little at Bhutu just in order to read those reports. Oh, how I sneaked and prowled at night, how cleverly I learned to fool the lock." Her voice trailed off, then she raised her head, looking at them squarely, one by one.

"Tell me, you psychological experts," the words were aimed at Casey and his Father, "did you come up with any tidy little theories as to why I avoid the company of dogs?" She didn't wait for an answer. "I'm sure that if it was noticed at all, and I have learned to be so sneaky in concealing my reactions that it probably wasn't, if it was noticed at all," she repeated, "the theory was probably that I feared them based on my long, and I might add happy, association with bonobo apes."

Again, she laughed. There was no humor in the sound. "Well, add this to those less than accurate records. Miss Agnes kept me on a collar and leash a lot the time. Much easier to control, you see." Her hand rose of its own accord to touch her neck.

"The first obedience words she taught me to understand were 'stay', 'quiet', 'sit', 'come' and 'fetch'. Yes, fetch!" Delilah took a deep, ragged breath. "Fetch me this, fetch me that is what she would say. Sometimes, just for fun, she would demand I fetch something just out of my reach on the leash. Oh, how she enjoyed that, watching me trying to decide between two wrongs, both of which would earn me a beating . . . to pull on the leash which was

487

forbidden, or to disobey the command to fetch, which was also forbidden."

She paused, looking at each of them in turn. "Well, I read a lot, and one of the things I've read about is called the double-bind situation where you're damned if you do and damned if you don't." Her voice took on a triumphant tone. "Oh, but she never taught me to speak like a good little doggy. No matter how she beat me, and screamed, and called on her God to strike me dead, I did not speak!"

Delilah was silent a moment, and Sarah's voice, shaken and husky, surprised them as she asked, "Delilah, what does the leash have to do with the garden?" She had suddenly remembered Delilah's occasional strange behavior when she was in the garden.

Delilah looked at her in surprise. "How would you know about that, Sarah? Did I talk about that when I fainted?" Without waiting for an answer, she went on. "The seeds for the garden and the collar and leash came on the same day. Miss Agnes introduced me to the collar and leash, and then we went out and planted her garden. Oh, it was a hard lesson, and my neck was raw and bleeding by the time all those seeds were in the ground to her satisfaction."

Delilah's voice became harsh with emotion, as though the words, themselves, were hurting her throat as she spoke. "She said that I should bend over and let the blood drip on the ground because it was good plant food. When I didn't bend over fast enough, she jerked on the collar until I fell down, and made me lay there for a long time, bleeding into the dirt while she talked to her God."

Her voice changed again, becoming almost dreamy. "You know, I used to hate her God and wonder where my God was, or if I even had one. I still don't know for sure. Sometimes, I would be hurting so bad that I would ask Miss Agnes' God to strike me dead or let me get away from there, but nothing happened, and I had to stay. I think you have to have a soul before God notices you."

Delilah was so deep inside herself now, she was unaware of the pain and empathy on every face as the others shared her agony. "Miss Agnes always said that eyes are the windows of the soul. She didn't like my eyes, didn't allow me to look directly at her, so I decided it was because they were empty, and I didn't have a soul. That's why God never talked to me the way He talked to her."

Her hand rose to touch her neck and she was quiet, lost in memory. Then, in quite a different tone of voice, she asked, "Oh, and why do I avoid dogs? Well, that's so easy it's almost funny. When I first got to Hiller School, one of the student's parents brought a dog to visit. They put on a little demonstration for the children to show how well the dog was obedience trained. When someone noticed that I was obeying every command as quickly and accurately as the dog, they got embarrassed enough to take me away."

She looked up at them again. "Why aren't you laughing?" she demanded. "Everyone laughed, then. But no one thought to ask how a feral child fresh from the jungle had learned all those dog obedience commands. I never found anything in the records about it, either. Simply put, I avoid dogs, even now, because when someone gives a command to them, I still automatically start to perform. That's how well I learned."

Delilah took a deep breath, feeling suddenly empty. No one spoke, and after a long time, she asked, "You asked me to trust you, didn't you?" She laughed weakly, her eyes pleading for their understanding. "I guess it took saying all of that for me to understand that you really don't know anything about what happened to me, and you certainly aren't responsible for any of it."

It was both an apology and an absolution. She reached to pat Sarah's arm, then leaned back in surprise as Sarah burst into sobs, jumped up from the table, and almost ran from the room, leaving the swinging door swishing loudly in the silence. Joe half-rose to follow her, then changed his mind and sat back down with a frown.

Jordan, who had to this point uttered not a word, suddenly

490

asked, "Delilah, you are very intelligent. Just who do you think is responsible for all of this?"

The question surprised her, but in a way she was grateful for the chance to explain. It must have been hard for them all to sit through her diatribe. Maybe they felt as emotionally drained as she did. A small voice in her mind giggled softly and wondered if a Dia tribe was related to the Navajo tribe, or perhaps the Cherokee tribe? Ignoring the little voice, she considered her answer to Jordan's question carefully. Finally she decided that, in this area at least, honesty couldn't hurt her.

"Brighton Foundation," she said firmly. "Someone very high up in Brighton Foundation." She slowly looked from Joe to Jordan to Casey to K.C. "I realize that none of you had any part in it, even if you all work for Brighton Foundation. But someone made decisions and someone else carried them out. I've spent the last five years or so prowling through their computer records and I haven't found anything." She sounded puzzled. "And that's strange," she continued. "There's no record on Agnes Kittridge and no record of who gave the orders that sent me to Bhutu, or Hiller School, or even here."

It suddenly struck her and she looked at Joe. "Oh, I'm sorry I upset Sarah. I never thought about how awful it all must sound until I actually said it out loud." Her dismay was obvious, and K.C. spoke quickly.

"We need to finish up now because the others will be back soon. And I'm sorry, too, Delilah, for coming down on a very sore spot in your life. Believe me, it wasn't intentional." He smiled and she returned it with a warm smile of her own. He found that he was as aware of the smile in her eyes as he was of her upturned lips and crinkled cheeks. It made him feel good inside for a reason he didn't pursue.

When he continued his voice was serious, and he was interrupted from time to time by Joe, Jordan, or Casey as they added their own thoughts about the situation he was describing, to the plan he was outlining to handle it, and the need for subterfuge in order to buy time for investigation. They stressed the fact that her not talking was important. They weren't sure why she should keep the fact secret, but they all agreed that it seemed to be some kind of pivotal point in what had been going on, what was still going on.

After her initial shock over the fact that they not only believed her theory, but had arrived at the same conclusion on their own, Delilah quickly absorbed what they were telling her. She also came to realize that these people were her friends and could be trusted . . . up to a point. She felt no slightest trace of guilt as one part of her mind, acting almost on its own, busily began to explore the possible ways they might be useful in completing her quest.

Her laughter was clear and unclouded by anything except humor. "I can hardly wait to see you as a farmer," she said to K.C. "And you must have a name, too." Her giggle brought grins to faces that had been grimly serious. "How about Homer?" she asked. "Can you think of a better name? Homer Hayseed would be a little too obvious, wouldn't it? Then plain old Homer Jones, part-time farmer's helper." She giggled again, then sobered.

Gentlemen, do you realize that you are telling me not to talk? After all the time and energy spent in getting me to talk? Doesn't that strike you as funny?"

It did, and they were still laughing as the picnickers returned from the stream. In the general confusion, Delilah slipped away to find Sarah. After checking the gatehouse and the barn, she found her down by the stream leaning against a tree. "Sarah," she called to announce her presence. "Want some company?" Without waiting for an answer, she went up beside Sarah, leaning against her companionably.

"Sarah, I'm sorry, really sorry that I just blurted it all out like I did. It's not very pretty, I know, and I'm sorry if I upset you."

Delilah could feel Sarah's shoulders shaking, feel the sobs silently shuddering through her body, and she could feel the effort that Sarah was making to bring herself under control. Delilah could see the tears coursing down Sarah's cheeks, and for a moment she had to fight the impulse to touch Sarah's cheek with

493

her finger, taste her tears as she had shared Auntie's bad hurt so long ago.

After a few moments, Sarah took a deep breath and turned to face Delilah. "Oh, Delilah, you will never know how sorry I am that you went through something that must have been a living hell! And whoever is responsible for it will pay in full, you can be sure of that!" There was no doubting the sincerity in Sarah's voice.

"I know that Sarah," Delilah said quietly. "The men finished filling me in on it." Sarah turned to look at her as she giggled, the unexpected sound riding along on the lower chuckling of the stream. "We had to have a name for K.C. in his undercover role, Sarah, so I named him Homer Jones!"

After a moment, Sarah chuckled, and said, "That's good, and I've got to go through Joe's old clothes tonight to find something suitable for Homer Jones to wear. First thing in the morning after the family leaves, he'll be here to help Joe out. Hope he's a good worker."

Arm in arm, they walked up the path to the farm, still laughing at the thought of the very professional Doctor K.C. Lowell shoveling cow manure in the barn. Even though there were only three cows and a calf, and they spent the day out in the pasture, their combined efforts at night produced enough aromatic waste to require at least an hour of energetic shoveling every morning.

* * *

The Prentiss family and Samantha got under way shortly after breakfast the next morning. The long RV eased around the stone gatepost onto Palmer Road, and the fact that James made the sharp corner on the first try attested to his driving skill. With several toots of the horn and much enthusiastic waving from the children, they drove out of sight. Doctor K.C. Lowell wasn't with them, but shortly after they disappeared down the road, Homer Jones slouched out of the bunkhouse and walked toward them.

Casey burst out laughing. "Homer, old son," he shouted, "we won't have you padding your hours. A man's gotta work if he wants to eat at Sarah's table! Step lively, there!"

They all walked up to the farmhouse together, then separated. "You'll pass, Homer," Joe said with a grin, "as long as you don't get too up close and personal, and it might be better if you just grunt now and then instead of talking. A grouchy old man goes a long way toward being ignored."

There was a final outburst of hilarity as Homer donned a disreputable hat, floppy and dirty, with what appeared to be permanently ingrained sweat-rings and various other marks and stains impossible to identify.

"Where in the world did you get that thing?" Sarah asked.

"My contribution, Mom," Jordan couldn't help laughing. "I found it up in the back of the barn loft a while back. You might say I was reluctant to touch it. Must have been there fifty years, or so, but when I beat the spiders out of their happy home yesterday evening I knew that it was Homer's hat. No one could possibly look past that hat. Downright hypnotic, isn't it?"

There was a loud chorus of agreement, and Homer grunted sourly. Jordan, still laughing, headed off to the greenhouse. Delilah and Sarah watched Homer and Joe turn into the equipment shed, and after a few minutes the tractor rumbled into life and disappeared off across the fields. With a wave, Casey disappeared inside, going upstairs to the office to run through Delilah's records again, looking for anything that he might have missed.

Sarah and Delilah were sitting in the kitchen, sipping coffee while they made out the grocery list and decided what other stops needed to be made on the trip into town, when Delilah held up her hand for silence, listening intently. Sarah also listened, but it was several seconds later that she caught the crunch of tires on the gravel driveway.

"Well, Delilah, it's no talking time," Sarah said. "Here comes our Brighton representative. Come on, we'll meet whoever it is together."

They reached the front porch just as the driver awkwardly jerked a piece of luggage from the trunk of the small blue Brighton car and turned around to peer at them across the driveway. The frown was in place, the voice already rising in a whining complaint.

Delilah turned and started back in the house. "Lots of luck, Sarah," she muttered softly. "They've sent us dear Margaret or Marguerite, or whatever her name is. I'm going to go and hide!"

Suiting action to words, she went back inside, leaving only the faintest trill of laughter drifting through the air behind her as she ran up the stairs.

CHAPTER TWENTY TWO

Delilah stood just inside her closed door listening as Sarah escorted Margaret upstairs to her room. She hasn't changed much, was Delilah's first thought. As they came up the stairs, Margaret's annoying whine listing the hardships she had encountered on the trip would have been audible to anyone on the second floor, even with the doors closed. Her various complaints ranged from unsanitary restrooms in the plane to the strange knocking sound in the engine of the Brighton car that had been conveniently waiting in the airport parking lot for her private use.

"Sarah," she said, the words clearly an order given to a menial, "you must see to it that your husband checks that engine before I use the car again. He is a mechanic of sorts, isn't he?" The question was rhetorical because she didn't wait for an answer. "The very idea of being stranded out on some godforsaken country road is just too much. It's bad enough to have to cancel all my plans . . . ." Her voice trickled away into momentary silence.

Delilah smiled. So Margaret hadn't planned this visit? Had to change her plans?

The respite was brief. Apparently Margaret decided that Sarah was too stupid to read any significance into her momentary lapse, and went off in another direction. "And Sarah, I was in that horrible green room right by the bathroom the last time. I didn't complain then because all the rooms seemed to be occupied," her voice took on a suitable tone of long-suffering martyrdom, "but I must tell you that I found it disgusting to be subjected to the bathroom noises of other people." The offensive whine returned as she said, "And one of them actually made songs as he gargled!"

Apparently she turned to Sarah for sympathetic understanding of the depths to which she had been offended because Delilah clearly heard Sarah's muffled "Oh my goodness, how awful!" as they stopped just outside of her door. After a moment, Sarah said, "Well, the green room is occupied. A Doctor Casey Lowell is here working with Delilah. She still has the rose room here in the middle, but the other four are empty at the moment, so take your pick, Margaret."

"Oh, yes, Doctor Lowell. I forgot he was here. Well, I'll just take this one across the hall from Delilah. It's the yellow one, isn't it? A good color with my complexion." There was the sound of a door opening and closing. The whine became muffled, the sound of an annoying insect mindlessly determined to get through a

499

window screen on a warm summer evening.

Thank you, Sarah, Delilah thought, as she quickly slipped out her door and closed it very quietly behind her. A good color? With her pasty, yellowish skin, Margaret would blend right into the yellow room and disappear. Delilah had to stifle a giggle as she went quickly and quietly down the hall to the office. Casey turned toward her as she pushed the partly-closed door open. His face was red with repressed laughter, and when she motioned him to come on, he quickly gathered up the folders he was working on and came out on the landing. He motioned to his room, indicating the folders, and she waited until he put them in his room, closed the door with exaggerated care, and tiptoed back down the hall.

When they reached the comparative safety of the kitchen, Delilah went to the pantry and got a basket, then went to the refrigerator. "We've only got a minute," she whispered over her shoulder, hurriedly shoving various things to eat and drink into the basket. She closed the refrigerator and went to the back door. "We've got to talk, right now," she was still whispering. "I think we've got time to get to the greenhouse before she gets back downstairs." She grinned happily, an expression on her face that could only be called impish. "Poor Sarah," she said, the grin giving the lie to the sympathetic words, "she's running interference, but she won't be able to hold her back long."

Taking a roundabout route that kept them out of sight of the upstairs windows on the yellow room side of the house, they were tapping insistently on the back door of the greenhouse. It was kept locked because it opened directly into the laboratory section where traffic was not encouraged. They had almost given up when Jordan's head appeared, peering at them through the upper glass panes. "What's going on? Why the back door?" he asked as he turned the latch and let them in.

"Remember that obnoxious Margaret person who was doing a paper on me about six months ago?" Delilah asked.

Jordan groaned. "Do I ever remember! Do you know she pursued me like a hungry piranha? I had to keep the front door to the greenhouse locked while she was here. Something to do with relative isolation and eligible men, I think. She reminded me of an ambulatory Venus' Fly trap." He stopped and looked at them. "You mean she's the one we were waiting for?"

Delilah stopped laughing at the images Jordan had painted and her face was serious when she answered. Glancing at Casey for verification, she said, "She slipped at least two times that I heard. Once when she complained about having to cancel her plans in order to come here, and again when she acknowledged that she knew Casey was here." When Casey nodded she went on. "The fact that she's been here before, and knows me . . . ."

The men waited patiently as she wrinkled her face in disgust, then looked up at them. "Well, here's another confession of stupidity. She's probably here because of me."

Casey and Jordan both laughed. "Of course, it's because of you. What other reason?" Jordan asked.

"Because I fed her an awful lot of crap, excuse me, misinformation, about myself, played a lot of mind games with her, and very carefully edited her report into something half-way intelligible because I felt guilty." She waited, and when they both looked puzzled, she explained. "Margaret is incredibly stupid and unobservant. If I had left it alone, her report on me would have gotten a failing grade, she wouldn't have come to the attention of someone at Brighton, and she wouldn't be here now as surrogate eyes and ears. Now do you see?"

"Oh yeah," Jordan said, "I can see it."

"But it isn't all bad if she's stupid and unobservant," Casey said thoughtfully. "Well, in one way it is because, no matter how stupid she is, she knows something about your behavior patterns. So you're going to have to go right along just as you did before, no changes from the last time. Except," he shook his finger warningly at Delilah, "no editorial tampering. Just let her muddle along by herself and hope she digs a very deep hole in her credibility."

He looked quizzically at Jordan. "We'll need time to talk to each other. Everyone is working on digging up information. Except you, Jordan." He paused, looking at Jordan with his

502

eyebrows raised, the corners of his mouth quirked in a silly grin.

"No!" Jordan yelled, "Absolutely not!"

"What?" Delilah asked, looking from one to the other. "What?"

"It's a dirty job, Jordan, but someone's got to do it." Casey burst out laughing as Jordan groaned loudly, grabbed his stomach and bent over, making realistic barfing noises as he did so.

"What? What's wrong? What's happening?" Delilah's voice was rising.

"Gaah!" Jordan said, then straightened up. "Delilah, although it may not have looked that way to you, we were in traditional manly fashion deciding on a way to divert Margaret long enough to give us all time to talk about the things we need to talk about, and do it without making her suspicious. And I've just been volunteered to be the diversion."

Delilah's trill of laughter when she understood what the men had just decided between them was cut off abruptly. "Someone's coming," she whispered, pointing to the back door.

Both men straightened up, listening intently, but it was several seconds before they heard the rustling sounds and the faint clink as two pieces of metal came in contact. Jordan motioned them through the door into the main part of the greenhouse, and when they were out of sight, he stepped to the back door, and opened it with a jerk.

"Uhh, well hello, Jordan. That was quick. I don't even remember knocking." It was Homer. The awful hat was pushed back on his forehead, a stubble of gray beard had started to make its appearance on his chin, and he looked like he had been rolling in the dirt. A rubber-tired wheelbarrow with a shovel leaning against it was parked on the walk behind him, and as a gentle breeze swept past, the distinct aroma of cow barn drifted into the cleaner air of the greenhouse.

He looked past Jordan as Delilah and Casey stepped into view. "I take it you've already brought the news of our guest." He pivoted, treating them to a full view of his body. It was even worse from the back. The pants drooped far below his waist, secured by a scuffed belt, and frayed cuffs dragged on the ground by the heels of his battered work shoes. "How do I look?"

Delilah sniffed. "I would say that you don't only look the part, Homer, you smell it too! What did you do?"

"Quite simple, my dear." His voice took on a pompous professorial tone so completely at odds with his appearance as to be ludicrous. "I merely thought of the most efficacious way of purveying the homely rural odor of farm and cow barn from my person to Amanda Brighton's emissary without engaging in the undignified process of rolling in the source of the aroma."

Casey let out a whoop of delight. "He's got cow shit in his pocket!" He banged Jordan on the shoulder. "Dad, you didn't put cow shit in your pocket?" Homer joined in the laughter as Casey and Jordan erupted. They didn't notice that Delilah had become silent and did not join in the laughter. Casey erupted again. "Wait until I tell Mom! She'll never let you live it down!"

Homer held up his hands, and they became quiet. "I think you two better get out of here, one at a time, and go your separate ways until lunch. Delilah, why don't you go down to the stream and make a show of trying to cross? Casey, I see you've got a basket of goodies, so you go on up to the big meadow, in clear view, and have yourself a little solitary picnic."

"But you stay here a few minutes, Homer," Jordan said. "We need to talk about Margaret." When Homer raised his eyebrows questioningly, Jordan continued, "We know her, and we've already got a kind of plan." He glared at Casey, who grinned widely, then threw off a mock salute as he went out the door with his basket. "And we need to pass the word around," he finished.

Delilah slipped away as they were talking, and a little while later she saw Homer trudging along the path toward the compost bins. The wheelbarrow was full of various wilted leaves and vines that Jordan must have provided. Good idea, she thought. Even someone as unobservant as Margaret would eventually notice if he kept pushing an empty wheelbarrow around.

At this point, everyone on the farm was involved in the charade, carrying on their activities right under Margaret's oversized nose. This was not going to be easy, Delilah realized, because it was no longer a private little game involving her and an obnoxious graduate student. A lot of very intelligent people were taking it very seriously. Her feeling of excited anticipation at the prospect of a new, intriguing game was gone. It had disappeared in the instant K.C., aka Homer, had mentioned Amanda Brighton's name. She had never encountered that name before. Amanda Brighton.

Delilah halted in mid step, awkwardly catching her balance as though she had tripped over the thought. Margaret. Amanda Brighton's emissary. At the time of her last visit, Margaret had been a graduate student, that was more than clear. But how had a mere graduate student, and one so inept and unqualified, gotten permission for a two week, in-depth study of Delilah Cross? Across the years, that privilege had always been restricted to professionals like the Lowells, people well-known and established as authorities in their fields. No matter how she had despised them, their credentials had never been in doubt. Margaret was completely unqualified at the time of her first visit, and in spite of the newly-earned diploma she apparently possessed now, she still had no real credentials whatsoever.

Delilah suddenly felt unaccountably small and vulnerable as she remembered the discussion at the table yesterday morning. She thought about K.C., suddenly understanding that he would never have assumed the Homer persona as a lark, a game. The matter was very serious. Keep walking, she told herself sternly, just keep on walking.

Amanda Brighton, she thought. Her mind was suddenly filled with a picture of a gigantic tree, the one she had constructed in an attempt to understand the interlinking parts of Brighton Foundation. She hadn't been able to decide if the final order giver sat at the very top like God or burrowed down among the roots like a worm. Now she knew the identity of the final order-giver and where she lived. Amanda Brighton, whoever she was, hid herself deep under the tree.

Not a worm, Delilah thought, not even a snake. They each had their own form of innocent purity. No, a powerful mutant octopus creature with hundreds of tentacles that had been groping around Delilah Cross for the past eight years. They are all very sure, the Lowells and the Clements, that Amanda Brighton wants something from me, something that is connected with my talking. But what? I don't know anything that she would . . . .

It blazed across her mind, then, in letters glowing like huge, neon lights, blinking on and off, on and off, to be sure she didn't miss the message. THE SECRET! Blink. THE SECRET! Blink.

Delilah had an overwhelming urge to run to Sarah and bury her face in her comforting warmth, hiding from that mocking, blinking neon billboard and everything it meant. She half-turned

507

meaning to do just that, then squared her shoulders and marched resolutely toward the stream and its six mossy stepping-stones. Without thought, she crossed the stream without slowing her stride, ignoring the second stone that shifted slightly under her foot, and walked across the pasture to the stile.

She climbed to the top and sat down, her legs dangling, facing Palmer Road. After a while, her breathing slowed and she began to think again. Turned totally inward, she didn't see the occasional car that passed, or hear the rise and fall of traffic sounds as drivers halted at the stop signs, then continued on their way at the four corners. After a while, she jumped down from the wall, and walked resolutely back up the road to the driveway, turned in, and walked up to the farmhouse. For a moment she felt a fleeting sense of accomplishment and satisfaction, but it only lasted a moment. She had just taken the walk that she had so badly wanted to take . . . but the shadow-dark figure of Amanda Brighton had taken it with her.

She paused on the porch, fished her notepad and pen out of her pocket and wrote a few words before going in the house. She was smiling broadly as she entered the kitchen and walked past Margaret, going directly to Sarah, tugging at her arm for attention. She knew Margaret was there from the nasal whine that had drifted down the hall, and she knew that Margaret was watching her closely as she handed the notepad to Sarah.

Sarah read the words, then looked up, smiling. The smile was still on Delilah's face, but her eyes were not visible to Margaret as they were to Sarah. They were deadly, cold with something that Sarah recognized as pure, undiluted hatred . . . and something else. She repressed an urge to shudder and managed to keep her smile in place as she said, "Why that's wonderful, Delilah, just wonderful!" before turning back to the counter, anxiously wondering what had happened to cause this sudden change in Delilah.

Then her eyes widened as she remembered the dinner table discussion they had about the stepping stones. Jordan insisted that anyone who reached the fourth stepping stone in either direction had actually crossed the stream because they could jump to the bank from there. Delilah was telling her that she had crossed the stream! But why hadn't she simply written that on her notepad? Then Sarah thought about what she had seen in Delilah's eyes. There was a reason. She turned around to watch, sure something was going to happen.

Delilah's head was lowered, lids concealing her eyes, but the smile was even wider when she turned back to face Margaret. She slowly started to put her notepad back in her pocket. Come on, Margaret, come on, she thought. Come on and grab the bait like a good hungry little Brighton piranha.

"Oh, Delilah dear, would you like to share that with me?"

Margaret's words and intonation were those one might use to coax a backward six-year-old, but it was clearly a command, not a request. Delilah didn't mind. What was it Paulie used to say? Hook, line, and sinker, she thought. She managed a slightly puzzled look, then walked over to where Margaret sat at the table and handed her the notepad. Hook, line, and sinker.

Margaret read the words out loud. "'I got all the way to the fourth stepping stone!'" she read, pretending to have difficulty making out the clearly printed words. "How nice." Her voice was flat.

She paused, looking at Delilah, then made a comment about something she would have had no way of knowing unless she had been privy to the report written by Doctor Casey Lowell, Junior, a privileged document from one psychiatrist to another that had been filed with Brighton Foundation a few days ago.

"You know, Delilah, you might do better with this water phobia of yours if someone went along to oversee your efforts. I totally disagree that you should be allowed to continue on your own." She sniffed, her nose twitching.

"What is that dreadful odor?"

Margaret had been directing all her attention to Delilah, glorying in what could only be her newly-acquired authority. And we know where that came from, Delilah thought, as she stood with downcast eyes, awash in Margaret's flow of condescension.

Homer had slipped through the swinging doors in time to hear everything that Margaret said, bringing with him the earthy smell of cow manure. Delilah saw him over Margaret's head, and Sarah saw him as she turned from the counter, but neither had given the slightest indication of his presence.

"Shit," he said in a gravely, sour voice.

Margaret jumped to her feet and turned to face him, an expression of horror on her face. "What?" she gargled, clasping her hand protectively over her nose as Homer took a step closer. "What did you say?"

"I said shit, ma'am," he repeated, idly slapping his filthy hat against the pocket area of his pants, releasing an even stronger flow of eye-watering smell. "You asked what that smell was an' I tole ya. It's cow shit. I bin cleanin' the barn and I guess a little of the stink kinda hung on."

He took another step closer, standing beside Margaret, still idly slapping his pocket as he addressed his words to Sarah. "Miz Clement, if I smell too randy to sit at the table, I'd be plumb glad to sit out on the porch fer lunch. Gotta go right back to shovelin' shit, so no sense in cleanin' up now."

With a muffled sound somewhere between an outraged shriek and a gag, Margaret flew from the room, nearly taking the swinging door from its hinges. The three conspirators stood silently. Sarah looked like she was courting a case of apoplexy and Delilah was bent over clutching her stomach as it spasmed with soundless laughter. The sound of a car starting and departing in a spray of gravel was punctuated by Casey's arrival. His face was puzzled.

"What happened? Margaret just ran out, jumped in her car and took off toward town like a bat out of hell."

The silence broke then. Sarah tried to explain, but all she got out was something that sounded to Casey like "Cow shit" before she rushed out the back door and collapsed on the steps, emitting howls that Casey decided was laughter, not symptoms of a seizure.

Homer had seated himself at the table, calmly watching Delilah as she shamelessly rolled back and forth on the floor, emitting a fascinating series of hoots and snorts and gurgles as she did so. Casey sniffed loudly, and looked pointedly at his Dad.

"I'll leave in a minute, son, and let the ladies fill you in. That is, as soon as I'm sure they're going to survive." He rose, emitting an almost visible cloud of smell. "Strange how your nose adapts to almost anything. Apparently, I overdid it without noticing. Sorry about that," he said as he went past Sarah and down the steps.

At the bottom, he turned around and walked back up a couple of steps. "Casey," he called, "keep one thing in mind. This woman belongs to Brighton Foundation, no question. I heard enough to nail her ass legally for violation of professional ethics, and if she's got no actual professional status, it's enough to get whoever gave her your report on Delilah, too, and blacklist both of them everywhere except maybe China."

He turned to Sarah. "Sorry about that whole thing, but when I heard her sounding off like that to Delilah, I got mad." With that, he turned and headed toward the bunkhouse and a shower.

On the way, he passed Joe and Jordan who were heading toward the house and lunch. In the midst of their partly-feigned revulsion and waving arms telling him to get himself downwind, he told them to get on up to the house so Sarah and Delilah would only have to tell the story once. He didn't think they could get through it twice without bursting something vital in the process.

In spite of all his bravado, by the time he reached the bunkhouse, the smell was beginning to get to him, and after a quick look around, he shucked off every stitch of clothing and left the stinking pile on the steps as he trotted to the shower buck naked.

* * *

Margaret was much calmer later in the afternoon when she swung the car back into the Bent Tree Farm driveway. She had, quite to her surprise, found a very charming tea room tucked away in one corner of the big shopping complex on the outskirts of Centerville. As she fled the farm, she pulled over briefly to roll

513

down all the car windows, disregarding wind damage to her hair. She also rolled through the stop sign at the four corners, and drove down Brookline Avenue over the speed limit in her anxiety to rid herself of the odor that seemed to hover around her like a noxious mist.

She was positive that even breathing in such fumes could cause some internal damage, coating tender mucous membranes and perhaps clogging some vital airway in her lungs. The thought was accompanied by a tight feeling in her chest, and she inhaled deeply a few times, realizing that she had been on the verge of hyper-ventilating in her effort to take shallow gasps of air rather than risk ingesting any more of the possibly toxic fumes.

She had cruised aimlessly around the huge parking lot for a few minutes, undecided what to do, but fully determined not to return to the farm until she could do so without encountering that foul, shit-stinking beast. Then she became appalled at the idea of such a traumatic thing happening to her, upsetting her to the point that she would even stoop to thinking in such crude terms. She pounded one fist on the steering wheel until she accidentally hit the horn button, drawing an outraged stare from the driver in front of her.

As she turned a corner, she spotted the small, ornately-lettered sign announcing that the Olde English Tea Shoppe occupied these premises. That the yokels in this rural area of the state were aware of something as refined as a tea room came as a pleasant surprise, but the feeling was quickly replaced by suspicion.

Sure of being disappointed, she found a parking space and leaned over to the rear view mirror to arrange loose wisps of hair with her fingers. She lifted a fold of her new lavender blouse to her nose, sniffing for any trace of lingering odor. It was part of the whole new wardrobe she had hastily purchased for this occasion, one she felt suitably reflected her newly-elevated status. Of course, the subtle nuances of such a sartorial announcement was no doubt wasted on these farmer types.

Unfortunately, her nose was somewhat clogged, as it usually was, so she couldn't be really sure that the smell had not penetrated her clothing. She was sure she had been quick enough in her getaway that it had not coated her body or had time to penetrate her pores. That thought caused an involuntary shudder to ripple through her, and for a moment the urge for a long, hot shower with her anti-bacterial soap and stiff-bristled bath brush warred with the reality that she was hungry and the thought of going back to the farm kitchen to eat made her feel slightly nauseous.

She entered the Olde English Tea Shoppe, jumping as a small silver bell attached to the door tinkled merrily to announce her entrance, and looked around warily, eyes darting and nostrils flaring. Why, she thought in surprise, it's charming!

515

And it was. There were perhaps a dozen small, round tables covered with flounced print cloths with smaller matching solid-color cloths spread diagonally across them to display the printed corners. The seating was spaced tastefully around the room, and a low, discreet murmur of conversation rose from the occupied tables. Small lamps with cloth-covered shades hung above each table, shedding a soft, cheery light that reflected back from the polished wood of the chairs, giving each table its own feeling of cozy privacy. Teapots of every size and variety, separated by shiny-leaved ivy plants in decorated ceramic containers, sat on a narrow wooden shelf that ran around the room three feet below the beamed ceiling, inviting the eye to tour and sample the visual feast.

Even through her clogged nose, Margaret could smell the aroma of tea and scones baking. When a round little woman in an Olde English costume bustled out from the kitchen to seat her, greeting her in a charming Cockney accent, Margaret stopped wondering how such a place came to be here, of all places, and claimed the place for her very own secret hideaway, a place of taste and discrimination where she could come for respite when the crude, uncouth farm life became too much for her refined sensibilities.

Her sense of satisfaction and well-being returned in direct ratio to her consumption of a chicken salad sandwich, toasted to perfection, lightly mayonnaised with the crusts removed, a delicious cherry tart, bubbling and juicy from the oven, topped with a generous dollop of what she was assured was freshly-whipped cream, and several cups of Earl Grey tea.

To her delight, the tea was brewed in a rose-patterned pot right at the table, the boiling water bubbling from the long, narrow spout of a copper teakettle that the proprietress brought to the table herself. After pouring the first cup with a flourish, and checking to see there was an adequate supply of heavy cream in the matching rose-patterned pitcher, the round little woman left the teapot at Margaret's table with a cheery, "Pour when you will, dearie. The pot's on the boil, so call out if you'll be wantin' more."

Margaret took her time, prolonging her pleasure, and it was like stepping into another world when she finally paid her bill and left, the bell tinkling to announce her departure. The sun was reflecting blindingly from the stark white side of the department store, and as she hurried to the car she momentarily considered going inside to buy a pair of sunglasses of the sort that clipped on over regular prescription glasses. No, she decided, squinting her eyes against the glare, cheap department stores were a thing of her past. Money was not a problem now, and she could have dark glasses made with prescription lenses if she wanted them. She didn't have to settle for department store specials any more.

She was feeling quite content when she drove out of the

517

parking lot and headed back toward the farm, thinking about the time she had spent there a few months ago. How inept and unprofessional she had felt then. The corners of her mouth turned up slightly. Well, things had certainly changed. She had done a bang-up job on her Delilah Cross paper, so good that within a month she had received a personal phone call from none other than Amanda Brighton herself.

The memory of that call still gave her goose-flesh- -she could feel the small shivery bumps rising on her arms even now- -and she thanked whatever Gods had been looking out for her for bringing her to the attention of old Doctor Quillan, and through him to Amanda Brighton.

Things had been going very badly for her at that time. Money was short, the classes were hard, and somewhere along the line, she had a small nervous breakdown. That is how she described it to herself, a small nervous breakdown due to stress. It had come on her gradually, hardly noticed, a need to feel clean, the compulsion to wash her hands frequently. If she thought about it at all, she attributed it to her natural sense of fastidiousness. That also explained her feeling that bad odors had a physical presence and could somehow get on your skin and penetrate it unless they were washed off quickly. After all, no one wanted to smell bad.

She was slightly embarrassed, even now, that it was only after her room-mate had come in unexpectedly one afternoon when she had scrubbed her hands into a state of bleeding rawness, seen the damage, and unceremoniously hauled her off to the campus infirmary, that she became aware that she had a problem.

The doctor had recommended a psychiatrist rather than a psychologist, feeling her problem was serious enough to require intensive therapy. Because of her Brighton Foundation educational grant and the fact that the University was located in the same town as Brighton headquarters, the decision was made that one of their staff psychiatrists would be best for her. While Margaret thought they were making a big fuss about a small problem, she had no choice but to do what they said.

Well, she thought, it all worked out for the best, didn't it? Her psychiatrist just happened to be a protege of retired Doctor Quillan - Sarah Clement appointed at the time of the good doctor's retirement - and Doctor Quillan just happened to be a personal friend of Amanda Brighton. Apparently, her doctor had discussed her case with Doctor Quillan, no doubt seeking his expert advice, and Doctor Quillan had mentioned her to Amanda Brighton. For some unexplained reason, Amanda had taken a personal interest in Margaret, granting permission for her to finish her thesis with direct interaction with Delilah Cross.

No. Margaret's forehead wrinkled in a frown, her glasses uneasily shifting their perch on the bridge of her nose as she did so. That wasn't quite the way it had happened. Her psychiatrist had told her that the necessary arrangements had been made for her to go to Bent Tree Farm, adding that a stay in the quiet, rural atmosphere would be very beneficial for her. He only mentioned, almost as an afterthought, that the one and only Delilah Cross, the very subject of her thesis work, was also there, and wasn't that a serendipitous happenstance?

Margaret vividly remembered how fascinated she had been with his mouth as his lips shaped the words serendipitous happenstance. It seemed to her that he was forming secret kisses directed at her, and had chosen those specific words to convey his message of love. Of course, she might have led him on a bit.

She was smiling at the memory when she passed the cluster of signs announcing that you were now leaving Centerville, and be sure to come again. A group of middle-aged women were working in the flower beds around the base of the signs, and they cheerfully waved at her, thinking she was smiling at them. Come back again? Not if I can help it, she thought, and returned to her pleasant reminiscing.

She had been very cooperative with the young psychiatrist, answering his questions truthfully, even volunteering information of an intimate nature when it seemed called for. He hadn't been at all surprised that she was still a virgin. Apparently, he felt this was very praiseworthy, and she squirmed a bit in the seat as she remembered. Perhaps the idea of her virginity had aroused him.

The thought rewarded her with small, pleasurable tingles, and she squirmed again.

My, he had been a handsome man, but any possible relationship had been doomed from the beginning because of his mustache. Nothing could ever persuade her to kiss such an unsanitary mass of hair, no matter how carefully trimmed and groomed. And that other part surrounded by hair? Her mouth curled in distaste. The very idea was unthinkable. She was as fastidious about that as she was with all her personal hygiene, and methodically kept her own body hair-free. One could not disinfect a hair, after all.

As she drove sedately down Brookline Avenue, Margaret sighed sadly over this lost love, then the bumps rose on her arms again. A few days after she had submitted her thesis on Delilah Cross, Amanda Brighton had called her, offering her congratulations on the fine work. Margaret never thought to question how her thesis, submitted to the University, had come to the attention of Amanda Brighton. After asking if the stay at Bent Tree Farm had gone smoothly with proper care and attention from the staff, she had listened quite sympathetically to Margaret's complaint about the sheets and pillowcases.

Changing them once a week simply was not often enough for a fastidious person like herself, Margaret told her, unaware of the rising whine in her voice. While she was accustomed to changing them daily at home, she went on, she understood that it would cause too much extra work for the farm staff, but it did seem that changing them every other day would be a reasonable compromise.

To her satisfaction, Amanda had agreed with her, and after a few more questions about Delilah, Amanda casually mentioned an upcoming staff opening at Brighton Foundation headquarters, a position with a salary that took Margaret's breath away. Might she consider such a position after graduation, Amanda had asked, and just that quickly it became a world of no more cheap, department store clothes, no more special sales. All of the things Margaret had only dreamed about were suddenly within her reach.

As she slowed to a stop at the stop sign at the four corners, waited for a bright, stainless steel milk truck to clear the intersection, and turned up the short stretch of Palmer Road toward the farm, she told herself that she shouldn't resent the fact that Amanda's phone call a few days ago spoiled some of her plans. After all, the decision had been hers, Amanda had only suggested that perhaps because of her work with Delilah before, she was the best-qualified of anyone on Brighton staff to undertake this short assignment to ascertain that all was well with Delilah, that there had been no changes in her behavior as a result of Doctor Lowell's presence. We care about her, Amanda had said, and it never hurts to double check, does it?

No, it doesn't hurt to double check, Margaret thought as she pulled into the parking space across the driveway from the farmhouse and turned off the motor, but from what she had seen so far, nothing had changed with Delilah Cross. Same old notepad kept in the same old pocket of the same old baggy shirt. Same dark glasses when she went outside. Same down-turned head, same demurely-lidded eyes when she was inside. Same old eerie silence. Nothing at all had changed, of that she was sure. You are a very good observer, Margaret told herself. You would have spotted any difference, no matter how small.

She felt special, smugly filled with the knowledge that Amanda Brighton considered her to be qualified and professional enough to check on the work of a psychiatrist. As an afterthought, she twisted around to check her hair in the mirror again. It was the young Doctor Lowell here, not the old one; although she hadn't actually seen him yet, and disagreed with his decision to let Delilah work on her water phobia alone at her own pace, his report had been a good one, brief and to the point. Besides, he was unmarried . . . and so was Jordan Clement.

She stretched her lips into a wide grimace, stared into the small mirror intently, then used her fingernail to dislodge an unsightly remnant of chicken salad sandwich from between her front teeth. No, it certainly didn't hurt to double check.

By nine o'clock that evening, Margaret was sleeping the sleep of the righteous, her skin reddened by the fierce scrubbings she had given it. The feeling that Homer's stink was still somehow clinging to her, clogging her pores, silently breeding bacteria, germs, and even some exotic strain of fungus, would not be denied.

In addition to the long, hot shower she had taken when she got back from town, she showered twice more before she went to bed. She had been compelled to stand under the hot water, soaping and scrubbing every part of her body, including her head and hair, over and over again before she felt satisfied that she was clean. Each time, she paid special attention to the tender place between her buttocks, sliding the bar of germicidal soap down and under, massaging the crevices and folds of her hairless vulva until spasms of pleasure shook her, then taking the stiff-bristled brush and scrubbing fiercely.

Her plain cotton pajamas, washed into an indeterminate color that blended with the pale yellow sheets, rubbed and stuck on three or four abraded spots, but the pain was somehow satisfying, proof that she was, indeed, free of contamination.

Her last thoughts before dropping off were filled with pleasure. Sarah had apparently taken firm action with that disgusting old man. Yes, these people seemed to understand a tone of command far better than a politely phrased request,

524

probably something to do with both their lowly status in life and their intellectual inferiority. Of course, she hadn't exactly given Sarah a command about the old man as she beat a retreat from the kitchen. Her mind wanted to drift off along that tangent, but she pulled it back, the better to savor the overall sense of pleasure she was feeling.

The old man had come shuffling into the kitchen at dinner time, still unshaven but apparently bathed, dressed in old denim pants and a plaid shirt, both of which were clean as far as she could tell. His hair was slicked straight back from his forehead, and he had apparently attempted to comb it, but when she saw in the reflected light of the hanging lamp that his glasses were fingermarked and smeared, her lip curled slightly in disgust, and she quickly looked away.

He had taken a place as far from her as possible, and that suited her just fine. He had only spoken once during dinner, a sour grunt of assent when Joe Clement asked him if he would like to join them at the gatehouse after dinner for a little game of poker, adding that Sarah felt like a winner tonight, and Jordan and Doctor Lowell would complete the fivesome.

After a few suspicious sniffs in the old man's direction, she dismissed him from her mind - as she did everyone else at the table - concentrating on Jordan Clement who was, unlike the handsome but remote Doctor Lowell, responding quite positively to her conversational gambits and coyly provocative glances.

He's attracted to me, she thought with satisfaction as she turned over in bed, wincing as a raw spot on her buttocks was further irritated by her pajamas. She slid into sleep with the mental picture of herself and Jordan strolling down a path in the sweetly-scented moonlight of some fairyland garden, softly speaking of romance and love. Platonic love, of course.

CHAPTER TWENTY THREE

Waiting, Delilah sat in her room and rocked, taking comfort in the regular, soothing motion as she waited for an hour to make sure Margaret was sleeping soundly and not likely to pop out of her door unexpectedly. Earlier, she and Casey had come upstairs together and turned into the office, sitting well out of sight of the hall and the landing, partly closing the door behind them. Unless she came looking, Margaret wasn't apt to be aware of them.

Delilah was surprised to find how likable he was when he wasn't skulking around like an amateur detective. She decided that he wasn't any more comfortable with that role than she enjoyed being the recipient of that kind of attention. For the moment, an unofficial, undeclared truce was in effect, at least during what she had laughingly termed the taming of Margaret with poo.

She and Sarah had been working on dinner and Jordan had just come in with a bag of potatoes over his shoulder when she made this comment in a loud stage whisper. He dove for the pantry,

Sarah right behind him, and their snorts and wheezes of poorly-contained laughter were punctuated by the thuds and thumps of potatoes rolling into the big metal bin kept in the pantry for that purpose. When they came out, faces flushed and eyes somewhat wet, Delilah was calmly slicing tomatoes for salad.

Five minutes later, when Margaret strolled through the swinging doors and stood looking around, Jordan cheerfully acknowledged her presence. "Hi, Margaret. Have a pleasant trip into town?"

He didn't notice that there was a strange, almost distant look on her face as though she was puzzled about something. She was. She had heard something the first time she approached the swinging kitchen door, something that caused her to turn around and walk down the hall and out the front door. She had stood on the porch for nearly five minutes, trying to make sense out of it.

"The taming of Margaret with poo?" It was incomprehensible, she thought. I couldn't have possibly heard something like that. She didn't even recognize the voice that spoke those words, and while they made a weird kind of sense, who would say something like that?

She had heard something, some strange voice. Maybe she had not heard the words correctly, but she had definitely heard something strange. Her name had been clearly spoken. Could it have been Delilah? Talking? That would explain why she didn't recognize the voice. While this idea was more than she was able to accept, its alternative that she was hearing things, having auditory hallucinations, was unthinkable. No, she could not deal with the thought that she might be developing another little stress-induced quirk. No, she decided, it was Delilah. She was able to talk.

Well, they couldn't fool her, she would find out, no matter how sneaky they were. Then, she was forced to consider just who 'they' were. Oh, she thought, what a report she would have for Amanda Brighton!

Finally, when she didn't respond, Jordan repeated his question. Flattered and a little flustered by his unexpected attention, Margaret turned her attention to him, and launched into a flowery description of the lovely little tea room she had found, describing it in excruciating detail. She didn't notice when Sarah left, mumbling something about calling Joe for dinner, and Delilah picked up the egg basket and headed out the back door toward the barn. She didn't even notice the glazed expression that appeared on Jordan's face.

Yes, it's nice to have a truce, Delilah thought, but sternly warned herself not to drop her guard with anyone. Too much was going on, and she needed all her wits about her to do what she wanted to do without anyone realizing that she had a hidden agenda.

Hidden agenda. She turned the words over in her mind. Concealed plans, or maybe an artichoke with layers and layers of concealment, each partially covering the one beneath. She liked the meaning of that- -it spoke of secrets- -but artichoke was an ugly word for something that looked more like, with the use of a little imagination, an exotic kind of pineapple.

The sound of the shower could be heard, beating against the tile enclosure, so Margaret was located for the moment. "The poker game will be starting in a few minutes," Casey said softly. "I hope you don't mind sharing the house with Margaret. I don't think she'd buy your interest in some down 'n dirty poker with the common folk."

"That's fine with me. I'm behind on my homework, and a little quiet computer time is just what I need." Her voice was smooth, noncommittal, but Casey glanced at her sharply before he asked, his tone also casual, "What's on the agenda for tonight? Genetics? Anthropology? Math?"

There's that word agenda, again, Delilah thought. Telepathy? Then she chuckled. "Believe it or not, Zoology and the articulation of a giraffe's neck. The FAX works beautifully with the diagrams I have to make." Part true, part false, she thought. The FAX works beautifully with the diagrams, but my agenda for tonight doesn't include a giraffe's neck.

They heard the bathroom door open, and Delilah caught the

sharp odor of antiseptic wafting down the hall. Casey waited until Margaret's door closed with a thud, then stood up to leave. "Well, wish me luck with the cards. We're playing for beans, I think, or was it popcorn?" He had taken two or three steps toward the door, when Margaret's door opened with a whoosh, and a moment later the bathroom door closed decisively. Within seconds, they could hear the shower again.

Delilah had a sudden thought. Her gambit this afternoon had worked very well. Margaret had no way of knowing that there had been a general discussion at the dinner table one night several months before about the brook and the stepping stones. Joe insisted that they rearrange the stones, increasing their number to seven. That way, when you were standing on the fourth stone, you knew you were right in the middle, with three stones to go in either direction.

Jordan had insisted that by the time you got to the fourth stone in either direction you were practically across anyway, because almost anyone could jump the other two stones to the bank. And besides, he had added, those rocks have been there so long they've probably grown in place. That little printed note saying that she had reached the fourth stepping stone told Sarah that Delilah had finally crossed the brook, and her smile had been warm and delighted. Margaret had read it to mean that she was still bogged down, unable to cross.

"Casey, wait. I've got an idea for a little charade for Margaret's benefit, something that she will recognize and understand. When she was here before, she had endless lists of questions for me to answer, essay questions, and I gave her one or two word answers, most of them flip and sarcastic. It drove her to distraction and she complained to Sarah about it."

Casey was giving her his full attention, standing a few feet away, listening intently. "It goes like this," she continued. "After breakfast in the morning, you make a production out of arranging for private time for us. We'll go down to the barn, sit on hay bales right in the middle with the doors all open, and you ask me questions out loud, which I will answer on my notepad. You read my answers out loud, and pretend to go along with them at first, then get impatient, and finally walk away in disgust. That is exactly what Margaret did, and this should give her solid verification that you aren't making any more progress with me than she did."

She looked up at him. "Do you agree that she won't be able to stop herself from straining her ears to hear every word?"

Casey's grin was downright wicked and he gave her a thumb's up sign. As he went toward the door, he said, "Well, if at first you don't succeed, scrub, scrub, again," and motioned down the hall.

Delilah giggled; then, just as he went out of her sight, she said,

"Oh, and I crossed the stream this afternoon."

He popped back around the door like a jack-in-the-box, looking at her in amazement. "You did it, you actually did it, and then toss the news out like yesterday's stock report?" He shook his head. "You never cease to amaze me, Delilah Cross."

He left then, leaving Delilah giggling again. After a moment she sobered and slipped quietly down the hall into her own room to wait. It was a while, because after another trip to her bedroom, Margaret went back to the bathroom and took another shower, causing Delilah to laugh so hard, she had to muffle the sound in Teddy Bear's soft back.

She was late when she put her game book and the zoology textbook on the counter beside the corner desk. She didn't need the game book, but time had made its presence a taken for granted thing. When she booted up the computer and logged on to the game site, they were there before her, Darkling, Merlin, and Hunter, discussing something in game language. Before announcing her presence, she read the dialogue visible on her monitor.

Merlin had agreed to preserve this evening's game and "prepare illuminated scrolls on papyrus for the warriors bold to study by the lamps of midnight." He would, he said, "dispatch his swiftest runner to bring them to the mighty Hunter, who could, in turn, deliver them to the others by the swiftest means at hand."

533

They did this occasionally when an unusually complex and involved puzzle was to be solved and a printed copy of it aided in the process.

"Chameleon here. She has a secret," she typed and waited. The hair rose on her neck as she read the entry appearing on the screen.

Darkling was talking. "Oh, I went to the animal fair," he wrote, "and the birds and the beasts were there, but not all of them." There was a short pause, then, "I spoke to a maiden fair, with long and flowing hair, and asked her pray to tell me where the other beasts had strayed . . . and when. She was lovely, was this maiden, innocent and uncomplicated in her thinking, and fair swept away by my charm. For long we sat upon a rock by the moat while she told me tales quite wondrous to hear."

Delilah made an anguished sound. Darkling was saying that he had gone to the Landon Zoo and Auntie and her babe were not there.

Darkling again. "T'was near four months gone, she told me, that an uncommonly coy and cautious dragon passed their way, found several beasts uncommonly fair and toothsome, and took them right away. She knew not where the dragon dens, but there be some with other stories just as wondrous. They speak of roaring things that carry burdens and emit noxious fumes, bags of gold, and remote castles heavily guarded. A sad and intricately-woven tale, my stalwart comrades, but one with many threads that are unraveling even as we speak. They can be woven again into tapestries of uncommon beauty and truth."

So, Delilah thought, leaning back in her chair. Someone- -the dragon- -had taken Auntie, her babe, and several others away. Darkling had been following their trail, working on how and by whom they had been transported, and to what destination. He did not end on a down note at all, and the mention of money and heavily guarded estates might mean he already knew the location.

Her hopes were soaring as she typed. "Bravo, stalwart Darkling! You have flung a torch far into the darkness, lighting the way for others to follow through this treacherous labyrinth. And I, too, have news. I give you the name of the dragon! It is Amanda Brighton."

Hunter came first. "Hallo, daughter of rainbows! Indeed, we are in agreement about the treacherous path our Darkling traveled to carry the torch this far, and at great personal danger to himself, and we all agree on the name of the dragon. But hark now to the tale of Merlin. His delicate magical touch has placed glowing fairy lanterns along quite another path, one just wide enough for us all to tiptoe down in single file, providing we nimbly leap over those treacherous places where the path has crumbled away with time, and the maps be forgotten in most men's memories, but not all. It is not a pretty tale, so prepare yourself."

Delilah's forehead wrinkled in a frown. Hunter was warning her, but about what? Before she could examine this further, Merlin was speaking, and she gave the monitor screen her full attention.

"Here, then, speaks Merlin, reader of ancient tomes, collector of forgotten spells, follower of time lines linked to the past. I sought a path wide and broad down which we might travel unnoticed. In the beginning, the road was, indeed, wide and inviting with clear signposts along the way. Then, as I progressed, mapping each twist and turn with care, the road became narrower and there were fewer travelers to be met. I explored each branch and byway, looking for the one true way to our goal.

I had begun to greatly fear that I had lost my way, but I used my magic distance viewer, questing in every direction for thousands of miles, asking questions of friends, and consulting official mapmakers and keepers of old records half-way round the world.

Finally, I found myself on a narrow, twisting path in the center of Europe, with no way to go but forward on a trail that led backward through time. Through time portal after time portal I traveled, and finally I reached a strange and faraway land, one filled with exotic and wondrous creatures. Only a few real monsters still wandered about, and those beasts were elderly enough to have lost most of their teeth and their fires were but memories of long ago. After all, nearly sixty years of mortal time had passed since the events of which I sought news had occurred."

Merlin stopped then, and it was just as well. Delilah had been holding her breath most of the time since he began, understanding clearly what he was telling them. No, telling her. All of this had already cleared through Paulie and Darkling. Merlin had researched the dates and, using his computer, followed the trail to Europe. From there, it had led him to the Africa of sixty years ago . . . but along what trail?

Hurry, Merlin, she urged him with her mind, wondering if they were really being obtuse enough with their game talk to fool a casual observer, and deciding they were. In a strange way, it followed the pattern of many of their imaginary adventures wherein they took turns describing where they had been, what they seen, and what they had done in the fantasy worlds they invented and peopled as they chose, making the experience as real as possible for the other players.

Then, he was there again. "The ancient tomes I searched were yellowed and sometimes blurred with age, but the story they told was clear to see, and I shall tell it to you . . . a tale within a tale, as it were:

'In the long ago, perhaps six decades or even more past, a crazed and mighty king came into power in Europe. Enthralled

537

with his own power, he raised an army with promises that they would rule the entire world if they would but unquestioningly obey him. He started a war, and, for a time, all went very well. He started another war, and another, and one by one conquered all his neighbors, his armies spreading ever farther outward.

The people of his land were very proud and pleased, and wished to have all this new land and wealth for themselves, so, by doing nothing, they gave their tacit approval to all manner of cruel and barbarous practices designed to eliminate everyone who was not a follower of the mad king, and take whatever of their possessions they chose, as has been the manner of mad kings and their followers since the beginning of time.

Now it came about that to the south and west, across a sea called Mediterranean, lay a great, sparsely populated land called Africa. It was not, at that time, truly involved in any war, and deep in the middle of it where few men dared or cared to go seemed an ideal place for the mad king to build workshops where the wise men and magicians of his army could work in private and secret as they sought to improve their spells and incantations and invent all sorts of new ones to better destroy his enemies.

There were rumors that these wise men and magicians were using methods and sorcery that would sicken decent people to their very souls had they known, but it was a very worthwhile project as seen through the eyes of the mad king and his followers.

At first, everything went well, and no one noticed the secret places, but as more countries became involved in the war, the mad king and his magicians did not feel secure. By taking some land in the northern part of Africa, and placing part of his army there, they could ensure privacy by causing everyone to look at the battles being fought there instead of in the hidden places. But there was still a problem. In order to be truly secret, these hidden places would have to appear to be something other than what they really were. They had to perfect a spell of misdirection.'"

Then Merlin added a personal comment. "That is something Chameleon knows very well and practices often."

This time, the pause was very short, and even though Delilah was smiling at Merlin's pointed personal remark, she found herself sitting on the edge of the chair, aware that she had been scarcely breathing again. Merlin was an excellent teller of tales and this was clearly a part of World War II history.

"'Now there was another country far away across a mighty rolling sea. It was not yet involved in the wars, so a plan was devised. Living in that country was a very good friend and supporter of the mad king and he was delighted to help. Although here the story becomes somewhat dim and difficult to follow, the plan was this: The mad king sent a great amount of gold, so much that it is hard for common folk to imagine, to another country which was also neutral. From there, it was delivered to the country of the mad king's friend. He, in turn, found a way to fool the mages studying their arcane arts and wise men of that country into believing that all the gold was his, and that he only wanted to use it for good works in the world.

"Of course, everyone was full of praise for the mad king's friend and his lavish public display of benevolence. And, were the truth told, many good people did benefit from the largess of his gold-filled coffers. But in addition to the many good works he did, the friend of the mad king also set up, funded and supplied several secret places for the mad king's magicians and sorcerers to pursue their evil works, each one concealed, lost among the many.

"And so it went for a time, and the supply of gold seemed unlimited, coming as it did from the countries conquered and people destroyed by the mad king.'"

Again, the pause was brief. "My tale of exploration and discovery, and the saga of the mad king and his friend draws near its end, my fellow warriors, so be patient a while longer.

'Things took a bad turn for the mad king. Other countries talked together and finally decided that he truly was mad and becoming a threat to everyone in his madness. So they banded together and in a time defeated him and made every effort to seek and destroy all of his friends, no matter where in the whole world they had hidden themselves. Some escaped for a while, and even today they are being searched out. But they never suspected one friend and supporter of the mad king. He was much too visible, possessed of much gold, and too well known as a doer of good works to ever be suspected. But something had happened.'"

Merlin stopped, then inserted a personal note again. "My warrior friends, here the tale becomes partly fact-based, partly based on Chameleon's tale, and partly based on well-founded and carefully thought out logic predicated upon those facts. I warn you of this so that you may query and assist in corrections, should they be necessary."

Delilah could not control her fingers any longer. "Merlin, for God's sake finish it. I'm dying!" she typed, knowing there would be a delay before the words appeared on all of their screens. It was the Brighton Foundation, she thought, and Merlin had taken it all the way back in time to the beginning of Bhutu. But how much more had he discovered? Her throat was dry, and she reached for her glass of milk before she realized that she hadn't gone to the kitchen for her snack as she usually did. There was surely something to drink in the small refrigerator across the room, but she couldn't tear herself away from the computer.

"Very well, dear friend Chameleon, but be warned that it may raise more questions than it answers," was his reply. "And the questions it raises about the friend who is held captive, the one who is marked in a special way, cannot be wished away, because the reason for that captivity has become obvious."

This time, the pause was very long, so long that Delilah was becoming worried that he might not finish. She could feel the worry- -and the warning- -in his last words. Then she realized that maybe it would be best if he didn't go on. Just as she placed her hands on the keyboard to tell him to stop, the words came again.

"'The friend of the mad king had become infected with the idea that even though the mad king was dead and his armies defeated, he could carry out the secret work of the magicians and sorcerers himself. They had been so close to finding the incantation, the magical formula that would make him as powerful a creator as God, a man whose name would go down as the greatest magician in the history of all the world. You see, he became insane and infected his wife, and eventually his son, with the same terrible insanity.

"Alone and in secret these two, father and son, continued the work for many years while the wife took care of dispensing the gold and making sure the good works were properly appreciated throughout the world, their reputation kept above reproach so no one would look at them too closely. Although the wife knew all about it in a general way, being fully joined in their madness, she was not aware of all the details and there were many gaps in her information. This was a state of affairs quite in keeping with what a woman's place was considered to be in those ancient times.

"One by one, the dedicated guardian dragons, those who knew what they were charged with guarding, became old and useless. Many of them died, and many were found and made to pay for their crimes. Most of those who had shared in the mad king's dream also became old; the great dream of conquering the world and ruling for a thousand years became not a dream, but just a memory of a dream. And sometimes, as old people do, they spoke of the mad king's dream and their words were recorded, leaving faint trails that when followed led back to the mad king's friend. And so the father and son continued, their insanity fueling their obsession . . . or the other way around.

"Then, a long time ago, perhaps as many as eighteen circles around the sun in our human way of reckoning the passage of time, in the secret laboratory of the mad magicians, a man was killed.

"And there, in that time and in that place in Africa, begins the real story of our own dear Chameleon."

Delilah's thoughts were chaotic as she quickly typed, "Thank you, all, out," and turned off the computer. It was too much to comprehend, too clear in its details not to be comprehended. She moaned, a hurting animal sound.

She ran from the office to her room, uncaring about the office lights or any noise she might be making. Kicking off her shoes, grabbing Teddy Bear almost by reflex, she crawled into bed and pulled the covers over her head. It was then that the realization came, hitting her like a blow.

The big neon letters began to blink on and off in her mind, burning the inside of her eyelids. She could feel them burning with each pulsing beat. THE SECRET, Blink THE SECRET, Blink THE SECRET, Blink. Merlin knew THE SECRET, Blink. Darkling knew THE SECRET, Blink. And Hunter knew THE SECRET, Blink. And if they didn't already understand all the implications, they would soon figure it out. No, they all knew THE SECRET, Blink.

She tried to reason with herself when she became aware of the short, guttural whimpers she was making. She knew the story. She had always known about THE SECRET, Blink. Auntie had told it to her over and over and over again, the story of all the mothers before her, Mandy's story, Auntie's story, her own story. THE SECRET, Blink.

It was seeing it written out, reading it letter by letter as the nameless was named - the obsession, the insanity, the reason that she was here, the very reason that she had been born, now being revealed and given stark reality, word by word by word - that was crushing her, destroying her.

She rolled over in anguish, crushing her mouth against Teddy Bear's soft back- -in the same place she had muffled her laughter not so long before- -as the sobs came, deep, hurting, punishing sobs that wrenched their way through her in agonizing spasms. After a while, they spent themselves, and she lay there feeling the tears hot on her face. Slowly she reached up and touched her wet cheek, then licked the finger, thinking of the time she and Auntie had tasted the sweet saltiness of each other's bad hurt through the steel mesh separating them. Ape not cry, she thought. Ape not cry.

She was dimly aware of the telephone ringing in the office, but it didn't matter. The moonlight, the steel mesh, the warm breeze filled with the earthy scent of growing things, the small sounds of night creatures, the glint of Auntie's tears as they slid from her eyes and rolled down her face . . . these things were her reality for this moment.

After a while, the ringing stopped, and she wondered, as though considering it from a distance, how long it would be before her three friends, the stalwart warriors who had accomplished such miracles at her request- -yes, at her request- - came to fully realize that she was the youngling taken from Auntie, the daughter of Mandy the ape, Mandy the murderess.

No, not Auntie. She was just an ape called No Name, her aunt, the sister of her mother. As though it had happened long ago in another lifetime, she remembered telling Paulie Auntie's true name. Paulie knew everything now, she thought, and it didn't seem to matter any more. Paulie knew her true name, too, while Darkling and Merlin knew her only as Chameleon, but that didn't matter, either.

She felt numb and lost here in this world, and returned to the small, bare room at Bhutu, sitting on the narrow cot, feeling Auntie's comforting warmth through the steel mesh on the window. Then, it had been a simple struggle for daily survival, with little idea of what tomorrow meant. And now? She didn't want to think about tomorrow.

A long while later, just before she drifted off into a deep, dreamless sleep, another thought passed slowly across her mind. That murder, the murder of the Brighton son, had brought a final end to the mad king's plan. Or had it? Amanda Brighton.

The name sat there in her mind with an almost physical presence. Had that murder not been committed, she, Delilah Cross, would now bear a neat row of acid-burned X's near her left shoulder, five of them instead of four like Auntie and her sister, Mandy. Five X's to indicate that she was the fifth successful experimental generation in a line, a line that she now knew began with a human male named Brighton and a nameless female bonobo ape. Would it take another murder, the death of Amanda Brighton to finally put an end to the nightmare?

She touched her left shoulder, and then, as exhaustion carried her into darkness, her fingers made the sign of who she was . . .

her two index fingers clearly forming not a cross, but an X.

CHAPTER TWENTY FOUR

Sarah measured the flour, deftly scraping a knife across the top of the cup to level it, then dumping it into the big sifter sitting in the stainless steel mixing bowl. After adding the other dry ingredients to the sifter, she turned the handle on the side, watching the miniature snowstorm drift down into the mixing bowl. She was sure that it was no longer necessary to tediously sift the flour to remove suspicious lumps and bumps, but she enjoyed doing it, making white snow mountains of flour, salt, and baking powder around the bottom of the bowl. It seemed to her that sifting gave baked things a finer, lighter texture. Besides, she liked the quiet grinding sound the sifter made as she turned the handle; there was something basic and satisfying about it, grinding grain into meal to cook for your family. Sarah smiled at the thought.

Besides, she was fussy about her sugar cookies, and it pleased her that Delilah always patiently and painstakingly followed each of her own steps when she baked. Although she wouldn't admit it, she couldn't tell Delilah's sugar cookies from her own, and that gave her a warm feeling, as though she had handed down a family treasure, preserving it for future generations.

She heard the swish of the swinging door and turned, intending to give whoever it was a cheerful greeting. Seemed like she wasn't the only one making an early start this morning. She had felt tense this morning, so after getting Joe and Jordan up and on their way for the day, instead of following her usual routine of household chores at the gatehouse, she came up to the farmhouse, sure that the soothing, comfortable routine of baking would work out some of her mental kinks. It had until now.

"Oh, good morning, Margaret." Her greeting was muted, and she turned back to her baking without waiting for a response. She got one anyway.

"Well, I suppose it's a good enough morning for people who insist on getting up and clattering around disturbing other people before the sun even comes up." Margaret hardly paused for a breath. "And I want to tell you, Sarah, that from now on I will be showering in the downstairs bathroom. I assume that no one else uses that shower. I certainly don't mind disinfecting a shower after I use it, but I find the idea of sharing bathing facilities with strangers," Margaret illustrated with an exaggerated grimace of disgust, "I find it absolutely distasteful. Germs, you know, and all sorts of bacteria and fungi!" Margaret's nasal buzz-saw was revving up, gaining momentum as it began its inevitable climb into an unendurable whine when it was interrupted by another voice.

"Well, and how is Mrs. Moneybags this morning?" Casey, carrying a zippered portfolio, came through the door behind Margaret, and pointedly ignoring her, moved to the counter beside Sarah. As he busied himself getting a cup of coffee, he said, "I have never seen such a run of luck at cards!"

He continued to address Sarah, talking about her winning streak in a game of cards which had never taken place as he took his usual place at the table, stirring his coffee with more than necessary zeal. He was irritated. In just a few sentences, Margaret had made it clear why Homer had lost his cool with her yesterday. The bitch was complaining about him and Delilah. They were the only ones currently using the upstairs bathroom. Germs! Germs?

He fell silent, thinking about her trips to the bathroom last night, the prolonged sound of water beating on the tiled shower walls. Scrub, scrub, again? From what Sarah and Homer said last night about the scene in the kitchen at lunch yesterday, her reaction had been on the abnormal side, an over-reaction in fact, if nothing more than an odor had caused her to flee the farm. He idly wondered how she would react if she accidentally stepped in a freshly-fragrant, mushy cow patty? Nervous collapse? Hysteria?

Jordan had been laughing when he passed on Delilah's clever

550

description, but the taming of Margaret with poo might be more appropriate than they had thought. Casey filed this away for later discussion with his fellow conspirators. They just might be able to speed the taming process along and get Margaret on her way with nothing more than a few subtle pushes by innocently using normal farm routines. After all, this was a working farm, was it not? And wasn't fertilizer a vital part of a farming operation?

"Sarah, have you seen Delilah yet this morning?" He turned toward the counter where she was rolling out the cookie dough on a big floured board, the wooden rolling pin making small creaking sounds with each pass. It was time to set the scene for this morning's performance in the barn, and he had something to tell Delilah about last night.

When he returned from the gatehouse last night, the phone had been ringing in the office as he came up the stairs. The lights were on, but when it wasn't picked up after the fifth ring, he assumed that Delilah wasn't there so he went in and answered it. The voice, deep but unmistakably young, had asked for Delilah Cross. When Casey told him that she appeared to be in bed, the caller had hung up without saying anything else.

The zoology text and the game book were sitting on the counter, and Super Snoop Lowell found it impossible to get out of the room without looking through them, even as he castigated himself for even thinking of it. It took him a minute's study to

551

realize what the game book was, then he smiled.

So Delilah was a computer game player, he thought. Well, that was right in keeping with what he had already decided was a deeply-ingrained trait. That was why she had been so evasive, embarrassed about such an innocent thing. For some reason, he found that idea charming, a hint of shyness there. It explained the enigmatic words he had seen on the monitor and the oddly archaic language she had used during the telephone conversation he overheard.

According to the dates at the beginning of the book, the game had gone on since the time Delilah was at Hiller School. That seemed to support his assumption that it was probably Paulie Newcombe she had been talking to during his eavesdropping fiasco, and that it was Paulie Newcombe who had just called. Perhaps the game had gone badly for her tonight, was his first thought. If she was upset by losing it would explain her forgetting her books and leaving the office lights on. Paulie had probably called to console her, that sounded reasonable enough. He had put the books in front of her door last night, and they were gone when he came down this morning.

Sarah made two more passes with the rolling pin, then, deciding the dough was just exactly the right thickness, laid it to one side and picked up a large round cookie cutter, before turning to Casey. He had waited patiently for her answer, knowing she was not ignoring him. Besides, he appreciated the work of a culinary artist, and in his opinion the sugar cookies were a work of art.

"Now that you ask, no, I haven't seen her, but she was here earlier. When I came in, the coffee was already made and waiting." Sarah smiled fondly. "She does that sometimes when she gets up early. She's probably out walking, or maybe down by the stream." She turned to the waiting dough and carefully incised the outline of a big, round cookie.

"Well, I can tell you that she got up early this morning."

Margaret was at the stove, dividing her attention between the two eggs boiling in a small pan and her wristwatch. It was only after standing unnoticed for several minutes that she had finally gotten the message that Sarah had no intention of taking her order and serving her breakfast like a proper menial. Of course, those ridiculous house rules did say that everyone should take care of their own breakfast, and perhaps it was just as well.

As she washed the eggs before putting them in the pan to boil, she soothed herself with the thought that Sarah probably couldn't be trusted to cook her eggs to that state of perfection she preferred. After carefully washing the orange, she had squeezed her own orange juice, too, avoiding the glass juice bottles in the refrigerator. Everyone handled them, and without first washing their hands, a positively revolting thought. At least they kept an abundance of fresh fruit and vegetables on hand.

After a few moments, she realized that Sarah and Casey were looking at her questioningly, she continued. "It must have been at least five o'clock, an ungodly hour. These old houses are really terrible, you know, every sound echoes through the walls."

Margaret paused, mentally compiling her grievances as she drained the boiling water from her eggs and filled the pan with cold water. She looked suspiciously at one of the eggs. Was that a hairline crack? If it was, it meant she would have to cook another one or make do with just one egg. No, when she scooped the suspected egg up in a large spoon and held it level with her nose, inspecting it closely, she could see that it had just been a trick of lighting. The egg was pristine in its unblemished perfection.

Sarah and Casey had formed a fascinated audience of two, unobtrusively watching the entire performance from the careful washing of the eggs before boiling them to the orange washing, through this peculiar egg inspection, and Casey made careful note of her red, chapped-looking hands. This young lady has real problems, serious problems, he thought. He exchanged glances with Sarah and her almost imperceptible nod told him she shared his opinion. One more of the flawed containers that Amanda Brighton seemed to prefer for her special projects.

Satisfied that the eggs were in edible condition, Margaret collected herself, and drained the cold water from the egg pan before she continued. "She took a shower, and I almost never got back to sleep!" She conveniently overlooked the fact that by five o'clock this morning she had already had a full eight hours sleep. She looked accusingly at Sarah who was methodically cutting the cookies and sliding them onto a baking sheet. "I don't suppose you have any egg cups?" Her tone implied that Sarah probably didn't know what an egg cup was.

Sarah very deliberately slid the full baking tray into the oven before she turned and reached up into the cupboard. "Would you like one egg cup or two?" she asked. Casey couldn't help admiring the calm, polite way she had answered, and the sweet smile on her face as she turned toward Margaret, an egg cup in each hand, was positively beautiful. Margaret, totally deflated, reached out and took both of them. As Sarah turned back to check on the cookies, she said over her shoulder, "Perhaps you should wash them before you use them, Margaret. They've been sitting there in the cupboard ever since yesterday morning."

Casey finished his coffee in a hasty gulp, praying that he wouldn't choke on it and, God forbid, snort it out his nose as he had once before. As he put the cup in the sink, he said, "I'm not hungry right now, Sarah. I'll be back later for some of those cookies, and if you see Delilah, would you tell her that I have some questions that I need to ask her?" Making a show of picking up his portfolio, he beat a retreat out the back door. While he felt some sympathy for Sarah, it wasn't strong enough to make him sit there and watch Margaret eat those eggs.

* * *

Delilah was sitting on the top of the stile over the stone wall down by the four corners. Once again, she had crossed the stream without hesitation. She discovered after she crossed the brook yesterday that the stile was a good place to sit. Although she hadn't paid attention then, she could see now that the intersection was a fairly busy place as people went about their daily business, concerned with themselves and their own lives.

The stone wall was far enough from the road to make it clear she wasn't seeking contact with passersby, but occasionally someone would wave. At first, she ignored them, but after a while she matched these strangers smile for smile and wave for wave. They didn't know who she was, but their smiles and waves acknowledged her as one of them. In her present state of mind, it was as though their casual acceptance was a gift they were giving her, blowing away bits and wisps of the overwhelming feeling of isolation and difference that had swirled around her like a fog from the moment she woke up this morning.

It's like that roller coaster at the carnival in Landon, she thought. At first it was easy, exciting, a new game to play. Then the high places got higher, the low places lower, bouts of laughter alternating with an almost physical need to scream in terror, until the ride ended and the excitement slowly dissipated. Now though, the excitement of the emotional roller coaster she had been riding hadn't dissipated, it had metamorphosed into an anger so cold she could almost feel herself freezing inside as the face of the enemy was revealed. And then, last night, she was forced to look at her own face in the mirror held up by her friends.

How could she have been so stupid, she wondered, so childish in her belief that she could, like a chameleon, reveal so much of herself to them and still remain unseen? So driven by the need to rescue Auntie and her babe that she lost all sense of caution? The quest had been a central part of her dream for so long it had taken on its own reality. She had been so sure that any and all obstacles to her goal could be overcome as easily as those in her fantasy game world. A child's view of the real world, she decided.

She glanced up at a passing car. The two children in the back seat waved vigorously, smiling. She smiled and waved back, wondering what their reality was. They looked happy, so maybe their world was a nice one. She had looked at the real world of Delilah Cross last night, the real world created by a madman, the real world in which the crazed wife of one of his last followers was still pursuing her, determined to have the secret so long sought by the sorcerers and magicians. To have it or to destroy it by destroying her.

Delilah realized that nothing that had been done could be

undone, erased like her first hesitant words on the blackboard at Hiller School. Yes, Auntie, she thought. Not know what do, not do, and I did it anyway. Now she had to deal with the consequences. She straightened her shoulders, suddenly aware of her own strength and ability to endure. Telling part of her story, speaking the words out loud, had given her some distance from it, allowed her to see the strength of the child she had been, understand what that child had endured, and survived.

Suddenly, a small smile tugged at the corners of her mouth. Certainly, she had managed to put Casey in his proper place. The smile disappeared as she wondered about that. Why had she felt it important and right to dominate him? What was his proper place? That word. She hated that word. It was Miss Agnes speaking that word.

Before she could pursue the thought, Delilah suddenly became aware that someone was coming down the path from the stream behind her. Casey, she thought. He was humming as he walked along, sounding quite cheerful, if not doing very well with the tune.

She started to turn around, but halted the motion as a car going up Palmer Road toward the farm entrance suddenly braked, then backed up, pulling to a stop even with her across the road. Its two occupants got out, and started across the road toward her. At first, she didn't believe it, sitting motionless, watching them cross the road and approach the wall. When one of the men took her by the arms, swung her down from her perch and enveloped her in a hug, she had to believe it.

"Hello, Delilah," Harold Newcombe said as he released her, standing back to take a good look at her, his eyes warm and affectionate behind the lenses of his glasses. "You haven't exactly grown, but you've certainly matured, haven't you?"

Delilah looked at the other man. No, it wasn't a man, it was Paulie, taller and broader than she could have ever imagined, his red hair darkened into a deep auburn. When he grinned and said, "Hello, Delilah," it was the same old mischievous face, but his eyes were serious, his look intent and questioning.

She was at a loss. What were they doing here? She hadn't yet called the Newcombe family. Had Paulie told his father she could talk? As she was fumbling for her note pad and pen, from the other side of the wall behind her, Casey solved the problem very neatly, giving her time to think.

"Hello, there. I'm Doctor Lowell. Can I help you with something?" His tone was cold and businesslike, making it clear that he would tolerate no nonsense from them.

Both Newcombes immediately focused their attention on him; then Harold gave a totally unexpected answer, one that startled Delilah more than their sudden appearance at Bent Tree Farm.

"Glad to meet you, Doctor Lowell. I'm Harold Hunter and this is my son, Paul." He motioned toward Paulie, who nodded politely but said nothing.

"We met Delilah a couple or three years ago when my daughter, Becky, was a student at Hiller School. My wife has never forgotten how kind and helpful Delilah was with Becky. She's mentally handicapped, you know, Becky, that is, not my wife." He chuckled nervously.

"Anyway, when she found out we were coming through this area on our way to deliver Paul to his grandma's house for the summer, she didn't give me a minute's peace until I agreed to stop by and see Delilah, my wife, that is, not Becky." He paused a moment, as though gathering his thoughts, then added to Delilah, patting her shoulder. "But Becky sends her love, too. You remember how she sometimes has these spells where she can remember things."

Delilah's mouth wasn't the only one hanging open after this garbled explanation. It had taken a moment, but Casey recognized them as part of the family group in the picture in Delilah's room. Hunter? He had thought it was the Newcombe family. Harold? Paul? Then it registered. He had seen this man's signature several times on the reports in Delilah's records. This was Harold Newcombe, Director of Hiller School, and his son, Paulie. Harold Hunter? What in the hell was going on here?

It only took an instant for Delilah put it all together. Paulie had told his father. How much she didn't know, but apparently enough, and they had mounted a rescue mission, complete with a cover story just wild enough to be believed by anyone who didn't know them. And if Casey had happened to be an enemy, Harold had very cleverly given her the whole scenario to play from.

"Oh, I'm so glad to see you!" When Delilah spoke, her delight lit up her face and spilled over into her voice. Then she sobered. "Harold and Paulie Newcombe, I'd like you to meet Casey Lowell. He's my friend, and we need to talk right now."

Harold nodded, his face serious, and he looked at Casey, who also nodded as she told Paulie, "There's a dragon's spawn on the farm, so we need to get away from here and out of sight." She glanced at the corner in the direction of the Crossroads Diner. "Drive your car down there and park. We'll walk down and meet you."

As Casey and Delilah walked toward the corner, Harold and Paulie, returned to their car, made a U-turn and went past them, ignoring their presence. Delilah was deep in thought, trying to decide what and how much to tell whom. After chasing her thoughts in a circle for the third time, she gave up, finally understanding that the whole thing was out of her hands now. There was a strange kind of relief in the thought. Gnawing knot, she thought, it feels like one of those gnawing knots in my stomach is gone.

Her friends from the farm knew part of the story, Paulie knew almost all of it, Merlin and Darkling knew nearly as much, and she had no idea how much Harold knew. The important thing was that they were all willing to help her. She was beginning to feel warm inside. Paulie knew who- -and what- -she was. She stumbled over the thought. What she was. But they were here. That was important, they were here.

It was over an hour later that they finished talking. Casey and Delilah had joined Harold and Paulie in a back booth in the diner, and all of them had ordered the country breakfasts that were the house specialty. The generous mugs of coffee served with thick country cream turned out to be almost as good as Sarah's special grind.

Paulie spoke directly to Delilah. "I worried about you last night, Delilah. Merlin figured it was a bad time for you and he didn't waste any time after you signed off. I tried to call you right back, but you had already left." He glanced at Casey who nodded affirmation. "Anyway, Merlin fired off copies of both stories to me, yours and his, because he was worried, too. As soon as I got them, I woke Dad up and insisted he read them both right then."

The grin he aimed at Harold was big and appreciative. "For an old guy, he caught on pretty fast, got the message on the first reading. I wish you could have seen his face. It turned every color and back again by the time he finished. I added a few details about the things you had told me on the phone before, and we were in the car and gone before I could get my shoe laces tied." Paulie's face became serious. "I think your friend, Doctor Lowell, should read these now, Delilah, but only if you say so."

When she nodded, he pulled an envelope from his jacket pocket and handed it across the table to Casey, who took out the folded sheets of paper and began to read. Casey will know, now, Delilah thought. He'll know it all. She was still having trouble with the thought. Then the realization came. I have never accepted it, never accepted it no matter how many times Auntie told the story. I didn't want to think about it. It, she thought. It. I can't even say the words to myself.

Casey read fast, and when he was through, he methodically folded the papers, put them back into the envelope, and handed it back to Paulie without looking up. He took a sip of his coffee and carefully sat the mug down. Still not looking up, he began to cut the bacon on his plate into smaller and smaller pieces. Delilah was sitting close beside him, and with each movement of the knife, she was aware of the odor of adrenalin that poured from him until it was an acrid, almost visible cloud.

It wasn't until Delilah shifted away from him, half-frightened by the anger smell that continued to increase in intensity- -the smell of danger- -that he laid down his knife and fork, and looked up, not at her, but at Harold Newcombe.

"Are you Delilah's friends?" he asked. When Harold nodded, he continued. "I hope so, because if you aren't, you'll have to deal with me, and it won't be pretty." His voice was low and flat, the truth unmistakable, his words echoing those that Jordan had spoken such a short time before.

"Delilah was safe with me for four years beginning when I bodily took her away from Agnes Kittridge at the Landon Airport." The truth in Harold's voice was also very clear. "She was completely dehydrated, in a tranquilized stupor, it was winter, she had on only a thin dress, and she had raw collar marks on her neck." He said nothing else, just sat there looking straight at Casey.

Delilah looked from one to the other, aware that they were communicating in far more than words, a kind of male behavior that she had first become aware of in the greenhouse when Casey and Jordan had been talking about Margaret. When she thought about it, it seemed like her speaking had only served to make her understand how ignorant she really was, how little she knew about the world, the people in it, and how they interacted with one another. There was so much she hadn't learned. She realized that there were also many things she didn't know about herself, things that other people knew, and she found that disturbing, almost frightening. This was the first time she had heard anything about her arrival at Hiller School, something she had no memory of.

She had been so childishly sure that she was the only one with secrets.

"All right, Harold," Casey said, "can you stay at the farm for a while, a day or two anyway? There are four other friends there, including my father, Doctor K. C. Lowell. I think you know of him." It was a statement, and Harold nodded, his eyebrows rising in surprise at the mention of Casey's father.

Casey was talking fast now, the strong adrenalin odor abating somewhat as he got his feelings under control. "With Margaret there, you can't come to visit Delilah. Her visitors are all cleared through Amanda Brighton, personally, and Margaret will report it immediately. Comes to that," he glanced at his watch, "she's probably out looking for us now, so we've got to hurry." He grinned at Paulie. "Margaret is the dragon's spawn that Delilah warned you about, Paulie."

He looked around the diner. "There's a phone over there. I can call Sarah and set things up. The Hunter name is fine, but you've come to visit your old friend Joe Clement. You were both agriculture professors at the university. You haven't seen him, his wife, Sarah, or his son, Jordan, for three years, or so since they retired to the farm. Same story, taking Paulie to his grandmother's house, and my hasn't he grown? No problem with setting you up in the bunkhouse. The only one there is my Dad."

Delilah laughed at the puzzled looks on Harold's and Paulie's

565

faces. Casey joined in, chuckling as he explained. "Actually, since Margaret's been there, my Dad has been Homer, the hired man, living in the bunkhouse, reeking of cow manure, and playing the role to the hilt, too. And you're not expected to know him or Delilah, okay? Or me, either, for that matter."

He got up and went to the phone. After talking a few minutes, he came back and said, "It's all set. Wait until about twelve-thirty, then just drive up like you belonged there. Toot your horn. They'll meet you and smooth the way." He looked at the Newcombes a moment, then stuck out his hand, shaking each of their quickly offered hands firmly. "Thank you both for coming. I think we've got a good idea about the situation, but some hard decisions have to be made about where it goes from here."

After Casey and Delilah left, walking quickly back up the road to the stile crossing, Harold paid the check, and he and Paulie walked outside. "Well, Dad, what do you think?" Paulie asked.

"I think, Paulie, that through no fault of her own, Delilah is standing directly in the eye of a hurricane. No matter which way she steps, the storm is going to try to sweep her away. And," he clapped Paulie on the shoulder that was exactly level with his, "and I am damned glad that she has a friend like you, mighty Hunter."

CHAPTER TWENTY FIVE

The performance on center stage in the barn went off without a hitch. During the time Delilah and Casey were at the cafe, Sarah had somehow coerced Jordan into making the ultimate sacrifice. With little enthusiasm, he invited Margaret for a guided tour of the greenhouse, a tour that he promised Sarah would last only until Casey and Delilah set the stage in the barn. While Margaret was upstairs changing into what she termed appropriate clothes, which turned out to be a new blouse and gathered skirt that did nothing for her pear-shaped figure, Sarah hastily filled Jordan in about the expected arrival of their unexpected visitors and how the situation should be handled.

She had just said, "Remember, its Joe's old school chum and his son," when Margaret pushed though the swinging doors.

"What? What did you say, Sarah?" The nasal voice was demanding.

"I said Jordan better not drop any crumbs or I'd disown him as my son," Sarah answered, hastily shoving two cookies into his hand, one of which he quickly bit into to avoid having to say anything.

She heaved a deep sigh of relief as they left, pushing a stray wisp of hair from her damp forehead. This was getting more complicated by the hour, and the group of conspirators was quickly turning into an army. She smiled at the thought of this latest detachment of cavalry dashing to Delilah's rescue. She knew of Harold Newcombe and the excellent job he had done as Director of Hiller School, but he was about the last person in the world she expected to personally arrive prepared to protect and defend Delilah. It seemed Delilah made friends wherever she was, good friends, loyal friends. The thought gave Sarah a great deal of comfort as though, in some way, it made up for her own betrayal. She pushed that thought away, and busied herself with lunch preparations.

How many for lunch? As she counted, Sarah found herself laughing out loud. Seven for lunch and nine for dinner . . . and all but one are members of Delilah's army. If Margaret wasn't so damned obnoxious, I might feel sorry for her. No, never that, she amended the thought. Even though she was an absurd caricature of a person, Margaret was also Amanda's willing eyes and ears, an extended poisonous tentacle. As I was. Her laughter died, and she pushed the thought away, trying to bury it under the peelings of the vegetables she was preparing for salad.

Lunch was a quiet affair. No one had much to say, and Homer, spreading no apparent odiferous pollution into the air, kept his distance from Margaret, scarcely grunting at all. Casey seemed lost in thought, frowning from time to time, and Delilah, still full of country breakfast, ate little, scarcely moving the food around her plate. Jordan left the table early, heading for the gatehouse after pleading an incipient migraine that could only be forestalled by taking several aspirin and lying in a dark room for a while.

Margaret smirked in Casey's direction several times, fully satisfied that he had gotten his deserved come-comeuppance in the barn. It pleased her that Delilah had given him the same kind of short, flip answers to his list of questions that she had received on her very carefully prepared essay question six months before.

Other than the nagging feeling that what she overheard in the kitchen about poo was actually Delilah talking, nothing seemed to have changed here at all. Although she tried to catch Delilah making the slightest sound, she had met with no success. She would keep on trying as long as she was here. If she had spoken once, she would do it again, Margaret was convinced of that. She mentally began to write her brief report and rehearse the conversation she would have with Amanda Brighton. Right at the top of the list would be her suspicion that Delilah was talking. Maybe she could word it in such a way that it appeared to be a fact, not a suspicion. Yes, that is exactly what she would do.

Serve them all right. That damned Sarah still hadn't given her the extra sheets she asked for.

She smiled, pleased at the thought of the streams of investigators and professionals that would descend on the farm. Of course, all of them would give her proper credit for discovering that the mute Delilah Cross wasn't so mute after all. And Sarah would find her fat, dumpy body up to her double chin in sheets. Oh, and she would certainly emphasize the fact that Doctor Casey Lowell, Junior wasn't accomplishing any more than she had, and perhaps not as much. With any luck she could be out and away from this terrible place by tomorrow afternoon in plenty of time to catch the evening flight back to civilization.

Overhearing the interview in the barn had been a stroke of luck. She had been in the greenhouse with Jordan, and just happened to be facing out toward the barn when Casey and Delilah walked slowly down the gentle slope and disappeared inside. She was totally unaware that Jordan had carefully manipulated her into that position when he caught a glimpse of them coming out the front door of the farmhouse. It was the longest way around, but it made them visible from the greenhouse for a longer period of time before they entered the barn.

Jordan had smiled with what he hoped was an understanding expression as Margaret hurriedly made her excuses and took up her listening post, leaning against the barn wall on one side of the door in what she assumed was a casual posture of bored disinterest. All in all, Margaret felt that this assignment had been very successful. She did feel slightly sad about dear Jordan. He was obviously smitten with her, but, as was the case with so many others, it could never be. She thought of them as her star-crossed loves, the ones who had loved and lost her for one reason or another. Although she could see that his eyes were almost glazed with his desire and longing for her, he was just too attached to the bucolic life. And she was sure she had detected a faint ring of potting soil under his fingernails this morning, although it appeared to be gone when he came in for lunch.

She was deep in thought about this doomed romance, so much so that when Sarah said something to her, she looked up with a start. Everyone except Sarah and Delilah had already left the kitchen, and they were quietly clearing the table.

"I said a penny for your thoughts, Margaret," Sarah repeated pleasantly. "You seemed pretty far away."

Margaret got up quickly, mumbling something unintelligible as she left the room. What she thought was none of this menial's business. She had just had an idea, and she went out on the front porch, examining the various mismatched but comfortable chairs scattered along its length. Choosing one that didn't look too dusty, she ran her fingers across the seat, looked at them, and grimaced in disgust. She quickly went back inside to the hall bathroom and thoroughly scrubbed her hands. Taking a large white bath towel from the rack, she went back to the porch and carefully draped it over the chair she had chosen. After making sure that no portion of her clothing came in contact with any unprotected part of the chair seat or back, she seated herself comfortably and prepared to wait. She took a tentative, shallow breath, and was pleased to discover that the breeze was coming from the direction of the road, bringing with it the odor of fresh-mown grass. That would exacerbate her delicate nasal membranes, perhaps causing an onset of hay fever, but it was infinitely preferable to those vile smells Bent Tree Farm seemed to perpetually generate.

She had made up her mind. As soon as Jordan came in view from the gatehouse, she would greet him warmly and invite him to accompany her to a pleasant early dinner at the Olde English Tea Shoppe in Centerville. That way she could let him down gently and privately in pleasant surroundings, making him understand that their romance could never be, that his longings for her could never be satisfied.

She was still sitting there, lost in pleasant dreams of dalliance, when a car turned into the driveway and rolled to a stop in the parking area. As it stopped, there were three sharp toots of the horn, and two men got out, stretching and looking around curiously. Margaret squinted her eyes, peering hard through her thick lenses, and just as she decided that it was a man and a boy, not two men, Sarah rushed out of the house and down the steps toward them, a big smile on her face.

At the same time, she became aware that Joe and Jordan were hurrying down the driveway from the direction of the barn. For a moment she wondered how she could have possibly missed Jordan, then decided that he must have gone by the porch while she was in the bathroom. Having settled this in her mind, she watched what was clearly a happy reunion of old friends. Delilah came out on the porch and seated herself on the top step, obviously interested in what was going on, but not taking part. She doesn't know them, Margaret thought, and then, with a flash of condescending pity, but then the poor dumb thing doesn't know very many people at all.

Within a few minutes, the man was walking with Joe and Jordan toward the barn. They were talking animatedly about the farm, Margaret could see. Joe said something and waved his arm enthusiastically in the direction of the fields, and Jordan tapped on the man's arm, drawing his attention to the greenhouse. The young man, or boy, Margaret couldn't make up her mind at this distance, had pulled two bags from the car and was following Sarah to the bunkhouse. Obviously, they were going to spend the night.

Margaret frowned. How often did this happen? Freeloading, that's what it was, imposing on the benevolence of Brighton

574

Foundation by entertaining and feeding personal friends. Oh, she would be sure to mention this in her report, too! Little things like that could add up to a lot of money over a period of time. She was sure Amanda Brighton would appreciate knowing, and appreciate her loyalty and concern, too.

She was feeling very pleased with herself as she left the porch and went upstairs. It was a chore to carry her bath things up and down the stairs, but she needed a shower badly, and she would never again step foot in the upstairs bathroom, at least not for the purpose of taking a shower. Of course, she had showered before lunch when she came back from the greenhouse, but she had an uncomfortable feeling that some distasteful intruder might still be sharing her body with her. She had leaned against the barn wall for quite some time while listening to Casey question Delilah. Had something gotten on her there while her attention was distracted? Was that a crawly feeling in the small of her back? Had the damp, humid atmosphere in the greenhouse promoted the growth of some insidious tropical organism that hadn't been removed by her first shower? Margaret was almost frantic by the time she ran up the stairs, grabbed her bath things and a complete change of clothes from her room, and raced back down the stairs to the hall bathroom.

Delilah was still sitting on the porch steps when Sarah and Paulie returned from the bunkhouse. Sarah raised her eyebrows questioningly, and Delilah stood up, pointed toward the hall and cupped her ear. They came up the steps quietly, hearing the rush of water in the shower as Delilah led them down the hall to the kitchen. Not willing to take chances, Delilah quickly drew a large question mark on her notepad and held it up to them.

Sarah took it from her and wrote, "Meeting tonight." She held it up for both Paulie and Delilah, then turned the page. "Jordan taking her to town tonight." She made a sad clown face, turned the page again, and wrote, "Poor Jordan!" She handed the pad back to Delilah, making tearing-up motions, and said conversationally, "Well, Paulie, I'll bet you haven't forgotten my sugar cookies, have you?"

"One of my very best memories," he answered. They all heard the sliding scuffle of footsteps in the hall, and as Sarah put a plate of cookies on the table, he said, a little louder than necessary, "Wow, Aunt Sarah, they're just as big as I remember! Got any cold milk to go with them?"

Sarah took a pitcher of milk from the refrigerator and placed it on the table with a big glass. "I can't get over how much you've grown, young man. And your voice has changed, too. Tell me, how long have you been shaving?" In the momentary silence, they heard the quiet shuffle of slippers as Margaret left the other side of the swinging door and went up the stairs.

Paulie started to say something, but Sarah motioned him to

silence, then whispered just loud enough for them to hear. "She'll be right back. I'll get you two off alone, but it's better that I do it right in front of her. Not suspicious that way."

They both nodded, and when Margaret pushed through the swinging door a few minutes later, dressed in still another new skirt and blouse, Sarah pleasantly introduced her to Paulie Hunter, son of an old friend from the Agriculture Department at the State College.

Paulie stood up, acknowledged the introduction and offered his hand, his manners impeccable. Margaret noticed that his fingernails were clean and well trimmed, as she allowed him the barest touch of the tips of her fingers. Well, she thought, this one doesn't behave like a farm hick. Perhaps his parents have a bit more class than the Clements. She glanced at Delilah. Her back was turned and her head was down as she worked on peeling a huge bowl of potatoes. Margaret noted her air of concentration on the simple task. Another item for my report, she thought. If nothing else, Sarah has certainly trained her for a job as a kitchen helper, which was, she supposed, a form of gainful employment suitable for her, considering her background, of course.

Margaret was sure the presence of young Doctor Lowell and herself signaled that the time was fast approaching when Delilah could no longer rely on the largess of Brighton Foundation, freely receiving all the things that people like herself had to work for.

For some reason that she didn't examine, the thought of Delilah as a kitchen drudge filled her with pleasure, almost as much as the sweet anticipation of telling Amanda Brighton that she could talk.

A moment later, she changed her mind about the couth index of the Hunters. As the three men came up on the back porch and started into the kitchen, the two older men were in the lead, deeply involved in a heated discussion about the relative merits of various types of fertilizers. Her nose twitched involuntarily as she moved past them, ignoring Sarah's half-completed introduction of the elder Hunter in her determination to catch Jordan on the porch. Yes, the faint odor of fertilizer hung in the air around them, and she wondered if they were compelled to handle the stuff, or if the smell just jumped off and clung to the clothes of anyone who came too close.

"Oh, Jordan, there you are." Her voice was syrupy. "I was wondering . . . "

He cut her off before she could finish. "Margaret, would you go to dinner in town with me tonight?" His words were clipped and he was looking down as he spoke.

Oh, the poor dear, Margaret thought. He's shy, but determined to be alone with me. How charming . . . and sad. Her voice still dripping sugar, she replied: "Why, of course I will, Jordan dear. What a nice time we'll have. We can go to the Olde English Tea Shoppe and just simply indulge ourselves. I saw what I am sure will be deliciously authentic English pot pies listed on their menu, and their desserts are simply delicious. What time shall I be ready?" She placed her hand gingerly on his arm, hoping his shirt wasn't too contaminated with farm-generated odors and germs, and blinked her eyes rapidly behind her glasses in what she was sure was a nicely flirtatious manner.

For a wild moment Jordan fought an outburst of laughter. It looked as though her bat-like glasses were struggling to take off from their perch on her nose and flap away. His face reddened, but he managed to say, "I'll pick you up on the front porch about six-thirty. Is that all right?" Without waiting for her answer, he jumped off the steps and trotted toward the barn, leaving Margaret basking in the warmth of the knowledge that she had swept him quite off of his feet.

She was feeling good as she went back into the kitchen. "Oh, Sarah." Her voice cut through the men's continuing fertilizer conversation like a saw-blade. "Jordan and I won't be having dinner here tonight. We're going into town to dine at that clever little English tearoom, you know, the one tucked away in the corner of the shopping center?" Her tone implied that they wouldn't know, and she started across the kitchen, already preoccupied with deciding between the two new skirt and blouse sets that she hadn't yet worn.

Sarah nodded to her, then asked, "Would you like to take a

look around the farm, Paulie? It must be getting boring sitting around listening to the old fogies blabber." She turned to Delilah. "Finished with the potatoes, I see. Why don't you give this young man the three dollar tour of Bent Tree Farm?" She glanced at her watch. "Be more than an hour before we get down to serious cooking, so go on and get some fresh air, you two."

Margaret had slowed her steps across the kitchen in order to hear this interchange, and she went through the swinging door thinking that there was nothing here that needed her attention. Delilah had probably never been alone with a boy in her entire life, and an hour stroll around the farm in broad daylight was harmless enough. Certainly, Delilah had displayed no interest in the boy, had scarcely even looked at him, so she had an hour free to bathe and choose her outfit for the evening. Besides, she didn't think she could stand to listen to any more talk about fertilizer.

As she went up the stairs, she wondered about Doctor Casey Lowell, Junior. She hadn't seen him since lunch, but when she glanced through the open office doors as she turned down the hall, she saw him engrossed in the file folders on the desk at the far end of the room. All present and accounted for, she thought happily, and closed the door to the yellow room with a satisfying thunk.

***

Everyone but Homer had gathered in the kitchen before sitting down to dinner when they heard the unmistakable sound of the farm pickup. It came up in front, paused a minute, then moved away down the driveway.

Harold and Paulie looked puzzled as the others burst into laughter. "You'll have to excuse us," Sarah gasped, "but Jordan is performing way beyond the call of duty, so we can't hold the pickup against him, can we now?"

Laughter rose again, and Joe tried to explain. "Did you by any chance notice that brand new, bright red sports car sitting down at the end of the row by the Rover? Well, that little car is Jordan's pride and joy. He doesn't feel dressed when he leaves the farm unless he's wearing it." His face crinkled, and he snorted happily.

"Let me explain." They all turned as Homer came in the back door. "Hello, Harold, and you must be Delilah's friend, Paulie. Good to see you, especially here and now." They shook hands, and Harold grinned as he took in the disreputable clothes and slicked back hair.

"Doctor Lowell, I presume," he said, and laughed. "Sorry, couldn't help it," he apologized. "Go ahead and explain about the car."

"Well, much against his will, Jordan drew the distasteful job of distracting the piranha, as he calls Margaret. He's doing it, and doing it well, but he absolutely refused to be seen with her in his own car. He is known in town, and he's been dating a town girl for some time, so you can understand his problem. But he seems to have solved it in his own way. Instead of taking the Rover, or even using Margaret's company car, he hauled her off in the farm pickup, which has, incidentally, several bags of aromatic steer manure sitting in the back perfuming the evening air even as we speak." His composure broke, and he whooped loudly.

Between gasps, Joe asked, "How did the manure get in the pickup? We unloaded that this morning." Then he understood. "You didn't!"

"Oh, but I did," Homer admitted happily. "I was lurking about, waiting to see that they got away in style, and met Jordan muttering and moaning in the vicinity of his precious red car. I must admit that it was I who suggested that he wait a few minutes while I prepared his chariot, and then sent him off to town in the pickup. It also crossed my mind that the noise of the thing would serve us as an early warning of their return."

"You're evil, Dad, downright evil," Casey said approvingly. As they sat down at the table, he explained about his diagnosis of Margaret's seriously obsessional behavior. Sarah chimed in, agreeing that Margaret was in dire need of professional help. Casey explained to Harold and Paulie that it was their intention to get rid of Margaret as soon as possible, making her stay as unpleasant as possible while reinforcing the idea that nothing had changed here since her last visit. Certainly, she had been kept

582

unaware of the fact that Delilah was talking.

They ate quickly, anxious to get down to business because there was a great deal of information to be shared. At this point, a number of facts were spread out among various members of the group. Sarah, Joe, and Homer didn't know about the computer printouts in Paulie's jacket pocket. Only Harold knew what he personally had done to dispose of Agnes Kittridge, and he and Paulie and Delilah didn't know about the part Sarah had played. Only Paulie and Delilah actually knew the identity of Auntie. And Delilah.

No one commented about Delilah's silence or her apparently inward-turned air of intense preoccupation. Paulie didn't have much to say, either, and Sarah wasn't the only one who wondered what the two of them had talked about during their walk alone around the farm that afternoon. Everyone was helping to clear the table and get the dishes into the dishwasher, and everyone jumped at the unexpected sound of the kitchen telephone ringing. Sarah answered it.

"Yes, yes it is," she said. Then, her forehead wrinkling in puzzlement, she listened a moment, and said, "Why, yes, he's here. Just a minute, please."

Turning to Paulie, she said, "Paulie, it's for you, and he says it's extremely urgent."

His face was just as puzzled as hers as he took the phone.

Everyone was listening, making no pretense of doing anything else, and they soon assumed the same puzzled expression at the cryptic words they were hearing.

"Hello," Paulie said, then listened a moment.

Then, "Oh Jesus, he didn't! He couldn't!" His face was visibly pale as he listened again, and Harold took a step toward him, suddenly concerned about his son.

"How long ago?" Paulie asked. "Next check-in time?" He listened intently, all of his attention focused on what he was hearing. "That's about an hour from now."

Paulie appeared to be handling whatever was going on, and Harold stepped back, not only giving him physical room, but the implied room to take care of whatever it was on his own. Strange, Harold thought, with more than a little sadness, how something as simple as taking a step back can mark a rite of passage into manhood.

Paulie was speaking again. "Hey, don't worry. We'll handle this. If he could do that, then we can sure as hell do this. Stay by the phone and I'll get back to you before he checks in again. Bye."

He slowly replaced the receiver, and turned to face them. Taking a deep breath, he spoke directly to Delilah, ignoring the circle of expectant faces. "Chameleon, I'm sorry, but there's no easy way to tell you this, and no way to keep it private so here goes." He paused, then moved close to her, all the while looking straight into her eyes . . . and she knew. Maybe it was his use of her game name, maybe it was something else, but she knew before he started to speak, and her heart started to pound.

The silence in the kitchen was almost painful in its intensity, and his voice sounded loud as he spoke, deeper in its emotional intensity. "Darkling found Auntie and her babe. The dragon had them hidden away, but he found them. Delilah, he talked to them, do you understand? He talked to both of them for a long time, telling them all the things he knew." He took a ragged breath, his eyes never leaving Delilah.

"Then, Auntie cried. She cried real tears, do you hear me? He said real tears. She begged to be taken to you, Delilah. Merlin didn't give me all the details, but he said the place they were in was very bad. Darkling couldn't leave them there, so as soon as it got dark, he took them away with him. I guess you could say he stole them. He looked at her intently, then said, "Kidnapped them . . . and he's bringing them here."

He cleared his throat, and turned to the others. "You all heard. I think most of you know what it means. That was Merlin on the phone. Darkling will check in with him in an hour. What shall we tell him?" He looked from face to face, then asked no one in particular, "What can we tell him?"

CHAPTER TWENTY SIX

There was a moment of silence while the full import of what Paulie said to Delilah registered, understood in differing degrees by each person depending on the amount of information they had. Then a storm of questions rose in the kitchen.

Harold Newcombe took charge. His voice was all Director of Hiller School, quiet, modulated, and brooking no disobedience. "Paulie, give me the papers." As Paulie hurried to comply, Harold motioned to Joe and Sarah to go the table. "Sit down and read," he told them, removing the papers from the envelope and handing them to Joe. "When you finish Chameleon's story – Delilah's story - give it to Sarah." He patted Sarah's shoulder. "Sarah, when you finish it, give it to Homer."

Homer joined the Clements at the table, and Harold added a few words of explanation. "We don't have much time and reading the two stories is the quickest way for you to understand what has happened. Paulie, Casey, and I have read it, and Delilah wrote the first part shortly after she began to talk. Merlin, the one who called, wrote the second part last night. These four, Delilah, Paulie and their friends started playing a computer role-playing adventure game when they were much younger, and they've continued to play during the time Delilah's been here. That's why the rather strange and archaic language. They were discussing this under cover of their game roles using game language."

Joe quickly finished the first part and handed it to Sarah. His look of compassion and sympathy brought a small smile of acknowledgment from Delilah; she stood close to Paulie, leaning into his side within the circle of the arm he had put protectively around her. Neither of them had spoken since Paulie's explanation of the phone call. Paulie looked relieved that the matter seemed to be out of his hands. Delilah was fighting the urge to withdraw into some far place in her mind where she could hide. Not now, she told herself. Not now. You started it, you started the quest. Now you stay right here on the roller coaster and ride it all the way to the end. She forced herself to look around the kitchen. Casey had put on a pot of coffee and Harold was getting coffee cups out of the cupboard. Joe had finished reading and was passing the second part to Sarah, who had already passed the first part to Homer. When Sarah took it, Joe put his elbows on the table and buried his face in his hands.

She looked at Sarah again. Sarah seemed to be smaller, Delilah thought, as though she were curling inward upon herself, as though the words were sucking something vital from her as she read them. Maybe they were . . . the thought shocked her. If she looked at it from Sarah's point of view, or anyone else's for that matter, it was an incredible and evil story of insanity and obsession, one that had left its mark on many innocent lives. Everyone in this room had been touched by Brighton Foundation to a greater or lesser degree, and this truth must be devastating.

I've lived with most of the story all of my life, Delilah thought, and the whole story, the one they're reading right now, almost destroyed me last night. What must these people think, what must they feel, getting it all on a few pages of computer printout? She realized that she was avoiding the urgent problem, the thing that had to be decided within the next half-hour. But this decision wasn't going to be hers that much was clear. Someone was going to do something, had to do something, because Darkling was on the road somewhere with Auntie and her youngling, and no one was going to desert him, no matter how crazy his act of derring-do. No, it wasn't a crazy act, was it? Wasn't that exactly what she wanted, the freedom of Auntie and her youngling? She could feel the tension, smell it swirling out from everyone, including herself. She looked up at Paulie and asked the question uppermost in her mind. "Paulie, Darkling is a risk-taking adventurer, but he wouldn't have done something like this unless the situation with Auntie and her youngling was really bad, would he?"

"I've known him for years, Delilah, and he doesn't do crazy things. He talks a lot and plays the swashbuckling adventurer in our games, but he thinks before he does things. I guess that's why he didn't last long with Becky. He was too serious, actually too mature for her tastes, at least that's the way it looked to me. No, it was something he had to do and do now rather than wait for us to make a plan. He thought it was an emergency and I think we should take his word for it. He's risking jail if he gets caught, and if we help him, we're all taking that same risk." He gestured around the kitchen. "Believe me Dad and all the rest know that, and I don't see anyone hesitating, do you?"

She smiled weakly, and moved to help with the coffee. The coffee-maker was just emitting its final bubbling gasps of steam to announce that the coffee was ready when she stepped up to the counter beside Casey.

"Are you all right?" he asked, his voice full of concern.

"Yes, but it's all happening so fast, I feel like I can't quite keep up," she answered.

"Well, Delilah," he said, "look around. These are all very good people with very good minds, and they're all your friends. No matter what happens now you're surrounded by friends and you won't be alone. Neither will Darkling and Auntie."

Delilah involuntarily jerked as hands fell on her shoulders from behind. Homer gently turned her around to face him. His voice was full of sympathy as he said, "Girl, you've carried this burden all by yourself for a long time, and frankly, I don't know how you've done it." He sighed deeply.

The kitchen was very quiet and she realized everyone was listening intently as he continued. He was standing very close, and his eyes held hers in a steady gaze. His hands remained in place, cupping her shoulders firmly, and she realized that it gave her a sense of security to be this close, to smell him, to look into his eyes, to feel the faint touch of his breath. She could feel herself relaxing.

She didn't see the look Casey and Sarah exchanged. Both of them realized that Homer, the farmhand, had disappeared. Doctor K.C. Lowell, Senior had once again, as he had on that day in the hall bathroom, taken charge of Delilah. He was giving her what she needed to cope, what he felt she had to have in order to deal with this latest crisis rationally and come out of it as intact as possible.

"There are a few questions that we must have the answers to before we can make any decisions." He waited until she nodded, then began, his voice still very gentle, but audible to everyone in the kitchen. "Tell us about Auntie, Delilah, she can talk?" It was a statement, not a question, and she nodded again.

"Why didn't you talk?"

There is that question again, Delilah thought. The corners of her mouth curled up slightly. "Because Auntie told me not to." That answer did not sound sufficient, even though it was the simple truth, so she continued. "For a long time, I thought it was because the rest of the group didn't talk, and they might hurt us if they found out how different we were, especially me. They're frightened by anything strange and different, you know."

She was still looking straight into K.C.'s eyes. "And then, there was the secret, the secret of all the mothers before us who spoke. Auntie said it must never be told or men would come and kill everyone. We were the last of the different ones, and we must protect the group. That's why she didn't rescue me from Bhutu Holding Facility. She could have easily pulled off the chain link screen and taken me away, but they would look for me, find the group, and kill us all. But she came there to Bhutu Holding Facility just the same. She came at night for almost a year to that hell place where she was born . . . where my mother was born."

She took a deep, painful breath before she continued. She heard Sarah then. She was sobbing softly. "Don't cry, Sarah. It's all right," she said around the shoulder blocking her view, her eyes never wavering from those of the man in front of her.

"How did you find out about Auntie's capture?"

Her small laugh held no humor. "Paulie knows. She was there at the Landon Zoo the day I went there with the Newcombes. She had a babe, and she bit me to make me go away before anyone

591

heard us talking or saw us together. She was very frightened, full of fear for the babe, and me, and herself. The babe talks. She told me to go away, too." Her voice was getting lower, slower as the words came with an effort.

"You've read the tales of the four warriors. You know what Darkling has done because I sent them off on my quest. I never thought, I never knew . . . " She stopped.

"One more question, Delilah, and then I think we'll be ready to make some plans." Though his voice was still low and gentle, it sounded loud in the continuing silence. No one had moved while she was talking, and Sarah had stopped crying. His grip on her shoulders tightened. "Delilah, was Mandy your mother?"

She didn't seem surprised by the question, and answered without hesitation. In a strange way she was almost anxious to say the words out loud, to speak the unspeakable and face rejection by these people who had been her friends.

"Yes, Mandy was my mother, Auntie's full sister. Auntie said she was very much like me, or I was very much like her, only I was even more different, more other inside where I feel and think. We had the same eyes, Auntie said . . . the same eyes only mine were the color of my father's eyes. Sky eyes Auntie said."

They all heard the change in Delilah's voice; it took on a child-like, plaintive sound as she continued. "Miss Agnes really hated my eyes, you know. She thought I didn't have a soul. She made me keep my eyes down because eyes are the windows of the soul." She took a deep, ragged breath, speaking directly to him. "K.C., I really looked for a soul. I tried and tried. Paulie helped me look for a way to get one, but I didn't dare tell him what I was really looking for. We searched through all the religions in the world didn't we, Paulie?"

She didn't wait for an answer. "But they only talk about people who already have souls. They're born with them. I know there must be a God, but I don't think he cares about creatures that have no souls. See? If you don't have a soul, you can't be a human person, you can only be a creature like a cat or dog . . . or ape. When they talked about me like I wasn't there and called me 'she' or 'her' the way people talk about animals, I knew Agnes Kittridge was right. I had no soul."

Her voice wavered uncertainly, then grew stronger as she said, "But Paulie never seemed to notice that I didn't have a soul, and most of the time I don't ever let anyone really see into my eyes, so they don't know it either."

Delilah's voice changed suddenly, became very matter-of-fact. "Auntie is a throw-back, an atavism is the word I've read in my genetics books. They didn't even bother to name her and they didn't teach her to talk. She learned at night from my mother. I think they only let her live at first to keep my mother company because they were the last. You see, there were never any males born, only females, and they usually died giving birth to one of us different ones, or shortly after." There was pain in her voice now, and though she wasn't aware of it, everyone in the kitchen had tears in their eyes, hurting with the depth of her pain, hurting with a need to help her.

"Auntie told me they made the mothers pregnant too soon, too early, before they were old enough to be mothers. They took them into the back building at Bhutu Holding Facility and did something to them to make them have babes when they were still only younglings. In the group, you only have babes when you are the right age, and you must nurse the babe and care for it, find food for it, and protect it for four years, or so. In the group, your body tells you when it is the right time. Auntie ran away because she was afraid they would make her pregnant. She heard them talking about it. They didn't know she could understand what they were saying. They didn't know she could speak."

She shrugged away from K.C.'s grasp, and took a few steps away from the counter. "Mandy was my mother and she died. When I was starving to death, Auntie tried to nurse me. She had never had a babe, but she made milk for me. Auntie is my milk mother."

Her voice became defiant. "Mandy the murderess was my mother, and she killed the man who fathered her. He fathered Auntie, and their mother, and me, and most of the mothers in our

594

line. Now I know that his father contributed his share in earlier years. I think they call that line breeding in pedigreed animals, don't they?"

She looked around the room. "What would you call it? Brighton line breeding? Makes me a purebred creature, doesn't it? Too bad I didn't get a soul in the process, but he probably didn't have one. From what I learned about God and souls, anyone who would do what they did couldn't possibly have one for me to inherit like Mandy and I inherited the color of their eyes."

Her voice got louder; now she looked around at each of them in turn, then focused on Casey. "I told you the records were wrong, didn't I? I'm not sixteen years old, I'm eighteen. I wasn't eight when they took me away from my group, my family. I was ten years old, ten rains and ten not rains. Auntie counts time in half-years because of the seasons. She's very good at keeping track of time, a natural born historian, too."

She couldn't control her voice and her laugh was a painful croak. "Why did I survive Agnes Kittridge? Because Auntie taught me to talk, because she came to Bhutu Holding Facility the whole first year, and because Auntie taught me everything she knew about living and surviving and keeping secrets during the first ten years of my life." The words were coming faster and faster, tumbling over one another in her urgency to get them all said. "And I never made the sign of the cross that Agnes Kittridge so conveniently turned into a name that fit her religious insanity. Here is what I did."

Clearly and decisively she made the sign of who she was, holding her hands at shoulder level. "See? It's not a cross and was never meant to be. It's an X. My name is Delilah X . . . X for experimental animal. If my mother hadn't killed him and left that place, my father would have strapped me on a table in that building out in back at Bhutu Holding Facility and, without anesthetic, acid-burned five neat X's right here!" She touched her shoulder, her face twisted in pain. "Five X's. Mandy and Auntie got four."

She looked at Paulie for a long moment. "Paulie helped me figure it out this afternoon. He's always been very good with fractions." Her voice was shaking, and Paulie took a step toward her, his face showing the depth of his pain. "I'm one-thirty-second bonobo ape fathered by a human monster named Brighton who was also my grandfather. And his own father was my great-grandfather." She touched the place near her shoulder again and burst into tears.

Before she realized it, K.C. had enveloped her in a firm hug, gently stroking her head and shoulders as he murmured softly, crooning and rocking slightly as her sobs gathered strength, reached a crescendo, and gradually subsided. At the same time, Joe, Harold, Casey, and Paulie took turns asking each other terse questions, giving brief answers. Sarah, unable to control her tears, unthinkingly blew her nose on a kitchen towel and busied herself with serving the coffee. She forgot all about the cookies.

Merlin knew about the farm because Paulie had called him and told him while Harold was explaining matters and making excuses to a half-awake Dee Dee. Merlin also had the farm address.

"Can you do it?" Harold asked Joe, glancing anxiously at his watch. Merlin would be calling in a very few minutes.

"Yes," Joe answered immediately. "Right into the gatehouse until that bitch clears out. That will buy us the time we need to really get down to figuring this out."

"But what if she hangs around?" Casey asked.

"I can guarantee she won't be around long after breakfast," Joe said grimly. "You have no idea how easy it is to have an accident with a manure spreader full of liquid manure. The way she took out of here yesterday over a little dry cow shit in Homer's pocket pretty well says it all. Ordinarily, I'd feel sorry for someone that far gone in their phobia, but I feel no compunction about really giving her a shove. Maybe she'll get herself some help."

"Delilah, are you listening?" When she released herself from K.C. 's hug and looked toward Joe, he could see the worst of the emotional storm was over. He turned to Paulie. "I think it's best that you talk to Merlin so that he doesn't get the idea that there's any dirty work at the crossroads."

He shot a guilty look at Sarah. It was his favorite joke about the farm, and Sarah hated it. Before she could react with anything other than a frown, he hurried on. "Did Merlin say where Darkling and his passengers were?"

Paulie thought a moment. "I think he said Darkling had crossed the state line before he stopped to call, but he didn't say between what states." He thought a minute longer, then said, "Yes, he told Merlin he was calling from a pay phone on State Route 24 because he was keeping to the less-traveled roads."

"Excellent!" Joe exclaimed. "He's in this state already, and if he stays on 24 South, he'll wind up right in Centerville."

He addressed them all. "Look, we all better get out of here. Even if we hear the pickup I don't think we can scatter fast enough to avoid Margaret's prying eyes. Paulie, you stay here with Delilah. Go in the living room and turn on the television. You know, sort of hang out? Two teen-agers watching a movie with the lights on doesn't look suspicious. You can hear the kitchen phone from there. Casey, take the office until the bat roosts for the night. I guess you can run interference for Paulie if you have to."

He looked around. "Okay by everyone?" There was a chorus of assents, and Joe borrowed Delilah's notepad to write down the private number at the gatehouse for Paulie. "Give Merlin this number for Darkling and tell him to call as soon as he gets to Centerville. We'll guide him in from there. Or if he has any trouble at all, tell him to call either number. Maybe you also better tell him that anyone who answers at the gatehouse number will be a friend of . . . " He paused a second, then said, " . . . a friend of Chameleon."

* * *

When Margaret clambered out of the pickup an hour later, she rushed up the steps, frantic to get upstairs and into the shower, barely noting that Delilah and Paulie were sitting well apart in the brightly-lit room engrossed in a television movie. The evening had been a fiasco from beginning to end, and she was sure she could never totally eliminate the acrid odor of steer manure from her hair and body. The new clothes were ruined. No amount of washing would help, because in her mind the odor had permeated the very molecules of the threads from which the material was woven.

The nerve of that hick, she thought. Taking a date to dinner in that filthy pickup was bad enough, but with bags of steer manure in the back? When Jordan first drove up in it, she started to suggest that they take her Brighton car, then didn't because she was afraid of insulting him. At first she hadn't noticed the acrid odor, mixed as it was with gasoline fumes and something else equally unpleasant that she couldn't identify. That state of affairs lasted only until they stopped at the crossroad corner, because the movement of the truck swept the odor back and away.

Never had a ride seemed so long. She could have sworn Jordan was deliberately dawdling, prolonging her agony, carrying on a spirited, one-sided conversation about his beloved greenhouse, not seeming to notice that she answered in monosyllables as she concentrated on breathing as shallowly as possible without hyperventilating.

From there, it was all down hill. She quickly led the way into Ye Olde English Tea Shoppe, hoping that no one would notice the smell she was sure surrounded them both like an evil cloud. Her relief was short-lived. She had left Jordan to find a place for them to sit, and hurried to the bathroom. It was new and cleaner than most public restrooms; she spent a frantic ten minutes washing and rinsing her hands and face, finishing with an antiseptic towelette from the supply that she carried in her purse. When she came out of the restroom, she was feeling slightly better, determined to get through the evening with as much dignity as possible. Perhaps she would even enjoy the authentic English food, and looked forward to a cup of good tea. Jordan had found a table in the corner and was talking to the round little dark-haired lady who had treated her so nicely the time she was there before.

As she crossed the room, she could see that the woman had her hand on his shoulder, laughing about something. Perhaps a little too familiar, she thought, but then wasn't a casual kind of friendliness a trademark of this kind of establishment, a part of its charm? That thought lasted until she was close enough to hear their conversation.

With no hint of an English accent, the woman said, "Oh come on, Jordan. Your Mom always comes through with those big, old sugar cookies that make such a hit with everyone at our bake sales. I wish I could convince her to keep this place supplied. Make a fortune for both of us." She turned and smiled as Margaret walked up to the table. "Oh, and here's your lady, Jordan. I'll bring a pot of tea while you think about what you'd like to eat, although why you'd eat here instead of pigging out on Sarah's cooking is beyond me." With that, she bustled away.

Jordan rose and politely seated Margaret then resumed his seat.

"But she isn't English," was all she could think of to say.

"Well, of course not," he replied, smiling. "Dora just puts on that phony accent for people she doesn't know. She knows everyone in Centerville and most of the other towns around the area, and they'd laugh their heads off if she used it on them. But she's done a pretty good business with this franchise operation." He picked up the menus and handed her one.

"Franchise operation?" Margaret wasn't able to grasp it. Her eyes wandered around the room, looking at the teapots and plants on the shelf, the neat tablecloths, the warm lamplight under the beamed ceiling.

"Yes," he answered, glancing up from the menu. "Kind of a far out idea that some smart operator figured out a couple of years ago. It was kind of iffy at first, but it seems to be catching on with the crowd it's meant for. You know, not a kid's place, not a steak place, not a Rotary Club meeting place, but a good place for the ladies to get together, drink tea and gossip when they're coming and going to the supermarket and the department store. Mom and Delilah always stop here after they finish their shopping."

Margaret thought about that. Somehow, it had never entered her mind that Delilah lived any kind of life that might include shopping trips and tearooms. Did she go to movies, too? Parties? Church socials? All those normal things? It seemed all wrong to Margaret. She couldn't think of a reason why it should be wrong, but the idea irritated her.

Jordan studied the menu again. "One thing about these places. The food is all centrally prepared under rigid quality controls, frozen, and delivered every other day. It's better than your usual fast food operations, and you can see the menu is quite small, so it doesn't take a big inventory investment. At least you always know what you're getting. People like that, you know. And they're all identical, right down to the teapots and artificial plants."

He gestured at the shelf above their heads. "Walk into any one of Ye Olde English Tea Shoppe in any shopping center in the southern part of the state and you won't be able to tell where you are unless you go outside and look." He laughed. "Matter of fact, the way these shopping centers are so standardized, you might not be able to tell even then."

He finally noticed that Margaret wasn't talking. "Sorry to rattle on like that. I think I'll have the Scotch pot pie, how about you?"

Margaret would have gotten up and left, but just then Dora came back with the tea. It smelled good and she needed something in her stomach to dilute the bile she could feel building into a full-fledged attack of heartburn. And the thought of returning to that stinking truck was more than she could bear right now.

The evening dragged on and on, taking on a kind of dreamy slow-motion horror film quality for Margaret. The other customers left before they finished their Scotch pot pies, piping hot from the microwave. Jordan decided to have a cherry tart, also piping hot from the microwave, with a generous dollop of fresh whipped cream especially defrosted for that purpose.

After Dora served it, inquiring if Margaret was really sure she didn't want one for herself, she locked the front door and turned off the outside lights. Then, she got herself a cup, plopped herself down at their table without being invited, poured herself a cup of tea, and spent the next hour discussing everything from franchises to crop rotation with Jordan, who seemed to be thoroughly enjoying himself.

As she watched and listened, Margaret decided that Jordan could just suffer through the heartbreak of unrequited love without her help. She had tried, really tried to let him down easily, but a person could only be expected to do so much out of kindness and compassion. The trip home seemed slower than the trip into town, and after a very long, hot shower, followed by a second that left raw places all over her body, Margaret finally went to sleep.

Her first waking thought was of sewers and cesspools and things better not thought about. As she sat upright in bed, the realization came that this was no leftover figment of a nightmare. It was real, and the unbelievable stench was rolling through her open window in waves. She staggered to the window with her hand over her nose, gagging convulsively as she took in the scene in the driveway directly below her window.

A piece of farm equipment had apparently struck one of the curbing stones and tipped slightly to one side, allowing the horror it contained in its tank to spill in oozing ripples down one side. Joe, Jordan and the hired man stood looking at the mess, apparently unaffected by the smell that was causing her to convulse. She slammed her window down, hoping to keep the smell out, but it only seemed to trap it inside the room with her. Sobbing, she pulled on a skirt and blouse, and stuffed her few belongings into her bag, including the skirt and blouse from last night that she had intended to deposit in the trash.

Sarah was standing on the front porch, holding her nose as she called advice to the men which they ignored as they continued to loudly discuss the situation among themselves. Margaret caught the words "plumb rotten stink" and "enough to gag a maggot", and fought the urge to vomit as she rushed down the steps, also ignoring Sarah and the questions she called after her. She flung her suitcase in the back seat and jumped in the car. In spite of her shaking hands, she found the keyhole on the first try, started the motor, and was half-way down the driveway toward Palmer Road before she managed to get her door shut.

Two days later at the Seymour Motel on the outskirts of Centerville, the manager, accompanied by the Sheriff, used his passkey to unlock the door of Number Eight. He had decided to take this step after becoming aware that the water in this unit had been running ever since the somewhat wild-eyed young lady checked in two mornings before. After taking a brief look in the bathroom, the Sheriff radioed for an ambulance. Other than a short outburst of mumbled objections when the ambulance attendants turned off the shower and removed her still fully clothed from the tub, Margaret went along quietly.

Her brief report stating that nothing had changed with Delilah Cross or Bent Tree Farm was filed a week later. When Amanda Brighton called her a few days after that, Margaret apologized profusely. She had, it seemed, had a brief relapse of her problem. Nothing serious, of course, and that nice young doctor assured her that one therapy session a week would be sufficient.

When Amanda pressed her, she was very positive. No, nothing had changed with either Delilah or the farm since her last visit. She had made very close observations of everything and everyone. No, there was no unusual activity of any kind, no one coming or going in any way not related to normal farm operations. Yes, Sarah had taken care of the sheet problem that Margaret had mentioned before, and everything seemed to be going smoothly in a regular routine.

Doctor Casey Lowell, Junior? Seemed to be doing a very good job, very business-like and professional. Yes, Delilah seemed cooperative enough, and she was sure his reports and recommendations could be relied on to be accurate and objective. No, there was no indication of any kind that Delilah was talking. Her opinion? No, as far as she was concerned, Delilah Cross would never talk.

After what seemed like a very long inquisition, Amanda seemed satisfied, and Margaret hung up with a deep feeling of relief. She offered up a fervent prayer that no one would ever find out that of the last three days she claimed to have spent observing the activity at Bent Tree Farm, two had actually been spent in the bathtub of the Seymour Motel eight miles away, and one had been spent in the Centerville hospital. Above all, she prayed that the report she had filed and the answers she had just given to Amanda Brighton would ensure that she would never again be sent to Bent Tree Farm. "Please God, don't ever send me to that hell again. Amen".

CHAPTER TWENTY SEVEN

Within fifteen minutes after Margaret's departure, the manure spreader had been righted and parked behind the barn. Later, its contents would be spread across one of the fields, exchanging its natural nutrients for a healthy late corn crop. The small amount that had been deliberately spilled in front of the farmhouse was quickly hosed into the lawn; the smell dissipating as the concentration was diluted across the spread of grass and dried in the warm morning sun. Paulie and Delilah were waiting by the phone in the gatehouse, and farm work came to a standstill. One by one, as though drawn by an irresistible magnet, the others drifted down to join them in their vigil. The conversation was devoted to quickly preparing a suitable place for Auntie and her youngling. It had to be both concealed from all but the most intense scrutiny, yet, Sarah insisted, much to Delilah's delight, it had to be 'homey', a home place for Delilah's aunt and cousin.

"They've had enough of cages," Sarah said, her tone clearly indicating that she had already, sight-unseen, taken the two under her warm, voluminous wing. "And thank God that we have a whole farm to work with."

"That's it," Jordan said. "The barn. Remember the back of the loft where I found Homer's hat? The floored area up there is as big as an apartment. Why, it wouldn't take much, and we could open up a big area of the back wall on the pond side for windows and lots of fresh air and sunshine. They couldn't be seen from the road at all. There's even electricity up there." His face lit up as he talked out his idea, and soon the other men were busy contributing their thoughts, and Joe was scribbling a list of the building materials they would need.

Sarah drew Delilah to one side, hesitated, obviously wanting to talk to her, but not sure about how to begin. Finally, she led the way into the family room, and turned to face Delilah.

"Sarah, the questions are written all over your face." Delilah said quietly. "And you're too worried about my feelings to ask them, right?"

Sarah nodded. "It's such a strange situation, unique is the word for it, and I don't want to hurt your feelings, but we have to deal with the realities." She paused, obviously embarrassed, and Delilah laughed, feeling a burst of love for this woman who had given her so much, freely and without reservation.

"Auntie looks like a bonobo ape, Sarah. Bigger, taller, with several differences in her hands and feet and body, but she's worked hard to conceal them. From what I saw of the youngling, she's pretty much like her mother, bred back to a bonobo father there in the zoo, but she speaks, that much is sure." Delilah paused, thinking of that day at the zoo. The babe told her to go away, and did it in very passable English. "Sarah, they haven't had the benefits of being civilized the way Agnes Kittridge civilized me." She stopped, dismayed by the look on Sarah's face. "No, Sarah, don't be upset. That's long ago and far away now. What I meant is I don't think they are toilet trained, they don't know about things like furniture. They eat and drink with their hands, and they sleep wherever they can." Her voice broke slightly. "Sarah, they've been in a cage for years. Auntie went directly from a room at Bhutu Holding Facility that was hardly more than a cage, to the free life in the jungle, then back to a cage. The youngling has never known anything else."

She stopped, looking down at her hands. The men's voices rose and fell in the kitchen as the barn apartment was designed in every detail on scraps of paper that they passed around the table. Then there was the sound of someone leaving, and in a few minutes the pickup rattled out of the driveway. Jordan was on his way to the lumberyard with the material list in hand and the cover story of enlarging a portion of the greenhouse firmly in mind.

For the first time, Sarah smiled. "I would say they aren't wasting any time, wouldn't you?"

610

Delilah nodded agreement, then said, "You'd better tell them that they aren't building an apartment for . . . " She stopped, cleared her throat, then finished, " . . . for humans, Sarah. These are experimental animals like me." The last sentence came out in a rush. "They can be taught, they're intelligent, but it will take time."

She turned and went back into the kitchen, unable to say more without breaking down. Sarah was right behind her, and started talking as she came through the kitchen door.

"I want you all to hear this," she said, addressing the men at the table. "It is my opinion that Auntie and her child are feral children, feral children with a decided head start because they can speak." Delilah didn't notice that Sarah's voice and delivery had changed, taking on a tone of professional authority, but the others did. "They need to be housed in clean, secure, comfortable surroundings, and taught. These children," she emphasized the word, "these children have been severely traumatized, and judging by the actions taken by the brave warrior Darkling, they have probably been badly abused." She paused for breath, looking at each of the men in turn. "I know you all realize that we are involved in an act of criminal conspiracy, aiding and abetting in a theft of property, which is what the authorities will call it. Well, I call it a rescue operation to save abused children, and as far as I'm concerned, this is just the opening shot of a battle that I won't stop until Amanda Brighton and, if necessary, the entire Brighton Foundation is brought down once and for all!" Sarah's round cheeks were flushed with the intensity of her feelings, and they grew even redder as the loud agreement from the men threatened to rattle the dishes in the cupboard.

In the momentary silence that followed, K.C.'s voice was thoughtful. "I think we're going to need an attorney sooner or later, and hopefully not to defend us against criminal charges. What do you all think about calling James and Kaydee? They're family, they know Delilah now, and they're damned good civil attorneys."

He looked down at his hands a moment, then addressed Delilah. "Child, you probably haven't thought this out, but I'd like you to think about this." He glanced at the others, then back at Delilah, his calm words falling into the room like small bombs, detonating one at a time as their meaning became clear. "Delilah, if the two Brighton men are the sole male genetic contributors that resulted in all the Mothers, you, Auntie, and even her youngling being here, then your last name is not Cross, it is Brighton. By any and every criteria of genetics, you are almost pure Brighton with more legitimate claim to the name than even Amanda Brighton herself is. She only acquired it by marriage." He paused, looking at her intently trying to evaluate the effect his words were having.

"You are her son's daughter. That makes her your grandmother. You are her husband's granddaughter, but even more than that, and here it gets very complex . . . he was the father of your grandmother, and the son was the father of your mother. This relationship can be unraveled but for now, accept the fact that you are, indeed, more Brighton than anything else."

The silence that followed this statement made the sound of the phone seem even louder, and everyone jumped even though they had all been expecting it. Paulie got it on the second ring. It was Darkling calling from a pay phone in the shopping center in Centerville. Within a half an hour, as they all stood outside the gatehouse waiting, a small, customized, metallic-red pick-up with sporty racing stripes and a small camper shell on the back pulled in and rolled to a stop in front of them.

A tall, darkly handsome young man wearing a red baseball cap jumped out. His grin threatened to split his face as he swept the cap from his head and made a deep, graceful bow in their direction. Darkling had named himself well. They had all read his part of the story, but when he straightened up, instead of the flowery phrases his looks and demeanor led them to expect, he said, "Hey, people, let's get with it! Me and the kids are starving to death!"

From there, nothing went as they had more or less planned. Delilah moved to the back of the pickup as Darkling prepared to open up the back of the small camper shell, and was talking to Auntie before the door was completely open. Auntie came to her immediately, dragging a reluctant, complaining youngling with her. The others followed and were gathered in a semi-circle a few feet away, almost as anxious to meet them as Delilah was; the youngling's objections were clearly audible to everyone.

At first her complaints were a combination of grimaces and screeches; then, when Auntie, still hanging on to Delilah with one hand, persisted in dragging her to the ground, she spoke, and the words were understandable to all.

"No!" she said, trying to pull away from Auntie. "Bad one!" She gestured at Delilah. "Live good, she come, go bad place! Bite! Bite!" She moved toward Delilah, her facial expression and body language indicating that she intended to do just that.

"Not bite!" Auntie's words were sharply enunciated, emphasized with a harsh bark. She jerked the youngling back sharply, obviously much more powerful than her offspring, and capable of dominating her physically if she chose.

Apparently the youngling knew this and subsided at once, standing quietly in Auntie's firm grip, but she continued to glare at Delilah. Abruptly, she squatted, and the strong smell of urine and feces filled the air around them. As she made a motion toward the fecal deposit, Auntie jerked her roughly away from the spot. Then Auntie squatted and urinated, both the amount and her obvious relief attesting to the fact that they had both managed to avoid relieving themselves in the camper.

"Come," Delilah said. "Inside, good eat, no danger." She tugged on Auntie's arm, glancing at the semi-circle of fascinated observers. She realized that she was embarrassed by the unselfconscious actions of Auntie and the youngling, grateful that Auntie had stopped the youngling from flinging dung at her as she had obviously intended to do. She felt defensive, but she had no time to explore the feelings.

"No." Auntie's response was unequivocal. She looked toward the gatehouse, then slowly studied the group, inspecting each face in turn. She turned to Delilah, struggling to make herself understood. "Not go inside. Not go inside." After a moment, she turned loose of Delilah's hand and touched herself and her youngling. "Fear."

Delilah could smell it rising in waves . . . fear, so much fear. She turned again to the group. "Joe, can we take them to the barn? It's bigger, more open. The smells aren't so strange. They're both in pretty bad shape and very frightened. They need to eat and rest, relieve some of this stress before they both go hysterical. If that happens, we won't be able to control them. The youngling doesn't know me at all, and it has been years since Auntie and I were able to see and touch each other. This is going to take time."

Joe didn't hesitate. He started up the driveway, walking slowly, keeping close to the trees and shrubs that lined it. Darkling held out his hand to the youngling who took it without hesitation, apparently trusting him as a friend. Delilah put her arm around Auntie's shoulders, and the four of them started up the driveway behind Joe. After a few steps, Auntie moved closer to Delilah, and wrapped her arm around Delilah's waist. Delilah tightened her arm around Auntie's shoulders, holding her firmly, and easily fell into that strangely coordinated, three-legged walking step that Sarah had used to walk her from the bathroom to her room the day of her blackout.

Sarah, Casey, K.C., Jordan, Paulie, and Harold followed, walking slowly some distance behind. Casey looked at Sarah. "Look familiar?" he asked, grinning.

"Sure does, and apparently it works, too. Something about the closeness and the synchronization of movement, I think." She frowned slightly then. "Anyone have any ideas about what I should get in the way of something to eat? I feel stupid, but I'm just not sure what's needed right now."

Harold and Paulie spoke at once, and Paulie politely gave way with a grin. "Any fruit will be good, I think. Right now they need a blood sugar boost. Oranges are good, but I don't know if they will eat them or not. Fresh vegetables, I think, and you've got a large assortment to choose from. Just sort of gather up whatever looks right."

Sarah turned off, hurrying into the farmhouse, and K.C. spoke quietly. "Did you see their condition? There's a lot of bare spots where there should be hair, and Auntie has several sores that look like she's had them a while. Vitamin deficiency can cause that. They're both very thin, too, but I don't think they're sick. I think they've been slowly starved over a period of time. They just have that look of emaciation about them." He sighed, obviously disturbed. "They remind me of pictures I've seen of concentration camp survivors. They were both blinking like they hadn't been out in the sunlight for a long time."

He addressed Paulie. "Paulie, I think your Darkling made the right decision to get them out of wherever they were. Certainly their fear of going inside a building must have developed since they were taken from the zoo. Inside and outside living are normal for zoo life, and the youngling was born there."

Joe rolled open both of the big front doors on the barn and walked through to open the smaller door and the shutters on the windows on the back side facing the pond. The big central area was flooded with light, emphasizing the high openness that reached upward to the ceiling. Auntie hesitated only a moment before entering, nostrils flared as she cataloged the rich smells of hay, straw, grain, cows, chickens, and even the pigeons high above in one corner. Apparently she quickly decided that there were no bad smells here, and walked to the center and sat down on the straw-covered floor, dragging the youngling and a laughing Delilah and Darkling down with her.

Joe stood quietly by the small door, arms folded, watching. Although he had no concern about Auntie, he was not satisfied about Delilah's safety with the youngling. Her opinions had been stated and her aggressive feelings clearly shown. He almost smiled when he recalled her movement to throw dung at Delilah, and Auntie's quick, no nonsense reaction.

Darkling spoke to Delilah for the first time, his even teeth flashing whitely as he smiled. "So there you are, Chameleon, she of many colors, keeper of secrets. You know you're beautiful, don't you?"

Delilah was embarrassed, but she said, "Thank you, Darkling. You know you've completed a magnificent quest, don't you?"

Before he could answer, Sarah entered the barn carrying a big basket of fruit and vegetables still gleaming with the water she had used to rinse them after she took them from the garden. Without hesitating, she walked to them, knelt down, and placed the basket in the center of their circle. Touching Auntie and the youngling on their shoulders, she said, "Good eat. Eat now," and settled her plump self on the floor between them as though she belonged there.

Darkling took an apple, bit into it, and chewing noisily, said, "Oh, good eat!"

Delilah quickly followed suit, and after one suspicious look at Sarah, the youngling joined in, followed immediately by Auntie. As the others stepped quietly into the barn, seating themselves on bales of straw against the front wall, the basket quickly emptied and the motion of chewing jaws slowed.

Delilah took a banana from the basket, peeled it, and offered it to the youngling. The youngling observed this peace gesture thoughtfully. Sharing food was a ritual of bonding like grooming. Only friends shared their food with friends. Now that the first fear had eased and the gnawing hunger pangs were abated, she took time to look around. She smelled no danger signals, not from the young male who had taken them from the bad place, not from the big female who brought good eat, not from the other males who kept their distance, and not from this female offering food. She looked at her mother who was leaning on Delilah's shoulder half-asleep.

And she took the banana although she was no longer hungry, looking intently into Delilah's eyes as she took several methodical bites. Then, she handed it back to Delilah, who took it, and still holding the youngling's gaze, ate the rest of it. They both understood that a truce between them had been offered . . . and accepted.

Margaret was already huddled in the bathtub in Room Eight at the Seymour Motel when Jordan made the first of several trips past it on his way back and forth to the Centerville lumberyard. Auntie and the youngling were napping in a pile of straw in one corner of the barn. Joe, still a bit uneasy about them, had volunteered to stay with them, and everyone else gathered in the kitchen.

Between bites from the plate of food Sarah placed in front of him, Darkling gave them an account of what he insisted on calling Chameleon's quest.

It all started off with a bit of good luck, he told them, when he quickly discovered the name of the trucking company that had picked the apes up from the Landon Zoo. He had a pretty good idea that the same company would take them directly to their delivery point, so he made a phone call, pretending to be someone he was not, and very easily got the delivery address. This admission was accompanied by a wicked grin, and Delilah wasn't the only one trying to catch a glimpse of the serious mathematician that Paulie had insisted also inhabited this body along with Darkling, the adventurer.

The name was Brighton, the address was the Brighton estate and, determined to follow it up, scope it out, as he put it, he called home with a flimsy excuse of visiting friends, then took off for Philadelphia. There were some surprised looks on the faces of his listeners. That Amanda Brighton actually lived in Philadelphia, the headquarters of Brighton Foundation, hadn't entered their minds. And so close to Landon, too. They all shared the picture of Amanda hovering in the neighborhood of Hiller School, and it made them uncomfortably aware of how little they knew about her personally.

To make a long story short, Darkling said, he found the estate easily. It was a big, old place, surrounded by a high wall, and locked iron gates guarded the front driveway. After cruising around a while, he found a narrow access road leading around to the back. There was a smaller locked gate there, and while there were some trees and shrubbery near the back wall, an even heavier growth screened the smaller buildings in the rear from the main building. Darkling grinned sheepishly. "I just couldn't waste the opportunity to check it out while I was there, could I?" He got over the fence with little difficulty, and wandered around a bit before he found them.

He looked at Delilah apologetically. "This isn't very pretty, but I think you all need to know. I finally found them by the smell coming from a small house that looked like it might have been old servant's quarters built almost up against the wall in a back corner. The smell was of dead things, and I had to work up a lot of courage to even get close. The place was pretty big with lots of rooms, but it looked all boarded up."

He went on with the story. First he circled the place and discovered that some of the windows were only partially boarded, while others were fully covered. There wasn't a sound from inside, and he called softly as he circled the building, saying who he was, talking about Delilah as "Auntie's friend," using Auntie's name, asking her to answer him, telling her that Delilah had sent him there to help them. The smell seeping out of the cracks in the fully boarded-up windows was sickening. Clearly there were decomposing bodies in those rooms. "I have to tell you, I was so afraid that Auntie and the youngling were in one of those boarded up rooms." His face mirrored the sick anxiety he had felt then.

Finally, without hope, just as he was making the last circuit around the place, still calling, it was the youngling who answered from somewhere inside. "Who?" "Hungry!" "Give eat!" "Drink!"

That was all Darkling needed. He found tools in an old tool shed and ripped the boards from the windows in the rear, methodically removing them from window after window. Sometimes gagging at the stench that rolled out of those closed rooms, he kept on until he found them in a partially boarded room, huddled together against the bars that formed their prison, blinking their eyes painfully in the full sunlight as they took deep breaths of fresh air.

Darkling paused and looked around the table at his rapt audience. "I didn't know what to give them to eat, so I found an old can and brought them water from a faucet and held it between the bars. They drank and drank, and I got scared that they would

622

get sick. I asked Auntie directly what I should bring them to eat that wouldn't make them sick. She thought about it, then pointed to some plants growing nearby. So I brought them plants and leaves and pieces of everything I could break off or pull up."

He paused, obviously shaken by reliving the experience. "The youngling showed me what they had been eating for nearly two weeks. It was old wallpaper they had been peeling off of the walls. They had been licking the moisture off of the bars at night for liquid."

Darkling had lost all his charm; his face was tight as he continued, saying that the smell wasn't so bad from Auntie and the youngling. It came from the decomposing ape bodies in the other rooms, horrific experiments gone wrong or ignored. Taking a deep breath, he finished with an attempt at his old flair. "So I waited until dark, pried the bars off of the window, we all climbed back over the fence, got in the truck, and you know all the rest of the story." He looked around. "Hey, people! Don't look so serious! They're here, they're safe, and I need a shower and a bed!"

After a lengthy farewell to Auntie and the youngling, Darkling left for home the next morning. The youngling was particularly distressed, hanging on him and wailing piteously until he made her understand that he would come back to see her. The flimsy excuse of visiting friends that he had given his family was backed up by a phone call from Harold to his father, assuring him that he brought Paulie down himself, and had acted as an additional chaperon for the gathering of young people.

Harold smiled wryly as this blatant lie fell easily and smoothly from his lips. Hopefully, this whole mess could be straightened out before lying became habitual with all of them, he thought, then called his office at Hiller School with another lie to his secretary to explain his extended absence. When he called Dee Dee, he also lied, but told himself it was not so much lying as just omitting some details. Actually, he didn't tell her anything other than they were fine, and had decided to stay a few days longer. He only felt guilty about it after he hung up.

* * *

The six men went to work with more will than expertise, and in less than two days had turned the loft into very comfortable quarters for Auntie and her youngling. They put plywood sheets across the whole width of the loft, forming a wall set back just far enough from the edge of the loft floor to leave enough room to stack a single high row of straw bales against it to conceal the plywood. From the barn floor, it looked like a loft space stacked with straw. The small door was reached by stepping around another stack of straw bales several feet from the ladder. They had decided that putting in a stairway was too obvious, so the flat nailed-on ladder was inconspicuously reinforced.

624

This posed a problem for getting the building materials up to the loft until Joe rigged a temporary rope and pulley arrangement to hoist the boards, windows, and heavier things up to the amateur but eager carpenters waiting above. This also led to the installation of a heavy rope tied around a ceiling beam above and allowed to dangle to the floor in the center of the new loft room. The youngling happily spent hours climbing up and down and swinging back and forth on it, which was much better for all concerned than her original game of swinging up and down on the pulley rope.

Delilah and Sarah immediately turned the center of the barn into a schoolroom, and went about explaining how things must be, at least for a while. Auntie and her youngling, who Delilah insisted must have a proper name, one that Auntie must choose, had to understand that they must not be seen or heard by anyone other than the people here. They were safe here only as long as no one knew about them. Auntie understood quickly, and set about, in her own way, to make sure her youngling understood the importance of secrecy. Auntie knew about secrets, and this was not the first time that she had escaped from a bad place or had bad people looking for her.

Both of them quickly learned to distinguish the sounds of the various cars and equipment that belonged to the farm, and understood that any strange engine sounds were the signal to remain very quiet until they went away again. If they were downstairs in the main part of the barn, and they saw or heard anything unusual, they should immediately go upstairs to their room and be very quiet. They were introduced to each of the men, and carefully repeated their names. Names to distinguish individuals was a new concept, and they had some trouble with K.C. and Casey. Auntie solved this with a not-too-flattering "Old one", "Young one" designation.

After some thought, Delilah instructed the men to build a small enclosure about the size of a small child's sandbox across one corner of the loft room by the windows. After it was lined with plastic and filled with fragrant cedar shavings, Auntie quickly understood the idea of using it for a bathroom. She had been toilet trained during her five years at Bhutu Holding Facility, and the lesson had made an impression. When Delilah realized this, she wondered if the methods used to train Auntie had been anything like those Agnes Kittridge used on her. She quickly pushed the thought away. As she had told Sarah, that was long ago and far away and today held enough things to worry about without thinking about the past.

Auntie was older. The realization hurt Delilah as she watched her climb the ladder to the loft room for the first time. It wasn't that she was less agile or was in pain, far from it. It was just that her movements were slower, taken with greater deliberation. She no longer moved quickly the way Delilah remembered from childhood, and there were touches of gray here and there. K.C. and Casey had immediately began using antiseptic salve on her sores, insisting that Auntie and her youngling each have a multivitamin tablet every day, in addition to eating as wide a variety of foods as they could be persuaded to sample. The loft windows provided ample fresh air and sunshine, so going outside was not a problem.

Sarah fussed and worried like a hen with one chick. They must carpet the loft floor, she insisted. No, it just needed a thick layer of fresh straw, was Delilah's response. They must have beds, Sarah said. Not yet, was Delilah's answer. It's too early for furniture. Bales of straw stacked two and three high against the back wall gave an ample choice of seating and sleeping places. But they must have bedding, at least, Sarah begged. Blankets, Delilah agreed. They would enjoy having soft blankets to make their sleeping nests. She smiled to herself, thinking of the pleasure her soft comforter gave her.

The first two nights, before the loft room was finished, Delilah slept with them, going to bed at dark. She was surprised that after listening to Auntie tell the story of the mothers, and singing the going to sleep song, she, too, fell asleep snuggled against Auntie on one side while her youngling snuggled close against the other, not to waken until the sun came up the next morning. There were no words to express the simple, soul-deep contentment and rightness that she felt. This was her family, and on those nights she slept with them, she didn't miss her friend Teddy Bear at all.

CHAPTER TWENTY EIGHT

On the evening of the third day after Auntie's rescue, they all gathered around the table in the farmhouse kitchen an hour after dinner. Delilah had just come back from bedding Auntie and her youngling down in their loft room for the night, and Sarah immediately noticed the strange, almost distant expression on her face as she slipped into her seat at the table.

"Is something wrong, Delilah?" Her voice was concerned.

"No, nothing's wrong, it's just that Auntie's chosen a name for her youngling."

"And? And?" Sarah was almost bouncing in her chair in her anxiety to find out.

"She's named her Mandy after her sister, my mother." Delilah's voice echoed the sadness in her face.

"Does that upset you?" Sarah asked, feeling there was something more that Delilah wasn't saying.

"Oh, Sarah, I asked her why she picked that name. I'm so stupid. She's intelligent, Sarah, she has feelings." Delilah sighed deeply. "There were tears in her eyes when she told me why. She only knows three female names, mine, yours, and her sister Mandy. She never had a name. They called her No Name after a while, and she understood that it meant she was not good enough to have a name. She's always known the significance of names, that names give you identity, distinction as an individual." After a moment, she finished, the pain in her voice clear. "And she knows only too well that she isn't an ape. If she were an ape, she wouldn't care, and she didn't care while we were with the apes. But the first thing that happened to me was I was given a name, an identity."

"Anntee," Casey said unexpectedly. "She has a name, Delilah. You gave it to her long ago. Can you make her see that it's just like K.C. or Kaydee? Listen to it . . . Anntee and Kaydee."

"He's right," Paulie said. "They sound very alike. Can't you make her see it?"

Delilah looked from Casey to Paulie, a smile slowly breaking through the sadness that marred her face. "Talk about overlooking the obvious! Anntee. I've always called her that. If she thinks about it she'll realize that all of you have been calling her that, too. First thing in the morning, Sarah, we'll sit down and explain it to her, okay?"

Sarah smiled back, glad that at least this one problem had found an easy solution. She turned to K.C., her face serious.

"Well, we agreed about calling James and Kaydee. Now then, what did they say? And where do we go from here?"

Harold spoke up. "Before we get into that, I have to tell you that Paulie and I have stretched our time out just about as far as it will go. We've got to get back home, probably leave in the morning. Sharing the driving the way we did coming down will get us home sometime tomorrow evening."

He looked around the table. "There's one thing I do want to tell you all. I've worked for Hiller School for twenty years, now. That means I'm actually eligible for retirement, though I intended to go on there until I was a doddering old man or Dee Dee brow-beat me into retiring, whichever came first. And I think Dee Dee would be the winner hands down."

His chuckle was full of affection, and Paulie grinned, nodding agreement.

"The important thing, the thing I want you to know, is that Amanda Brighton and I went head-to-head about Agnes Kittridge one week after Delilah got to Hiller School. Amanda tried. She threatened and I threatened right back." He paused, his face showing his distaste as he remembered that confrontation. "Hiller School has an excellent reputation. It does good work and good people work there. I believed then, and I still believe, that even if Brighton Foundation withdrew its funding, the school would go right on, either with help from some other foundation or even

631

private funding, if it came down to that."

"You're right, Harold," K.C. agreed. "Too many years doing too good a job to just fade away. You had a strong bargaining position."

"No," Harold disagreed. "No bargaining. She tried it from every angle. First she threatened to fire me, threatened to close Hiller down, and finally suggesting that everything would stay the same if I kept her privately informed about Delilah, and cooperated by following little suggestions she might make from time to time, all for the child's own good, you understand."

Delilah made a small sound, and he looked at her questioningly before he went on. "I don't know if anyone here has had direct contact with this woman. As I understand it, she usually keeps a buffer of front people between herself and the Foundation business, but no matter how old she is, or how insane, she's the controlling force, and everyone knows it. She's sly, used to buying anything or anyone, a manipulator. She offered me a big salary increase in return for little favors." There was anger in his tone now.

"Margaret is a fine example of her handiwork, and I guess even otherwise good people can be enticed to cut a corner here and there, cut a little slice off of ethics in return for the security she offers, always with her assurance that her motives are benevolent."

632

Sarah squirmed in her chair, then got up to putter aimlessly with the silverware in the drainer on the counter. "How does everyone feel about some hot chocolate?" she asked, and when they chorused approval, Joe got up to help her, standing close with his arm draped over her shoulder. He understood how Sarah felt. Although Harold didn't know it, his words were cutting into Sarah like knives.

If Harold was surprised by this interruption, he didn't show it, and turned to Paulie. "Did Merlin keep good records on the way he got his information? I mean can anyone follow the path he took and come up with solid documentation of everything he wrote about in his story?"

"You bet he has records," Paulie said. "Merlin is the smartest person I know, clear up in the genius range." He turned to Delilah. "He was on his computer for nearly twenty-four straight hours after you told your story, Delilah, and if I know him, by now he probably has even more to document it because now he knows where to look."

He glanced around the kitchen, becoming aware that everyone's attention was focused on him. "You've all met Darkling, the dashing hero, but you should know that he's also a math genius, a serious student, and the Darkling persona does a lot to balance out what he calls his dark side. Dad knows him because he's been around our house a lot for the last year, or so.

He dated my sister, Becky, for a while."

He grinned as he added, "Becky just loved Darkling the handsome, dashing hero, almost as much as our Mandy does, but she wasn't too impressed with Chris the mathematician. Just couldn't understand why she had to have both of them along on a date."

Everyone laughed, even Sarah, and there was a soft clatter of silverware and the clink of dishes as she and Joe served the steaming mugs of cocoa. She resumed her seat after putting a huge platter of sugar cookies in the center of the table, and smiled at the murmurs of appreciation.

After a moment, Paulie continued. "I think you should also know about Merlin. Merlin is a paraplegic, confined to a custom-built, electronically driven wheelchair, although it's a lot more than that. He says that as long as he has to spend his whole waking life in it, he might as well enjoy all the comforts of home, so he dreams things up and his Dad builds and installs them for him."

He looked at Delilah again, then turned to face the others. "The game that we've been playing so long is Merlin's other life, his only other life. And I don't think anyone will ever really know how much taking part in this real life, honest-to-goodness life and death quest has done for him. This may sound dumb, but Merlin has done a man's job in a man's world, and done it damned well, too."

Delilah eyes were filled with tears, and all she could manage was a weak, "Oh Paulie, I had no idea."

His voice was roughened by emotion. "Good, because that is exactly how he wanted it, and you can do him a big return favor by never letting on that you do know."

Pride and sadness, Harold thought, that's what I feel. My son is indeed a man. Then he cleared his throat. "I think there's something else that may prove to be our single most important tool in dealing with Amanda Brighton. After I refused all her offers and rejected all her threats, I threatened to expose the whole nasty mess about Agnes Kittridge, her abuse of Delilah, her obvious mental condition, and who would take ultimate responsibility for it. Then I brought up anything else I could think of, including making Delilah a ward of the court by bringing in the authorities to investigate."

He paused a moment, thoughtful. "Now that I know what I know, I think that last thing scared her worse than anything else, because it was hands off from then on except for a constant stream of Foundation people coming in to observe Delilah. I couldn't complain about that because there was a tremendous amount of legitimate interest in her throughout the scientific community." He grinned, looking at Delilah.

"Do you remember who was always there with you during

every single one of those visits?"

Delilah looked puzzled a moment, then smiled. "Nurse Romer was always there. I thought it was because it was part of her job. Except once . . . " She paused, remembering clearly the one time Nurse Romer had not been with her, and the encounter with the old pedophile doctor.

"It was," Harold answered. "I gave her that job to make damned sure none of those observers did anything out of line whatsoever. Whether they liked it or not, I insisted that every one of them, no matter their credentials, give us a precise list of every question they intended to ask you, and every test they intended to use. Then, every minute they were with you, Nurse Romer sat there with their own copy of the list in her hand, checking off each section as it was completed." Harold paused, his face becoming serious.

"I think you should know that during the first couple of years, several of those observers were stopped in their tracks by Nurse Romer. I don't know what they had in mind, but I do know their intentions weren't good and I'm sure Amanda Brighton sent them to do something very specific . . . to you, Delilah."

The kitchen was quiet as everyone digested the information Harold was giving them. It was filling in many of the blanks in the story of Delilah's four years at Hiller School, blanks that until now she never realized existed. The fact that Amanda Brighton had been, even then, pursuing her caused a chill deep inside. She glanced around the table and saw the same reaction on every face.

Then, Harold was speaking again. "I was angry and disgusted by the whole thing, and I started questioning the reason Delilah had been sent to Hiller School of all the possible places that she might have been sent. About that time, it struck me that a school for the retarded was not the place for Delilah to learn to adapt to normal environments. All she could actually learn there was how to adapt as a handicapped person would."

He grinned, speaking directly to Delilah. "So, little Chameleon, whose first question printed on her little notepad was whether or not God lived in the clock on my office wall, I took you home with me, and, as much as I could, made you one of my children." He looked around the table, conscious of the smiles on every face, the approval that seemed to fill the kitchen like a warm mist. "And I had you checked out, too, Sarah. I realized that Amanda wouldn't give up that easily, and Bent Tree Farm is pretty far off the beaten path."

Then he surprised them all by laughing. "But I did have my own little line of defense, just in case." He turned to Paulie as he continued. "Paulie, do you really think that as the official bill payer of the Newcombe household I didn't know about your weekly game playing? One look at the phone bills told me you were connected to Bent Tree Farm for about two hours every

637

Friday night and I didn't think you were talking to the cows. I was pretty sure, and as it turned out, correctly so, that if anything went wrong with Delilah, you would be the first to know, and I would be the second." He chuckled at the surprised embarrassment on both Paulie's and Delilah's faces.

"There, I've spoken my piece, and I hope you realize that I am with you all the way. When push comes to shove and this whole nasty affair finds its way into a courtroom, which just may happen, I'll be there."

"Well done, Harold," K.C. said, his voice rising above the murmurs of approval from the others. He turned to Sarah, but his words were meant for everyone. "I caught James and Kaydee on the road. I just barely gave them an outline of the situation on the phone, and they didn't hesitate a second, so if they can park the RV by the bunkhouse for a couple of days, we will do some legal brainstorming. I think by now they've already put Samantha and the kids on a plane for our place. She's delighted, as always, to have the kids to herself for as long as it takes, so there's no worry on that score." His grin quickly faded and his tone became serious.

"One thing, though. If this thing comes to a legal battle, I hope you all realize that the publicity is going to be incredible. It's a unique situation in and of itself, and when the Nazi connection comes out, the European press will go wild as well, so we all better get ourselves ready for it."

It was quiet for a minute or two as everyone considered this last information. Then, Joe asked, "Any ideas on this? Will Amanda Brighton bring the fight to us, and do we wait to see if she does, or do we just simply attack her with everything we've got?"

Jordan and Casey both spoke at once. "Attack," was the word they said, grinning at each other.

"Attack!" Paulie said. "And if Darkling and Merlin could vote, they'd say attack, too!"

"Attack!" Harold added his vote.

"Well, seeing as how it appears to be a vote," K.C. said, "I say attack, too."

"Me, too," Joe said. "Attack!" Then he looked at his wife. "Sarah, what do you say?"

"Well, she's a very old woman, and I don't want to take a chance that she might die . . . " She paused, aware of the amazed looks from everyone, " . . . before I get a chance to confront her personally. Attack!"

"So, Delilah," Harold spoke. "Here you have a unanimous vote to carry the battle to Amanda Brighton. How do you vote? You really must be the one who decides."

It was a moment before she answered. When she raised her eyes to them, the tears she had been fighting spilled over, making shiny trails down her cheeks. "When I sent the warriors out on the quest, I never really thought it through. Everything that's happening right now is because I never thought about what might happen afterwards. It was a quest, that's what I called it to myself, a child's game in an adult world that I knew nothing about." Her face twisted in anguish. "I thought about it for a long time last night, and finally realized that I'm only eight years old in your world, only eight years out of the jungle where I was born." Her voice cracked, and she angrily brushed the tears from her eyes, then blew her nose on the paper napkin Sarah handed her, smiling her thanks. Her voice was stronger when she continued.

"I still can't believe that Anntee and . . . ." She hesitated, "…Mandy, are really here, and now that they are, I won't be separated from them again. I feel like all of you are my family, but they are my family, too, my blood family. If I have to, I'll live in a cage in the zoo, but I will stay with them no matter what happens from now on." There was no mistaking the sincerity in her voice.

"I thought about something else, too, something you have all been careful to avoid talking about. Where does ape stop and human begin? Is one thirty-second bonobo ancestry all that is required to make me an ape? Or is thirty-one one-thirty-seconds Brighton ancestry enough to make me a human? Who makes this decision? And who answers the question of a soul?"

She was quiet for several seconds. In spite of her tears a moment before, they were all becoming aware that it was a different Delilah addressing them today, a calmer, controlled Delilah who was in some indefinable way exuding an aura of quiet power.

Casey took a deep breath and looked at K.C., wondering if he felt it, too. K.C. returned his look with a slight nod of agreement as Delilah spoke again.

"Now, you are all older and smarter than me - except Paulie - and if you think that taking the fight to her is best, then I say attack!"

* * *

When Sarah answered the phone by her chair in the gatehouse family room later that evening, the sound of Amanda Brighton's voice caused her to freeze. Joe and Jordan immediately came to attention. They knew that no one but Amanda Brighton could have put that sick look on Sarah's face. As they watched, her expression slowly changed into a cold, almost smiling look that radiated hatred. Husband and son exchanged looks, then focused on Sarah's end of the conversation, trying to squeeze as much information as possible from her responses.

"How are you and the family doing?" Amanda wanted to know.

"Fine, just fine," Sarah answered.

"And Delilah, anything new with the child?"

Sarah's smile was a grimace, a rictus that twisted her lips out of shape as she replied, "Delilah? No nothing new with her. She seems to be doing well with her college studies." Sarah's eyes narrowed into slits, but her voice remained calm and noncommittal. "I think she wants to major in English. She seems to be fascinated with words, you know." She managed an almost believable chuckle. "Probably has something to do with the fact that she realizes that she will never be able to speak."

Joe and Jordan looked at Sarah in amazement. She was baiting the monster, deliberately feeding her misinformation. Bravo, Joe thought. It was about time Sarah got some kind of revenge, or was at least able to do something instead of being used.

"And how is Margaret?" Amanda asked. "Did she get away all right today?"

"Margaret?" Sarah was thinking fast, trying to remember the reservation call she had received. Yes, Margaret was supposed to have stayed until today. "Yes," she answered. "She got away bright and early." Sarah paused, then said, "You know Amanda, I really don't think Margaret is comfortable in a rural setting like this."

Amanda laughed. Sarah jerked the receiver away from her ear, and looked at Joe and Jordan. They could hear the tinny cackle that seemed to go on and on. There was no doubt that Amanda knew about and enjoyed the discomfort that being at Bent Tree Farm caused Margaret.

When the laughter finally stopped, Sarah returned the receiver to her ear. Amanda was talking. "Oh, I almost forgot. About Agnes Kittridge. Sad case. She's hopelessly insane, confined to a mental institution for the last eight years. No amount of treatment seems to help. She insists that God talks to her, you know." The laughter came again, and again, Sarah held the receiver away from her ear, looking at it in disgust. She felt like she wanted to wash her hands. The old bitch had said Agnes Kittridge had been in a mental institution for eight years, when, in fact, she knew Kittridge had been at Bhutu Holding Facility with Delilah for two of those years. Amanda had deliberately sent her there.

"You know, Sarah," Amanda was speaking again, "your diagnosis of her was very accurate. You've always been an excellent diagnostician, haven't you?" Her voice was thoughtful.

Sarah didn't answer, she couldn't. Then, it came again, the hungry, grasping tone filled with a need to know. "You're sure, are you Sarah, that Delilah will never speak?"

Sarah answered immediately. "No, Amanda, Delilah Cross will never speak. I don't think she can, some hereditary weakness in her background, perhaps. After all, we have no idea who her parents might have been or what kind of disabilities they might have had." Her tone was thoughtful, her expression vicious. Take that diagnosis, you old bitch, she thought. Think about it! Believe it, Amanda! Apparently Amanda did because she hung up after a perfunctory good-bye.

* * *

After the general leave-taking in the kitchen, Delilah went up the stairs, intending to go to her room. Her mind was whirling with bits and pieces of information and feelings that she needed time to figure out. She was amazed to learn what a big part Harold Newcombe had played in her life, always in the background, always protecting her, surrounding her with safeguards, and doing it so unobtrusively that she never felt it. Sarah, Joe and Jordan, too, had spread themselves around her like a warm, comforting blanket, always there, making a group for her whether she was consciously aware of it or not.

I'm ignorant, she thought. Naive and ignorant. Her own words about being only eight years old in this world resounded in her mind. And it all had to do with speaking. The whole world had changed when she voiced her own opinions and thoughts. The people around her changed, responding with their own opinions and thoughts, making her aware of her own ineptitude, her own mistakes in judgment, her own self-involvement. Oh yes, she thought. I am intelligent . . . and incredibly dumb.

When Casey spoke her name, she jumped, surprised to find him on the stairs behind her. Had she thought about it, the fact

644

that he had gotten so close without her being aware of it would have set off some alarm bells in her mind, but she didn't think about it. During the last few days, he seemed to be within a few feet of her all the time, and she had begun to take his presence for granted.

He was a step below her as she stood on the landing, which brought his head level with hers. She gazed at him, exploring his face from this new perspective, completely unselfconscious about her scrutiny, realizing that he seemed to be looking at her in the same way, his expression serious, his eyes calm. Without thinking, she reached out and pushed the hair back from his forehead, then jerked her hand away, taking a step backward at the same time. He couldn't hear them, but the alarm bells had finally gone off in her mind when she touched him. She was immediately aware that her touch had aroused feelings in both of them, feelings that expressed themselves in sudden hormonal changes that almost visibly colored the air between them, potent, bewitching in their lure, and frightening to her.

Casey hadn't moved, and when he spoke, his voice was easy and calm. "I'd like to talk to you, Delilah. Can we sit in the office and talk a while?"

He had noted the sudden flare of fear in her eyes, her involuntary retreat telling him that she was reacting to her own feelings. He remained still, making no slightest motion that she might interpret as aggressive or threatening. Then he remembered her sense of smell. Damn it all, he thought, I can control my body movements but I can't control my inner physical reactions. Her touch had gone through him like a jolt of electricity, triggering an uncontrollable response. Far back in his mind, a small voice asked if he really thought he could handle a relationship with a girl, no a woman who could sniff out the truth of his feelings, no matter what he said aloud.

Delilah made up her mind quickly. There was no doubting the feelings she had for this man, almost as strong as the feelings he had for her. Besides the sexual attraction, she had come to like him, and that made it even more difficult. She had to tell him because he apparently hadn't figured it out for himself. Sex was forbidden to her, surely he could understand that? The fact that she equated their feelings with sex and nothing else held no significance for her. In her realm of experience, attraction between males and females simply meant sex. Without a word, she turned and entered the office, flipping on the lights as she went through the door. She walked to one of the couches in the corner, sat down, and waited until he seated himself in a chair opposite her, obviously waiting for him to begin.

Casey cleared his throat. So talk, he told himself. She's waiting for you to talk. Talk, damn it!

The silence lengthened. Finally, Delilah shifted her position and looked at him quizzically.

"Delilah, I'm in love with you." The words came out in a croak. Oh my God, Casey thought, is there no end to my idiocy?

He didn't know what he expected, but her response took him completely off guard.

"Casey," she asked, "do you know the difference between being in love and being in lust?" When he didn't answer, she continued matter-of-factly. "I know you have more than a passing acquaintance with bonobo apes. Certainly, I do." She laughed, a natural, easy sound. "Their basic premise is to make love, not war. I read that in a book, and it seems just right to explain how they behave. Sex is an every day fact of life, whether as a token gesture of affection, a declaration of non-aggression, or a serious thing for pleasure and getting babes. I've given it a lot of thought, and I think that long ago bonobos somehow discovered that sexual contact eliminated most aggressive behavior in the group."

Casey couldn't help grinning. "Like discovering fire?" he asked.

"Exactly," Delilah answered, returning his grin. "Sex before you eat eliminates most fighting over food. Sex with your friends makes the bonding stronger. Sex when you meet someone you haven't seen for a while eliminates a lot of territorial arguments, and sex as often as a male wants it eliminates a lot of aggressive and frustrated behavior."

Delilah's voice became softer, introspective as she continued. "There are a lot of strange things about the bonobos. I don't think their sexual behavior is instinctual, Casey, it's learned within the group. And females are dominant, not like other ape species at all. They actively offer sex in exchange for food, did you know that?

"There are other things that no one seems to be able to explain, Casey. Females leave the group and join other groups. Males aren't driven away by older males, they stay together in the group for life. And sometimes the males do a rain dance." She looked at him as though expecting to see disbelief in his face. "I've seen it many times, Casey. In the time of rain, it sometimes rains for a very long time. Everyone hates it. One male gets up and dances. I don't know how else to describe it. Sometimes he beats a branch on the ground. Then another joins him, doing the same thing. Then another, and another. The females and young don't dance, they only watch. Isn't that strange? Other males, human beings, do rain dances to make it rain while the women and children watched. Is the bonobo dance to make the rain stop any different? I mean the rain always stopped, didn't it?"

She was silent for several moments, remembering things Casey could only guess at. When she continued, her voice had lost the dream-like quality, sounding very serious and business-like. "You know Anntee and I were different from them. I wouldn't have known, but she taught me. Sex of any kind that involved penetration was forbidden to us. I know now it was because she was afraid of becoming pregnant. It was Anntee's law. She reasoned it out for herself based on her early years at Bhutu and what Mandy told her . . . and she was right, Casey, sex is forbidden."

Delilah was quiet, thinking about what to say next. Casey could think of nothing to say, so he was quiet, too. After a while, she said, "I've seen movies, I've read books, and I've even had a sex education class. I know there are different kinds of love, and I know there is lust." She leaned forward, looking at him directly. "Casey, when you say you're in love with me, I don't believe you. But there is much lust between us. And I cannot do that, I cannot." Her voice sounded sad, almost plaintive, as she pleaded for his understanding. "I am an experimental animal, Casey."

When he started to speak, she waved her hand to stop him, then stood up and moved close to his chair. "I have never been kissed on the lips, Casey. I would like to be kissed. Will you kiss me one time?"

Casey didn't need a second invitation. When he stood up, he put his arms around Delilah like she was a precious, breakable object of art. The kiss was gentle, light, exploratory. She responded to each subtle change in his lips, each shift in pressure, learning, feeling. She didn't realize that her eyes were closed until she moved back, breaking off the contact of their lips and bodies.

He didn't try to hold her and when she opened her eyes, she found he was looking at her with an expression that she didn't recognize, couldn't interpret. She swayed slightly as anxiety swept through her like a cold wind. She took a deep, shaky breath, suddenly aware that the air between them was heavy with the smells of arousal and desire. "Was it all right?" she asked. "Was it a good kiss?"

Shaken to the center of his being, feeling disoriented, Casey tried to collect himself, pull himself back from the strange place he had been. It was a place deep within himself where he had never been before, a place where thought ceased to exist, feeling was everything, and his will had all but disappeared as he yielded to her. Yielded to her, gave himself to her, submitted, acknowledged her dominance and power.

Before he could manage to answer, she ran from the office, down the hall, and into her room, closing the door with a thud. For the third time since he had been at Bent Tree Farm, Delilah had left him alone to sort things out. And, like the other times, he was left to brood the errors he had committed, professional ethics breached and how to remedy all of it. Too late.

CHAPTER TWENTY NINE

James and Casey were standing by the open trunk of the car in the parking area arranging the luggage when Delilah and Sarah came out the door and down the steps. They were accustomed to Delilah's baggy, nondescript style of dressing and her severely pulled-back hair, so the young woman walking toward them might have been a stranger. Several hours later they were still casting surreptitious glances at her as though making sure their eyes weren't deceiving them, that it was really Delilah and not some strange young woman substituted for the occasion.

She was wearing a well-cut navy blue pantsuit with a white blouse and matching navy flats. A stylish navy-and-white purse was slung over her shoulder, and her dark hair was much shorter and casually styled, feathered becomingly around her tastefully made-up face. She wore small white earrings, an understated white necklace, and dark glasses with navy frames completed the outfit.

"Wow!" James said, making no effort to conceal his approval as he took her small overnight bag, also new, and turned to put it in the trunk. "You're totally beautiful, Delilah!" He closed the trunk, and turned toward Sarah, who was still standing on the

651

steps. "Are you sure that this is Delilah?" he called.

Casey opened his mouth to say something complimentary, thinking about the picture of her as a typical teen-ager with the Newcombes, and the almost uncanny appropriateness of the name Chameleon. He swallowed the words as Anntee and Mandy called from where they stood in the barn doorway. They were usually very careful to keep out of sight, clearly understanding the reasons for remaining hidden, but now their voices joined together, carrying clearly.

"Bye, Delilah." Then Anntee, a note of anxiety in her words, called, "See soon?"

Delilah turned and waved. "Back soon, Anntee. Not fear. Back soon." Her voice was clear and reassuring as she answered, revealing none of her own anxiety and tension. She was puzzled by Anntee's choice of words.

It was early and, in the rush of getting ready to leave, she hadn't talked to them this morning, but the afternoon before she had explained to them where she was going and why she must go. Everything had been fine until they realized that she was going to see the bad old woman in the bad place where Darkling found them. It took Delilah nearly an hour to soothe their fears and make them understand that Casey and James would both be there and would protect her. Delilah felt a little better when she looked back as they were turning on to Palmer Road and saw Sarah on her way to the barn. Sarah will take good care of them, she thought.

The trip was a quiet one, each of them closed inside their own minds with their own thoughts. Casey hadn't said a word to Delilah, nor had she spoken to him. He had tried a dozen times to find her alone since the night in the office when he kissed her, but she was always with someone, in the barn with Anntee and Mandy, or in her room. He could have simply knocked on her door and forced the issue, but it was clear that she was avoiding him and his instincts told him that now was no time to try to mend fences with her. There would be time enough later, he hoped.

James and Kaydee, with the invaluable help of Merlin, had performed small miracles of information gathering and research. Kaydee, after checking and rechecking the legal aspects and whatever case law seemed applicable in such unusual circumstances, had prepared several documents intended for Amanda Brighton's signature. When they all felt they had done as much as possible to cover every foreseeable contingency, James had made a phone call directly to Amanda Brighton, herself, using the private number Sarah had given them.

Sarah's face had been grim when she gave them the number. "This is Amanda's private little report line. She'll answer it personally because she wouldn't want to miss any of the dirt her puppets might have for her." A small, vindictive smile tightened her lips. "The fact that you have this number will send a message that she won't miss, believe me!"

It had been surprisingly easy - almost too easy - for Amanda to agree to see them, but after discussing the matter at length with Kaydee and K.C., James put his misgivings aside. He trusted K.C.'s objective judgment, his ability to see things as a whole, rather than isolated fragments of information. It had to be done, and they were as ready as they would ever be.

After a relatively short and pleasant flight, they took a taxi into town and checked into a hotel, a first for Delilah. She lost some of her reserve as she explored the rooms of the suite James had reserved, trotting from room to room, bouncing experimentally on each bed and sniffing the small packages of soap and bottles of shampoo in the bathroom. She looked out of all the windows, and spent some time playing with the drapes, fascinated by the idea that pushing a button could make them open and close.

"James," she whispered. "I've got to pee, but the toilet has a paper band on it. Is there another bathroom somewhere that isn't broken?" Before James could answer, she added, "And I don't think they want you to use the glasses, either. They've all got paper on them, too."

James chuckled, and explained the niceties of hotels and their way of doing things. Delilah is incredibly unsophisticated and naive, he thought. Sometimes, her intelligence and quick adaptation to changing circumstances, actually a learning process, obscured the fact that she had had little contact with the real world. He decided that he would have a talk with Sarah about the need to expand this side of Delilah's education, but first things first.

Their appointment with Amanda was the next morning, and James carefully explained why they were staying in the hotel overnight, that it was better that they be fresh and well-rested. James had no idea how long this mission would take, but he was prepared to stay as long as necessary, no matter what happened. Delilah accepted this explanation without question, ate well in the hotel dining room, and went to bed early, lulled to sleep by the low murmur of voices as James and Casey talked in the living room. Her last waking thought was of being grateful. Since Anntee and Mandy had arrived at the farm, she'd had no nightmares and none of the painful flashbacks that had plagued her for so long.

The next morning, as the taxi turned into the curved driveway between high granite pillars, the heavy iron gates were open. They rolled past an acre of manicured lawns and came in sight of the house. As he looked at it, Casey realized who had been responsible for Brighton Foundation's use of old, carefully restored and remodeled mansions. When he considered Amanda

Brighton's age, it was clear that she was attracted to the homes she had known in their prime in an era when such houses were the epitome of wealth and sophistication.

The Brighton mansion was one of them, built by Albert Brighton and occupied by the family through all the years. It was much too large for the three Brightons, especially when the father and then the son spent so much time in Africa, and Casey wondered at the thought processes that kept Amanda Brighton living there alone since Albert Brighton died. Without knowing how he knew he was sure she lived there alone. A small ripple of unease stirred as he had a clear mental picture of a black widow spider, red hour-glass warning clearly visible on her belly, sitting quietly in the center of a web woven of phone lines waiting . . . waiting for them.

They were admitted to the house by an elderly butler with a foreign accent. He was wearing a correctly formal black suit, and introduced himself as Walter. James handed him a business card that did not name Casey or Delilah, feeling that it might be a tactical advantage if it was assumed that they were his assistants, anonymous members of his staff.

Something unexpected happened there in the entry; James to reacted quickly, and held a hurried whispered conversation with Delilah and Casey as they waited to be announced. When they first came into the comparative gloom of the wood-paneled entry hall, Delilah removed her dark glasses, and when Walter happened to look directly at her, his face paled and he involuntarily gasped in surprise. He was obviously flustered as, carrying the card on a small silver tray, he moved up a sweeping staircase to the second floor. At James' suggestion, Delilah replaced the dark glasses and kept them on.

When Walter returned a few minutes later, he escorted them up the staircase to an elaborately furnished anteroom outside of Amanda Brighton's private office. He crossed the room and tapped on the ornately carved double doors. Apparently receiving an answer from the other room, he nodded to James and left the room without a word. James motioned Casey and Delilah to chairs beside a small table in front of the large windows, smiled at them reassuringly, and with his briefcase swinging at his side, walking with an assurance he didn't feel, entered the dragon's lair.

James was very aware that some of the things in his briefcase were illegal, unauthorized copies of information that was both confidential and closely guarded. After careful consideration of the legal risks involved, they had decided that it all came down to this one make-or-break confrontation and the situation warranted ignoring some legalities along the way. Certainly, it was apparent that Amanda Brighton - and the Brighton Foundation - had operated far outside the laws for an unthinkable number of years, and any risks they took would be worth it. And, no matter what

657

happened, they had enough information to destroy Amanda Brighton and Brighton Foundation if it became necessary.

James' smile was entirely correct and professional as he walked up to the big, highly polished rosewood desk and addressed the small figure seated in a large chair behind it. "Hello, Mrs. Brighton," he said. "Thank you for seeing us. I'm James Prentiss, and I represent Anntee Brighton, Mandy Brighton, and Delilah Cross Brighton." There, he thought. You have the whole thing clearly and concisely stated in those three names.

His smile faded when he looked directly at her. My God, he thought, as he placed his briefcase on a chair, opened it, and carefully removed separate stacks of documents. She's old . . . old! He was very surprised that she was alone. He had expected to see her surrounded by legal experts of all sizes, shapes, and talents and had mentally prepared himself for a legal duel. Maybe, he thought, this is just a tactic, a manipulation to make him feel guilty, unwilling to mount an all-out attack a frail, old woman. Or, on second thought, perhaps she had never shared even a small part of this nasty piece of Brighton history with anyone and didn't intend to start now. That's more likely, James told himself. When she finally did look up at him, James could barely conceal his reaction. Ancient, he thought. Ancient . . . and evil! He found her totally repugnant and this feeling overrode his satisfaction that he had been right about her eyes, that he had correctly interpreted the butler's reaction downstairs. He busied himself with the documents, then directed her attention to the two stacks he had placed on the desk.

"Mrs. Brighton, these are to be read first, if you will." He indicated one stack. "And these documents are to be signed." His words were polite and pleasant as he indicated the other stack of papers, but it was a statement, not a request. When she nodded, he seated himself in the chair facing her across the expanse of desk, empty except for the two stacks of documents. So far, she had not spoken a word, simply responding by nodding her head.

The top papers on the stack to be read were recent certified blood and DNA test results on Delilah, Anntee, and Mandy. Directly under them were blood and DNA test results from Amanda, her husband, and her son, also certified. These last had been exhumed from old records by Merlin. He had also found the names of some of the Brighton's old Nazi friends and contacts, some of them still living, both in this country and in Europe. These names were listed in alphabetical order on the next sheet of paper. James was sure Amanda would remember those names. He had been shocked when he recognized some of them himself, infamous people who had figured prominently among Hitler's close associates. James hadn't asked Merlin how he had come up with this information, feeling it better if there were some details

659

he didn't know.

Under that was a report by a well-known genetics expert attesting to the certainty of paternity. While such tests usually only disclosed who could not be the father, these were unusual in stating who must have been the father. What the reports did not show was the sworn-to-secrecy expert's amazement at what else his tests had revealed when comparing the blood of the two males and four females represented in the samples he was given.

It took Amanda some time to carefully read both stacks of paper. James was surprised that she did not seem to need glasses, and wondered if she had corrective lens implants or just naturally had excellent eyesight. When she was through, she leaned back in her chair, smiled, and shook her head.

"No," she said, speaking for the first time. "I'll fight you. I will not have the honor of the Brighton name besmirched." There was no mistaking the determination in that ancient face or the hatred in her eyes, and James was shocked to hear her use the word honor in connection with the Brighton name.

"Mrs. Brighton," James said, his voice firm, "we have no desire to air this matter publicly, but you must understand that we will if we have to. The facts are all there, and you know it. The whole thing can be managed very quickly and discreetly. I think you realize the amount of publicity something like this would receive if the media got wind of it?"

Amanda looked at him for a long time before answering, her eyes flicking and probing at him. James resisted the urge to look away, shift in his chair, scratch his nose, adjust his tie, or make any display of the unease he was feeling under this scrutiny. He was suddenly aware of the powerful personality of the woman he was facing, and the way she was using her eyes like weapons.

When she finally broke the silence, looking down at her small, claw-like hands, her voice had a sly, wheedling tone, the sound of a market-place hawker peddling his wares. "How much will it take to buy you off, Mr. Prentiss? What do you want that money and power can buy? There is much more money than anyone imagines, Mr. Prentiss." Her voice took on a dreamy tone as she fastened her eyes on him. "And power? Who can measure power? What are your hopes, your dreams? I can make them all come true for you."

James didn't answer because he couldn't. Although he had heard all the stories about her, nothing could have prepared him for the revulsion he was feeling. He looked down for a moment, getting his feelings under control, then stood up.

Amanda was still talking. "Let's see." Her voice was soft, musing. "You're K.C. Lowell's son-in-law. You have two young children, a nice little law practice with your wife, Kaydee, and a nice little home in the suburbs, an upwardly mobile family. Isn't that what they call it nowadays?" She didn't wait for an answer.

"You got involved in this matter through your brother-in-law, Casey Lowell, and some of the information you have placed before me could only have come from a traitor or spy inside Brighton Foundation." Her voice turned cold and angry. "That little matter I shall take care of personally."

James repressed a shiver at the malevolence in her voice. The threat to him and his family was implicit in every word she had spoken, and her talk of money and power had not been idle boasting. She had made him an offer and backed it up with a threat. He thought about Sarah and her words about a donkey, a carrot . . . and a stick.

"Excuse me a moment, please."

He walked to the double door, opened it, and motioned Delilah inside. Casey rose and looked at him questioningly. When James nodded, Casey turned and walked out of the room toward the staircase. In their whispered conversation downstairs, James had suggested what Delilah might do should it become necessary, but it was understood that she must face this confrontation on her own, with James as back-up should she need it. Casey already knew what he had to do.

Delilah hesitated a moment just inside the door glancing around; then, with her head up, shoulders squared and back rigidly straight, she walked to the desk and stopped, looking every inch a well-dressed, composed young woman. "Hello,

Grandmother," she said. "Or is it Great Grandmother? Or even Great Great Grandmother? When a family line gets as inbred as ours is, it's difficult to tell, isn't it?" Her voice was even, noncommittal. She could have been making polite dinner table conversation.

James seated himself in the chair after moving it a bit to one side, positioning himself so he could see both of the women. He saw the slight flaring of Delilah's nostrils before she continued, and glanced at Amanda. She was sitting very still, looking down at her hands, but he could see a flutter of movement as her eyes shifted under thin, papery lids. Delilah's words had struck home, he thought.

"My mother's name was Mandy, did you know that?" Delilah paused a moment before she continued, staring at the old woman who had not looked up or acknowledged her presence. "Mandy was named after you, you know. Or did you?" Delilah smiled. It did not warm the cold expression on her face.

This brought a small, involuntary grunt from Amanda, and her bony, liver-spotted hands tightened their grip on each other, but she still did not look up.

Scored again, James thought, and looked at Delilah for any sign that he should step in to help her. From this angle he could see that her upper incisors were visible as her upper lip tightened and pulled back. He found himself hoping that she never looked

663

at him like that.

"You see," she continued evenly, "when she was born, your son saw immediately that she was the greatest success you had ever had in your breeding program, so he named her Mandy in your honor. It's the diminutive of your name. It means little Amanda. Too bad he didn't live to see me, his last daughter."

Delilah put her hands on the desk and leaned forward, closer to the still figure in the chair. "Eye color is hereditary, but of course you know all about genetics and heredity, don't you? " Her voice was delicate, the words had an almost singing quality, belying the venom with which she emphasized 'you'.

Suddenly, her voice changed, its tone harsh and commanding. "I can smell you, old woman," she said. "You smell of mold and decay and dead things." Then, "Look at me!" Almost involuntarily the old woman looked up just as Delilah took off her dark glasses.

Delilah's shock was almost as great as Amanda's. As she gazed at that old, wrinkled face, all she could see were the eyes. It was like looking into her own eyes, deeply-set, and surrounded by a heavy webbing of wrinkles, but the same startling blue with the distinctive darker ring around the iris.

Their eyes remained locked, and James became aware that Delilah was very still, not appearing to breathe as the seconds ticked away. They're communicating, he thought, bemused by the idea of telepathy. Then, he realized he was witnessing a battle of wills, a contest for dominance on some level far beyond the realm of attorneys or documents or legalities, a battle that only one of them would win. He felt a sudden chill, and understood that this was primal, as old as time, a struggle that had its beginnings when the instinct for survival was the only imperative, and dominance the road to survival.

It was Amanda who finally gave way, lowering her eyes. Delilah took a deep breath and straightened up. Beside her, James, too, took a deep, ragged breath, feeling as though he had been emotionally whipped raw by the silent but almost palpable currents of energy swirling around these two women.

For Amanda, the shock was more than looking into the eyes of her son, eyes that he had inherited from her and passed on to this, his misbegotten offspring. Delilah could talk, would talk, had talked. She knew the story and could destroy everything, exposing the secret, her husband's dream, her dream, the dream that her son had died for. And Delilah was powerful, living proof that they had been right, the dream had been fulfilled, the long-sought goal reached. She knew without asking that Delilah's physical strength was far beyond human. Yes their uebermenschen dream had been fulfilled. But it was over.

Delilah read it in Amanda's eyes. It was over . . . or was it?

Amanda took a deep, shaken breath, and reached deep inside

herself for the strength. She found it in her hatred, in her belief in her own power and superiority, in her grief for her son. He died because of this creature, this freak of his own creation that was trying to destroy everything for which they had worked so long and hard.

"No," she said. Her voice was shaking, but the word was clear. "No!" Taking another deep breath, she spat the words at Delilah like acid-coated bullets. "You're not human! You're an animal!"

James stood up and touched Delilah on the shoulder. When she turned to face him, he could see that she was drained and shaken, wounded by Amanda's last vitriolic words. "I'm sorry, Delilah," he said quietly. "I didn't want it to come to this, but it has." He walked quickly to the office door. This time he opened both sides of the double door. "Come in," he said.

Anntee, her head moving from side to side, nostrils flaring, slowly knuckle-walked through the door, Darkling close on one side, Jordan on the other. Behind them, Casey brought up the rear, his hand on Anntee's shoulder, the three men forming a protective, reassuring, physically close, semi-circular shield.

Behind the group, Walter stood wringing his hands, close to tears. His inability to stop this invasion would cost him his job he was sure, but it was the other punishments that Amanda was sure to inflict on him-or his family-that he feared. And the ape. He recognized that ape. He was sure it recognized him. It had snarled at him when those men brought it in. When its eyes threatened death, he stopped resisting their entry. Amanda had not told him about this. He had not been told to call the police, so he did nothing, following them up the stairs and into the anteroom, keeping a safe distance.

Yes, Walter thought, it was the same ape that had been kept in the small servant's quarters on the rear of the estate. He had heard it and the young one screaming from time to time. He knew they had been abused, tortured, but felt powerless to intervene. After Amanda had ordered him to stop going to the back of the grounds with food for them, he was sure they had died. He had been having nightmares about their starved, decomposing bodies laying out there. Tears trickled down his cheeks, and he sniffed loudly as he reached for his handkerchief.

"Anntee!"

Delilah's shocked exclamation was loud in the stillness of the room. She looked from Darkling, who grinned and lowered one eyelid in a wink, to Jordan, who smiled and gave her a reassuring nod. Now she realized what Anntee had meant by "See soon." Anntee had known about this plan, but they hadn't had time to talk before leaving for the airport. Obviously, Darkling and Jordan had driven her here from the farm, starting out shortly after she and Casey and James left. They all knew. Keeping secrets, always secrets, Delilah thought. She moved to one side, making room for Anntee to stand beside her in front of the desk. Anntee had just as much right to be here as she did. Anntee, too, was a Brighton daughter.

Amanda had watched everything intently. After a brief glance at the others, she stared at Anntee. Her lips curled in a sneer, then formed a moue of distaste. "And why have you brought this stinking ape here?"

At her words, Anntee straightened to her full height and stood there a moment. Then in an unexpected movement that mirrored what Delilah had done a few minutes before, she placed her hands on the desk and leaned forward, closer to Amanda. Amanda sucked in her breath and shrank back in her chair, fear clearly etched on her face, the tightness of her body telegraphing her urge to flee.

"Bad old female," Anntee said clearly and carefully. "Hurt me. Hurt babe. Hurt others. Make others dead." The quiet, rumbling growl that followed her words brought a sudden chill into the room. "Make you dead!" Anntee made a motion with her hand, bringing it very close to Amanda's face, then pulled back her lips in a fearsome grimace, exposing almost all of her teeth. Her canine teeth glistened wetly as she hissed-growled loudly.

Without thought, Delilah moved closer to Anntee until they were touching, standing shoulder to shoulder. She felt her ears tighten against her head and was aware that the hairs on the back of her neck were rising. Her own lips tightened, pulled back away from her teeth. She felt the growl rising in her own chest as she instinctively responded to Anntee's attack signals and the thick cloud of anger smell mixed with the fear smell coming from Amanda in waves.

"Delilah!"

James' voice was loud and imperative, demanding attention. It cracked into the charged silence like a pistol shot, jolting Delilah. She jerked her head around to look at him, and for a moment before full awareness returned to her eyes, James saw the jungle ancestors of Delilah Cross. He saw his own jungle ancestors there, too. In that moment he stood in another time and place, looking at his own reflection in her eyes. This knowledge would haunt him, coloring his thoughts, influencing his viewpoint for the rest of his life. In that instant he knew not only who he was but what he was.

"Anntee," Delilah said quietly. "No." She touched Anntee's shoulder gently. "We are humans, not animals."

Almost visibly, muscle by muscle, Anntee relaxed. Then, still staring at Amanda, she moved back from the desk. "Yes," she said. "Not animals. Humans." In that moment, they both crossed a bridge so real that it had an almost physical presence in the room. In that same moment, Delilah assumed the dominant female position in their relationship.

There were audible breathing sounds as the others inhaled deeply. They had all been holding their breaths for what seemed like minutes since they realized that the situation could explode into violence, and became aware that there was nothing they could do to prevent it.

"I tried to have you killed, you know." Amanda's voice startled them. It quavered, an old, old woman's voice, the words drifting like dried leaves fluttering into the silence. "When I heard they found you so close to Bhutu Holding Facility I knew . . . I knew." It was a moment before she continued. "I sent two men to take you from the recovery team and dispose of you. I read the reports. It was close, so close. Two bullets in the trunk, but they missed you." Amanda laughed, the sound even more like dry leaves blown by a winter wind, her frail old body shaking with the effort.

"Oh, but I had Agnes Kittridge, didn't I? She was insane, and she should have made you insane, too. Or killed you. Either way, a dead or crazy feral child was no threat, you see?" Amanda sagged tiredly back in her chair. After a while, she spoke again. "I only used Agnes on the children found in that general area." She looked up at Delilah. "You're the only one that didn't go insane, the only one that survived her with unscrambled brains. How many of them were there? It's hard to remember, and it really doesn't matter, does it?"

"It matters." If Amanda's voice had been dried leaves blown by winter winds, Delilah's came from glacial places buried under ice for untold millennia. "Job. Samuel. Rebecca. Joseph. Zachariah. Jacob. And me, Delilah." Each name rang out as she pronounced it, a crystalline sound of shattering icicles as she hurled the names at the old woman behind the desk.

Amanda was silent, showing no emotion, giving no indication that she had any feeling about the unspeakable thing she had done to those children . . . to Delilah. Then her voice suddenly came again. "I couldn't have you killed at Hiller School. Too many people knew about you by then, and that damned Harold Newcombe stood his ground about you." Amanda's tone had grown thin and petulant.

"I sent recovery crews out to get some of those apes you were with, but they didn't talk, so I gave them to a zoo. If they didn't talk, they weren't important, weren't the ones that my son created. Those were the ones who might talk and tell." There was more than a hint of madness in her voice. She stared, first at James, then at Delilah. Finally, she looked at Anntee, who was standing quietly but fully erect by Delilah.

"Like he created you," she added, her voice venomous and taunting. "You fooled me, didn't you? I brought you here because I was suspicious. You came from the same area, but no matter what we did, you didn't talk."

"No," Anntee said. "Die first."

"How many, Amanda, how many were killed in all those years before your son and husband began their own private research after the war?" Delilah's voice was calm, curious, interested.

Amanda seemed anxious to talk, seemingly unaware of the nature of the atrocities she was describing or the responsibility she was taking on herself with every word she spoke. "Oh, thousands, I suppose. At first we assumed that most of the crossbreeds that they infected and turned loose back into the jungle as carriers died, too." Her voice took on a distant, thoughtful tone. "But now I know for sure they didn't all die. They do keep coming up with new, strange diseases in that part of Africa, don't they? AIDS, Ebola. It was a wonderful idea, you know, a secret and deadly way to cleanse the entire continent of blacks." Smiling now, she paused and looked around at them before continuing. No one moved. They were scarcely breathing as she piled horror upon horror, her voice taking on a lecturer's tone, intent on enlightening them.

"Blacks are truly untermenschen, you know, totally unmoral in their breeding habits. They sometimes breed with apes, you know. And they eat apes, consider them quite a delicacy, I understand. My dear Albert always said that if only one black mated with or ate one infected bonobo carrier, it wouldn't be long before the whole black population would be infected. Bacteriological warfare before they even had a name for it."

Her voice changed again, became stronger as she began to recite facts. "It was a German who actually recognized the bonobo apes as a distinct species, much closer to man than anyone imagined." Her voice carried a note of pride. "It was very secret and only a few people knew that there were bonobos being used in experiments right there in Austria, Belgium, and Germany even before our Fuhrer came into power. He did have friends and followers all over Europe, you know."

Then she giggled, the sound as shocking as if she had suddenly spouted obscenities into the quiet room. "They had bonobos at a zoo near Hellabrun, Germany, and they all died of fright when the Allies dropped bombs nearby during the war." She looked at Delilah and Anntee, her words taunting and malicious. "Are you two that sensitive to loud noises? Would you just curl up and die if I arranged an explosion for your benefit?"

The demented giggle came again, and she seemed unaware that the four men had tensed and   moved protectively closer to Delilah and Anntee.

"What a genius our Fuhrer was, what a concept he had! In the beginning, you see, he didn't have all those Jews to experiment on. It was so clever, breeding the bonobos even closer to men, infecting them with all manner of exotic diseases, then, making vaccines from the ones that developed immunity. And the carriers went back into the wild to pass it on, generations able to infect

673

any humans they came in contact with that didn't know their secret and take proper precautions."

Amanda's voice became stronger, sounding loud in the room. "Oh, but it was a beautiful plan! There they were, safely contained in their jungle, thousands of little man-ape time bombs. So easy to catch a few and ship them off to research facilities and zoos here and there around the world. No one would ever be able to figure out where the killer epidemics started - or why they started - until it was too late."

Her voice softened, becoming sad, barely audible. "But we lost the war, and most of the antidotes and vaccines were destroyed. So my husband, quite taken with the idea of the man-apes, continued to work with the safe ones. But it was my son, my son who created you." She had come full circle and she glared at Delilah, her voice becoming vicious. "Your mother killed my son. I gave those others, including this ape here, to the Landon Zoo as a joke and to try to smoke you out. I wanted you to find your tribe. There you were in Landon, so close to your own relatives and didn't even know it." Her voice was taunting.

Then Amanda stopped talking and was silent a long time, looking down. James was standing beside Delilah and Anntee now, and they were both still, too shocked by these revelations to say anything. He reached out and took Delilah's hand, holding it tightly in his own. She was trembling and her hand was cold, so

674

he edged closer until his side was touching hers. At the contact, she gave him a grateful look, and he responded with a reassuring smile and a comforting squeeze of her hand.

"Oh well," Amanda said. "It doesn't matter now. None of it matters now." She was obviously very tired, her shoulders sagging. "Margaret was so sure nothing had changed at the farm, and she wouldn't lie to me. But that damned Sarah Clement. She lied to me! Dared to lie to me! Not three weeks ago, she told me you would never speak, and she lied!"

She seemed exhausted as she leaned forward and pushed a button on the edge of her desk. James moved forward. "Will you sign the papers?" he asked.

"Yes," she said.

While everyone watched, Amanda signed the papers, handing each one to Walter, who had edged his way into the room in response to the buzzer. Staying as far away as possible from Anntee, he carefully affixed his signature to each one as a witness, and handed them to James.

With a few strokes of a pen, the sound scratching loudly in the quiet room, it was done. Everything, all the money, all the real estate around the world, all the property, all the power, everything including the Brighton Foundation and all its holdings, the Brighton mansion, and the Brighton name, itself, was transferred to Anntee Brighton, Mandy Brighton, and Delilah Cross

Brighton.

CHAPTER THIRTY

Everyone was subdued and emotionally spent as they left the Brighton mansion. After a brief muted leave-taking, Darkling climbed in the back of his truck with Anntee, and Jordan took the wheel for the trip back to the farm. With a smile and a thumbs-up wave, Jordan engaged the gears and the small truck quickly disappeared around the curve in the driveway. James used his cell phone to call a taxi when they got outside and they waited for it in the driveway, reluctant to spend any more time inside Amanda Brighton's den.

Merlin's words about old dragons, their fires little more than smoldering embers, ending their lives with only memories of dreams to keep them company kept running through Delilah's mind. The gardens on the other side of the driveway were well-tended and bright with color. Birds were busy in the berry loaded shrubs near the house, and from time to time one burst into song, leaving an almost visible trail of trills in the air as it moved from bush to bush. Even in a dragon's garden, she thought, the birds sing; she shivered slightly though the day was quite warm. A light breeze stirred the air and faintly, ever so faintly, she caught the lingering odor of death and decomposing bodies.

They decided to stay the night at the hotel, and return to the farm the next morning, feeling too drained to cope with traffic and airports. As they stood there waiting, James said quietly, "Amanda Brighton is insane all right, but not in any legal way. Merlin had it right when he termed it insanity fueling obsession, or obsession fueling insanity. It's my feeling that we're lucky she's so old. She was ready to do battle, but she's tired, tired in the way only very old people can be, emotionally used up, the fires almost out." Delilah looked at him, surprised to hear him echo her own thoughts so closely.

The enormity of what they had just experienced was too much for anyone to absorb all at once, and if the men thought anything about Delilah's silence, they attributed it to that. James, more aware than Casey of the intensity and near-violence of the confrontation, thought he understood her need for quiet time. He needed some quiet time himself. Deeply shaken by the experience, he could only imagine what Delilah was feeling.

Casey was having his own problems. Just being in the same room with Amanda had made it difficult for him to follow James' instructions and remain silent like Jordan and Darkling. He wanted jump in, do something or say something, anything to make it clear that he, too, was ready to fight Delilah's battles. He was still pumped up with adrenalin as they waited, feeling the need to do something physical, anything, run, or yell, or hit someone, and unable to stand still, he paced up and down in the driveway, enjoying the sound and feel of the gravel crunching under his feet. The professional part of his mind whispered about displaced aggression, but he continued to walk until the taxi arrived.

By the time they got back to the farm the next day, Anntee was already there. Delilah told James she needed to talk to Anntee, and walked away toward the barn without another word. Anntee was upstairs in the loft room rocking in her rocking chair. Delilah found the chair at the furniture store in Centerville and presented it to Anntee with a great deal of happy laughter.

"Oh! Oh!" Anntee had exclaimed happily when she understood that it was her very own. "Rocking chair! Rocking chair!"

She and Mandy quickly understood that the houses in this place were safe, full of interesting places to explore and things to learn about. A necessary part of their on-going learning process about small things like turning water faucets off were the most difficult to learn. Anntee had quite easily comprehended the idea that all of the interesting things sitting and lying around unattended belonged to someone else and were to be left alone, that touching them without first asking permission was the same as snatching something from someone's hand. This was a bad thing. Mandy was more difficult about it, grabbing, examining, tasting, and dropping anything that caught her eye. She was fast, frequently quicker than the person chaperoning her, and she was strong.

Sarah and Delilah had discussed this at length, agreeing that the idea of asking permission before doing or touching anything was the first and most urgent thing that Mandy needed to learn. It was a form of disciplined self-control that had to be enforced, more to protect Mandy from injury than to preserve things like vases, dishes, papers, magazines, wall sockets, telephones, all of the things that every child has to learn are off limits for them.

While they were talking about it, Delilah suddenly became silent; Sarah, ever attentive, asked her what was wrong. "I learned the group ways from Anntee and the group," she answered. "She has her own way of teaching, and the group set the example to follow. Then, I had to learn the same lessons Mandy has to learn, Sarah. I was older than Mandy, more set in the ways of the group, but I learned them, with the help of a collar and leash and liberal applications of Agnes Kittridge's correctional implementer. Every time I get impatient with Mandy and feel like swatting her, I think about that time. I can't help it, Sarah, but I can't hit her, and sometimes she needs to be physically punished."

They discussed it some more, then talked with Anntee for a long time. When they were finished, it was agreed that Anntee would be Mandy's primary teacher. If discipline was necessary, she would apply it in her own way. Everyone else would provide examples for Mandy to follow, using exaggerated requests for permission to do or touch something until Mandy grasped the idea that this was a new, different group and they had new, different rules that must be followed.

It was by coincidence that Mandy's first lesson in self-control and self-discipline occurred over Anntee's rocking chair. Anntee had rocked in Delilah's chair nearly every day since their arrival, delighted when Delilah took her upstairs, always a little sad when it was time to stop rocking. Ever since Joe and Jordan used the pulley to haul her chair up to the loft room, she had spent at least an hour every day sitting by the window rocking, looking out toward the pond, thinking her own thoughts, sometimes napping, and sometimes singing to herself.

She quickly made Mandy understand that this rocking chair was not some new toy to play with. It was hers and Mandy must leave it alone. When Mandy whined and disregarded her order, jumping in the chair the minute Anntee got up, Anntee had wasted no time. First she said, "No! My chair!" as she unceremoniously jerked Mandy out of the chair and dumped her on the floor with a thump that caused Mandy to howl.

Displaying a kind of wisdom that surprised Sarah and Delilah as they sat against the wall of the loft room on a bale of straw watching with interest, Anntee did not go back and take possession of the empty chair. She sat down on the floor and waited. Mandy, more angry than hurt, immediately climbed back in the chair, broadcasting her defiance by rocking furiously.

Anntee growled threateningly and said "No! My chair!" as she got up from the floor, yanked Mandy from the chair and delivered a pushing kick as Mandy hit the floor. Ignoring the ear-shattering howls of pain and anger, Anntee sat in the chair and rocked.

When Sarah made a move to go to the howling Mandy, Delilah put a restraining hand on her arm. "No, Sarah," she said quietly. "This is the group way of teaching. Mandy understands very well." And she did. Still whining, Mandy edged up to the chair, making the begging motion. Anntee responded immediately, hauling Mandy up on her lap, holding her close, making soothing sounds. When Delilah and Sarah climbed back down the ladder, they could hear the creak of the rocker, and the soft sounds of Anntee singing.

From then on, it was clear that Anntee was being much stricter with Mandy than she had been with Delilah, but Delilah thought she understood what Anntee was doing and why she was doing it. This was not the jungle. This was not a cage in the zoo. It was not the terrible place of the bad old female. Life was not the same, and there were many new rules of behavior to learn. They were very well treated here, and they were safe.

Although Delilah didn't realize it, Anntee was also aware of many things that she did not - or could not - put into words. She and Mandy were treated with the same respect and consideration these people accorded each other. Like having a proper name, this had great meaning to her. She was determined that Mandy should clearly understand this and treat these people with the same respect and consideration. Although she had no words for the concept, she did know the difference between being asked what you would like to eat, and having food that you did not particularly want dumped on the ground in front of you, and how that difference made you feel inside yourself.

Sarah always asked what they would like to eat, and brought it to them, clean and fresh in a basket. There was no dirt on it, no sandy grains to hurt your teeth. And Sarah often sat down to eat with them, sometimes bringing special treats like cookies or peanut butter. She had showed them how to drink from plastic cups so the water didn't run away between your fingers, and how to peel oranges to get to the sweet part inside. She showed them how to use spoons to scoop the peanut butter from the jar instead of getting it on your fingers. Then she joined them, licking the peanut butter from her spoon, laughing as they all made faces and smacked their lips when it stuck on the roofs of their mouths.

Anntee and Sarah had become close friends since the afternoon they cried together, and Sarah's opinions were important. Anntee realized that Sarah was dominant female to her here in this place and that she was wise and knew many things Anntee must learn. Her guidance was good, necessary, and frequently sought.

On the afternoon they cried, Sarah had slowly climbed the ladder to the loft room and found Anntee sitting in the rocker rocking. She seated herself on a blanket-covered bale of straw, and, after a contented silence, Sarah asked, "Anntee, can you sing?"

"Yes," Anntee said, and launched into the going to sleep song. "Baby dear," she sang, her voice surprisingly soft and sweet. That was when Sarah cried the first time; then, after a moment, she sang, too, her voice wavering a bit, tears streaming down her cheeks. Sarah cried for Anntee, for the intelligent, caring, loving person inside the ape body who taught Delilah about singing, and survival, loyalty and family love.

Later that same afternoon, Sarah returned to the loft room carrying a set of bright blue, heavily padded cushions. Together, laughing at Anntee's fumbling efforts to help, they attached them to the rocking chair seat and back.

"Good," Anntee had said, gazing into Sarah's eyes. She stroked the cushion then Sarah's cheek. "Sarah good," she said, and tears

684

trickled from her eyes and down her cheeks. "Ape not cry," she said, touching the tears on her face. "Ape not cry."

Sarah touched Anntee's cheek and said, "Human cry," pointing at herself. "Anntee good human." And Sarah cried again. So they cried together, easing some of the pain, sharing many unspoken sorrows, bonding in a silent sisterhood.

When Delilah climbed the ladder and entered the loft room after the confrontation with Amanda, she found Anntee sitting quite still in her rocking chair staring out across the pond. Anntee knew she had crossed a revelation yesterday in Amanda Brighton's house. Perhaps it was because of Sarah that she suddenly understood the difference between animals and humans, a difference that was internal, soul-deep, and one that went far beyond mere physical differences. She had always been highly aware of her difference from the group, something she had struggled to conceal. In that moment, standing shoulder to shoulder with Delilah confronting the bad old woman, their tormentor and enemy, Anntee understood exactly how great her difference from the group really was even in her sameness. Based on this new understanding, she had declared her own humanity.

As Delilah came into the loft room, Anntee turned to look at her, then got up and went to her, taking her arm. "Speak," she said, seating herself on the floor, drawing Delilah down with her. And Delilah talked. After a while, Anntee began to ask questions, much in the way she had questioned Delilah so long ago at Bhutu Holding Facility. Almost immediately, Delilah fell into the old way of speaking with simple words and gestures.

"No more bad old female," Anntee said.

"Yes, no more bad old female," Delilah agreed.

When Anntee finally understood that Delilah was hurt by what she considered to be Sarah's betrayal, she thought about it, absent-mindedly playing with her lower lip. Delilah waited patiently, and after a while Anntee said, "No. Sarah good. Sarah not hurt." She thought some more. "I there. I hear. Bad old female say Sarah bad. Sarah good to you, bad to old female."

Delilah thought about this. Anntee had a way of going directly to the heart of the matter. Sarah had never hurt her, had always treated her with love and affection. And she had lied to Amanda, protecting Delilah, not betraying her. Delilah trusted Anntee's judgment, so that part of her problem was solved.

She turned to look into Anntee's eyes. "Want to be with Casey."

Anntee didn't respond. She was aware of the pairing of Joe and Sarah, aware they had no mating feelings for anyone else, aware that Jordan was their one babe grown big. She had also been aware of Casey's feelings for Delilah since her first day on the farm. Only lately had she noticed that Delilah was feeling the same way about him. But something puzzled her. "You not ready get babe," she said, audibly sniffing in Delilah's direction. "What love? Sarah speak love. Not understand."

"Oh," Delilah moaned. "Not know. Not like group. Pair, stay together. Like Sarah and Joe. Have babes, stay together, both take care of babe. Not mate go away like group. Not mate with other like group. Stay together." She tried to think of something else to explain it and couldn't.

Finally, she said, "You mate, get Mandy. I mate, get babe?" The question was accompanied by the begging gesture, although Delilah was not aware that she had made it.

"Young one?" Anntee asked to be sure. K.C. was the old one, Casey the young one. When Delilah nodded, Anntee thought about it some more.

"Old one smell better," she stated unequivocally, and was silent for a while. Finally, she said, "No more bad old female. Can speak. Not hide. Mate young one. Make play. He ready, you ready play." That was her final word on the subject and she went back to her chair, softly humming the going to sleep song in time with her rocking.

* * *

The transfer of power in Brighton Foundation wasn't noticed by most of its employees because most of the changes took place in the higher echelons. The entire Board of Directors retired, replaced by new faces that included Doctor K.C. Lowell as

Chairman of the Board. The new members were drawn from a cross-section of reputable professional people with no prior connection to Brighton Foundation. Many upper level officers and executives also found it convenient to retire at this time, and the general housecleaning continued, going from top to bottom and back again, making sure that all the checks and balances that should have been there before were firmly in place and fully operational.

K.C., taking great pleasure in what was for him an unusually vindictive act, removed a small package from his pocket, unsealed it, and poured its contents into a small glass candy dish on one side of his desk. Then, he instructed his secretary to not mention his name, but just have Margaret report to the Board Chairman's office. A few minutes later flustered and out of breath, she was seated in the chair across the desk from him. He simply sat there and looked at her without speaking.

It took a little while. She hadn't looked directly at the man across the desk from her, her eyes nervously darting over the objects on his desk as she waited for him to speak. First, her nose twitched and she rubbed it nervously. Then full awareness of what she smelled hit her. She looked directly at him then and her eyes widened in horrified recognition.

"Shit," he said, his Homer voice making it sound more like shee-it. "Caow shee-it," he added by way of explanation as he shoved the small glass bowl and its contents nearer to her.

As he told Casey later, Margaret didn't even hesitate. In Homer's words, "She jes straddled her ole broom, 'n flew outta there like uh bat outta hell." Margaret resigned on her way out that day. Everyone agreed that she probably found another job, but she did it without contacting anyone at Brighton Foundation for a reference.

Much to Paulie's satisfaction, Merlin was hired as a full-time outside computer specialist with full authority to access, examine, and copy any Brighton file he felt useful or necessary. As his first job, he was assigned the job of tracing and documenting the activities of every facility that had ever been operated by Brighton Foundation since its inception with special attention to Africa and outbreaks of suspicious diseases.

Delilah and Sarah talked long and seriously, becoming even closer in the process. In a transaction handled by attorneys, Bent Tree Farm was put into joint ownership. Half remained in Delilah's name with equal portions of that half held in trust for Anntee and Mandy. The other half-interest belonged to Joe, Sarah, and Jordan in equal shares.

James and Kaydee Prentiss handled all of the legal details, carefully stepping around the question of the ancestry of the persons involved. It was, at best, a sticky legal situation that could become very nasty if ever challenged, and for that reason, all connection between Delilah, Anntee, Mandy, and the Brighton Foundation itself had been concealed under several layers of legal arrangements. Such things as the sudden appearance of unexplained and unexplainable children and their inheritance of personal estates when there were no other heirs to be found did happen from time to time. But everyone agreed that in order to avoid any close scrutiny, concealing all ties to the Foundation was the best thing that could be done under the circumstances.

Anntee and Mandy refused to move into the farmhouse, preferring to stay in their loft home; by autumn it had been winterized for them, including a heating and vaporizing system similar to the one used to produce a warm, humidified atmosphere for the plants that needed it in the greenhouse.

All in all, things had gone smoothly and well, and if Delilah had occasional doubts about herself, who she was - what she was - she kept them to herself. Sometimes she had nightmarish flashbacks that left her panting and sweating in the middle of the night; sometimes she thought about God and wondered about that intangible thing called a soul. More often, she thought about Africa and secrets.

EPILOGUE

It was another one of those warm, late spring days poised on the edge of summer, and a few puffy clouds drifted slowly across the sky over Bent Tree Farm. The stream chuckled happily to itself, and a breeze played tag in the leaves of the trees that shaded the bank. The stepping stones, six of them, invited one to cross and follow the path to the stile by Palmer Road, and the second one still rocked slightly under the weight of the unwary. Bent Tree Farm hadn't changed much in the last year, but many other things had.

Delilah Cross Brighton Lowell and Anntee Brighton sat together on the bank near the stream. In the distance they could hear the persistent sound of a tractor rising and falling as Joe made neat furrows, turning the dark, rich earth, making it ready for a new crop. The back screen door of the farmhouse slammed behind Sarah as she went out to work in her garden, and there were faint sounds of conversation as several people left the bunkhouse and walked up the driveway on their way to work on various projects in the greenhouse.

Farther downstream toward the barn, the high sweet sound of

Mandy's laughter rang out as she and Casey splashed wildly through the water in unsuccessful pursuit of minnows. Anntee grunted her disapproval. She would never change her mind about water being dangerous, but she wasn't concerned enough about Mandy's safety to move from her comfortable position on the bank.

Strange, Delilah thought, how everything has stayed so much the same while being so different. Perhaps not so strange, really, she amended the thought. The land stayed the same, following the cycles of the seasons as it always had. It was the people who changed as they followed the seasons of their own lives. She couldn't help wondering where the seasons would take her from here.

There had been many changes in her life over the last year. When she thought about it, she realized that there had been many changes in her, too. Her lips curled in a smile as she remembered the naive, naked girl poised on the second stepping stone, unable to go either forward or back. Was it only a year ago? Then rapidly changing circumstances brought about the changes in her, almost forcing her into new ways of acting and thinking. Looking back, her life had been simple then; she had been so sure of herself, so sure she had all the answers.

She and Casey were married; their new house sat on the gentle slope above and behind the greenhouse, high enough to see most of Bent Tree Farm and the crossroad corner where Palmer Road and Brookline Avenue crossed each other on their way to somewhere else.

The farm was still used for the same purpose as before, leased under contract to Brighton Foundation, the operation running smoothly under Sarah's expert guidance. Amanda Brighton died quietly in her sleep six months before and there had been no one to mourn her passing. Yes, Delilah thought, it had been a year of changes for them all, but Bent Tree Farm remained much the same . . . her home place.

She turned to Anntee. "Need to talk," she said. "Group still there. Want to go back?"

Anntee was silent for a long time. Finally, she simply said, "No. Stay here." She thought a while longer, then echoed Delilah's thoughts. "Here good place. Home place now."

Delilah nodded, then placed her hand on her stomach. "Babe."

"Yes," Anntee answered. "Know. Smell." She wrinkled her nose, sniffing in Delilah's direction.

"Scared," Delilah said. "What babe be?"

Placing her own hand over Delilah's as it lay on her stomach, Anntee gave it a reassuring squeeze.

"Not be scared. I here."